T0122148

THE BRIDGE AT BAN BAK

by James F. Casey

Order this book online at www.trafford.com or email orders@trafford.com

Most Trafford titles are also available at major online book retailers.

Printed in Victoria, BC, Canada.

ISBN: 978-1-4269-1705-9 (sc)

Library of Congress Control Number: 2009937240

Our mission is to efficiently provide the world's finest, most comprehensive book publishing service, enabling every author to experience success. To find out how to publish your book, your way, and have it available worldwide, visit us online at www.trafford.com

Trafford rev. 9/16/2009

www.trafford.com

North America & international
toll-free: 1 888 232 4444 (USA & Canada)
phone: 250 383 6864 • fax: 812 355 4082

CONTENTS

I: GOING DOWNTOWN

The news media and the Generals knew it as the F-105 Thunderchief. The men that flew it into combat, whose lives depended on its rugged strength and raw power, simply called it the "Thud".

Friday, 15 DEC 1967 (0937L hrs)

THE FORMATION OF aircraft was really quite impressive; four giant KC-135 tankers spread in a wide echelon formation with six fighter jets along side each one. The smaller fighters looked like worker bees tending to the larger Queen bees, the tankers. At this altitude, the morning sun was bright and warm; the sky was a pristine blue.

Each of the fighters cycled on and off of the boom of the tankers in a well-rehearsed drill. The smaller jets had been airborne for less than 20 minutes but burdened by their heavy weapons loads, they were already thirsty for gas. Each jet carried more weight in bombs than the B-17 of World War 2 did. When every fighter's fuel tank had been topped off the fighters slowly dropped below and behind the lumbering tankers. As soon as they were clear, the fighters turned to the east and set off toward battle. The formation of tankers quickly disappeared behind them. One by one the sleek jets pushed over and descended toward the dirty gray cloud deck below them. The F-105 was arguably one of the most beautiful airplanes that the Cold War had ever spawned. Even dressed up in their tan and green combat camouflage the airplanes had a graceful, almost elegant appearance. But, they weren't coming to North Viet Nam be admired. They were coming to create mayhem and destruction in the most-heavily defended airspace in the world.

Sixteen single-seat F-105D's each carrying six 750 lbs. bombs formed the strike-force. Wolf, Lobo, Grizzly and Panda were their call signs. A flight of four two-seat F-105G's , call sign Fist was assigned to suppress SAM's and AAA and a four-ship of F-4C's using the call sign Cobalt, provided cover from enemy Migs.

"Wolf fence in," came over the radio as the airplanes began to rapidly gather speed. Major Tim "Doc" Holiday leading the strike, ordered his flight to prepare for battle. A *fence check* is preformed as the airplane crosses over into enemy territory. Master Arm switches, which had been off to prevent accidental releases of ordnance, are turned on. Electronic Counter Measures (ECM) transmitters are turned on to jam enemy radars all other emitters and lights are turned off.

"2,3,4." Came the quick responses as each member of Wolf flight acknowledged.

"Lobo fence in."

"2,3,4"

Each flight lead in turn ordered his flight to fence in.

Every pilot silently tensed for battle.

In turn, each flight lead then waggled the wings of his airplane slightly, a silent signal for his flight to close up into close formation as they descended through the cloud layer. They were vulnerable like this but they stayed close so that they could keep sight of each other in the clouds. Tucked in close together with just three feet separating the airplanes wingtips, wingmen could not afford to look away from the plane next to them for even a second. There was always turbulence in the clouds that made the task of holding on to the formation just that much more difficult. It was nerve-wracking. They couldn't see out in front and if their navigation was off even a little they might just slam into the ground before anyone had a chance to react. It was the ultimate expression of trust. Wingmen had to trust their flight leads and flight leads had to trust their instruments.

The weather guessers had promised them that the clouds ended somewhere between three or four thousand feet above the ground and that it was clear underneath. It was tense for everyone. This time the forecasters got it right. At about 3000 feet above the ground the airplanes broke into the clear once again.

By yawing the rudders back and forth the flight leads quickly and silently sent their flights into combat spread, a wide tactical formation. With a mile of spacing between element leads the pilots didn't have to be as concerned about running into each other and could spend more time flying their own airplanes.

They were moving very fast now, seven and a half miles every minute, racing headlong into harms way. They continued to descend toward the velvety green foliage of the jungle beneath them hiding behind the safety of "Thud Ridge". Thud Ridge, as it had become to be known to the Americans who fought in the skies over North Viet Nam, was actually a rugged line of mountains that seemed to form a finger pointed right at the center of the City of Hanoi. The U.S. pilots stayed below the peaks of the ridgeline as they ingressed safely concealed from enemy radars. Wolf flight leveled off just 100 feet above the jungle canopy and the rest of the strikers followed suit.

Normally they would come in at three or four thousand feet above the ground to put themselves beyond the range of most of the guns. Guns were far more deadly than SAM's[1] in Viet Nam. Over 90% of the planes shot down in Viet Nam were the victims of guns not SAM's. These early SAM's had real problems at low altitude. The radar that

---

1 SAM; Surface to Air Missile. Most notably the Soviet-made SA-2 Guidline. Later in the war the SA-7 hand-held, shoulder fired infra-red seeking missile became a problem in North and South Vietnam.

guided the SAM to its target would usually break lock if it was forced to look down into ground clutter. But, a SAM didn't have to shoot you down in order to be effective. A SAM could be successful just by forcing the enemy down back into the range of the guns that seemed to be everywhere throughout the country of North Viet Nam.

This was an audacious plan that Major Holiday had conceived. They would come in low, *very low,* and challenge the gunners that made their job so dangerous. At this altitude and speed a gun crew would have only a few seconds to spot them and react before they disappeared again below the horizon. Just flying a high-performance jet at this altitude and speed required intense concentration and exceptional skill but each pilot would also be required to precisely navigate to a selected point. The idea was for each flight to arrive over the IP (Initial Point, the start of the bomb run) at a precise time. Wolf flight headed straight to the IP and each of the following flights would fly a slightly longer route so as to arrive at the IP precisely one minute after the preceding flight. At the IP, the flights would split into four separate entities and each aircraft would attack the target from a different direction. They would stay low and fast until they arrived at a predetermined pop point. At the pop point the pilot would climb his aircraft as rapidly as possible to three thousand feet above the ground while he acquired the target. Then he would roll in, drop his bombs slam his afterburner on and race away at tree top level. "One pass, then haul ass," Holiday had said. If the timing worked properly, the last bomb would fall just four minutes after the first. Each pilot would only be exposed to the guns from the time that he popped until just after he released his bombs. No more than 15 or 20 seconds. A crew-served gun would have a very difficult time acquiring the target, slewing the gun around, tracking it and firing all within that time.

Holiday had stacked the deck in his favor. He had handpicked each of the fifteen other pilots in the strike package. This was the varsity squad.

1Lt Tom Morgan was the least experienced pilot in the strike force. Flying Panda 4 he was "*tail-end Charlie*", the last guy over the target, easily the least desirable position in the flight. Whatever else happened, the gunners would be fully alert by the time he rolled in on the target, but someone had to do it. Holiday had chosen Tom because he was sure Morgan could handle it.

Morgan had been in country for three months and had completed 34 missions so far. Holiday was his hooch-mate and he expected to see Tom become one of the best pilots in the squadron before he rotated back to the States.

Tom was apprehensive. With a solid layer of clouds above them and the deep green of the jungle below, it felt as if they were flying inside a very large room. The fighters would high-lighted against the dark gray clouds above them. His heart pounded more quickly now as he silently went about doing his job, trying to stay in formation, backing up his flight lead on the navigation and constantly scanning around them for threats. This was Indian country and an ambush could come from any direction at any time. He'd never gotten accustomed to being shot at but it didn't bother him as much as it did the first time. He took just a second to take in the magnificent beauty of the dark green of jungle as it slid quickly beneath him. For a moment it occurred to him that it actually looked inviting. He quickly snapped back to reality. This jungle was death. There was nothing attractive about it.

Nguyen Duc Nung was a bit nervous too. Le Nhu Thinh, the local communist party boss had chosen this morning for his weekly visit. Once a week Thinh came by to *supervise* the activities at the small warehouse complex known officially as the Peoples Allocation and Relocation Complex for the greater Good of the South West Province. Unofficially, most people referred to it as the Buc Mai warehouse if they referred to it at all. The complex hadn't been originally constructed for the military but over time nearly 90% of the goods passing through it was military supplies or hardware. The warehouse was originally just four large storage buildings oriented north and south and an adjacent railroad track and siding to the east. A year ago an even larger storage building was built perpendicular to the others on the north side. Together the complex formed in inverted letter "L" when viewed from above. Trucks came and went all day and night. Many were parked in the open area to the west of the four main buildings as they waited their turn at the loading dock. Military officials had hoped that the complex was too small to attract the attention of the American bombers but, they had taken the precaution of assigning two 37mm guns directly on the warehouse property. Two kilometers east at a military training facility, a giant 57 mm radar-directed Soviet-made gun battery added it's considerable weight to the defense of the area. In total there were sixteen 14.5 mm, six 37 mm, two 57 mm guns and an SA-2 missile site plus hundreds of AK-47s in the hands of individuals within a twenty kilometer radius of the warehouse facility. The area was exceptionally well defended against air attack.

The real purpose of Thinh's visit was to collect the proceeds from the black market operation that Nung ran for him. Thinh controlled nearly everything that went on in the district. As goods arrived by train at the warehouses a certain portion were put aside for Mr. Thinh. Everything was pilfered from time to time but the most desirable items were food and armaments that could be sold quickly. The government in Hanoi expected to lose a certain percentage of the goods that they sent south and who was to say what had become of them as they worked their way along the Ho Chi Minh trail. The warehouses were close enough to Laos to have a thriving trade network with the Pahtet Lao guerilla forces. Nung was chosen by Thinh to run the operation because he was smart enough not to get too greedy and attract the attention of Hanoi and not courageous enough to swindle Thinh. Nung did all of the work and took all of the risks and Thinh reaped all of the profits. In return Nung got to keep his nice job. As an added bonus Thinh had intervened with military and seen to it that Nung's oldest son had been assigned to a nice staff position in Haiphong instead of being shipped south to die in the jungle. Nung was most appreciative. He didn't like Thinh or the fact that he was being forced to break the law but he owed him much.

"This seems a little light," Thinh said suspiciously as he counted the contents of the envelope.

"I assure you, Sir. It's all there," Nung said quickly. "Next week should be better. We'll turn a nice profit on the beef that arrived last night."

Nung gulped slightly. Thinh enjoyed making his employees squirm just a little.

"I have something special for you, sir," Nung's eyes lit up as he motioned to the older man that was waiting expectantly just outside of the office.

"Genuine Russian Vodka, sir. A whole case," Nung smiled hopefully as he opened the crate that the old man had brought in. He looked at Thinh for some positive reaction but got none.

"It was intended for some General in Cambodia I believe." "The Shipping carton was marked Personal Goods," Nung laughed.

"Very nice," Thinh said blandly. "The General should do less drinking and more fighting," he went on. "A man needs to have a clear head if he's to command troops in battle."

Nung agreed.

"Put it in the truck of my car," he said to the old man without ever making eye contact with him.

The old man hurried away with the crate.

Thinh didn't want to stay too long. The warehouse complex made him nervous. If the Americans ever figured out how much material was passing through the facility, they would bomb it to kingdom come. Still, it was important to be seen by the masses. Let them know that he was in charge and was keeping an eye on them. He didn't have to pretend that he liked them or even cared for them. Only politicians in democracies had to put on that kind of charade. But they had to be constantly reminded of his power over them.

Thinh would have been even more anxious to leave if he had known that a vital telephone exchange had been destroyed the previous evening by an F-111 bombing raid. Thinh's district had been effectively cut off from all telephone communications for over eight hours. The air raid warnings that had been sent to them earlier that morning had never been received.

Thinh got up slowly.

"I have to go, Nguyen. There's a British reporter with a television camera filming something down near An Luc. I want to keep an eye on him."

He patted the envelope full of cash.

"Let's see if we can do better next week. Yes? By the way how is your son? Does he enjoy Haiphong?"

Thinh didn't really care at all about the boy; it was just his way of reminding Nung that he was obligated to his superior and that Thinh controlled the welfare of his family.

"Yes Sir. He's very well, thank you."

Nung was very proud of the way his son had been quickly promoted. He wasn't sure if Thinh had been responsible but he suspected that he was not. Thinh always took credit for the favors that he extended to others and always expected to be repaid in one way or another. The boy had earned it. Nung was anxious to talk about his son but he knew his boss well enough to know that Thinh had no real interest in any of them. Knowing it was pointless to go on he quietly followed Thinh out to the loading dock.

They stepped out onto the loading dock. About half a dozen trucks were backed up to building number one. Each truck was quickly loaded by a host of civilian workers and a few uniformed military people. At least two dozen more trucks were waiting in the cleared area just to the west of the main buildings. It was a sign that the pace of operations had been greatly increased. Even six months ago they would never have kept trucks waiting to be loaded. The vehicles presented too great a target to the marauding American warplanes that seemed to wander at will throughout the skies above them. Now they had no choice. So much material was moving through the complex that they simply could not load them all as quickly as they arrived. Nung had suspected for weeks that some major operation was about to take place. But he was not a military man and it was none of his business.

Thinh's car was parked near the steps at the north end of the loading platform. The old man who had been in the office with them was now carefully loading the case of vodka into the trunk of Thinh's small black Russian-made import. Thinh's driver held the truck open for him and the two men were laughing at something as Nung glanced over at them.

Thinh didn't notice. He was looking east where something moving quickly through the sky in the distance caught his attention. It was very low on the horizon about three or four miles away moving from south to north. He just caught a glimpse of it. The object had been moving horizontally across the ground but suddenly it pitched up and began to climb rapidly.

"Wolf One's Up..."

At first Thinh thought it might be an SA-2 missile being fired. It was long and slender and climbing very rapidly but unlike a missile launch this object didn't accelerate as it climbed and it didn't have a large plume of smoke behind it as the missiles did. Besides, the SA-2 site wasn't east. It was south of them. Thinh's brain worked quickly processing the data as he stared almost hypnotically at the object.

"Wolf One's in hot!"

Just as the object seemed about to go into the dark gray layer of clouds above them it rolled quickly to the left and began to pull it's nose back to the west, towards the warehouses. As it rolled in the distinctive shape of an American F-105 fighter jet was plainly visible.

The sight of the airplane mesmerized Thinh. He watched as the plane quickly accelerated downhill toward them. He heard one or two voices around him shout something incomprehensible but still there was no sound from the airplane. He saw the six smaller objects detach from the belly of the airplane and stood transfixed, as they appeared to be falling straight toward him. His knees felt weak. He knew that he should run for cover but he was unable to force his body to move from its present position.

"Wolf One's off north..."

"Wolf two's up..."

The six small objects that had fallen away from the jet were M117 750 lbs destructor bombs. Each contained nearly 400 pounds of the highly explosive compound known as Minol wrapped in a 200-pound cast iron shell.

Thinh finally heard the roar of the airplane as is sliced through the air immediately above them in a right turn now back to the north. Milliseconds later, in rapid succession, the bombs slammed into the new building just north of where Nung and Thinh were standing.

"Wolf two's in hot.."

There was an enormous blast of sound and heat.

"Wolf two's off west. Lead in sight"

"Wolf three's in hot..."

Thinh was laying flat on his back twenty feet away from where he had been standing as the second set of explosions went off. These also struck the newer building and sent another huge shock wave through the entire complex.

Thinh's ears were ringing so loudly that he could barely hear anything around him. He could feel blood coming from his nose and ears. Another of the sleek jets roared overheard just fifty feet above him.

"Wolf three's off north two's in sight"

"Wolf four's in..."

The 37 mm gun crew in the northwest corner of the complex began to get into action now wildly swinging the barrel of their gun skyward and blasting away at nothing in particular as they attempted to extract some measure of revenge. The American warplanes seemed to be popping up from everywhere around them.

"Wolf four's off south, blind"

"Lobo One's up..."

Thinh knew he had to get out of there. So far the first three or four bombers had concentrated their fire on the new building but that wouldn't last, he was sure. Soon they would turn their attention to the four main buildings, right where he was. Another fighter roared past overhead. It was so low that Thinh could feel the heat from its afterburner as it sped off to the south. He tried to get to his feet just as another set of explosions ripped into the new building again. There were many smaller secondary explosions now as flammable and explosive goods that had been stored in the warehouse went off too.

"Lobo two's in hot..."

Another gun was firing now. Thinh could feel the concussion of it more than hear it through the constant ringing in his ears.

"Lobo One's off east"

"Lobo two's up..."

Another set of explosions went off behind Thinh now probably in building four of the original complex or on the railroad tracks just east of it. There was nothing left of the new building except fire and thick black smoke. Now they were starting to do the same thing to the original four buildings.

"Lobo two in hot..."

Another jet screamed past overhead followed immediately by more explosions. Thinh started to crawl back along the loading dock toward his car.

"Lobo two's off north"

"Lobo three's up..."

Guns were firing from all around now. People shouted and screamed. Many were wounded some just lay on the ground paralyzed with fear.

"Lobo three's in hot!"

Thinh felt another concussion behind him as he crawled along the wooden loading dock. He couldn't really hear anything because of the overwhelming ringing in his ears.

"Lobo three's off west. Lead in sight."

"Lobo four's up"

Planes were racing overhead and explosions were going off almost constantly as Thinh reached the small stairway at the end of the loading dock.

"Lobo four's in hot"

Thinh could see the gun crew in the northwest corner of the facility firing away almost without any hope of hitting anything. He looked around for his driver.

"Lobo four's off south. Three's in sight"

"Grizzly one's up..."

The driver was cringing between the car and the building next to the old man who had loaded the vodka. Thinh had to chance it. He got to his feet and moved as quickly as he could manage down the small steps. The new building was burning and exploding and Thinh had to stay low to avoid flying debris.

Another jet streaked overhead and the 37 mm gun thumped away impotently after it.

"Grizzly one's in hot from the north"

Thinh shouted at his driver. Screaming for him to get up and get into the car. Thinh couldn't even hear his own voice.

Another jet roared overhead and the ground trembled violently from yet another string of explosions.

"Grizzly one's off to the southeast."

"Grizzly two's up"

Finally Thinh grabbed the driver by his shirt collar and threw him toward the front door of the car.

"**Drive, DRIVE!! GET US OUT OF HERE!**" Thinh screamed at the man.

"Grizzly two's in hot!"

The driver searched his pockets frantically for his keys to the car as Thinh crawled into the back seat. He found them right in the pocket of his pants where he always put them just as wood and shrapnel smashed through the windshield of the car.

"Grizzly two's off west Lead is in sight"

"Grizzly three's up..."

The driver was miraculously unhurt but once again he was frozen with fear. Thinh shook his shoulder violently.

"GO, **GO,**" Thinh screamed.

"Grizzly three's in hot"

Shaken from his terror the driver pushed the debris in the windshield aside and fumbled with the keys. He found the slot just as the building closest to them was ripped by a series of explosions.

"Grizzly three's off north"

"Grizzly fours up"

The driver turned the key and held it but with the cacophony of noises around them he couldn't tell if the car was started or not.

"Grizzly four is in hot."

Finally the driver just released the key, slammed the car into gear and released the clutch. The car was running apparently because it lurched violently forward and then stalled.

"You fool you're going to get us killed!" Thinh shouted.

"Grizzly four's off northwest."

"Panda one's up"

The driver finally managed to start the car again as the complex continued to be rocked by explosions and they began working their way around the debris toward the main road west of the warehouses.

Tom Morgan had his hands full just flying his airplane and avoiding the ground. On the radio it sounded as if the mission was going very well. The radio transmissions were short and crisp and most importantly he hadn't heard anyone say anything about being hit. He couldn't see the preceding flights because they were all so low but as the airplanes popped up to make their bomb runs they became visible for a short time. Tom could see them rolling over into their dives so he knew where the target was even without his map. He could see tracers from guns on the ground firing everywhere around them. He tightened up a little more.

Tom had seen a SAM launch a minute or so ago. The huge missile streaked rapidly upward initially then seemed to self-destruct before he or anyone else could call it out.

The shot should never had been taken, the target was too low already and descending as the missile blasted away from it's launch pad. A half second after the launch a faulty weld in the booster case failed and the rocket motor exploded. What was left of the missile tumbled across the sky like a flaming comet and landed one or two miles west of the warehouse complex.

Fist flight, the SAM suppression Thuds had seen it and were bombing and strafing the site within seconds of the launch.

There was thick black smoke rising from the warehouse complex as Tom approached his pop point.

"Panda four's up," he radioed and pulled quickly and smoothly back on the stick.

The jet rocketed upward.

Tom was headed west and the target was off his right shoulder as he steeply climbed. He had a few seconds to survey the target. Everything was just as it had been in the reconnaissance photos earlier that morning except that all five main buildings seemed to be completely destroyed. Tom was frustrated. There didn't seem to be too much left worth bombing. He had traveled all of this way and risked his life and now the target was already destroyed. He had almost decided just to add his own bombs to the black smoke that enveloped all of the buildings when he spotted the trucks parked just to the west.

There were just seconds now to make the mental computations. He selected a small square building just north of the warehouse complex as his aim-off distance. He would point the airplane at it and walk his pipper[2] to the target.

"Panda four's in hot from the south," he transmitted.

"Panda three's off northeast," he heard over the radio.

A quick glance to the northeast of the target area Tom could see his element lead, Fred Winters racing away from the target "Like a scalded ass ape."

Tom rolled the airplane about 120 degrees to the right and pulled sharply down toward the target. Tracer rounds from guns were all around now. Most of it was wild but some was uncomfortably close. He could see more guns being slewed toward him with every second. As Tom rolled out streaking downward at 45 degrees, he thought for a moment that it would take a miracle to avoid all of the anti-aircraft fire that was now beginning to be directed at him.

He tried to ignore the fire and concentrated on making a good bomb run. Tom pressed the release button just as his pipper touched the nearest truck in the parking area.

A pulse of electricity raced backwards through the plane to the center aft station on the bomb rack. Two solenoids were immediately activated. One moved a lever that unlocked the shackle while the other closed to retain a metal swivel loop on the end of the bomb's arming wire. At the same moment a small shotgun-type shell at the rear of the shackle fired pushing a metal piston down and forcing the bomb away from the airplane. With one end of the arming wire securely attached by the solenoid to the shackle the other end began to be pulled out of the nose fuse. The arming wire, a heavy gauge steel wire had been threaded through a hole in the nose fuse and then through another hole in a small propeller-like device attached to the front of the fuse. With the wire removed; the propeller was free to rotate in the air stream. As it rotated it turned a sphere inside the fuse that aligned the firing pin with the detonator. Once the firing pin and the detonator were lined up with each other the bomb was armed.

This same sequence of events occurred five more times in rapid succession as each of the six bombs released within fractions of a second of each other. The bombs were on their way and no power on earth could stop them now!

Tom could feel a jolt as the bombs released. The Thud seemed to leap forward as more than two tons of weight and drag were instantly relieved. Tom slammed the throttle all the way forward into full afterburner. Just as he began to raise the nose of the racing jet up, away form the ground, he saw a small black car slowly moving away from the warehouse and toward the truck park.

---

[2] Bomb sights in aircraft of this era were just marginally better than the gun sights that were developed for airplanes during World War II. There were two panes of glass mounted in front of the pilot. When it was turned on, a series of concentric circles with a dot of light in the center illuminated in front of the pilot's field of view. Essentially a poor-man's Heads Up Display (HUD). The dot, or pip of light in the center became known as the pipper to pilots. On a perfect bomb pass the airplane would roll out with the pipper below the target. As the airplane descended in it's dive the pipper would appear to get closer and closer to the target. This apparent movement was known as walking the pipper. If everything was set up properly, the pipper would appear to be directly over the target when it was the right time for the airplane to release it's bomb.

There was no time to watch his bombs hit. Tracers were all around him now. It seemed as if everyone in North Viet Nam was shooting at him. Tom pulled the jet into level flight, made a slight heading change to the northwest and looked for Panda Three.

Thinh was lying on his back in the rear seat of the car. He was trying to stay low hoping that the thin doors of the car would provide him with some degree of protection. As he looked to the south he caught sight of six large objects falling in a neat row out of the sky. He had seen the same thing just a few minutes before as the first bombs impacted and he instantly knew what they were. The human brain is capable of incredibly fast computations during times of great stress. Thinh saw the motion of the on-coming bombs and calculated their impact point. He knew immediately that he was dead. There was no time to articulate a warning to his driver. It wouldn't have done any good.

Surprisingly, what Thinh felt was not fear.

"There will be no mourners at my funeral," he thought.

Oh, there would be plenty of people there. A party official of his stature would rate a large funeral, but no one would actually mourn his death. Some would be happy, he was sure, seeing his death as an opportunity to advance their own careers.

He hadn't been a very good person he concluded.

The first bomb disappeared in a blinding flash of as it impacted between two parked trucks just thirty yards from Thinh's car.

He wondered how his life might have been different if he had married Ha, his sweetheart in school.

The second bomb blasted through the cab of a truck just twenty yards away.

He left her because she could do nothing to advance his career aspirations.

The third bomb augured into a tank truck just 15 yards away.

But, she was the only person other than his mother that he had ever really loved.

The fourth bomb took destroyed two small pick-up trucks just 10 yards away.

No, if he had married her he would surely have wound in some menial job, like Nung he assured himself.

The fifth bomb blasted a flatbed truck only five yards away.

"I wonder if I should have gotten religion'" he mused as the sixth bomb slammed through the right side of the small car.

Le Nhu Thinh, his driver, the car and the case of Russian vodka vaporized into oblivion.

Tom came off of the target and jinked quickly left and then back to the right, hoping to throw off the aim of the gunners. He thought that he heard a sound similar to pebbles being thrown onto a tin roof. He quickly inspected his instrument panel and everything appeared to be normal. The plane did not seem to have suffered any damage so he concentrated on getting back into formation and getting as far away from the target area as quickly as he could.

Panda flight was in a turn to the south making it easy for Tom to slide back into position. With the flight reformed, Panda One turned back to the west, away from the target and on their way home. Several gun positions opened up from time to time as the fighters sped off to the west but the jets were too low and fast now for the gunners to have any real chance.

The bombing ended as quickly as it had begun. Slowly the gun crews realized that it was over and one by one they ceased firing. The overwhelming volume of noise was suddenly replaced by an eerie silence. There was the sound of fire and some small explosions where the warehouses had been but this was nearly inaudible to anyone who was even close to where the bombs had gone off. All any of them could hear was a tremendous ringing in their ears from all of the previous noise.

Nung was lying on his side in the clear area just to the west of the four main warehouses. The blast from the first string of bombs had thrown him off of the loading dock and onto the ground. He was dazed but he quickly got back to his feet only to be blown back again when the second string of bombs hit. This time he just stayed on the ground where he was. He was quickly covered by debris that was blown from the warehouse. Lying on his left side the warehouses were behind him but he could clearly see the truck park and the 37 mm gun in the corner of the complex. As bombs and debris rained down he watched an almost unbelievable drama unfold before him. A soldier was standing not ten yards from where Nung lay waving his AK-47 from side to side as he furiously fired into the air. The soldier paused for a moment to reload and the blast of another bomb hurled him backward off of his feet. The soldier smashed onto the hood of one of the parked trucks and slid off like a rag doll. The gun crew near the entrance to the complex was in a frenzy, firing constantly as they swung their gun back and forth. The barrel of their gun was depressed very low most of the time and Nung was certain that they were hitting buildings on the ground instead of the airplanes. As the ground continued to tremble from massive explosions, Nung watched as an SA-2 missile, burning with it's body broken in half, landed in the large housing area across the road from the warehouse complex and exploded. A minute or so later he saw Thinh's car disappear in a flash of light and heat as it moved toward the gate.

Nung was shaking uncontrollably. He tried to force himself to stop but it was no use. The speed and ferocity of the attack was unlike anything he had ever experienced. He managed to get out from under the pile of debris around him and back up on his feet. His knees were weak but he willed his body into a more or less up-right position. He slowly managed to turn and face the warehouse complex. All that was left were five fiery black holes where the warehouses had been just moments before and debris strewn about as far as he could see.

Nung was bruised and sore all over but incredibly he seemed to be all right. He wasn't bleeding except for a scrape on his forehead and a small puncture wound on his right thigh.

He hated the Americans for what they had done to his workplace. He wondered why they had come halfway around the world to enslave the people of Viet Nam. But, there would be time for that later. Now he began rousing others and they searched through the destruction for more survivors.

Nung had been concerned for his own family since he lived in the housing area just across the street. He consoled himself with the knowledge that his wife should be at her job in the local textile factory, well away from the attack. His children would have been at school, also safely away from harm. It appeared that the SA-2 had fallen well to the south of his own house so he wasn't overly concerned about it. Still, he went out of his way to walk toward the impact site on his way home, later that evening. It broke his heart when he caught sight of the damaged hospital. There was a large group of people standing around helplessly as searchers rummaged through the destruction. The SA-2 missile that he had seen earlier had fallen squarely on the hospital and nearly completely destroyed it.

It was a relatively small community and Nung knew most of his neighbors by their faces if not by their names. There were numerous strangers around the wreckage of the hospital that Nung assumed were from the propaganda ministry. Most of them were moving through the small crowd, trying to incite them with anti-American rhetoric. One slipped away from the crowd with something concealed beneath his coat. As the strangers distracted the crowd the other man placed a large metallic object just under a pile of debris. A few minutes later one of the rescue workers ***happened*** upon the object. He yelled something to get the attention of the crowd and then made a somewhat dramatic display of pulling the object from beneath the wreckage. It was a twisted shard of metal, presumably a bomb fragment, with the letters USAF painted on it in yellow letters.

"Look at this," the man shouted! He held the object over his head with the writing toward the crowd. "This is who killed your brothers and sisters. This is who killed your sons and daughters. This is who tried to kill you! DEATH TO THE IMPERIALISTS! DEATH TO AMERICA," he shouted!

Western news journalists had been taken to the site and they captured the entire charade on film. Nung just laughed to himself. It was an amateurish bit of theater but the crowd seemed to eat it up. Nung spoke French well enough to understand that the journalists were being told that the Americans had intentionally bombed the hospital. Amazingly enough, some of the wreckage of the missile was still there and it should have been obvious to anyone that it had caused the damage.

Nung simply shook his head. Whatever else the Americans had done it was plainly clear that their bombing had been remarkably accurate and the warehouses ***were*** loaded to the rafters with military supplies. Still, in a roundabout way it ***had*** been their fault that the hospital had been destroyed. If the American warplanes hadn't come to bomb his warehouse, the missile would never have been launched at them and the hospital would still be intact.

What was it he had read years ago, Nung tried to recall? Something to the effect that truth is the first casualty of war. He wondered if he and his family would ever get to live out their lives in peace.

Once the fighters were out of North Vietnamese air space they climbed to a comfortable altitude and each flight lead called for his flight to perform a BDA (Bomb Damage Assessment) check. The number four man in each flight slid his airplane underneath each of the others to search for any visible damage. Then the number three airplane slid back and looked over number four.

As Tom's airplane was being inspected by Winters, in Panda three, he reported he saw fluid leaking from the right side of Tom's fuselage just below the wing. Tom felt a sickening feeling in his stomach. He knew that he must have been hit as he came off of the target. A fluid leak usually meant hydraulic fluid and hydraulic fluid was the life-blood of the F-105. Without it the airplane could not be flown. It wasn't a question of pilot skill. The flight controls required hydraulic fluid to work and without them the airplane would become a huge uncontrollable dart.

Panda three and four split off from the rest of formation and diverted to Nakom Phenom (NKP) Air Base near the Laotian border as a precaution. It looked for a while as if everything would work out OK. But, just 10 miles from landing with the runway clearly in sight the hydraulic system completely let go. What had been a minor leak split wide open and within 30 seconds the entire hydraulic system was empty of fluid. There was no question about it Tom *had* to eject. Winters had gone over the ejection procedure with him a few minutes earlier just in case it became necessary.

Tom tightened his belt and shoulder harnesses as tight as he could. He straightened his back and pulled the ejection seat handles. The canopy blew off and Tom rocketed upward and away from the crippled airplane. Seconds later he was hanging in his parachute watching as his airplane rolled to it's left and dived straight into the ground a few miles ahead of him. There was a surprisingly small explosion as the jet drove itself into the ground. Tom couldn't help but feel sadness to see his plane end up this way. Certainly, it was just an inanimate piece of metal but it had performed well and had gotten him back to safety before it finally came apart.

NKP was not only closer than their own base in Ubon; it was also the headquarters of the rescue forces. Panda One had alerted them as soon as he realized that Tom had a problem and they had been patiently standing by as the situation unfolded. Jolly Two-four, a rescue HH-3 helicopter, launched as soon as Tom announced that he was going to bail out. Tom could see it coming toward him just as he touched down on a large open plain just a few miles from the base. He landed a little hard and sprained his left ankle slightly but other than that he seemed to be fine. The rescue chopper touched down just a minute or two after he did and since he wasn't really hurt it was decided to fly him straight back to Ubon AB. The helicopter touched down at Ubon just an hour or so after the last of the strike force landed. His fellow pilots treated him to a hero's welcome. Technically he had been shot down but realistically it sounded much worse than it was.

The Flight Surgeon told him to take few days off to allow his ankle heal before flying again and then sent him on his way.

Later that evening Lt. Col Morris, Tom's Squadron Commander intercepted Tom as he was on route to the Officer's Club for dinner.

"Tom," Morris said. "The Air Force will probably send someone to tell your wife about your crash today. It would probably be better if she heard it from you first. Before you get started at the club tonight why don't you head over to the Command Post. Tell the

Duty Officer that I authorized a five-minute phone call home for you. Let your wife hear your voice and she'll know that you're OK."

Morris had been around airplanes for many years. He had seen many of his friends get injured and some even killed in aircraft accidents. He knew that the fastest way to defuse the stress on a wife was to talk directly to her. Phone calls home were a rare luxury but this situation warranted one.

Tom was elated. He quickly saluted and hurried over to the Command Post. He did some quick calculations as he walked. California was fourteen hours behind Thailand so if it was seven P.M. here it was about five o'clock on Friday morning there. It was a bit early to wake Nikki but he simply couldn't wait to hear her voice again.

II: THE INDISCRETION

Friday, 15 Dec 1967 (0511L), Westwood, Ca.

TOM HAD MARRIED Nikki Swanson just two weeks before he had shipped out for Viet Nam. Her real name was Nicole but since the age of three everyone had called her Nikki. Tom had been attending the F-105 training school at George AFB in Victorville, Ca.

Victorville was just a flyspeck on the map in the high desert north of Los Angeles, a refueling stop on the way to Las Vegas. It's likely that the town wouldn't have existed at all if it hadn't been for the Air Force Base on the north side of town.

Nikki's parents lived in Victorville and her father managed a couple of restaurants that were just off of Interstate 15. Nikki was attending the University of California at Los Angeles (UCLA) and she lived at home with her parents whenever school was out. Her father always made room for her at one of the restaurants to work as a waitress so she always had a job waiting whenever school was not in session. The money wasn't great but it was adequate.

Every Friday afternoon and evening there would be another parade of cars heading out across the desert, fortune hunters hoping to strike it rich in Vegas. Every Sunday they would return with their pockets emptied heading in the opposite direction. The restaurants did a brisk business on those days that supported them through the rest of the week. Not surprisingly, the customers tended to tip better on their way out to Las Vegas than they did on the return trip.

Tom was assigned to George AFB after he had completed undergraduate pilot training (UPT). A year at UPT, six months going through the fighter Lead-in course at Holloman AFB, New Mexico and then another six months at George learning how to fly and fight in the F-105. It was a long and arduous process to become a fighter pilot. Most of the graduates from George would have at least a few months of additional training at a stateside assignment before being shipped over to fight in Viet Nam but there was a shortage of pilots so Tom's entire class knew that they were going directly overseas as soon as they graduated.

Nikki met Tom the summer between her junior and senior year. Tom and a couple of the other pilots in his class stopped in at the restaurant mainly just to escape the oppressive heat of the summer. She wasn't the most beautiful girl he had ever seen but she was pretty close to it. Tom instantly became a regular at the restaurant and soon the two were dating. He spent every moment that he wasn't flying or in class with her.

Tom graduated the second week in August and was due to ship out to Thailand the first week in September. They both knew that the flying from Thailand was going to be very dangerous and there was at least some chance that he might never come back. The thought of never seeing each other again was more than either of them could bear. They hastily decided to affirm their love for each other and they got married just two weeks before Tom had to leave. It all seemed terribly romantic at the time. Nikki started her senior year at the UCLA, just as Tom shipped out.

The marital arrangement worked out well for Tom. All of the married pilots were separated from their wives. The tour was not a set length for the fighter pilots. They stayed until they had accumulated 100 missions over North Viet Nam. Less dangerous missions over South Viet Nam or Laos didn't count, only missions over the North. All of the pilots had to fly *non-counters* when they were scheduled for them. Still, most pilots could finish their tours in eight or nine months. The thought of going home and being reunited with their women was a powerful incentive for most of them to finish their tours as quickly as possible. It also sustained them through the difficult times.

It was different for Nikki. She shared an apartment just off-campus with three other girls, Fran Koster, Marcia Hood and Debbie Serrano. The four girls had known each other since their freshman year. As a married woman, Nikki found that she had less and less in common with them as the semester progressed. Most of the drama in their lives, and there was plenty, centered on their boyfriends and lovers which seemed to come and go with a certain regularity. Nikki just wasn't a part of that anymore and she felt somewhat left out.

On campus the situation was even worse. Many of the students and professors had become vehemently opposed to the war in Viet Nam. Many were quite vocal about their dislike of anyone in the U.S. military which they saw as nothing more than hired thugs and murderers. She had bravely defended Tom and the U.S. military many times in class and in private gatherings but she felt increasingly isolated from her fellow students and professors. Most of the pilot's wives lived on base or at least in the proximity of a military community. They had that support group to sustain them. Nikki didn't.

The semester had been difficult but Nikki had survived by looking forward the Christmas break. Tom was entitled to take leave halfway through his tour and the two of them were planning to get together in Hawaii after the Christmas holidays were over.

The four girls shared a two-bedroom apartment just off of the University campus. Two girls shared each of the bedrooms. There was a good-sized living room/ kitchen in between the two bedrooms and fair-sized bathroom in the corner near the front door. It was not unusual for the phone to ring at odd hours of the day or night. Attractive women tend to have attractive women friends and most men tended to find Nikki's roommates as attractive as she was. Between the four of them, the girls had a lot of friends, many of whom thought nothing of calling in the middle of the night. Debbie seemed to have more inconsiderate friends than the others. More often than not if the phone rang at some ungodly hour it was someone calling Debbie.

When the phone rang at just after five A.M. it was not the cause of any great concern for any of the girls. Debbie stumbled out to the living room to answer it.

"Hello," she answered sounding half asleep and somewhat annoyed.

"Is Nikki there," Tom asked? The connection was somewhat scratchy.

"Where else is she going to be at this time of the morning," she really sounded annoyed now. "Wait a second." She dropped the phone on to the couch and stumbled into Nikki's room.

"It's for you Nikki," she said with her eyes half opened.

"Who is it," she said as she scrambled for her robe? Nikki was very surprised. Of the four girls, she was the least likely to get a phone call at this hour.

"I don't know, ...some guy."

Debbie drunkenly lurched back across the living room and back into bed.

Half a world away Tom was hoping that she would hurry to the phone. He had been given five minutes and there was a Tech Sergeant in the command post with him whose job it was to insure that he didn't go over by even a second. It seemed to take forever for her to get to the phone.

"Hello," she asked?

"Hello, sweetheart, it's me."

"Tom?" "What...where are you?"

"I'm still in Thailand, Honey. It sure is great to hear your voice."

"Oh, you sound great too but how did you get to make a phone call?"

"They always let you call home after you get shot down." He tried to make it sound inconsequential, even humorous but he knew that it probably didn't come off that way.

"SHOT Down?!" "What, how...are you all right," her mind fought through the sleepy haze to understand the import of exactly what he was saying. She began to sound almost hysterical.

The stress of separation and of impending final exams seemed to boil over inside her and she began to cry. Tom knew that he should have told her about his bailout in some other way.

"Honey, ...Nikki please don't cry it was really nothing. I'm not even sure that I was shot. It could have been just a mechanical failure. There's no way to really know, but I'm fine. It was really nothing."

Her throat was still choked with emotion. All she could do was to make little gasping sounds into the phone.

"Nikki, please don't be upset I just called you to let you know that I'm fine."

"You're really OK," she managed to say finally?

"Absolutely," he said. "I just twisted my ankle a little when I landed so I won't be flying for the next few days." He hoped that it would make her feel better to know that he would be safely on the ground for a while.

The rest of the conversation went somewhat better. Tom did the best that he could to minimize the danger that he faced on a routine basis. In the end he made flying over North Viet Nam sound about as dangerous as taking a sightseeing tour of the Grand Canyon. He tried to change to subject and asked her how she was doing, simply wanting to hear her voice.

At exactly the five minute point the sergeant cut him off and he hastily said goodbye. Just being able to talk with her for a few minutes helped him tremendously. He felt as if he would be okay for another two weeks anyway.

Nikki had been glad to hear from him but very distressed to hear that his airplane had been shot. She felt as if she was under a lot of pressure lately and that this was just another reason for her to be upset. Unable to get back to sleep she got dressed and left early for class.

She had only one last class to go to, philosophy. The professor was a 45-year who was trying hard to be a 20-year-old hippie. He wore is hair long and his beard scraggly. He always came to class wearing jeans and sandals. He liked his students to think that he was one of them.

This class had been particularly difficult for Nikki. The professor was bitterly opposed to the war in Viet Nam and regardless of the stated subject, his lectures usually degraded to anti-war, anti-military rants. Nikki needed to get credit for the class if she was to graduate the following June. She managed to hold her tongue most of the time but occasionally he said things that were just so absurd that she felt as if she had to respond regardless of the consequences. She often felt as if he was just trying to get a reaction out of her because she had made the mistake earlier in the term of saying that her husband was in the Air Force in Viet Nam.

The class started benignly enough with the professor simply going over the material that would be covered on the final exam the next week. Guided by questions from some of the sycophantic students in the class, the professor eventually worked the lecture around to speak about his favorite subject, his hatred of the military. He started slowly but quickly got up to speed. Nikki was certain that he kept looking over at her for some reaction as he babbled on. His diatribe reached a crescendo as he made the point that anyone who wears a uniform to work (i.e., policemen and people in the military) is simple-minded and blindly obeys orders from others. He said that they were no better than the storm troopers of Nazi Germany. He made the point that the people of real value in society were the *freethinkers*, the poets, artists and philosophers among us such as him.

The emotions and stress of the entire semester just seemed to erupt inside Nikki at that point. Her husband had nearly been killed yesterday and now this jerk had the nerve to compare him to a Nazi storm trooper! Unable to remain quiet any longer and against her better judgment Nikki finally spoke up. She challenged him, stating that he was as much a slave to conformity as anyone else. She said that he wore a uniform to work everyday, the uniform of the freethinking anti-war protestor. She pointed out that if he cut his hair, shaved his beard and wore a three-piece suit to work, no one would know that he was a "*freethinker*", as he liked to think of himself. She went on to point out that the only reason the professor and the rest of his free thinking poets and artists had the right to say and to do the things that they did was because others had been willing to lay down their own lives to give it to them! She concluded by saying that if he didn't have the decency to thank them for the precious freedom that they defended, perhaps he should just remain quiet on the subject.

The force of her rebuttal took everyone in the class aback a little, including Nikki.

The professor had claimed to encourage free and open dialogue in the classroom yet it soon became clear that he was a proponent only of the kind of free speech that agreed with him. The professor's face turned beet-red and he stammered for words. Nikki was certain that he was going to kick her out of the class and consequently she wouldn't be allowed to graduate in June. She packed up her books and hastily stormed out of the classroom before he could say a word. She didn't want that imbecile of a professor to see her cry.

Once she was safely away from the class in the hallway she burst into tears for the second time that day. She wondered if she would be allowed to get credit for the class after her outburst. She wondered if Tom was Okay. She wondered how she could tell her parents that she would be unable to graduate in June? Life just seemed to be conspiring against her at the moment.

She spent the rest of the day at her job in the campus bookstore. She tried to hide in the back as much as possible; ashamed of the way she had lost her temper. During the course of the afternoon three people from the class came in at various times. Each of them agreed that the professor had it coming. Two of them even said that they wished that they had had the courage to tell the old fool off themselves. It helped her to feel a bit better,

Nikki was home again later that evening, relieved that classes were over but anxious about a week of final exams ahead next week. Tom had been in her thoughts all day.

One of the girls had turned on the television to the evening news. The anchorman stated that the lead story was filed from North Vietnam about an American air raid that had taken place earlier that same day. All three of the other girls knew what Tom had called about earlier that morning. They all seemed to realize that this was probably the same mission that Tom had told Nikki about. All four of the girls watched the report with great interest.

Nigel Blankenship, an independent reporter for the World News Network, filmed the report. Blankenship was a product of a working class British family. His father had been a coal miner and labor union activist. Nigel had grown up loathing the British class system and the inequalities of capitalism, which he saw as the biggest problem in the world at that time. He became a journalist in order to affect the social change to a more equitable system of Socialism or Communism. He filed daily reports for the World News Network (WNN) from North Viet Nam. His reports were often heavily biased in favor of the North Viet Namese Communists. He routinely appeared on news broadcasts in Europe but the U.S. networks rarely picked up his segments because they were so blatantly slanted against the Americans. Still, this was ratings week for the television networks and Blankenship's report had some very compelling film footage taken earlier the previous day.

The story opened with a wide-angle shot of Blankenship standing in front of a rice paddy, microphone in hand, as happy, peaceful peasant workers busily bent over the fields in the background. Blankenship did a voice over of the original segment.

Speaking in his heavy British accent, Blankenship seemed to be an impartial observer since Britain didn't have a dog in this fight.

"We were filming a piece this morning from a communal farm in the Buc Mai province of North Viet Nam some forty miles southwest of the city of Hanoi. This is a quiet, peaceful farming community, normally far removed from the violence of the war with the south. This morning that peace was shattered by the roar of American warplanes."

The camera then zoomed in to an extreme long-range shot of two F-105's one after the other, climbing rapidly initially and then diving toward the ground some five miles in the distance. A huge column of smoke was rising in the background. The scene actually showed Panda 3 and 4 as they accomplished their attacks. The shot was too far away to see the anti-aircraft tracer fire that surrounded them.

"This morning American F-one-zero-five fighter-bomber jets were attacking the area just to the north of our location. We were close enough to hear and feel the tremendous blasts from the munitions that they were dropping. We were told by locals, (*local propaganda officials*), that the Americans were bombing and strafing a residential area. We quickly packed up our equipment and went to the scene of the fighting."

In reality, Blankenship and his cameraman were delayed some three hours as the local party propaganda ministers decided how to best to take advantage of their presence. When they did finally take him to the area they carefully avoided the warehouse complex and drove a rather circuitous path instead through the large housing area to the west.

The scene changed to a camera held inside a moving vehicle. The vehicle was passing dozens of shanty style houses. Every so often the camera would focus in on a house with some visible damage to a wall or roof.

"We approached the bombing site through a large residential community. We saw nothing of any military value what so ever. We encountered numerous houses like this one that had been hit by twenty-millimeter cannon shells similar to the type carried by the American jets.

The shell holes were actually from the 37 mm cannons that had been firing from the ground but Blankenship wouldn't have known a twenty-millimeter shell from an eggshell.

" When we arrived at the scene we found a local hospital that had been nearly destroyed by bombs," he went on.

The scene then changed to a dozen or so rescue workers shuffling through the smoldering remains of a building. All around, people were looking on with shocked and angry expressions on their faces. If the camera had panned another ninety degrees to the right it would have shown the smoke that was still rising from the warehouse complex. But instead, the camera remained aimed at the shattered hospital.

Nigel went on, "A small neighborhood hospital, more of a clinic actually had been virtually destroyed by bombs. This was the type of facility that is so common here in North Viet Nam. Usually one or two doctors and a half dozen nurses staff a hospital such as this and they tend to all of the medical needs of the local peasantry. The hospitals are generally very simple by western standards but they provide a vital service in this poor country. On a normal day they are quite crowded. Local officials told us that thirty-one people were killed and hundreds more injured when American bombs struck at around mid-morning. Officials said that the building was clearly marked with red crosses identifying it as a medical facility. One woman told us that her two-month old baby had been killed."

A hysterical woman cried and screamed in rapid-fire Vietnamese to Blankenship as he held the microphone toward her in the next scene.

"The American Department of Defense had no comment for us about this attack except to acknowledge that American bombers *had* struck, what they called, *military* targets in this general area."

The scene changed to a single worker seeming to find some bit of evidence among the debris. He held aloft a piece of metal and then began to shout something in Vietnamese to the crowd. The USAF was clearly visible to the cameras. The crowd became greatly agitated. The piece of metal was tossed toward the bystanders and many of them kicked and stomped the object as it lay on the ground. The scene was quite convincing. To the casual observer the shard of metal was the smoking gun that proved beyond any doubt that the U.S. Air Force was either accidentally or intentionally responsible was this heinous attack.

The next day a spokesman for the U.S. Department of Defense issued a statement refuting the North Vietnamese claim. He actually laughed at how poorly staged the event had been. He insisted that the scene was pure propaganda.

"First of all the Air Force doesn't paint USAF anywhere on the bombs that it drops. Second, how did this piece of metal survive the heat and blast of an explosion with the writing still intact? Third, the tail fin assembly of an SA-2 missile was clearly visible in several of the photographs of the destruction. Fourth, if we had dropped that many bombs on that hospital there would have been nothing left except a huge crater."

But, the denial was too little and too late. No one really paid any attention and the damage had already been done. Even those who supported the American war effort conceded that the bombing must have been some kind of mistake.

Nigel Blankenship concluded his report by standing in front of the wreckage looking and sounding quite solemn.

"It's difficult to understand the full effect of this war until one experiences it first hand like this. Regardless of what else happened here, this woman has lost her baby and thirty other people are dead as a result of this bombing. And still the war goes on."

"This is Nigel Blankenship reporting from the Buc Mai province of North Viet Nam for the World News Network."

Nikki was stunned.

"Tom's not like that," she stammered finally. "He wouldn't do that. I know he wouldn't."

She looked around at the other girls and realized that of the three of them, only Fran had ever met Tom before. The courtship had occurred so quickly over the summer that both Marcia and Debbie had never gotten to meet him at all.

"Tom would never bomb a hospital," she repeated. "I know that he just would never do anything like that."

The other girls looked skeptical but said nothing. All of them were uncomfortably silent for several moments and finally Nikki ran to her room and slammed the door behind her. She fell onto her bed and for the third time that day she wept openly.

She wondered to herself just how well she knew Tom. They had only dated for a little over two months before they had gotten married and they had been separated for three months since then. In his phone call Tom had said that the anti-aircraft fire during the bombing mission hadn't been bad at all. She wondered was he just trying to make her feel better or was the opposition very light because they were bombing an unarmed hospital.

Nikki felt as if her whole life was just falling in around her.

A few minutes later Debbie came into the room.

"Okay," she said. "We need to have a girls night out, just the four of us. You've had a hard day. Next week is finals week and we'll all take off as soon as we're finished. We haven't done this at all this semester. It's Friday night. This is our last chance. Let's go get drunk!"

Nikki was always the most conservative one of the four and she had never gone out with the intention of getting drunk before. Somehow though, it just sounded good to her at this particular moment.

Debbie ordered the other two girls to cancel whatever plans they had because they were all going out together.

An hour later the four of them were at *The Oar House*, a noisy nightclub in Venice Beach that attracted a lot of UCLA students. There was live music, a four-man ensemble that believed in the concept that if you can't play well, play loud. They played very loudly and the place was elbow to elbow with people.

The noise and the crowd seemed to be just what Nikki needed. She began to forget about her troubles almost as soon as they walked through the door. The girls found a table and to their credit they initially all simply wanted to talk among themselves. But, young men are attracted to young women the way moths are attracted to a flame. The girls turned away several groups of would-be suitors preferring to just be left alone.

After they had been there for about an hour a group of four boys came by their table and the other girls didn't seem to be as anxious to get rid of them.

Fran seemed to know everyone so she made the introductions. She introduced Nikki by her married name, Nikki Morgan. Each of the boys paired up with a girl at least initially.

Jeff Laica struck up a conversation with Nikki.

"Nikki Morgan? You and me were in the same English Lit. class last semester, remember? I thought your name was Stevenson or Swenson or something like that."

Nikki remembered him and she was flattered to know that he remembered her. She didn't think that he even knew that she was alive. Jeff was big on the school's football team. Nikki didn't really care enough to know what position he played but she knew that he was one of the better players on the team. All of the football players were treated like gods on campus. It had somewhat bothered her that the football players were idolized for playing a game while her husband was compared to a Nazi for risking his life defending his country.

Jeff was one of four football players in her English literature class the previous semester. The few times that they attended class, the four of them sat in the back of the classroom and acted like immature high school kids, talking loudly among themselves and being disruptive. It bothered Nikki because she and her parents had paid for her to attend that class and she actually hoped to learn something from it.

"It was Swanson," she replied. "I changed it when I got married." She held up her left hand and showed him her wedding ring.

To Jeff it was like waving a red cape in front of a bull. She was forbidden fruit, a real challenge.

"So where's the old ball and chain on a Friday night," he asked? He quickly held up his hand and stopped her just as she was about to respond.

"Don't tell me, let me guess," he went on. "He's working late at the bank foreclosing mortgages in the ghetto."

Nikki shook her head and smiled.

"Not even close," she said. Ordinarily he might have upset her but he had a certain boyish charm that she found quite appealing.

"Okay, let me see," Jeff went on appearing to concentrate hard on his next attempt. "He's a life insurance salesman away to a convention in Newark with his secretary."

Nikki shook her head again.

"I know," Jeff went on. "The conveyor belt in the widget factory broke and he has to stay until he makes his quota."

"No," Nikki replied. "He's pilot in the Air Force in Viet Nam."

"Ohhh," Jeff responded knowingly. "Oppressing the down-trodden Asians."

"Yeah, something like that," Nikki smiled.

"I guess we won't have to worry about him showing up unannounced," Jeff laughed.

"Don't laugh," She continued. "When you graduate in June you'll lose your college deferment for the draft. You may find yourself over there with him."

"Not me," Jeff said confidently. "I'm four-F."

"*You're* four-F," Nikki was clearly skeptical? "What's wrong with you?"

"I may have flatfeet or beriberi or diabetes," Jeff said matter-of-factly. "I'm not exactly sure."

Nikki just stared back at him.

"No really, Dr. Katz will tell me when the time comes," Jeff went on.

"Who is Dr. Katz," Nikki asked?

"Dr Katz is the head of the Selective Service Medical Review Board in Los Angeles," Jeff grinned. "And he also happens to be President of the Alumni Association *and* a very big football fan."

"Are you saying that he's going to give you a medical deferment from the draft just because you play football," Nikki sounded incredulous.

"Exactly!" Jeff said, sounding quite proud of himself.

"The alumni association," Jeff continued, "Likes to show its appreciation to the best players. They take pretty good care of us."

Nikki was speechless for a few moments.

"You're healthy enough to play football but not to serve in the Army," she said?

"Yes, it *is* tragic but true," Jeff, said. "Looks as if your husband is going to have to win the war without me. I'm going to turn pro, make a ton of money and retire to the good life when I'm thirty."

"I see," Nikki said.

They continued to talk on and on about school and music and mostly about Jeff's favorite subject, himself. Jeff seemed to be the exact opposite of Tom. He was egotistical, immature, irresponsible, shallow and seemingly without a care in the world. But, he was easy to talk with, he made her laugh and he was very good looking. Nikki noticed several other girls in the room looking enviously at their table. As time passed, she felt more relaxed than she had in quite some time.

The eight of them stayed there late into the night as they talked and laughed and drank. For a few hours the war, Vietnam and Tom all seemed very far away.

...Nikki's brain slowly awoke from its alcohol-induced stupor. She still felt as if the world was gyrating around beneath her but it was not an entirely uncomfortable feeling. She became aware that it was light. She opened her eyes momentarily and was blinded by the sunlight streaming in through her bedroom window. She quickly shut her eyes again. She lay quietly for a few moments, completely at peace. Slowly the various parts of her body came back to life. She could feel the cool softness of the bed sheets against her naked form. It was a wondrous, liberating feeling to be completely free of any clothing. She told herself that she had to try sleeping without her clothes more often.

Gradually, it occurred to her to question ***why*** she didn't have any clothes on. She ***always*** wore her pajamas to bed. She became aware of an object lying across her bare chest. It was Jeff Laica's arm. Instantly her mind forced itself to review events of the previous evening. She remembered talking and laughing at the bar. She recalled Marcia becoming somewhat amorous with one of the boys. Before long they were openly pawing each other. The other two girls seemed to be less interested in a Platonic relationship with their companions as well. Nikki remembered being uncomfortable with the situation and getting up to leave. She immediately fell to the floor. The alcohol had affected her more than she had realized. She recalled Jeff getting up and insisting that he take her home. She thought that was chivalrous. She had no real memory beyond that point.

She instantly sprang out bed feeling ashamed and embarrassed. She quickly covered herself as best she could with a blanket that she pulled from the other bed. Jeff was still passed out. He groaned and rolled over toward the wall. Her mind was going a thousand miles an hour in about eight different directions at once. What had she done? She had destroyed her marriage. How could she ever tell Tom? How could she ever face him again? What would her parents think of her if they ever found out?

She had to get out of there. That was the only thing that she was sure of. She couldn't stand to look at Jeff. She couldn't stand to look at the bed. She quickly got dressed and ran out of the apartment.

She walked for miles and eventually wound up at the beach. The ocean usually seemed to have a soothing effect on her, but not this time. She walked along the beach for almost an hour, shamefully reliving the events of the last 24 hours and wondering how her life had all gotten so fouled up. She searched her mind for someway to try and make everything all right again but she couldn't think of any answer. She cried until she had no more tears left. Eventually, she realized that she would have to return to her apartment. She caught a bus and returned home at around noon. Mercifully, Jeff was gone. The apartment was empty. As she sat alone in the silence she couldn't help but think that her life had reached its lowest point in her 22 years. Then she noticed a message that one of the girls had written on the notepad near the phone. It was a phone number for her to call. She didn't recognize the number but it seemed familiar.

It turned out that it was the student medical clinic. Nikki had gone there just over a week ago because she wasn't feeling quite right. They ran several tests but everything had come back negative.

She told the receptionist that she had a message to call and the girl on the other end seemed to be expecting her call.

"Oh yes, Mrs. Morgan. Dr Randolph wanted to speak to you. Can you hold for a minute while I get her," the receptionist asked?

"Yes, sure," Nikki responded without any emotion in her voice.

Two minutes later Dr Judith Randolph came on the line. She had seen Nikki the day that she came to the clinic.

"Nikki," the Doctor asked?

"Yes Doctor, how are you?" Nikki replied.

"I'm fine, Nikki. I tried getting a hold of you yesterday but you weren't in. I wanted to be sure to get you as soon as possible," the Doctor explained.

"Is something wrong," Nikki asked apprehensively? As if enough hadn't gone wrong already this day.

"No, not at all, Well, not really anyway. When we called you last week and we told you that all of the tests we ran were negative. It seems that there had been some confusion about the records"

"I don't understand," Nikki said.

"Well, one of the tests came back positive. You're pregnant! From what you told me during the office visit I would guess that you're about three months along. If you can come in on Monday we can set up to meet with an OB doctor."

There was no response for several seconds.

"Nikki?"

III: THE SOVIET

Friday, 15 Dec 1967 (2040L hrs), Xe Kong Province, Laos

Lam Quang Son walked slowly along the heavy pontoon bridge, checking it's security one last time. All around was the inky darkness of the jungle. The sky was completely overcast, no stars or moonlight were visible. Here and there small pools of light stood out like beacons and illuminated their work.

Son became a bit nostalgic as he walked. When he was in school, studying engineering, he had dreamed of building beautiful suspension bridges or rugged cantilever structures that would last for a hundred years. But, ten years later the reality was that the only bridge he had ever built, or assembled actually, was this Russian-made abomination. Still, what it lacked in aesthetics it made up for in utility. The bridge promised to be precisely what the Army of North Vietnam needed. It could support the largest vehicles in the Army's inventory and still be assembled and disassembled quickly.

Son was thirty-two years old and the father of three girls. His only ambition in life was to be a good engineer but the entire economy of North Vietnam was wrapped up in this war so he found himself in the military. He had served with the Army down south for a year. He hated every minute of it but he did the best that he could to tolerate it. For the last three years he had been working in an office in Hanoi that was in charge of modifying and maintaining the North Vietnamese paddy dyke system that was so vital for the country's rice production. Son was one of three engineers who worked for a senior engineer. Son had no particular background for this kind of work but one engineer is as good as another as far as the Army was concerned. Fortunately, it was easy work and it allowed him to live at home with his family. Son was content to work quietly in the background while many of his contemporaries with better assignments passed him by on the ladder to greater success. Then one day the Army decided that they needed one of the three junior engineers for an important assignment. The job meant deploying down to the South and could be dangerous. It was up to the senior engineer to choose one of his three subordinates for the mission. One of the engineers was his son-in-law so it essentially meant that the choice was between Son and the other engineer. Son had not tried to endear himself to his boss the way the other man did so it came as no surprise when he had been chosen for the job. His boss assured him that it would mean great opportunities for him. Son was not particularly interested but he had no choice.

There had been a very tearful good-bye with his wife and daughters and then he was on his way. He fully expected that he might never return.

Son was deep inside Laos at the front end of a huge supply chain that wound through Laos all the way to the cities of Hanoi and Haiphong in North Vietnam. Laos was a surrogate in North Vietnam's fight to take over the south. To the international community Laos was a neutral bystander in the conflict. The reality was that both sides moved rather freely throughout the country and there was little that the Laotian government could do to stop it even if they had wanted to. It was a bit worse for the Americans and the South Vietnamese because there were many Communist Pahtet Lao militias operating in the country that openly supported the North Vietnamese. The Americans also had the world news media watching them. If it had become widely known that they were operating and fighting in Laos, the American public would have viewed it as an expansion of the war. This did occur a few years later but in 1967 the American involvement in Laos was still one of the worst kept secrets in the world.

Supplies for the North Vietnamese Army (NVA) had always moved through Laos and Cambodia. But the amount of supplies moving south was scheduled to increase dramatically as the North prepared for the upcoming offensive that would be launched over the Tet Lunar New Year in early February. The North Vietnamese normally avoided crossing rivers unless they absolutely needed to use them. There were no permanent bridges along the Ho Chi Minh trail, as this would be seen as violation of the supposed Laotian neutrality. Beside that, any permanent structure would be quickly bombed out of existence by the American warplanes that patrolled constantly overhead. The coming offensive required drastic changes if the amount of supplies that were needed was to be moved within the available time. By bridging the Xe Kong River near the town of Ban Bak the NVA could save some 35 miles of travel over rough roads. The location was also desirable because the river turned nearly 180 degrees and the current slowed dramatically as it made the turn. Once astride the river the NVA would be in perfect position to launch the main thrust of their attack toward the city of Hue. The idea was to take advantage of the long winter nights when the skies were free of the American warplanes. The pontoon bridge could be constructed immediately after sunset, used for several hours to move vehicles and supplies and then dismantled and hidden again during the daylight hours.

The North Vietnamese had appealed to the Soviets for help and the Soviets had supplied them with a new pontoon bridge that seemed ideal for this type of situation.

Son was in charge of the construction. Originally he intended that his men would practice assembling the bridge back at their home base in Hanoi before they deployed with it to the field. But the bridge had arrived two months late and there was barely time to get it down to Laos on schedule. He fully anticipated that the assembly of the bridge would go slowly the first night but he expected it to improve as they gained experience putting it together and taking it down.

It had taken nearly five hours to assemble the bridge, nearly twice as long as it should have taken. His crew had worked hard but the bridge wasn't as easy to assemble as they had been led to believe it was. Several of the shipping containers had been mis-marked, the interlocking pieces didn't fit well together and they didn't have all of the tools that they required. Even so, the worst thing about the bridge, as far as Son was concerned, was that Sergey Valenchenko came with it. Sergey had been sent by the Soviets to assist the NVA with the bridge construction.

Everyone just assumed that Valenchenko was an engineer who had helped to design the bridge. In reality, he was a supervisor in the factory where the bridge had been manufactured. He had assembled the bridge sections many times on the floor of the factory but he had never done so in actual field conditions.

Son thought that Sergey was arrogant and condescending toward all of the Vietnamese. It was clear that he had no desire be there. Field conditions as they traveled through the jungle were difficult for everyone. They provided the Russian with everything that they had available and still he did nothing but complain. Son would be glad to be rid of him.

Son walked slowly across the bridge looking left and right with a flashlight as he inspected the structure one last time. As he reached the north side he nodded to the officer that was waiting there and the officer yelled for the first truck to come forward. The Officer was really more of a Communist party official than a military officer and he had been giving Son a hard time all night because the construction had taken so long. Son just ignored him.

Son, the Political Officer and a small group of other men stood and watched as the truck made it's way slowly across the river. The bridge was composed of sections each twenty meters long. Each section was similar to a rectangular twin-hulled boat. Two heavy guide wires were stretched along either side of the bridge to hold them in place. Then the sections were bolted together. As the truck moved from one section to another the weight of the vehicle caused the section to drop down considerably lower in the water. As the truck moved from one section to another the pieces would bob up and down in the water. It looked a bit precarious, but it was designed to work this way. The driver was quite nervous at first but the truck arrived safely on the other side.

Son just glared at the Officer as if to say, "I told you so," and walked away. He was proud of the job that he and his men had done under difficult conditions. He gathered his team together and they discussed how they were going to disassemble the bridge as they ate dinner. They also discussed how the construction process had gone and Son had to admit that Valenchenko had been very helpful. He thanked the Russian and then reminded his men that the job for the night was only half over. Son was most concerned about concealing the bridge sections so that they could not be spotted from the air. They had built large awnings covered with foliage to conceal the bridge during the day. The sections would have to be dragged across nearly 100 meters of ground away from the riverbank and then stacked beneath the awnings. It promised to be a difficult job. The most important part might be concealing the tracks that the sections made on the ground. If a sharp-eyed American pilot saw the tracks he might just be able to figure out what they were up to.

Traffic the first night was light, mostly people on foot and only a few vehicles. It was planned that the volume would increase steadily until the offensive finally kicked off in just over a month. Just after 2 AM Son closed the bridge and his crew began to take it down. It was a little early but this would give him about four and a half hours to get the job done. Everything went well initially.

General Dinh Duc Thien and some senior officers came by an hour later and the General insisted on speaking directly to Son. Son was a bit annoyed at first but everything was going very smoothly so he left Valenchenko in charge and he went back to the north side to meet with his guests. He briefed them on the specifications of the bridge and went on to tell them that he expected to be able to put it up and take it down in three hours as soon as his crew got some more experience. Everyone seemed pleased so after about twenty minutes Son excused himself and went back to his work.

Nearly half of the bridge had been disassembled as Son walked back toward the work party. As he looked at them from the river bank Son saw something that nearly made his heart stop. Valenchenko was about to release the safety restraint on the upstream side of the bridge while the downstream side was still locked in place. It was such a simple mistake that Son hadn't bothered to emphasize it as he briefed the crew. If the upstream side was released first, the bridge section could be twisted by the current and make it nearly impossible to release the downstream side. Any engineer would have known that but Valenchenko wasn't an engineer. There were no river currents to deal with on the factory floor where he had practiced disassembling the bridge.

"NOOO," Son yelled as he ran toward the Russian! But his warning came too late. The upstream side of the bridge section released and the powerful current immediately began twisting it in place. The safety wires snapped and there was a loud metallic groan as the fixtures on the downstream end held fast. The bridge section pivoted almost 45 degrees to the rest of the structure before it finally stopped in place.

Seconds later Son stood panting on the outermost edge of the last attached section. His worst fears were realized. The force of the river was pushing against the bolts on the downstream side. The horribly twisted section was firmly locked in place with no way to release it.

Son could imagine that his career was over. The bridge had been his responsibility and now it was badly damaged. Son didn't know whether to cry or to throw Valenchenko into the river but there was no time for either one. The sun would be up soon and they couldn't take off any more sections of the bridge until they got the damaged section out of the way. Once he got past the initial shock of seeing the damage done to the bridge Son began to think more clearly. He had to stabilize the remaining sections or the whole thing might be torn away and float down the river. They had two extra sections of the bridge that they hadn't used. If they could just release the damaged section they could discard it and continue dismantling the rest of the structure. But the Soviet bridge was strong. The metal was badly deformed but it didn't break.

Son couldn't wait. He sprang into action immediately grabbing his crew and racing back toward the bank for more reels of the heavy metal safety wire. It took over ninety minutes for Son and his men to replace the broken wires. He could relax for just a moment once the remainder of the bridge was secure.

General Dinh and his staff were gathered around Son. They all seemed to have an idea of how the problem could be easily solved. Son was exhausted but he managed to control his anger. He thanked them as politely as he could manage but assured them that he knew what to do.

He had three options. He could beat on the stubborn bolts and hope that they would release. He didn't think that this idea had much chance of success. He could attach towlines to the end of the broken section and pull back on them from the far riverbank to relieve the stress on the bolts and then try to beat them out of position. Realistically, he didn't think that this would work either. The entire section joint was twisted too badly. The last option was to send for some heavy cutting equipment and cut the damaged section off. Son opted to do all three at once.

With all humility, Son old the General and his staff that he intended to continue working on the bolts with sledgehammers as another part of his crew rigged tow lines to the opposite river bank. He assured them that they would make every effort to free the damaged section but he was honest about the chances for success. He asked General Dinh to send for some cutting equipment and informed him that it might take days or even weeks for it to arrive. He went on to say that they still had to disassemble the remaining sections and conceal them. Even if they could release the damaged section in the next few minutes, which was unlikely, they would be well into morning before they could finish. The bridge could be spotted easily from the air. Son was ashamed to have to be so blunt about the situation.

General Dinh was clearly angry, he yelled at the Colonel that followed him everywhere. Dinh demanded that every available anti-aircraft gun be brought up immediately.

"If the Americans want my bridge," he stated confidently, "they're going to have to fight for it!"

IV: THE DUCK

Saturday 16 Dec 1967 (0510L Nakom Phenom (NKP) Airbase, Thailand)

FRANK ROBERTSON AND his Cessna O-2A were Nail 58. Nail was the call sign of the 23rd TASS (Tactical Air Support Squadron). The two-digit number that followed had no particular significance but was unique to each pilot. Frank was a 27 year-old father of two from Moody AFB near Valdosta, Ga. Robertson had been flying F-100 Super Saber at Moody until he had been ordered to Vietnam to do a tour as a FAC (Forward Air Controller). He had been upset by the assignment at first. If he had to go to Vietnam he wanted to go as a fighter pilot in the fearsome F-100 not, what he saw, as an airborne radio operator flying the ungainly looking O-2. But Frank had begun to enjoy the FAC mission almost immediately. The 23rd provided Forward Air Controllers (FAC) to support American Army units in South Vietnam and to police the Ho Chi Minh trail. Occasionally they carried an observer or another pilot in the right seat of the airplane but most of the time they flew by themselves. The FACs operated as a single ship normally rather than being a member of a formation and had a great deal authority when it came to controlling air strikes. Frank loved the independence. He started by flying support missions for troops on the ground. He was assigned to work with an entire brigade but he eventually developed a close attachment to one of its' companies. He happened to be on the scene when the company was ambushed. He stayed overhead for nearly seven hours directing air strikes on the enemy positions. He refused to leave when his relief showed up, insisting on staying with the soldiers until they were safe. He had done that sort of mission for five months until he was reassigned to work over the trail. It was different work, not nearly as satisfying as supporting the troops on the ground. He didn't care for it at all initially but after a few successes he began to warm up to it. It was sort of twentieth century version of the old cat and mouse game. The NVA tried to sneak men and supplies through the jungle and the FACs tried to stop them.

The role of the FACs along the trail was to spot targets and then direct fighter-bombers to destroy them. Each FAC had his own little section of the trail to keep watch on. The concept was for the pilots to become intimately familiar with the daily routine in their areas of responsibility so that they could spot anything out of the ordinary. The North Vietnamese moved tons of supplies though the Laotian jungle and they had become very adept at concealing their activities from the American airplanes.

Nail 58 was the first flight of the day to taxi out for take-off on the sprawling airbase near the Laotian border. It was still completely dark as Robertson pushed up the throttles for take-off. By leaving now he would arrive over the trail just as the sun came up. The O-2 roared to life; the racket from its two engines shattered the peaceful morning calm. The noise was completely out of proportion to the size of the aircraft. The propellers bit into the air and the small plane slowly began moving down the runway.

As the war in Vietnam started the O-1 was the primary aircraft used by FACs. The Cessna O-1 was one of the smallest production aircraft ever built. It was just barely wide enough to accommodate two pilots sitting in tandem. With a single motor, high wing and a tail wheel the O-1 was slow and highly vulnerable to ground fire. The Air Force needed something quickly to replace the O-1. The North American OV-10 Bronco was the best answer, but it would take time to go into production. The O-2 was a modification of a civilian airplane that was already in production. The Air Force went to the Cessna plant and bought six model 337 Skymasters. The civilian version was large enough to accommodate six people with two pilots sitting side by side. The Air Force immediately began to modify the airplane for their military role. They ripped out the interior of the cabin and replaced the six seats with just two armored seats for the pilots. At the rear of the cabin a simple metal radio rack was added to accommodate UHF, VHF, FM and HF radios. They took a saber saw and cut away all of the sheet metal around the pilot that could be spared to open up the pilot's field of view. Even with the modifications the pilot's field of view was never as good as it had been on the O-1 because the cabin was so much wider. The final modification was the addition of a simple bombsight and an armament system that could handle 28 smoke rockets in four pods below the wings. They showed the completed versions to the folks at Cessna and told them to make more just like this. The production models were called the O-2A Skymaster.

Pilots usually form some sort of emotional attachment to the aircraft that they fly but the O-2 never seemed to attract much except ridicule. In the aviation phonetic alphabet the word "Oscar" is substituted for the letter O so the O-2 initially became known as the Oscar two. That eventually morphed into the Oscar Deuce and that became the "Oscar Duck" or just the "Duck". Air Force lore says that the name, duck replaced deuce because the airplane was slow, easy to shoot down and made a lot of noise when it flew.

Robertson's O-2 reluctantly lifted off of the runway. Robertson slowly climbed to just beneath cloud deck that hung like a blanket over the ground as far as the eye could see. The cloud layer was the O-2s best defense. If he was fired upon he could quickly climb into the clouds. He turned the little plane south toward his target area. He had been working over the same area for more than three weeks and felt very comfortable there now. Skimming just below the bases of the clouds Robertson set cruise power and leaned out the fuel mixture. It would take twenty-five minutes to arrive on-station and it gave him a little time to relax before work began.

He debated trying to call home again using the HF (High-Frequency) radio. It was a little trick that one of the other pilots had told him about. The HF radio was older technology that had tremendous range but was often temperamental. The FACs used it to communicate with higher headquarters but it could also be used to contact Ham radio operators around the world. Two weeks earlier, on his way home after a mission, Frank had contacted a Ham operator in Hawaii who agreed to make a collect phone call to Franks' wife in Georgia and patch him through on the radio. It was expensive but worth it. It had greatly lifted the spirits of both Frank and his wife. He considered doing it again but practicality won out. It was just too expensive to make a habit of. He would wait another two or three weeks until he tried it again. Instead his mind wandered to the conversation he had had with the night before with his Squadrons' Operations Officer, Lt Col. Garrett.

"We're going to lose this war because we're backing the wrong side," Garrett had said.

Robertson was incredulous. He thought that perhaps Garrett had had too much to drink. "What are you talking about," he replied? "We're fighting the communists."

"They may be communists," Garrett went on, "but they're determined to win this war. The South Vietnamese just want to get rich off of Uncle Sam. If the U.S. wasn't here backing them up, South Vietnam would fall like a house of cards. I say, if they want to be communists so badly; let them."

"But what about the Soviets? They'll gobble up all of Southeast Asia."

" So what? There's not a goddamned thing in Vietnam that we need. The entire country isn't worth the powder it would take to blow it to hell. Think about it, Frank," Garrett continued. "How are we supposed to win this war. Johnson already swore that he would never invade the North. So that means that they can devote all of their efforts towards the offensive in the south. The only way the war can end is if they get tired and quit."

Won't the people of North Vietnam get tired of it eventually and force their government to knock it off."

"Not very likely. The one thing that totalitarian regimes do very well is maintain civil order. You're not going to see any massive anti-war demonstrations in Hanoi or Haiphong. Although I'm sure there are probably a lot of them that would like to. Anyone who publicly protests is either killed or imprisoned immediately. There's no first amendment in North Vietnam."

"What about our bombing campaign of the North. Won't *that* bring them to their knees eventually?"

"What bombing campaign, Garrett responded? "Johnson and McNamara handpick the targets and the tactics that we have to use to attack. They won't allow us to go after the targets that might really hurt them like the power plants and the paddy dykes. We could bring them to their knees in two weeks if Johnson would let us. But Johnson is more afraid of winning this war than he is of losing it. He keeps a twenty-five mile safe area around Hanoi and Haiphong and then expects them to capitulate because they're afraid of us. He periodically pauses the bombing that we *are* allowed to do to demonstrate what a humanitarian he is. They just use the pauses to rebuild their defenses. They're laughing at us!"

"Well he *does* have to worry about the Chinese coming in like they did in North Korea, doesn't he?"

"Read your history, Frank. The Chinese have never gotten along with the people of Vietnam. They'll send arms and material goods to keep the U.S. tied up but spilling their own blood to save the people of Vietnam; that's something else. The North Vietnamese have the initiative. The only way they can lose is if they quit. Victory is not an option for us. Johnson already took that off of the table. This is probably the first time in history that something like this has ever happened. We're here to maintain the status quo. It's like playing a game of football and your entire objective is to keep the score tied. It's a defeatist mentality and it's sure to fail."

It had bothered Frank to hear that but the more he thought about it. the more it seemed as if Garrett might be right.

Lam Quang Son was the senior ranking officer at the river crossing once again. The General and his staff had made excuses about some important conference but it was plain that they didn't want to be anywhere around the bridge when the bombs started falling. He promised Son that there would be plenty of anti-aircraft guns to defend the bridge if he could just hold out for a few hours and then he and his staff beat a hasty retreat.

Son looked up at the sky. It was light now and he could once again see his surroundings. The sky was overcast and gray. He wondered if the clouds were low enough to keep the American airplanes away.

Son's men were still halfheartedly beating on the stubborn bolts with sledgehammers. They had nothing else to do until the cutting equipment arrived.

"Quiet." Son yelled suddenly and he strained to listen! It was faint but Son could definitely hear it, the muffled drone of an airplane approaching. The sound echoed off of the clouds and the ground making it difficult to determine just how far it was.

"Quickly! Grab everything and get off of the bridge," Son yelled!

Robertson was talking on the HF radio as he entered his work area. The ABCCC (Airborne Command and Control Center), call sign Dragnet was on the other end of the conversation.

"Dragnet, Nail five-eight is on station. Weather looks grim for any air strikes right now. Ceiling is ragged with bases between 1000 and 1500 feet. Visibility underneath is about 3 miles in mist."

"Roger Nail five-eight let me know if the weather improves I have a lot of strikes available this morning if you can find any targets for them," Dragnet replied.

"Okay I have an area that I've been keeping my eyes on it should…"

Frank couldn't believe what he saw. For three weeks he had been looking under tree branches and behind rocks for the enemy and now right in front of him was the best target he had ever seen. He quickly fumbled for his maps so that he could relay the position to Dragnet.

"Nail five-eight this is Dragnet say again your last transmission. You broke up at the end."

"Dragnet, Nail five-eight; you're not going to believe this but I got a pontoon bridge... or at least part of one across the Xe Kong west southwest of Ban Bak. Standby for coordinates." Frank worked quickly to determine the coordinates.

"Nail five eight did you say a bridge," Dragnet sounded as if he couldn't believe what he had heard?

"Yeah, I count five intact sections of a pontoon bridge and another, sixth section that's skewed to the south about 45 degrees off of the rest. It looks as if they hadn't quite gotten it into position yet. Let's see coordinates are Romeo Mike 264397."

"I copy your coordinates, Nail. We need to get a picture of this thing. Do you have a camera?"

"What does he think this is a sight-seeing tour? Yeah it's in my tote-bag right next to the suntan lotion," he thought to himself. Then he remembered that a lot of the other FACs carried their own cameras with them on missions.

"Negative, Dragnet I don't have a camera."

"Okay, Nail, just standby there for now I'm going to see if I can divert a recce flight your way."

"Roger."

"Nail, do you see any activity around the bridge?"

"Negative, but the jungle is so dense right here that they could hide an entire division under these trees."

"Well be careful. This could be something big. Charlie doesn't normally build bridges. Stay clear of it for now and stay safe. I'll get back to you in a few minutes. Dragnet out."

"Roger that, Nail five-eight, out"

Frank felt suddenly very much alone and vulnerable. It was no exaggeration that a 10,000-man division could be hiding in the jungle just beneath him and every one of them could have an AK-47 pointed at him. It was very unnerving to think that he might have 10,000 automatic weapons pointed at him at that very moment. He felt as if he could feel their eyes on him. He pulled the O-2 up just a bit more; getting closer to the cloud bases.

V: THE GUNS

(0630L 16 Dec 1969, NKP, Thailand)

TOM WRAPPED NIKKI in his arms. He was home with her. He could feel the gentle curves of her body against his. He kept his eyes closed fearing that this might be a dream. He never wanted to leave her again. He tried to drink in the moment and enjoy every sensation of it.

Then he opened his eyes and she was gone. He was on the other side of the world in the dingy hooch in Thailand. His heart sank; he felt physically sick. It had felt so real and now it was gone. Holiday was already gone since he had to fly in the first sortie of the day. Tom slowly got out of bed. He knew that he had made a big mistake last night.

John Layman, the squadron scheduler had cornered Tom at the bar in the Officers' club early last evening.

"I know you're DNIF[3], Tom but is there any way you can fly for me tomorrow? I'm really in a bind. All of the high-rollers are going to be in a briefing all day tomorrow and I'm really short of pilots," Layman said.

"Well, you know I sprained my ankle this morning..." Tom replied. He really didn't want to fly and he recalled the old military adage about never volunteering for anything.

"I know, but if you can't fly I'm going to have to double-bang someone."

Double banging meant flying twice in the same day. Generally it was a recipe for disaster. There was never time to decompress after the first mission and to properly brief the second mission. Facing the guns twice in one day was a lot to ask of anyone.

"Tom, I can give you a 0930 brief, so you can sleep in. It's an easy interdiction mission over Route Pack 1. You'll be back and debriefed in plenty of time for happy hour," Layman went on. "It's a *counter*," he added, as if to sweeten the pot.

A "counter" meant that it counted toward the 100 missions that were required to complete his tour.

---

3 DNIF stands for Duties, Not Including Flying. In other words, it means that a pilot is sick.

Tom reluctantly agreed.

Now he regretted it. He just didn't feel right about flying this time. He thought that it was probably due to fear because he had just been shot down. He told himself that the best way to get over it was just to get back in the cockpit and start flying again. He still had to fly another 64 missions before he could go home and this would get him one step closer.

Tom thought about his own plight as he showered and dressed. He wondered what was he doing here. He was separated from the love of his life so that he could fight for the people of South Vietnam yet, he didn't really care about them one-way or the other. He had only been to South Vietnam once and the experience didn't exactly endear him towards the people of South Vietnam.

About a month earlier Tom had diverted into Bien Hoa Airbase in South Vietnam with mechanical problems. The unit back at Ubon sent a mechanic to fix it but Tom was assured that he was going to have to stay the night there. It was still early in the day and Tom thought that it was a great opportunity to visit his older brother who was serving as a medic in the Army at a base just twenty miles northwest of Bien Hoa. It also seemed like a good chance to see some of the country that was the cause of his being in this part of the world. The motor pool had issued Tom a jeep and a Vietnamese driver who only spoke a few words of English. The driver was a pleasant old guy who was constantly smiling and agreeing with Tom even though he didn't seem to understand anything that he said. It just happened to be market day and the small dirt road was filled to capacity but there was a certain order to the chaos. On either side of the road, powered vehicles stayed in the center of the road for the most part then came people on bicycles to their right, then people with beasts of burden, water buffalo mostly, and finally pedestrians on the right shoulders of the road. The whole thing looked like a photograph from a *National Geographic* magazine.

They wound their way through mile after mile of countryside. At one particularly crowded section of roadway the normal order broke down and an elderly couple stumbled out in front of the jeep. Tom's driver had to swerve to avoid them. He missed hitting the two people but ran over the pig that they had with them on a rope leash. The driver stopped and both he and Tom got out to see what had happened. The couple started yelling at the driver and he yelled back at them. The entire exchange was in Vietnamese so Tom didn't understand what was being said. It was plain that both parties were very emotional. Soon there was a small group of people surrounding them and everyone seemed to have something to say. After a few minutes of this a police car showed up and most of the crowd quickly dispersed. The two officers got out and one came over to see what was going on. The other stood by the door of the police car staring at Tom with a sort of wild, angry look in his eyes and his right hand poised over the handle of his revolver. He looked as if he had seen too many western movies. He was small and his uniform was too big for him. Tom thought he looked like a teenage kid pretending to be a cop. It would have been comical except that he had a real gun and Tom was unarmed.

The first police officer seemed to be nasty toward everyone involved as he got a brief explanation from both sides in the dispute. Tom thought to himself that they needed help with their "Good Cop/ Bad Cop ploy" because neither one of them wanted to be the good cop. Then he came over to Tom.

"This your Jeep," he sneered as he spoke?

Tom thought that he might be funny and explain that it actually belonged to the U.S. government but he thought better of it.

"Yes, officer," he said as politely as he could manage.

"This your driver," he gestured toward the driver?

Tom nodded.

"This big trouble," the officer said. "He kill these people pig."

"Yes, but it was an accident," Tom explained. "Look I'll give these folks five dollars and we'll call it even, Okay?" Five dollars was twice as much as the pig was worth.

"No. This special pig, like family. Big trouble for driver. We take him with us. Jeep too. Evidence." Tom sensed that this was a scam that the policemen had practiced before. The officer moved to handcuff his driver and Tom instinctively moved to stop him. The other policeman crouched slightly and quickly drew his gun pointing it straight at Tom. His eyes seemed full of hate and anger. Tom stopped right where he was and raised both hands to show that he was unarmed. He realized that this was getting way out of hand. Part of him would like to have taken the gun from the other police officer and shoved it up his ass but discretion was the better part of valor. He explained that he had only fifty dollars with him and offered that to the policemen if they could settle the matter right there. The first police officer grudgingly agreed. Tom handed over his money and they were allowed to go on their way. The entire time the other Officer never took his eyes off of Tom. As they drove on Tom couldn't help but wonder how much of the fifty dollars would be given to the old couple. He thought it was a pretty lousy way to treat someone who had come halfway around the world to risk his life fighting for these people. Tom hadn't been able to forget the incident. He seriously wondered whether it was all worthwhile.

Tom was scheduled to fly with Captain Clark Kent. Yes, it was his real name. He had been born in 1940 long before Superman became nationally famous. His parents had never heard of the comic strip. Clark was a family name. The first time Tom met him he snickered a bit when Clark introduced himself.

"Clark Kent? Is your girlfriend named Lois," Tom had asked without even thinking. Then he thought that he might have sounded foolish.

"I guess you get that a lot," Tom added.

"No. No. You're pretty much the first one who's ever asked that," Clark said as he laughed. Clark was a good-natured person who always seemed to have a smile on his face.

The briefing was quick compared to yesterday's marathon flight briefing. Yesterday all of their actions had been carefully choreographed. They knew what the target was and how they were going to attack it. They had some idea of where the threats were. Today they had no idea of what they might encounter. Clark and Tom would fly as a two-ship today using the call signs Cyclone three-one and Cyclone three-two, respectively. Their mission was to check in with the ABCCC and orbit safely away from the battle area until some FAC found a target for them to bomb. Once they were cleared off of the ABCCC, the FAC would brief them on the target, the threats and surrounding terrain. They talked about bomb deliveries and emergency procedures. It only took about 30 minutes to brief since they had both done this many times before.

Each airplane carried 6 Mk 82 500 lbs bombs on a multiple ejector rack (MER) on the centerline station, the belly of the aircraft. As always they carried extra fuel in drop tanks under each wing. Two Electronic Countermeasures (ECM) pods were mounted on the outboard wing stations to jam enemy radars.

The two men suited up for battle in the life-support shop. Each of them donned their g-suit, survival vest and parachute. The final step was to check out a .38 cal revolver that fit into a holster on the left side of the survival vest. Then the pilots made their way to the flight line burdened by over 40 pounds of extra equipment.

The two planes lifted off the runway at Ubon RTAB three minutes ahead of schedule at 1057L. Twenty-two minutes later they had rendezvoused with Texaco two-three, a KC-135 tanker near the Laotian border. Clark's F-105 was having it's fuel tanks topped off while Tom flew on the left wing of the giant plane awaiting his turn on the boom.

The weather in the refueling track was awful. Dark, menacing clouds billowed up all around. The tanker pilots worked to try and stay in clear airspace but it wasn't always possible. Turbulence rocked all of the airplanes as they attempted to complete the refueling. It made the job of the fighters just that much more difficult.

Clark managed to hang on to the boom of the tanker long enough to get his fuel.

"Cyclone, I think I gave you about 500 pounds more than you asked for," the Boomer radioed. "Is that going to be a problem?"

"Nah," Clark responded. "You *never* have too much gas in a Thud, …unless you're on fire."

The Boomer smiled at that. Clark disconnected and slid his airplane over to the right wing of the tanker.

"Cyclone three-two you're cleared to pre-contact," the calm voice of the boomer came over the radio again.

"Roger, three-two," Tom said as he took a deep breath.

The refueling boom was lowered beneath the fuselage of the tanker and it bounced up and down slightly as turbulence buffeted it. Tom's F-105 slid quickly behind and below the bigger tanker and stabilized about 30 feet aft of the extended boom. In this position the boom operator could get his first good look at Tom's airplane.

"What, no nasty paintings on either one of your planes today?" the Boomer asked. He knew that a little humorous conversation usually helped to relieve the tension of a stressful situation.

Clark and Tom both immediately knew what he was talking about. For a time the squadrons from Ubon had been famous, or maybe infamous, for the bawdy paintings they had on the noses of their F-105's. Ever since World War II the noses of American combat aircraft had borne paintings of beautiful women. Most were rather scantily clad at best, some were downright obscene but boys will be boys and this was long before anyone had ever heard of sexual harassment. Someone at Ubon had taken it a step farther. The air-to-air refueling operation required the tanker to fit its extended boom into a receptacle on the receiver aircraft. The process had a great deal of obvious sexual overtones to it. Some pilots had paintings of women drawn on the noses of the F-105s with the girl straddling the refueling receptacle as if it were a certain part of her anatomy. This went on for some time somewhat under the radar because there was a door on the refueling receptacle and it wasn't immediately apparent how lewd the paintings were with the door closed. Most of the time the doors *were* closed so essentially the only ones who could see the paintings in all of their glory, were the boom operators and they weren't complaining about it. Then some cameraman rode along with a tanker one day and took some photographs of one of these *naughty* Thuds. Some General was appalled and before long the paintings were taken off.

"No, I think some old biddy in the Officers' Wives Club found out about it and we had to take all of them off'" Clark radioed back.

"Man, you guys are boring. Okay, Cyclone three-two, you're cleared into contact position."

Tom acknowledged and moved his airplane closer to the tanker. Two illuminated strips of lights under the forward fuselage of the tanker guided him into position. One signaled fore and aft adjustments and the other signaled up and down. As he nudged the F-105 into position both lights turned green indicating that he was in the proper position for refueling. The refueling receptacle was on the forward left side of the F-105's nose and the Boomer quickly guided the boom into the Thud. Tom could clearly see the face of the boom operator as he held the Thud in the refueling position.

"Texaco two-three, contact."

"Cyclone three-two, contact."

The tanker began refilling the tanks of Tom's Thud. The turbulence was moderate and continuous. Tom had been on the boom for several minutes when all of the sudden the airplanes encountered a violent up-draft. Both aircraft began to climb rapidly. The pilot of the tanker instinctively grabbed the controls and pushed forward attempting to maintain altitude. In his haste he didn't consider that Tom was still connected to the boom. The tanker pitched down while the F-105 was still moving up. The boom operator felt it and he tried to shout a warning over the radio.

"Texaco two-three **breakaway, breakaway, breakaway**!"

The boom snapped in two before he could finish saying breakaway the second time. Tom was able to disconnect and the portion of the boom that was still connected to the Thud flew cleanly away. Clark and Tom quickly moved well clear of the tanker which was spewing fuel out of the broken boom. The flow of fuel should have stopped immediately but in the heat of the moment the tanker pilots made a switch error that prevented the automatic shut-off. It would take them several more minutes to realize their mistake.

The tanker pilots quickly declared an emergency as they turned back toward their base at U-Tapao near Bangkok. Clark looked Tom's airplane over and determined that it was undamaged. Tom was shaken a bit but both he and Clark still wanted to continue with the mission and get credit for it. Tom had gotten nearly all of his fuel so they decided to continue on as planned.

Clark joked on the radio as they headed toward Vietnam.

"Tom, I think you just shot down a tanker."

"Yeah, well a kill's a kill no matter how you get it."

"Let's see you got a Thud yesterday and a tanker today. Three more and you'll be a communist ace."

They both laughed at that.

"It's a good thing that we're not sailors," Tom said.

"Why is that?"

"Because I think that incident with the tanker would be a really bad omen."

"Yeah, it's a good thing *we're* not superstitious," Clark agreed.

A few minutes later they checked in with Dragnet. They were instructed to head south and contact Nail four-four.

Frank Robertson had patrolled his area in Nail five-eight for nearly three hours. He kept the pontoon bridge in sight but stayed well clear of it. It had promised to be one of the most exciting missions of Frank's tour but it turned out to be one of the most boring. The weather was lousy all morning long and prevented fighters from attacking the bridge. It began to clear by late morning. An RF-101 had blasted through the area just after 0800 making two low, high-speed passes, taking photographs of the bridge and the surrounding area. Frank had watched closely but didn't see any ground fire toward the aircraft. He was relieved by Nail four-four at around 0900.

Thirty-one year old Major Steve Turner was Nail 44. He had flown F-100's just as Frank had and he was also Frank's flight commander in the squadron. They were good friends. Frank briefed him on the situation, showed him the pontoon bridge and then departed for NKP.

Turner had some trouble keeping his mind on the job. He was on of the very few people in the Squadron who had been allowed to take leave over the Christmas holiday. Most of the pilots weren't allowed to leave over the holidays but Turner had a bargaining chip that most of the others didn't. The Squadron was desperately short of Instructor Pilots and Turner was one of the best and most experienced. He had been scheduled to rotate home at the beginning of December but agreed to stay on for two extra months if he could take leave over the Christmas and New Year holidays. The leadership of the Squadron had no real choice, so they agreed to the bargain. Steve could leave on the 20th and had spent most of the morning arranging his transportation home.

By 1130 the weather had improved to the point that Turner thought he could work the target. He called the ABCCC and asked for fighters to be sent his way.

Ten minutes later he got a call on the radio.

"Nail four-four this is Cyclone three-one."

"Go ahead, Cyclone."

"I've got two Thuds with six Mk 82s and 1,000 rounds of twenty mike-mike each. We're about five minutes out from your position at base plus two (***base altitude changed*** *everyday; this day it was 13,000 feet so base plus two meant they were at 15,000 feet*) and we have thirty minutes of playtime."

"Roger, for now just take up an orbit over Dallas and stand by for my brief."

"Roger."

Dallas was a point on the map that had been prearranged. The FACs knew the landmarks in their areas very well since they flew over them nearly everyday. The Thud pilots had to operate over a much larger area covering North and South Vietnam as well as Laos and Cambodia so various points were established as holding points. They were named after American cities. Dallas was just to the northwest of the target area.

"Cyclone, I think we've caught Charlie with his pants down. There's half of a pontoon bridge over the river about eight clicks (*kilometers*) southwest of the village of Ban Bak. It looks as if it was put up over night and was supposed to be taken down by morning but one of the pieces is cocked off to the south and I think it's stuck."

"Cyclone copies," Clark said. "We have the tools to take the rest of it apart for them."

"That's what I was thinking, Cyclone. The weather is kind of marginal but I think you'll be able to work. Right now I have a ragged ceiling at 3,000 feet. Visibility is about five miles. The first order of business is to get you guys down below the clouds."

"Nail, there are some breaks in the overcast here over Dallas so I think I can probably get down through them. Just stand by for a minute."

"Okay Cyclone. I'm seven miles southeast of Dallas at 4,200 feet on the meter (altimeter). I should be no factor to you. Let me know when you're ready."

"Roger, stand by Nail."

Clark brought Tom into close formation and the two jets worked their way down through openings in the clouds. Tom had been listening to the exchange between Clark and the FAC but like a good wingman he kept his mouth shut. According to Air Force lore there are only three things that a good wingman can say on the radio; two, bingo and "lead, you're one fire". *Two* is used to acknowledge any radio call from lead. *Bingo* indicates that you're low on gas and it's time to go home and if your leaders' airplane catches fire you're allowed to tell him about it. Other than that, a good wingman just keeps his eyes and ears opened and his mouth shut. Of course this was a humorous exaggeration but the point was that Flight Leads, lead and wingmen follow. The pilots often switched roles and they were accustomed to being in charge so, it was difficult for many to be good wingmen and to allow the Flight Lead to do his job. Tom didn't have that problem.

Turner turned his attention to the northwest towards Dallas. He knew that seven miles wasn't very far in a high-performance jet and he didn't want to accidentally run into either of the Thuds. He saw them a few minutes later as they descended through a small opening in the clouds about three miles north of his position.

"Cyclone, I have you in sight. I'm at your left nine o'clock for three miles, slightly low."

Clark split Tom back out to tactical formation and they both strained to see the smaller airplane.

"OK Nail, I've got you in sight," Clark said after about thirty seconds.

"Cyclone, are you ready for the formal brief?"

"Sure, go ahead Nail."

"Cyclone three-one your target is a pontoon bridge on the river approximately eight miles southeast of Dallas. There are no threats that have been spotted in the area yet but you can expect to draw some triple-A as soon as you roll in. This is a high priority target and it may be well defended. SAFE (*selected area for evasion*) area is three miles west of the target. Your best immediate bailout is anywhere west of the target. There are no friendlies on the ground anywhere in the area. The wind is out of the east at about five knots. The target will not be marked. I don't think you'll need it."

"Cyclone copies all, Nail."

Clark was got busy trying to work out the details of his attack. This was before the days of GPS-guided bombs and automated airplanes. Even a full size bridge could be a very difficult target to hit using the technology of the day. It seemed logical that the best way to attack a bridge was to fly down the length of it as you dropped your bombs but experience had shown that this was not true. If the bomber didn't fly directly over the bridge all of his bombs would miss. Clearly attacking from 90 degrees to the span was the worst way because it required even greater accuracy. The best solution was to attack from a forty-five degree angle to the span of the bridge. Clark decided that was how he intended to attack.

"Cyclone, if you look beyond me you'll see a river flowing essentially north-south."

"Yeah, Nail, I see the river."

"If you follow the river south about three miles it takes a sharp turn to the east. The bridge is about one click north of the bend in the river on the western bank."

"Okay Nail, I copy all that. I'd like to make one dry pass through the area to take a look at the target and assess the threat."

"It's your show Cyclone. Do whatever you like. I'll try to spot any ground fire for you. Just be careful."

The two Thuds blasted over the bridge a few minutes later. Both Clark and Tom had no trouble spotting the target. They kept their speed up and didn't seem to attract any fire from the ground. Clark worked out his plan of attack with Tom. Clark would come in from the northwest and Tom would come from the southeast. Due to the low ceiling they would have to attack with a shallower dive angle than they would have preferred. Clark would like to have come in with a 45-degree dive bomb attack but the ceiling wouldn't allow that. Instead they would have to come in with about twenty degrees of dive. It meant that they would spend more time exposed to any ground fire and it would make it more difficult to hit the target. They discussed the plan briefly over the radio and then split up for the bomb run. They both would drop all of their bombs in one pass and then be on their way home. It all seemed simple enough.

The two Thuds climbed right up against the cloud deck and then began to orbit the target in a large circle. Tom maneuvered his airplane so that he was on the opposite side of the circle from Clark. In that way, Clark and Tom could both see the target as well as each other.

After a short while Clark radioed, "Cyclone three-one is in hot from the northwest."

"Cyclone, Nail four-four has you in sight. You're cleared in hot."

Clark dove down toward the target. It seemed to be very small as he lined his sights up on it. He kept his speed up at around 400 knots.

"Cyclone Three-one you're taking fire from your right two o'clock," It was Nail four-four with the warning.

Clark was aware of it but he chose to ignore it and concentrate on his bomb run. He released his bombs and then pulled off aggressively to his left.

Tom rolled in as soon as he saw Clark release his bombs. He was aware of some ground fire but it didn't concern him too greatly. Clarks' string of bombs exploded just beyond the bridge. There were huge geysers of water and the entire length of the bridge lifted slightly out of the water but the bridge appeared to be intact. In reality, Clark *had* destroyed it. The bridge was never intended to take that kind of punishment and it would not have been safe to use again but Tom had no way of knowing that. He was more determined than ever to destroy the structure. Tom pressed in on the target. The heavy Thud accelerated quickly as it raced toward the ground. He should have pulled up sooner but he was intent on destroying the bridge. He kept the nose of the Thud diving towards the bridge until he couldn't stand it any longer then he released his bombs at the last possible second. He quickly pulled back on the stick and forced the big fighter to climb away from the on-rushing ground. Just as Tom released his bombs the area around the bridge erupted with gunfire from all around.

"Cyclone come off right you're taking heavy fire from your left," it was Nail four-four again but his warning came too late.

Tom felt his airplane shudder from numerous hits. In an instant everything began to go very wrong. Amber caution lights illuminated all over the instrument panel in front of Tom. He immediately began to climb as rapidly as possible. He wanted to get away from the guns as quickly as he could. The Thud jerked sharply to the left and there was a loud bang behind Tom. The engine was compressor stalling. The engine firelight came on and Tom knew he was in serious trouble. The Thud had been mortally wounded. He couldn't believe that this was happening again. How could he get shot down twice in less than 24 hours? The odds against it must have been astronomical and yet it was happening. This time, however, there was no friendly airbase just a few miles away. This time he was smack in the middle of Indian country.

"Mayday, Mayday, Cyclone three-two; I'm hit," Tom tried to control the fear in his voice.

Nail four-four had watched it all happen and he knew immediately that the Thud was in very deep trouble. He could clearly see the back half of Tom's plane was covered in flames and thick black smoke as it climbed steeply away from the target. It looked like a roman candle on the fourth of July.

"Cyclone three-two, you're on fire. Bail-out, BAIL-OUT!" he radioed.

Tom heard the radio call from Nail four-four but he just couldn't get himself to pull the ejection handle again; not over *that* territory. He tried to coax the wounded plane back to the west toward Thailand and safety. The plane was climbing almost vertically and his airspeed was quickly decreasing to nothing. Tom tried to force the nose of his plane back down but the control stick didn't seem to have much effect. He could hear a loud scraping noise as the engine began to tear itself to pieces. The airplane was shuddering constantly now.

"Tom, get out of there," it was Clark on the radio. "You're going to explode."

The airplane had stopped responding to any of Tom's inputs. He was no longer a pilot, he was just a passenger. Tom knew it was inevitable now and he reached down and pulled the handle on the ejection seat.

The ejection seat worked flawlessly just as it had the day before and within seconds Tom was hanging beneath his parachute. The steep climb off of the target had taken him into the cloud deck and initially he found himself floating through the clouds. It was suddenly quiet and serene. He had a hope; more of a prayer actually, that when the ground appeared again he would find that he was safely far away from the bridge that he had just bombed. His mind was working so fast that it seemed as if he hung in the clouds for quite some time but it was only about 30 seconds. As Tom got a glimpse of the terrain beneath him, his hopes sank. He could see that he was going to land not more than a kilometer from the pontoon bridge. To his surprise the bridge was no longer intact. It was in three separate pieces, two of which were already beginning to drift away down the river. Water and debris from the blast of his bombs were still falling here and there around what was left of the structure. There was obvious bomb damage to a large part of the bridge, which was twisted almost beyond recognition. The sight of it fascinated Tom. He couldn't help but feel a twinge of satisfaction that he had accomplished his mission. Then reality caught up with him again and he once again realized what a terrible situation he was in.

He scanned the area beneath him. As he had sped along in his high-speed jet it looked as if the ground was completely covered by impenetrable jungle. Now he could see that there were clearings here and there in the jungle and he was descending into a somewhat large one.

He was only about a thousand feet above the ground when he saw a group of soldiers looking up at him and running towards the spot that he was descending to. His heart sank. They would be waiting for him as soon as he hit the ground. He was as good as captured already. His hand reached for the pistol on his survival vest but he realized how foolish it would be to try and fight his way out of this. There were about eight or ten Vietnamese and each of them had an AK-47. He didn't have a chance.

Suddenly Tom heard a great roar behind him and the ground around the soldiers exploded with dirt and debris. It was Clark and he was speeding down blasting away at the ground with his twenty-millimeter cannon. The cannon growled loudly as it spit out hundreds of rounds of cannon shells. His fire was accurate and devastating. Clark held the trigger down until he was out of bullets. The Thud raced quickly past Tom missing him by only a few hundred feet and then turned hard back to the left to set up for another pass. Tom was elated. He couldn't believe how close Clark had pressed the attack. Guns were firing at Clark from all around but he seemed oblivious to it.

Tom was only a couple of hundred feet above the ground as he watched the small group of soldiers. There was no movement for a long while and then two or three of them slowly stood up just as Tom hit the ground. They were only a hundred yards or so from

Tom now. For several seconds they seemed unsure of what they should do next. Then Clark decided the issue for them. His jet roared in again from behind Tom. He had no weapons left so he dropped all of his bomb racks and pylons on them. He came incredibly close to slamming right into them with his jet. The Thud roared past them not thirty feet above their heads. None of the projectiles from Clark's plane hit any of them but it was close enough for this bunch and they run away from Tom and back into the jungle.

Tom quickly shed his parachute harness, grabbed his seat kit and started to run for cover. The first step that he took on his left ankle felt as if someone had thrust a knife up into his leg. He fell to the ground, doubled over in pain. The ankle that he had sprained yesterday must have been re-injured as he landed. He had no time for this. He was completely exposed where he was. He had to get to some cover. For Tom, fear trumped pain. He staggered to his feet and hobbled as quickly as he could toward the nearest tree line but he didn't stop there. He ran as fast as he could for as long as he could. He stumbled over vines and slammed into low branches. Every step over the uneven terrain was torture. His ankle seared with pain, his entire body ached from exhaustion but his mind was in a panic now. He had no idea which direction he was going. The only thought in his mind was to get as far away from his parachute as possible. He knew that it would attract enemy soldiers like a magnet. After what seemed like an eternity he fell to the ground again, unable to go any farther. His lungs gasped frantically for air. As he lay there, desperately trying to catch his breath he realized that he was making so much noise that he could surely be heard for fifty yards in every direction. He forced himself to get control of his breathing. He made every effort to be as quiet as possible and he listened. He could hear voices in the distance. He had no idea how far away they were but he knew that they were a lot closer than he would have liked. He convinced himself that he had to control his fear if he was going to survive this. He began moving again, more cautiously and much more quietly this time. As he moved along Tom noticed that he had his .38 revolver, grasped tightly in his right hand. Some time after hitting the ground he must have taken it from it's holster. He had no recollection of doing it so it must have been instinctive. He wasn't certain how useful the small gun would be to him but it made him feel a little better just to hold it in his hand. It made him feel as if he still had some control of the situation. He moved on; away from the sound of the voices.

Tom had been moving quietly through the jungle for several minutes when he heard a noise that made his heart leap for joy. It was the drone of an airplane! The FAC was still there and in his haste to run from his parachute, Tom had forgotten the most important piece of survival equipment that he had with him; his radio. He could have kicked himself for being so stupid. It was clear that his mind wasn't working correctly. He pulled the radio from the pocket in his vest. He remembered to use the earphone that it had with it. He didn't want to make any more noise than he already was. He turned on the radio.

"Nail FAC, Nail FAC, this is Cyclone three-two," he whispered into the radio. For some reason he couldn't remember the two-digit number that the FAC was using as his call sign, so he just called for any Nail FAC. It was another indication that his mind wasn't thinking as clearly as it should have been.

"Cyclone three-two if you read this, turn off your beeper," the transmission was barely audible because of a continuous beeping sound on the frequency.

Another mistake. The locator beacon was automatically activated when the seat ejected from the airplane. It broadcast a continuous beeping on the emergency channel. It was nearly impossible to talk on the radio until the beeper was turned off. Tom mentally kicked himself again. He knew that he would have to start doing things better if he was going to survive. He switched off the beeper and tried again.

"Cyclone three-two I have you loud and clear now. It's good to hear you. We thought we'd lost you," Nail four-four responded.

"No, I'm still here for now," Tom said.

"What's your status, Cyclone are you alright?"

"Yeah, I'm OK for the most part. I sprained my ankle pretty badly and I'm a little sore from the ejection but I think I'm OK."

"OK Cyclone, I'm glad to hear that. We're going to get you out of there, buddy. Find a safe place to lay low for a while, drink some water if you have some and try to relax. The Cavalry's on the way. Things are going to get pretty exciting down there in the next few minutes. I have a flight of four Huns (F-100s) with some greeting cards for the gunners who shot you down. So keep your head down."

The voice of Nail four-four sounded relaxed and confident as if he had done this a million times before. Tom's throat was choked with emotion. Perhaps it was just the stress but, here was someone he had never met before who was going to move heaven and earth to save his life. Tom realized that he wasn't alone in this. Tom decided to do as Nail 44 had told him. He was in a thick section of jungle now and this seemed as good a place as any to stay for the next few minutes. The voices were gone for the moment. He had been carrying the survival kit that had been attached to his ejection seat. Now he finally opened it and examined the contents. There were two spare radio batteries; two gray cans of drinking water, two signal flares, a signal mirror, a signal strobe, some extra ammunition for his pistol and a host of other small items to help him stay alive. It was like Christmas morning to Tom. His spirits soared. He opened one of the cans of water and took a long swallow. The water tasted stale but at that moment it seemed like the finest drink he had ever had. It helped him to calm down.

It was Nail four-four who had spotted the troops moving towards Tom as he descended in his parachute. He had seen them long before Tom had. He talked Clark's eyes onto them and then watched as Clark executed the two most incredible strafing attacks he had ever seen. They both lost sight of Tom after he landed and it was more than fifteen minutes before his first radio call. Clark was out of ammunition and low on fuel but he still didn't want to leave until he knew Tom was OK. Nail Four-four finally persuaded him to go home. There was nothing else that Clark could do for his downed wingman and Nail four-four assured him that he would stay with Tom as long as he was needed. In the meantime, Nail two-eight showed up. He was scheduled to relieve Major Turner in Nail four-four at noon but Turner wasn't ready to leave. He had the best situational awareness of the problem and he was the logical man to direct the recovery effort if there was to be one. He told Nail two-eight to orbit high, above the clouds and the two of them would work together with two-eight being a radio relay for four-four.

The cavalry was indeed "on the way". Within ten minutes of Tom's shoot-down the rescue forces were airborne from their base at NKP. Four A-1 propeller driven attack bombers and two HH-3 rescue helicopters were racing to Tom as quickly as they could.

The A-1s used the call sign 'Sandy' whenever they flew on search and rescue missions. No one seemed to know for sure where the call sign originated but it was rumored to have been the name of the dog of the squadron's first commander.

The helicopters used the call sign "Jolly", short for Jolly Green Giant, a nickname that the copters had borrowed from an advertising campaign for a company that specialized in frozen foods back in the U.S. The "Jollys" and "Sandys" had become legendary throughout Vietnam for their heroic and selfless exploits, rescuing downed pilots.

Nail 44 had plotted the positions of two of the guns that had opened up on Clark and Tom. The guns had to be taken out before the slow moving helicopters could come into the area to rescue Tom. It seemed that Tom was safe for the moment, so Nail 44 turned his attention to the guns. He didn't know exactly where Tom was but he knew where he had landed. One of the gun positions was on the far side of the river from Tom and the other was much farther away than Tom could have traveled in the short time he had been on the ground. Nail 44 directed two flights of four F-100s first against one of the gun positions and then against the other.

Tom lay still on the jungle floor. He could hear the fighters swirling around above him and hear their bombs exploding in the distance. He could also hear a lot of guns firing back from the ground. The bombing continued for nearly twenty minutes.

Tom was almost beginning to feel comfortable in his hideout. Then he heard something that nearly made his heart stop. Tom could clearly hear a line of soldiers moving through the jungle. They made no effort to conceal their progress. They yelled back and forth to each other as they rustled through the jungle. They were close to Tom and they were slowly getting closer.

Tom quickly grabbed all of his things and began to scramble away. He was careful not to leave the empty water can behind. He didn't want to leave any clues that would prove that he had come this way. His heart was pounding again. He stayed low; crawling as quickly as he could. He forced himself to resist the panic that threatened gain control of him again. It occurred to him; they were flushing him out as if he was some kind of game animal. They wanted him to go in this direction. He wondered why they wanted him to move this way. He considered stopping where he was and hiding. If he concealed himself well enough, the line of troops might just pass by him without seeing him. Once he was behind them he could double back and throw them off of his trail. In the end, he was simply too scared to try it. He just continued scrambling away from the soldiers as fast as he could manage.

Suddenly Tom burst out of the jungle and he instantly realized what they had been up to. The Xe Kong River was in front of him. He was trapped. He had only seconds to decide what to do. There was a small clump of vegetation right at the river's edge. It wasn't large enough to conceal him completely but he dove into it anyway. The mud along the river's edge was thick and deep. Tom sprawled out in the water's edge. He used his legs and arms to quickly bury the lower half of his body. His head and shoulders were just barely above the water, hidden by the clump of small bushes. He prayed that his concealment would be adequate. He lay on his stomach; propped up on his elbows with his pistol clenched tightly in his right hand just above the water. His heart felt as if it would explode in his chest.

In just a minute or so, North Vietnamese troops began to step out of the jungle one by one. There was about twenty feet between each of them. Each one was armed with an AK-47. One walked right up to the small clump of bushes where Tom lay. Tom was frozen with fear. He felt certain that his heart was pounding loudly enough to be heard from five feet away. His index finger strained slightly against the trigger of the gun. Tom was ready to fire at the slightest indication that he had been spotted. He remembered in survival school he had been told not to stare at someone who was looking for you in a situation like this. Some people can sense when they are being stared at. Tom tried not to look straight at the man but he was frozen with fear. He expected any second that he would be dead or captured.

What Tom didn't know, was that the soldier was not really a soldier. He was a member of Lam Quang Son's engineer battalion as was the entire line of troops along the riverbank. They had been up all night working on the bridge. Finally by mid-morning they had been allowed to go and get a few hours of sleep. It seemed as if they had just lain down when bombs hitting the bridge awakened them again. Then they were ordered to run around through jungle looking for the American pilot who had been shot down. The soldier was tired and angry. What were the chances of *him* finding one person in this huge jungle? This was a job for the regular army, not the engineers. He barely knew how to use the AK-47 that he carried with him. They had been told to form a line across a wide stretch of jungle and to move towards the river. The Officer in charge had told them to stay in line as they moved and to make lots of noise. It all seemed incredibly foolish to him.

The soldier felt uneasy as he approached the riverbank. He couldn't understand exactly why. He stood there for a moment gazing across the beautiful river imaging how nice it would be to live in a house right at this very spot. He thought that someday he might like to leave his life in the city behind and start an easier existence in someplace like this. Then the Officer on the south end of the line yelled for them to reform down at that end. He joked with his friend as they made their way down to the Officer. They both hoped that they would be dismissed and be allowed to get some sleep.

Tom couldn't believe his luck. The man had stood not five feet away from him and hadn't seen him. Another dozen or so soldiers shuffled past him and no one seemed to pay him any attention.

Tom could breathe again. He was soaking wet and filthy now, shivering uncontrollably from the cold river water, but he was still alive. Then he heard something that suddenly made it all make sense to him. Dogs! A group of two dozen or so North Vietnamese soldiers to the south of him had two dogs with them as they moved slowly to the north along the river's edge. This group of soldiers appeared to be alert and ready for anything. Tom had never heard of the NVA using dogs before but that seemed irrelevant for the moment. The two dogs moved back and forth briskly in the clear area along the riverbank sniffing everything in sight. They were quick and methodical. Tom knew that they wouldn't be as careless as the other soldiers had been. This group would spot him for sure. They were only about a hundred yards away and Tom was paralyzed with fear again. He thought about going out into the river but he would be completely exposed and the powerful current would take him south, right into the bulk of the enemy forces. His only chance was to sprint for the jungle again and hope to lose them but there was no way that he could get back to the safety of the jungle without being seen. Once they saw how close they were to him, they would have little trouble running him down. There was no way that he could lose the dogs once they picked up his scent. Tom knew that it would take a miracle to save him from this. He did the only thing he could think of; he pulled out his radio and contacted Nail 44 again. Tom quickly explained the situation and asked if there was anything Nail could do to help.

Major Turner listened carefully and he immediately understood just how desperate Tom was, but Turner had a problem too. The fighters had expended their ordnance and left. The Sandys were still another ten minutes out. There was no one else there who could help right at that moment. Turner's mind raced quickly as he tried to think of something to do. He sensed something in Tom's voice that he hadn't heard before; resignation. Tom sounded as if he was going to give up and accept his fate.

The soldiers with the dogs were only eighty yards away now.

"Cyclone, stay with me now, buddy. It ain't over till the fat lady sings and she hasn't even started to warm up yet!" he radioed to Tom.

Steve Turner did the only thing he could think of, he pushed the throttles of the little O-2 to the firewall and dove down to the deck. It wasn't a question of heroism or valor for Turner. An hour or so earlier Turner had asked Clark and Tom to take a risk by attacking the bridge and they had done so without hesitation. Now Tom needed someone to take a risk for him and it was Turner who didn't hesitate.

Turner was skimming along the trees, missing the tops by just ten or twenty feet. He flew over the river and turned to follow it south. He got the best look he had had all day of the area around the river. The river was in the middle of a large valley. As he flew south, Turner could see the terrain rose slowly to the west side of the river and more steeply on the east side. There was actually a good side cliff that he hadn't noticed before overlooking the bend in the river on the east side. As Steve dropped down to just a few feet above the river he was below the level of most of the terrain on either side of the river. He could be seen and shot at by anyone on either side of the river for a kilometer in both directions.

The troops were just fifty yards away from Tom now.

"Stay down, Cyclone, but be ready to move," Turner said over the radio. "This is going to be really close!

Turner had taken off that morning with 14 "***willy-pete***" white phosphorus smoke rockets in two pods, one below each wing. He had shot one earlier to gauge the surface wind from the motion of the smoke cloud so he still had 13 left. That should be enough, he thought to himself. Normally the rockets were fired one at a time. Each press of the ***pickle*** button fired one rocket. Turner set his armament panel to ripple fire so that they would all go with a single push of the button.

Tom lay in the river frozen with fear. The soldiers were close enough now that he could begin to make out the details of their faces. He squeezed the pistol even more tightly in his right hand. Then, out of nowhere there was a terrible racket from the other side of him over the river. The soldiers and the dogs stopped where they were to look.

Out over the middle of the river just ten feet or so above the water, was an odd-looking airplane with two tails and propellers on both ends of it's fuselage.

"I SEE YOU. I SEE YOU, NAIL," Tom practically shouted into the radio! "The gomers are at your right one o'clock along the west side of the river."

Turner saw the group of soldiers and their dogs. He turned slightly to his right and pointed the airplane right at them. As he sped along he thought he saw the little clump of bushes that Tom had described as his hiding position. This was going to be **very** close.

The funny-looking airplane was pointing straight at the group of soldiers on the river-bank now. Most of them crouched down, a few dove flat on their stomachs but some just stood where they were. They all quickly raised their rifles and began to fire. Together, the soldiers put up and impressive volume of fire. The little airplane seemed impossibly close to them.

Turner's O-2 was peppered with bullets from the soldiers. At this range, there was almost no way they could miss. A round caught Turner square in the chest and killed him in seconds but not before he could press the pickle button. The O-2 appeared to erupt in smoke and flames as 13 rockets blasted out from the safety of the pods.

What happened next was like a scene from Dante's inferno. The rockets plowed into the unprotected soldiers enveloping them in smoke and flames. Turner's O-2 followed right behind and slammed full speed into the conflagration.

VI: SANDY 7

(1310L, Saturday 16 Dec 1967, NKP Thailand)

Lt. Col Mike Groves was Sandy 7. As the Operations Officer of the 601st Special Operations Squadron (SOS) Mike was the number-two man in the squadron behind the Commander. To the pilots in the 601st he was known as "Iron Mike". It was a nickname he had acquired early in his flying career. According to the story, Mike had nerves of steel (or iron). Nothing ever seemed to bother Mike Groves. In reality he was a deeply troubled man. He just chose to keep his problems to himself. He was forty-three years old with a loving wife of sixteen years and the father of three children. On paper, it looked like an idyllic situation. The reality was that both his personal and professional lives were in a shambles.

Mike was the product of a generation where the roles of men and women were still somewhat clearly defined. The man went to work and financially supported the family and the wife stayed home and took care of the kids. It was a simple and time-tested arrangement. A man was defined by his job and most of the concerns of the family were subordinated to the professional success of the father. Mike had never really thought twice about it. As far as he was concerned the more successful he was in his career, the better off his family would be. It wasn't a matter of choosing one over the other; they were both tightly intertwined with one another.

His wife, Barbara, would have disagreed with that notion. In the past three years Mike had only been home for seven months, but Mike's assignment to Hamilton Air Force Base in Sausalito had been very fortunate for her. She had two girlfriends who sold real estate and they convinced her to give it a try. Barbara discovered that she had a talent for selling and she was in the ideal location to profit as the real estate market in California just began to explode. She was earning more money than Mike after only two years on the job. She felt that Mike had abandoned her and the children but she didn't need him anymore and he clearly didn't need her. As far as she was concerned, their marriage had been over for quite some time.

The professional side of Mike's life was not in much better shape. He was six months away from reaching the twenty-year milestone with the Air Force but his career had run into a block wall. He knew that he was not on the list of Lt Cols who were destined to command a flying squadron and he would not be promoted without that. He had reflected on it many times but it was difficult to say where exactly, his career had been derailed. His flying skills and his ability to lead men into combat were unquestioned. But Mike also had a talent for speaking his mind and being very candid at inappropriate times. Over the course of twenty years he had learned that despite their protestations to the contrary, most Colonels and Generals don't like subordinates to tell them when they're screwing up. One incident in particular stood out above the rest. A couple of years ago Mike had been flying F-102s at Hamilton as an instructor pilot. He flew with a two-star General from higher headquarters one day and after the flight he respectfully told the General that he was getting too old to fly fighters anymore. Mike thought he had been very tactful as he explained to the General that his flying skills had degraded over time and that he didn't fly often enough to maintain any real proficiency. Mike thought that the General was a danger to himself and the other pilots that he flew with. He politely suggested that the General should confine his flying activities to larger airplanes where a co-pilot could help keep an eye on him. The General had thanked him afterwards for his insight and candor and then promptly put the word out that Mike Groves should be avoided like a leper by anyone who hoped to succeed in his command. It was only one incident. There had been others.

Groves was probably the most experienced man on the planet when it came to search and rescue. He had participated in dozens of rescue missions. He knew the elation that went along with a successful rescue and the terrible despair of failure. Outwardly, they were all the same to Mike; it was just another day on the job. He encouraged the other pilots in the squadron to think about it that way too and to avoid the emotional roller coaster that often accompanied their work.

Groves had the ability to leave his earth-bound problems behind him when he flew. His life on the ground was in turmoil and confusion. In the air he was in complete control. He flew on toward Thailand at the head of his small task force. The cockpit of the lumbering A-1 was hot and noisy and the airplane itself had all the charm and grace of a brick. But, the A-1 was a tough and sturdy airplane that could carry a truckload of ordnance. The Sandys were carrying a veritable arsenal of assorted weapons along with them. Each A-1 carried a large fuel drop tank that would allow them to stay airborne at least until sunset. They also had two canisters of napalm, eight Mk. 82 500 lbs. bombs, 28 2,75 inch rockets with high-explosive warheads in four pods and 1200 rounds of 20mm cannon shells. They had the potential to make it a very long day for the *gomers*. There was nowhere else in the entire world that Mike would have preferred to be at that moment. Groves in Sandy 7 and Sandy 15 flew ahead as Sandy 9 and 12 stayed back to escort the two "Jollys".

Experience had shown that their best chance for a successful rescue was to get in quickly before the North Vietnamese could reinforce their people on the ground. The first few hours were the most critical and the longer a survivor spent on the ground, the less likely he was to be saved. Groves was hopeful that this one could be done quickly. Generally, the NVA didn't have a lot of anti-aircraft firepower at any one location along the trail in Laos. The situation was much more fluid than that. If the NVA encountered resistance at a certain point they normally just went around it rather than standing and making a fight. He knew that there was an airborne FAC on the scene and that usually helped to expedite the rescue process. The FACs normally had very good situational awareness of the entire rescue area and they were good at suppressing threats. The downside was that they often felt a sense of responsibility for the fighters that they worked with. If there was a crash the FACs often allowed their emotions to override sensibility. It was another consideration that he would have to keep in mind. As he approached the location of the crash, Mike was given some troubling information. Cyclone three-one (Clark) the flight lead of the accident aircraft had discovered damage to his aircraft once he landed back in Thailand. Two flights of four F-100s had worked against guns in the area and three of them had been hit as well. One had been forced to make an emergency landing in South Vietnam. It sounded as if the crash site had already been fortified well beyond what Mike might normally have expected. He was told to contact Nail 44, who was the on-scene commander. Everything seemed to go wrong at that point.

Nail 44 didn't answer, Nail 28 did. He sounded confused and distraught.

Lt Rick Zeimmer was Nail 28. He had been in the area orbiting above the clouds working as a radio relay and assisting Nail 44. He had heard the exchange between Cyclone 32 and Nail 44 but he hadn't been able to see anything through the clouds. All of the aircraft used TACAN (Tactical Air Navigation) radios as their primary tool for navigation. If it was tuned to an operating ground station, it displayed bearing and distance to the station in the airplane. The TACAN also had an air-to-air mode that could be used to determine the distance between two aircraft. If two aircraft tuned in the proper frequencies they could see how far apart they were from each other. Nail 44 and 28 had been using the air-to-air mode to insure that they didn't accidentally collide with each other. The TACAN readout went dead right after Nail 44's last radio transmission. Zeimmer suspected the worst but he had no way of knowing for sure. There had been no more radio calls from Nail 44 or Cyclone 32 after that last desperate exchange. He informed Dragnet of what he suspected and then worked his way below the clouds to take a look for himself. By the time he got down below the cloud deck there wasn't much left for him to see. Zeimmer had a great deal of respect and admiration for Turner (Nail 44) and he simply couldn't force himself to believe that Turner had been killed. He was desperately trying to contact either Nail 44 or Cyclone 32 when Sandy 7 came on the radio.

Groves quickly assessed the situation and determined that the first order of business was to calm Nail 28 down and to try to focus him on the task at hand. They all orbited safely away from the target area while Groves talked with Zeimmer (Nail 28). Groves had seen this many times before and normally the best course of action was to send the distraught pilot back home. Mike didn't have that option. He needed Zeimmer's help if they were going to pull this off. He was compassionate but firm. Mike explained that they had a mission to accomplish and they would all have to concentrate on the mission if they were to succeed. It worked.

Everything needed for the rescue was quickly coming together. The Jollys were approaching their holding point northwest of the area. A flight of four F-105s was overhead to suppress any threats that appeared. The Sandys were ready and after a few minutes to gather his thoughts, Nail 28 was ready too. The only thing they lacked was a survivor to rescue. Both Nail 28 and Sandy 7 had been calling for the two Americans on the ground but there was no response.

After nearly 15 minutes of silence from the ground both Sandy 7 and Nail 28 agreed that someone was going to have to go into the valley where both men had been lost and see first-hand what the situation was. Zeimmer (Nail 28) wanted to go in and take a look. He felt as if it was his responsibility but Groves would have none of it. The last thing they needed was another plane shot down. The O-2 was simply too slow and too vulnerable. The F-105s overhead were fast enough to be relatively safe but their speed would preclude them from getting a good look at the area. There really was no choice. Only the Sandys could fly slowly enough to get a good look at the situation and yet were tough enough to stand up to any fire that they might encounter. There was no doubt that Sandy 7 (Mike Groves) would make the run. He told Sandy 15 to stay well above and behind him and to watch for any guns that engaged him as he flew down the river. He told Nail 28 to position himself so that he could spot any gun positions that opened up. Then Mike Groves pushed up the throttle of the aging A-1 and descended toward the little river valley. As he looked back to the west to take a quick glance at the two Jollys in their holding orbit, he could see that the weather was beginning to move in again. Mike guessed that they would have 30 maybe 40 minutes more before the weather would close in again over the river.

Back at NKP Frank Robertson (Nail 58) was having a late lunch at the Officers Club with a couple of other pilots from the Squadron. They were eating and laughing as Major Reynolds hurriedly came up to their table. Reynolds was another FAC and he was one of the biggest pranksters in the Squadron. He was usually a lot of fun to be around but he looked uncommonly serious. He seemed to be almost out of breath as he spoke.

"Frank, you need to get back to the squadron. The Commander wants to see you right away," Reynolds said.

"Great! What have I done *this* time," Frank laughed as he answered.

Reynolds was very serious as he glanced over at the other two pilots and then back to Frank. He really wasn't supposed to tell him anything; just bring him back to the Squadron.

"Your area got really hot after you left this morning," he said in all seriousness. "We think Steve Turner might have been shot down. Rick Zeimmer is out there right now but you know that area better than anyone. If Steve's alive, we want him back. We've got your plane being fueled and armed right now."

The impact of the news hit Frank like a ton of bricks but he quickly recovered his senses and he and Reynolds ran out of the Club.

Twenty minutes later he lifted off of the runway for the second time that day and turned southeast towards Laos.

As he flew south down the river Mike Groves was unknowingly retracing the route that Steve Turner (Nail 44) had taken nearly thirty minutes earlier. He kept the airspeed up at just over 250 knots as he scanned the small valley ahead. It seemed quite peaceful.

Groves was about two clicks north of a large bend in the river when the first guns opened up on him. It appeared as though they were working together because they both began to fire at the same time from opposite sides of the river. The fire was inaccurate at first; the gunners had misjudged his speed. The gun on the left bank was closer so Mike quickly turned directly toward it and fired off a few hundred rounds of 20 mm towards it.

"Do you see that, Nail 28?" Mike asked over the radio.

"Yeah, Sandy I see two gun positions," Zeimmer said. He was already plotting their positions.

Mike quickly turned south and headed back down along the river. He changed his altitude and heading continuously to throw off the gunners aim. A third heavy gun began firing at him a few seconds later. It was really getting hot. Then he saw what he was looking for, a black smudge along the riverbank on the west side just north of the bend in the river. The smudge was small at the river's edge but fanned out wider as it went into the jungle. Mike looked closely; this was definitely an airplane crash but the plane itself was completely destroyed. Then he saw the tail. The right tail and part of the stabilizer of the O-2 was the only thing that was recognizable as part of an airplane.

"Okay, mark this position, Nail 28. I think we know what happened to Nail 44." Groves said over the radio. "The crash site is on the west bank of the river about one click north of the river bend."

"Is there…do you think he might have gotten out?" Nail 28 responded.

"I don't know, Nail." Groves thought that it would have taken a miracle for Turner to get out but there was no sense in going into that right at this time.

Dozens of small arms joined into the hail of gunfire that was coming from both sides of the river now. The ground fire was very intense and Mike was tiring from the constant effort of moving his airplane around to avoid it. He began a rapid climb, trading airspeed for altitude and quickly out-distanced the guns. His airplane had taken a few hits but it was all right.

Groves told Nail 28 that he needed to work over the gun positions that they had just uncovered but Zeimmer (Nail 28) was hesitant. He didn't know if either of the two Americans on the ground were near the guns and he was reluctant to take the chance of hitting them. Groves finally convinced him by reminding him that there was no way they could possibly rescue either of them until the guns were suppressed. It was a chance that they would have to take. Zeimmer (Nail 28) finally agreed and he briefed the F-105s that were orbiting overhead.

Tom Morgan had been laying in the river as Nail 44 came to his rescue. He saw the little O-2 racing down the river to his aid and was elated. Turner (Nail 44) had been doing a good job of moving his airplane around to avoid the ground fire until he spotted the group of soldiers on the riverbank. In order to fire rockets accurately the aircraft had to be pointed at the target like a gun. As Turner (Nail 44) stabilized his flight path to aim his rockets, the gunners began to find their marks. Small arms and automatic weapons that were firing from all around shred the O-2. Tom was close enough to see it all. The blast from the rockets had been impressive but when the airplane slid onto the shore and exploded it felt to Tom as if the entire world had turned into a ball of flames. There was fire, smoke and debris everywhere. Laying flat in the river, Tom was protected from most of it but a large piece of metal hit him on the left side of his back and the fireball burned the left side of his head. He was bleeding and in great pain but he managed to get to his feet again and staggered off into the jungle to the north. He kept moving, away from the crash site, as quickly as he could manage until he was too exhausted to move any farther. He collapsed into a dense clump of bushes, deep in the jungle. He was cold, wet, filthy, hungry, thirsty and exhausted beyond what he would have believed possible just a few hours earlier. Tom was also completely drained emotionally. He had been minutes away from capture or death twice within the past two hours and he had been an eyewitness to the death of Nail 44. He wondered what made *his* life any more valuable than the life of Nail 44. As he lay in terrible physical and emotional pain, Tom was overcome by despair. He wondered how he could possibly go on after all of the misery that he had caused. Then he heard the familiar drone of a large radial aircraft engine. The motors made a very distinctive sound and Tom knew that it must be an A-1. The Sandys had arrived to save him; there was hope once again.

"Any Sandy, Any Sandy, this is Cyclone 32!" he radioed.

After a short pause that seemed like an eternity to Tom…

"Cyclone 32 this is Sandy 7, what's your status, over."

Tom was so grateful to hear a friendly voice again that tears ran down his face. He was glad, for a moment that he couldn't be seen by the other pilots. He took a deep breath and forced himself to control his emotions before he talked again on the radio. He thought to himself that whatever "Uncle Sam" paid for these survival radios, it was worth it!

"Sandy 7, I'm a little banged up but I'm Ok." Tom felt as if the entire left side of his body had been torn open and he could barely walk from the pain in his ankle, but he was grateful at the moment, just to be alive.

"Glad to hear it Cyclone. We're going to come in and get you but we're going to need you to help us. Keep your radio on and your head down. We're going to hit some of those gun positions again before we bring in the Jolly Greens."

"I copy all that, Sandy 7. Kick their f***ing asses. I'll be okay."

Groves was encouraged to hear that Tom still had some fight left in him.

"Cyclone, this is Nail 28. Do you know anything about the status of Nail 44. We've been unable to contact him."

"Yeah," Tom's throat was instantly choked with emotion at the thought of what had happened.

"He's gone," was about all that Tom could manage to say.

"Is there any chance that he may have gotten out?" Nail 28 refused to give up hope.

"No."

Groves knew that he couldn't allow them to be overwhelmed by their emotions so he immediately stepped back in, forcefully on the radio.

"Nail, bring down the fighters and work over the gun positions. Cyclone, try to get some idea of your position relative to the targets that we're hitting so you can vector us toward you. Let's get this over with while the beer is still cold at the club!"

Flights of fighters were beginning to stack up over the area, each waiting their turn to take a shot at the gunners that had made this a miserable day for them. For the next thirty minutes four F-105s and eight F-100s dropped tons of iron bombs into the river valley. Nail 28 did a remarkably good job of getting them in one right after the other and keeping the pressure on the guns. From the air it appeared as if nothing could have survived.

Tom was able to give Sandy 7 a rough idea about his position. It seemed to Tom as if he had traveled miles north of the crash site of Nail 44 but the reality was that he was only several hundred meters away from it.

The weather was closing in quickly as the last flight of fighters departed the area. The firing from the ground had abated to nearly nothing. Mike was still a bit apprehensive about taking the slow-moving Jollys into valley. He knew that iron bombs were notoriously ineffective against gun positions. Experience showed that often the gunners would fire until the attacking aircraft released its bombs. Then they would quickly duck into cover while the bombs exploded around them. Unless a direct hit was scored the guns would be right back in operation as soon as the dust cleared. At least one flight of F-100s had fuse extenders on their bombs. The fuse extender was a clever device that was simply a three-foot long metal tube. The tube was inserted between the bomb and the fuse. The fuse would detonate while the bomb was still three feet above the ground. This would allow more shrapnel to be dispersed around the area with the hope of killing more of the gun crew. Sometimes they were more effective but the jungle could absorb a lot of shrapnel. Mike Groves knew that they would have to work quickly. It was now or never.

"Okay Nail 28 good job. Let's get Cyclone out of there. Cyclone 32 get your marker flares out, we're coming to get you." Groves said over the radio.

Tom was elated. As the bombing had progressed he managed to work himself a little farther to the north and up to the edge of another small clearing. He expected the helicopter to come from the north or northwest and his position gave him a reasonably good view of the sky in that direction.

"Saddle up, boys." Groves radioed to his task force. "We're going in!"

VII: POLITICS

1400L Saturday, 18 Dec; The Pentagon, Arlington, Va.

Colonel Jack Broughton, U.S. Army, strode quickly through the long hallway with a large rolled map of Viet Nam in his left hand. The silver eagles that he wore on his shoulders looked as if they had just come out of their original packaging and in fact, they nearly had. The eagles had come along with his new job as Assistant Director of Army Intelligence. The job title sounded important but in reality there were several Assistant Directors of Army Intelligence. It was a job he really hadn't wanted but for the first time in his life he saw the possibility that he might just make it to the rank of General. If that was to happen, he had to have his "*ticket punched*" with a tour of the Pentagon. He was determined to distinguish himself from the others. He was one of a very small group of Senior Staff Officers who had actually completed a tour of combat in Viet Nam. He had always preferred to lead his men from the front, but it seemed now to be an antiquated notion. The road to promotions came straight through the Pentagon so Jack would have to pay his dues for a couple of years if he ever wanted to lead them into battle again.

The hallway was very quiet, even more so than on most Saturday afternoons. A lot of the Senior Officers and other workers at the Pentagon had already left town for the holidays.

Jack was a man with a mission who really didn't pay much attention to the days of the week. Since he had arrived in his new assignment nearly a month ago he had been pouring over old intelligence reports hoping to find something important that may have been overlooked. Some raw intel reports had arrived just hours ago that seemed to be just what he was looking for. Ordinarily he would have shown his theory to his boss first who would than forward up the chain to the Army Chief of Staff, General Harry Stanton, but most of the Chain of Command above him had already taken off and begun their Christmas vacations early. There was no one left between him and General Stanton and Jack felt that he had to act quickly.

He entered Stanton's outer office and a civilian woman looked up from behind her desk. She was in her early thirties, very attractive. To Jack it appeared as if she was trying hard to look professional but it just didn't work. Her dark hair was arranged neatly albeit somewhat matronly, in a large knot on the back of her head. Her sweater was modest enough but it seemed as if it was at least two sizes too small. Her ample breasts appeared as if they were going to explode out of it.

"*It's good to be king*," Jack thought to himself as he looked at her.

"May *ah* help you?" the secretary said with a slight southern Virginia drawl that Jack found so appealing.

"Yes, I'm Colonel Broughton. I called a few minutes ago. I need to see General Stanton right away, please."

"Oh yes, Colonel. The General is very busy but I'll ask if he can see you."

The secretary picked up her phone and dialed the intercom number that rang in the office just a few feet away.

Broughton had briefly met General Stanton twice and he wasn't really impressed by him on either occasion. The word throughout Pentagon was that Stanton had mostly avoided combat tours in favor of staff assignments in his rise to the top. He was known as a sycophant, a "yes man" who was pliable to the whims of whatever superior he served. This was the reason that President Johnson had hand-picked him for the top job. He was unlikely to make any waves as Johnson made all of the critical decisions concerning the war.

"The General will see you now, Colonel. Go right in," she said as she hung up the phone. She smiled sweetly and motioned toward the door to Stanton's office.

"Oh my God," Broughton thought as he started for the door. "Is she making a pass at me?" The secretary's smile seemed to make him weak in the knees. "*Come on Jack*," he thought, in answer to his own question. "*Can't a girl even smile at you without it being some kind of sexual innuendo?" "Besides, we have more important things to concentrate on now.*" He chased the thought of her from his mind but he made a subconscious note to find excuses to visit General Stanton more often and check out the theory.

General Stanton was standing behind his desk gathering up folders and filing them into the briefcase that lay in the middle of the desk. He was so pre-occupied that he seemed not to be aware that Broughton had entered the office.

Jack closed the door behind him, stood at attention directly in front of the General's desk and snapped into a rigid salute.

The General continued to fumble through papers on the desk for a few long moments apparently unaware that Broughton was even there. It was quite awkward as Jack stood silently waiting for the General to return his salute.

Stanton finally looked up and casually returned the salute as if he was annoyed by the whole process.

"It's Jack isn't it?" Stanton said as he returned to the work on his desk.

"Yes Sir," Jack nodded.

"You were CO of the four-two-two weren't you? That's why I picked you for the job. I was S-2 for the four-two-two in Korea."

Whatever else was true about Stanton, it was obvious to Broughton that he had a good memory. He had hundreds of Officers on his staff and yet Stanton remembered this small fact about Broughton.

"Yes, Sir. It was a really good unit. I was sorry to leave."

"Well Jack, what's so damned important that you to come down here on a Saturday afternoon to enlighten me about?

"We received an intelligence report this morning from an Air Force Forward Air Controller over southern Laos. The NVA set up a pontoon bridge last night over the Xe Kong River on the Ho Chi Minh trail."

Stanton looked up over his reading glasses. Jack felt as if the General was looking down his nose at him but he quickly dismissed the thought.

"And you don't think our colleagues in the Air Force are capable of taking out a *pontoon* bridge without our help?" Stanton said.

"No sir. That's not the point. I was going over some old reports from a year or so ago and I found one from a factory worker inside the Soviet Union that said the NVA were shopping around for a bridge that could be quickly constructed and dismantled. One of the criteria that they seemed to insist on was that the bridge be able to support PT-76 tanks. I think that this might just be that bridge."

Stanton just stared blankly back at Broughton as if he was speaking in some alien dialect.

"Don't you see sir?" Broughton was annoyed that Stanton seemed so dense. "We know that the Communists are building up for some kind of offensive push. This shows us at least one of the major axis of the attack and it shows us that they're going to use tanks in the assault."

"Can I show you on the map, sir?"

"I suppose there's no way to stop you now," Stanton grudgingly pointed toward the large table in the corner of his office.

Broughton moved quickly and unrolled the map on the table. The General walked slowly over to see the demonstration.

"I plotted the location of the bridge, here. You can see that a build-up here puts the entire Quang Tri province in danger but specifically our outpost at Lang Vei and the Marine outpost at Khe Sanh. My guess is that the NVA are going to make a major push for them and for the city of Hue and they'll have PT-76 tanks leading the way."

"So what? We know that the PT-76 is a piece of crap it can't stand up against any of our tanks."

"That's true except that we don't have any of *our* tanks stationed anywhere near Lang Vei or Khe Sanh. We don't even have any LAU rockets at Lang Vei. Hell, the communists could drive through with an armored car and we probably wouldn't be able to stop them."

Stanton seemed to understand now. He stood quietly thinking with his hand on his chin for a long moment.

"Wait a minute," Stanton said. "Isn't the PT-76 supposed to be amphibious?" "What the hell do they need a bridge for?"

Broughton was ready with the answer. "This is a very powerful river, Sir, with a very powerful current. The Soviets had a training exercise a few years ago where they tried to cross a river like this with a company of twelve PT-76's." "Seven of them were swamped and sank and the five that made it across were spread out for miles." Broughton paused for just a moment to allow his words to sink in. "The PT-76 *is* amphibious, but it would be foolish to risk a crossing such as this if you didn't have to."

"Colonel, you said that the Air Force boys spotted the bridge. They'll undoubtedly find some way to take it out. Problem solved, right?"

"The NVA will just find another way, sir. You know that. It may take longer and be more difficult but they'll find a way. The bridge itself isn't what's important. It shows us their intention."

"Okay so what are you proposing that we do?" he said finally.

Broughton had to try hard to contain his excitement. He knew what needed to be done and he was anxious to lead the effort. Suddenly it seemed to him as if this boring Pentagon Staff assignment might not be so boring after all.

"We need to get some eyes on the ground, Sir" Jack said. "Three or four covert teams to keep an eye on this area ought to do the job. If we're right and we move quickly we can stop this attack before it even gets going."

Stanton was quiet again for a long time. This time he shook his head slightly as he stared at the map. He seemed to be arguing with himself.

"This is Laos, Colonel. There are a lot of political considerations when you're dealing with Laos." Stanton shook his head vigorously. "The President won't like this one bit. There's an election next year. We're supposed to be reducing our troop strength. This will be viewed as an expansion of the war. The President will never go for it. "

"Sir, the lives are of our men may be in jeopardy if we don't act on this information. Besides we're bombing targets in Laos every day."

"Colonel, there's a big difference between having airplanes overhead and having troops on the ground. Right now, the President's press secretary can look the news media in the eye and honestly tell them that we don't have any troops *in* Laos. We have plenty of troops *over* Laos but none of them are actually *in* the country. Do you see the difference?"

"That's just semantics. You're playing games with words."

"Welcome to Washington, Colonel."

Both of them were silent for a few moments.

"Well, there's nothing *I* can do." Stanton threw up his hands as he walked away from the map. "Any operations in Laos have to be personally approved by the President. I couldn't even take a piss there without his okay. Hell, we're not even supposed to *be* in Laos."

"This opportunity won't last forever, Sir. If the President is the only one who can approve this operation than we need to get his approval."

"You're so young and naïve, Colonel." Stanton shook his head and smiled as he sat down behind his desk. "I was like that once. Washington doesn't work that way. We need to form a committee, do some research, arrive at a consensus and publish a plan of action. It could take months; years."

"Sir, with all due respect, we don't have months." Broughton was speaking more forcefully as his frustration grew. "We may not even have days. This bridge is a pretty brazen move for the commies. They're serious about trying to out-flank us at Lang Vei. We need to get serious about stopping them."

Stanton was quiet again for a long while before he spoke again.

"Normally I'd have you go see the Secretary of Defense and have him tell you to get lost but as you know, Secretary Mc Namara announced his resignation last month. He's already thrown in his chips. For the time being we don't really have a Secretary of Defense." Suddenly Stanton's mood seemed to brighten a bit as he appeared to come to a decision. "You need to talk to General Moore on Monday morning. I'm leaving town this afternoon. As a matter of fact, I have to catch my plane in an hour and a half. The only reason that I came in at all on a Saturday is so that I could straighten up a few things before I left for the holidays."

Stanton was certainly taking a military jet out of Andrews Air Force Base to wherever he was going. The jet would leave whenever he wanted it to.

"For God's sake, General, they're not going to leave without you! It's going to take time to get the teams together, to equip them, to deploy them. Even if we started right now it would probably be two weeks before we got any useful information from them. Every minute that we delay, works to help our enemy."

Jack knew that he shouldn't have made that statement but he seemed unable to keep the words from coming out of his mouth. It wasn't only what he had said that he regretted but the force with which he said it.

Stanton was caught a bit off guard by Broughton's outburst. His first response was defensive.

"We're going to our beach house on Windward Island for the holidays. The last ferry leaves at 1900. That's the only way to get to the island. If we don't take off from Andrews by 1600, we'll never make it."

Stanton could hear how weak his own argument sounded even to himself. He suddenly felt a surge of anger. Why was he even explaining himself to one of his subordinates, he wondered? He was about to lash back at the brash young Colonel when he stopped himself. He had an even better idea for teaching this upstart a lesson.

"Okay Colonel, you've got the job," Stanton said as he grinned. "I agree with your proposal. You can be in charge of this project and as such you can sell it to President Johnson."

"Sell it to the President?" Broughton seemed a bit flustered by the statement but not nearly as off-guard as Stanton had hoped.

"Yes. Do you have a dress uniform handy?"

"Yes, Sir. In my office."

"Good! Well go and change into it I'll get the White House on the phone and see if they can squeeze you in for a minute or two this afternoon."

Ten minutes later Broughton was back in Stanton's office. This time he was outfitted in his finest dress uniform. In the time that had passed, Stanton began to have second thoughts about sending Broughton over to see the President. It was a bit like sending a lamb into the lion's den for an Officer who didn't realize what he was getting into. He wasn't really angry at Broughton. The Colonel was just a bit too impulsive.

"Sit down, Colonel," Stanton said, this time with a more genuine smile on his face. "I talked to the President's appointment secretary, Frank Wilson and twisted his arm a bit. The little faggot said that he'd tried to give you a couple of minutes just before the President leaves for a campaign fund raiser this evening. He was angry so he'll do everything that he can in the meantime to make you miserable, but he'd probably do that anyway. Have you ever met President Johnson, Jack?"

"Well, he spoke to our class at the War College and I shook his hand afterwards along with about 200 others guys. Sooo, no! I guess I can say I've never met him."

"You probably have visions in your mind of great statesmen like Washington, Jefferson and Adams in your mind." Stanton was struggling to find the right words. "Lyndon Johnson is more like a used car salesman. He uses people to promote himself. He's not really a very likable person but don't ever underestimate him. He'll smile and tell you some folksy story one minute and shove a knife if your back the next. I wouldn't trust him any farther than I could throw him. He can be very mean and spiteful and for a man who has the most powerful job in the world; that's a dangerous combination."

Broughton was shocked to hear Stanton say these things about their Commander in Chief but he tried hard not to let his emotions show. Everyone in the Pentagon had the impression that Stanton was just one of Johnson's lap dogs. Apparently this was one lap dog who wasn't really that enamored with his master.

"Johnson especially doesn't like the military. He's more afraid of his *own* military than he is of the Communists. He thinks he knows military strategy and he doesn't like being told otherwise. Clausewitz, Sun-Tzu, Caesar; they were all wrong! Lyndon knows better. McNamara and Johnson have the notion that war is a negotiation. You twist their arm a little then back off and let them ponder the hopelessness of their situation. The trouble is that the Communists don't see it that way. Every time Johnson stops twisting their arms, with one of these bombing pauses, they use it as an opportunity to fix the damage that we've done and prepare for the next attack. It's beyond foolish. It's borderline insanity. When they write books on military strategy in the future, they'll use this as an example of what *NOT* to do."

Broughton was surprised to hear this coming from the most senior man in the Army, but it reflected what nearly every Officer in the military was thinking.

"General, if you feel this way why don't you do something about it?"

"Like what? Go to the press?"

"Yes! That would be a good start."

"Don't think that I haven't thought about it but, I'm a realist, Jack. I'm sitting here because I can get along with the President. Four other Officers interviewed for this job. All of them were senior to me and frankly, all of them were better qualified. I got the job because Johnson knew that I wasn't a threat to him." Stanton paused for a moment to assess Broughton's reaction. "Are you shocked, Jack?"

"Honestly?" Broughton hesitated, then he continued. "**Yes**! Johnson is using you as cover. How can you allow yourself to be used like this? By remaining quiet it appears to the American public as if you and the rest of the Army's leadership go along with this hare-brained strategy!"

"Jack, whatever else Johnson may be, he is a tough opponent. He would crush anyone who opposed him, including me. At least while I have this job I can make some small difference. I'm making changes that will insure that the Army becomes stronger in the future and we'll be better able to fight our real enemy, the Soviets, directly. Eisenhower weakened the Army, Jack. His massive retaliation strategy gave most of the funding to the Air Force. We're paying the price for that now. I'm rebuilding the Army. I can't do that from the outside. I have to be here!"

Broughton shook his head slowly in disbelief.

"While you're rebuilding the Army you're destroying it from within. Morale is in the toilet. The American people don't even respect us anymore. They think we're incompetent or war-mongers and baby killers. They blame US for the failed strategy of the President! You're asking the troops to fight and die and they don't even understand why."

"I'm not asking anything; Johnson is! Jack, you'll have to come to the realization that this is the way things are. You can either work within the system or be destroyed by it. The people of this country elected Johnson as their President; I didn't. The Constitution made him Commander in Chief of the military; I didn't. I'm a loyal subordinate, Jack. What are you? I follow orders to the best of my ability. I give the President my advice when he asks for it. You and I both took an oath of loyalty."

"The Wehrmacht officers in Nazi Germany swore an oath of loyalty to Adolph Hitler." Broughton said. " My oath didn't say anything about Lyndon Johnson. I swore to support and defend the Constitution of the United States. As Officers, we have a duty to the men that we lead into battle as well as to the people of this country. If the *temporary* occupant of the Office of the President is foolishly risking and sacrificing their lives don't we have an obligation to speak up on their behalf?"

"The most important asset of any subordinate is loyalty to his Commander!" Stanton snapped back.

Stanton was clearly becoming agitated. It was clear that he was now questioning Broughton's loyalty. Jack thought that it was best just to back-off and diffuse the issue.

"You made an appointment for me to see the President, Sir?"

Stanton quickly regained his composure.

"It's not an appointment really. If you go over and sit around all afternoon, the scheduling secretary said that he would try to get you a few minutes with the President. If you believe in what you're proposing, Jack, be careful. Johnson's number one priority is himself. If you can make it seem as if it will benefit him in some way, he might allow you to proceed. If you attempt to teach him military tactics and logic, he'll cut you off at the knees and you'll probably wind up in command of some outpost in the Aleutians before you know what's happening."

"I appreciate your candor. I'll try to keep that in mind, Sir."

"Well, good luck to you, Jack. If you can get the President's approval I'll see to it personally, that you get everything that you need."

Broughton proceeded quickly across the river and to the White House. He had seen the building from the outside many times before but he had never actually been in it. At first he was in awe of the imposing structure. The huge columns and high ceilings were designed to convey strength and power. The security precautions were strict but surprisingly less intense than he had expected. Broughton wondered if perhaps there were more precautions that he just didn't see taking place without his knowledge. He dismissed the thought. He had probably been reading too many spy novels.

Frank Wilson, the President's scheduling Secretary, met Colonel Broughton as he signed in at the security desk. Wilson was overtly homosexual just as Stanton had said. He acted as if he was being terribly imposed upon by Broughton and relished his position of authority. Normally, his attitude would have irritated Broughton but Jack was somewhat overwhelmed by the opportunity to actually talk about a military operation with the President of the United States so he ignored it.

Wilson showed Broughton to a seat in hallway just outside of the Oval Office. There were three other men in the hallway all of them apparently waiting for their opportunity to speak with the President as well. Wilson whispered to Broughton that the President was in the Oval Office and admonished him to remain quiet while he waited. Broughton felt as if he was being treated like a school boy waiting to see the Principal but he quietly sat down and waited.

Jack got his first glimpse of the President an hour and a half later. Johnson walked out of the Oval Office and quickly down the hallway surrounded by at least a half a dozen other men. The entourage was laughing and joking with President Johnson as if he was the funniest man they had ever met. Jack thought that he recognized one or two of them as Senators or Congressmen. The group walked swiftly past Jack as if he wasn't there. Not one of them even glanced his way. They were gone in an instant. Jack did not own a color television and he thought to himself that it was the first time that he had ever seen the President in living color.

Broughton assumed that his opportunity to meet with the President had come and gone but Frank Wilson assured him that the President would return for a few moments after his speaking engagement and that there might be an opportunity for him to make his proposal at that time. Broughton was normally a fairly good judge of people and he thought that Wilson might just be toying with him to see how much he would be willing to endure before he just gave up and left. Jack's first impulse was just to leave, even if it meant that he would not get to state his case to the President. At least there was a chance that he might get to meet with the President, so he stayed.

As the time passed, Broughton had the opportunity to reflect upon his earlier conversation with General Stanton. The more that he thought about it, the angrier he became. When he was in Viet Nam there was an assumption that no one person would knowingly run the war so poorly. It was generally agreed that Johnson was being misinformed by his advisors. If he only knew the truth about how badly the war was going, the frustration and despair that permeated the entire military, he would fix it. But Broughton had come to realize over the past month that Johnson knew exactly what was going on. Johnson was the problem and the entire military establishment was scared to death of him. Certainly loyalty to one's commander has to be considered but the situation in Viet Nam was slowly deteriorating to the point that it could not be saved. Someone of importance had to speak up. The American people had to know the truth. Jack thought back to some of the letters that he had written to the families of the men in his command that had been killed in the war. He always tried to make it sound as if their deaths had not been in vain. He attempted to tell their survivors that they had died in a worthy cause when he knew that it was not the case.

Nearly four more hours passed as Broughton sat dutifully in the hallway. The other three had all given up and left. Wilson came by periodically and assured him that Johnson was supposed to return eventually.

Just after nine P.M. Johnson came back up the hallway retracing the route that he had taken earlier. This time he was with only one other man. Broughton sprang quickly to attention just as he had the previous time. The two men walked past Broughton without a word. This time Jack saw that President Johnson looked over at him suspiciously but said nothing. The two men walked into the Oval Office and a security agent closed the door behind them. Jack sat quietly for nearly another hour. Every once in a while he could hear the sound of laughter and raucous conversation though the heavy door of the office. Eventually the door to the office burst open again and the President walked past Broughton for the third time today without any acknowledgement. This time he didn't even glance at Broughton. Just as Johnson and his friend were about to disappear again down the corner of the hallway, Broughton thought to himself."***How bad can the Aleutians really be?***"

"Mr. President," Jack called to them in a loud voice that was just below a shout.

The two men immediately stopped in their tracks and Johnson glared back at Broughton.

"***If looks could kill,***" Broughton thought to himself, "***I'd be a dead man.***"

"I know you're a very busy man , Sir, but if you don't want to start looking for a new job next November, you'd better hear what I have to say."

Jack congratulated himself at least for taking Stanton's advice by telling Johnson that it would be to his advantage to hear what Jack had come to say.

Johnson walked slowly over to Broughton. He looked angry and his stare never left Jack. It seemed a bit overly dramatic to Jack.

"Who in the hell are you?" Johnson sneered at him. "and who do you think you are yelling at me?"

"I'm Colonel Jack Broughton, Sir . I meant no disrespect. I work in the intelligence section for General Stanton."

"Army intelligence, there's a laugh," Johnson said over his shoulder to the other man that he was with but his eyes never left Broughton's.

Broughton understood the insult but he took it without any outward sign.

"Sir, I have some time-critical information that could help you to counter the offensive that the Communists are building up for."

"Offensive! What do you know about any offensive? The Communists don't have the capability. We've weakened them and cut their supply lines. The Communists are hanging on by their fingernails. They'll be lucky to hold on for another six months." There was obvious contempt in Johnson's tone of voice.

Broughton was astounded. He wondered if Johnson could actually be unaware that the Communists were building up their forces for some sort of offensive push. Was he unaware or did he just refuse to accept the possibility?

"Mr. President, I don't know who *you* have been talking to, but I just got back from Viet Nam less than two months ago and I can assure you that the Communists aren't hanging on by their fingernails!"

"That's the problem, Pete," Johnson laughed slightly, looking back towards his friend. "All of these guys want to be the next Mac Arthur. They all have the magic answer for instant victory. And that's fine soldier boy, except that *I'm* the Commander! *I* make the decisions!"

Jack was conflicted. Here he was, having his first ever conversation with the President of the United States and it was turning into an argument. But, more than anything, Jack was angry. He didn't like the belittling tone that Johnson had taken with him. Over the years he had learned to control his anger. If anything he over-compensated by appearing to be exceptionally well composed. His voice was calm and cool when he spoke again.

"That's absolutely right, Sir, and if you don't want to go down in history as the only American President who has lost a war, you'll listen to what I have to say."

Johnson's face turned red with anger as he glared at Broughton. Jack could smell alcohol on his breath.

"Give us a minute, Pete," Johnson said to his friend and pushed Broughton towards the Oval Office. "Okay Colonel, you've got your five minutes."

Broughton was unaccustomed to be physically pushed anywhere, but once again, he controlled his rage.

"*So this is how Johnson intimidates his opponents*," Jack thought to himself.

Jack wasted no time and quickly went into his presentation. It was essentially the same speech that he had given to Stanton but he had had time to go over it numerous times in the interim and it was very concise and succinct.

Johnson just sat quietly behind the desk staring contemptuously at Broughton.

"And so, Mr. President, with your approval I'd like to organize three covert teams of four men each to operate autonomously in this area and provide reconnaissance from ground level. This is the best way to determine what's really going on."

Johnson just sat staring at Broughton after he had finished his presentation.

Finally, he broke his silence;

"With my approval what you'd like to do is start World War Three. Expanding this war into Laos and Cambodia would be great wouldn't it? Get the Soviets or the Chi Coms or both in on it? We'd need more Army divisions if that happened. More divisions means more division commanders. More opportunities for you to move up, right Colonel?"

"I'm not a diplomat, Sir. I'm a soldier…"

"You're damned right you're not a diplomat! You have the easy job. I have to keep this war from expanding. If the news media ever found out that we had ground troops operating in Laos they'd destroy me."

"Mr. President, if I'm right and you fail to act on this information, you won't have to worry about the media, the Army of North Viet Nam will destroy you and a whole bunch of American soldiers in the process. Then if anyone ever found out that you had intelligence that could have prevented the attack and you refused to act on it. You wouldn't even be able to be re-elected Dog Catcher, much less President next year."

Jack knew that he had probably gone too far but he was a gambler and he thought that this might be the only way to win.

"Are you threatening me, Colonel because I can break you in half?"

"No Sir, I'm just saying that the truth has a way of coming out eventually. If I'm right and you do nothing you will have missed the opportunity to save American lives and to shorten the war. If you're right but you follow my advice anyway, you *may* risk a small chance of taking a hit in the media but you do that every day that you allow bombing missions over Laos anyway. You know damned well that the Soviets and the Chinese aren't going to start World War Three over a dozen U.S. troops in Laos."

Johnson was quiet for a few more moments but he continued to glare at Broughton.

"Okay Colonel, here's what we're going to do. As of right now everything that you've just told me is classified Top Secret. If I even hear the name Ban Bak, Laos mentioned again in the next six months I'll know where it came from and you'll find yourself in Leavenworth. Do I make myself clear?"

"Exceptionally clear, Sir."

Broughton knew just from the tone of the President's voice that whatever Johnson did, it wasn't going to be the course of action that he had recommended. The President was determined to show Jack that **HE** was the one who was in charge. Jack felt a profound sense of failure. Maybe had had pushed too hard too soon. If he had been a bit more diplomatic and hadn't put Johnson onto the defensive right off the bat he could have persuaded him. The point was moot now.

Johnson angrily pushed the intercom talk switch on the desk in front of him.

"Wilson, get the Air Force Command Post at the Pentagon on the phone. I want to speak with the duty officer NOW!" Johnson shouted into the device.

Within minutes The President was yelling at an Air Force Brigadier General at the Pentagon.

"I'm being told that there might be a build- up of forces in Ban Bak, Laos. I want six, no twelve B-52s ready to strike in the next twelve hours. There's a Colonel Broughton I'm sending over to give you the exact location. He'll be there in thirty minutes."

Johnson was quiet for a moment as he listened to the phone. Jack didn't have to hear the person on the other end to know what was being said. The General was probably explaining the difficulties involved in quickly re-assigning a dozen of the big bombers on such short notice.

"I don't care if you have to move heaven and earth," Johnson erupted again. "I want bombs on target in twelve hours or less. Do you understand me, General?"

Johnson was quiet again for a moment or so before he slammed the phone down and smiled smugly back at Broughton.

"That's power, Colonel," the President's voice was filled with contempt. "I say jump and you ask how high on the way up!"

Broughton was defeated and he knew it. This whole scene on the telephone had been a demonstration to him that Johnson was the man in supreme command. Broughton knew that he should just shut up and accept defeat gracefully but he felt compelled to speak up again.

"Sir, I'm not sure that a B-52 strike is the way to go with this. Using B-52's to stop supplies coming down the Ho Chi Minh trail is like using a sledgehammer to swat flies. Besides that, the Air Force has probably taken out the bridge by now and the supply line is being diverted to somewhere else."

"God Damn it, Colonel! " Johnson stood up abruptly behind his desk. He was infuriated now and yelling at Broughton. "I don't care what you think! If there really *is* anything there the B-52s will blow it to kingdom come."

Frank Wilson entered the office looking somewhat sheepish.

"Frank I need you to take a memo. Everything concerning this Ban Bak thing is now classified Top Secret!" the President said loudly.

Johnson smiled at Broughton. His voice sounded almost pleasant.

"Colonel, I think your business here is done. There's a General over in the Pentagon that's waiting for you to give him the exact coordinates of this supposed build-up. I want bombs on that target, Colonel! Now get your ass out of here and security had better be air tight on this. Do you understand me, Colonel? Air tight!"

VIII: THE RALLY

Saturday 16 Dec 1967, (0825L San Rafael, Ca)

BARBARA GROVES HELD the envelope in the opening of the mailbox. It occurred to her that as she dropped the letter into the box, she would be crossing the Rubicon. It was an analogy that she remembered from her high school history class. When Caesar led his legions across the Rubicon River and marched on Rome, he committed an act that would have irreversible consequences. This letter to her husband, Mike would have irreversible consequences as well.

She had taken nearly a full week to compose the contents of the letter that spelled out in detail exactly why she had filed for a divorce from him. The envelope also contained a copy of the divorce papers that she had filed with the local court. It was something that had been coming for quite some time. For sixteen years she had followed Mike around from one assignment to another some of them to the most god-awful places in the country. She spent three years in a dirty isolated cracker-box of a house in Alamogordo, New Mexico. If ever there was an armpit of the world, Alamogordo was it. Still, she had been a good wife and tolerated everything with, ***what she would describe as***; quiet stoicism while Mike flew all over the world. She stayed home with the children, a boring housewife, while he enjoyed one adventure after another.

The final straw had come nearly a year ago. Mike had just been home for four months having returned from a one-year unaccompanied assignment to Korea. He had an assignment to serve out his last two years working in the Pentagon in Washington D.C. Barbara was overjoyed. Her family home was in Baltimore, only an hour up the road from Washington D.C. She was so excited as she talked on the phone with her sister in Maryland and the two of them planned how they would spend their time together. But, Mike didn't want to go to the Pentagon. He did nothing but complain about how unhappy he was about it and how badly a Lt Colonel would be treated in the "Puzzle Palace", his pet name for the Pentagon. There was nothing she could say that would change his mind about it. Mike was certain that he would spend his last two years before retirement making coffee or getting the morning newspaper for some Colonel or General.

Lt Colonels were a dime a dozen in the Pentagon, he insisted. He wouldn't even give it a chance. Then he came home one day and said that he had managed to trade his assignment. There was an A-1 unit in Thailand that needed a new Operations Officer, in a hurry. Mike had volunteered to take it. He hadn't even talked to her about it, he just took it! He tried to explain to her how this might be his last chance for promotion to full Colonel and that at the very least it was an assignment that he would enjoy. That **HE** would enjoy! What about her? He tried to calm her by promising that after this assignment he would retire and take a job with one of the Defense Contractors in Washington. Barbara would have none of it. The entire incident was just another indication of how little he cared for her. In her mind, their marriage ended when he left for Thailand.

Two months ago Mike brought the family to meet with him for a week in Honolulu. It was obvious that he was trying to make amends with Barbara. She wasn't interested in reconciliation at that point. She carefully avoided every attempt that he made to be alone with her. She had been down that road before with him and her mind was made up. The only reason that she went at all was because she was anxious to visit Hawaii. She had never been there before.

Her mind was made up. There would be no reconciliation *this* time! She dropped the letter into the box and hurriedly walked back to her car. She had a busy day planned.

An hour later, she met with a couple in Sausalito. She was showing them a "cozy three-bedroom, fixer-upper home in a quiet neighborhood that was being offered by a highly-motivated seller". It was all a code used by real-estate agents. "Cozy" meant incredibly small. Fixer-upper indicated that the structure was desperately in need of repair. A quiet neighborhood is one that the police department has conceded to the criminals and highly-motivated meant that the owner of the property was willing to pay an exorbitant commission to anyone who could unload this piece of crap in a hurry.

It was all part of a game that Barbara enjoyed playing. It had given her the independence that she had always wanted but it had also made her realize that she was still young and attractive. Her body was not as tight nor her complexion as flawless as it had been when she got married at age 23 but she was still very attractive for a woman her age. She actually started to care again about the way that she looked when she left the house. She never went to work without taking the time to fix her hair and make-up and she spent a lot of money on nice clothes. Her husband may not have cared for her any longer but she knew that her clients found her to be quite attractive. The women were always the hard sells for her; the men were easy.

It wasn't going particularly well this morning. The buyers were a twenty-something couple from out of state. The husband had an annoying nasally voice and couldn't understand why the houses in California were so expensive. The wife was whiney and kept finding faults with the most trivial of things. Barbara found both of them to be obnoxious and their two kids were even worse. She sensed right from the start that they couldn't really afford to buy a house and were simply wasting her time but the period in between Thanksgiving and New Year was extremely slow in the real estate business and she had no other prospects that day.

She had a date at noon to meet Henry Gonzales for lunch. The two of them had been having an affair since Barbara had returned from Hawaii. She liked the sound of that. Barbara was no longer, simply a dull housewife. She was a woman with a secret life; a woman of adventure and mystery. It provided excitement that had been missing from her life for so long.

Henry was an elected member of the Solano County Board of Supervisors. He had tried several schemes to get rich quickly but Henry had a bad habit of not properly doing his homework before he jumped into an enterprise with both feet. He read that the County of Solano was offering preferential treatment to minority businessmen so he bought a franchise to repair automobile transmissions and set up shop just around the corner from the huge County motor pool. He hoped that his Hispanic surname would insure that he got the contract to repair the transmissions on hundreds of county vehicles. It was after he had spent all of his money that he discovered that the County didn't contract out transmission repairs; the County Garage did it themselves.

Another time on the advice of a friend, he bought a small parcel of land, hoping to develop it into commercial property. Then he belatedly discovered that the area wasn't zoned for commercial property. Henry approached a couple of the council members and tried to persuade them to change the zoning status of his area. One refused outright and the other agreed to propose the change if Henry could make it financially worth his time. Henry couldn't afford the price that was demanded. He wound up losing nearly half of his investment. He vowed to himself, that he would never allow that to happen again. Gonzales became obsessed with the idea of being on the Board of Supervisors so that he could control his own destiny and be the one who extorted money from others. He became friendly with some of the officials in the Solano County Registrars Office and found out what he would have to do to become a member of the Board. He discovered that few people ever pay much attention to local elections. Most voters have no idea even what the local issues are. There were a few simple rules in local elections. Voters were normally presented with a list of twenty or more names and were asked to vote for three or four. Unless there was some hot-button issue to arouse voters most incumbents tended to be re-elected. There was a steady turnover on the Board so there were usually more openings than there were incumbents to fill them. In that situation, people tended to vote for the name that they had seen before and that's why every serious candidate puts up hundreds of posters with their name on them all over the election area. The posters normally don't say anything about the candidates point of view they simply display the name in large easy to read letters. The last trick was to get your name at or near the top of the ballot. On a long ballot people tended to vote more often for the names near the top of the list. It was a proven fact that a candidate's chance of election was proportional to his placement on the list. The closer one's name was to the top, the more likely the chance of success.

For his first election to the Board, Henry plastered his name on nearly every building and telephone pole in the county. He increased his chances with a pay-off to one of his friends in the Registrars Office. For a few hundred dollars the friend had managed, somehow, to insure that Gonzales' name wound up at the top of a long list of candidates.

It had been money well spent. Henry had only been on the Board for three years but in that time his financial fortunes had greatly improved. He suddenly seemed to have acquired an uncanny ability to find undervalued property and quickly turn it around for a tidy profit. People were always asking for favors and for the right price, Henry was happy to assist them. There had been a few complaints in one of the local newspapers that he was using his office for personal gain, but nothing could be proven and no one paid much attention.

Barbara had met Henry at the County Recorders Office. She was having trouble getting the Clerk to record a deed for her. She couldn't collect her commission for the sale until the deed had been recorded and the bureaucrats were taking their sweet time about it. Henry overheard her arguing with one of the drones in the office and he stepped in and offered to help her. The job was soon done. She admired the way that he bullied her tormentors in the Clerk's office. She could see that he was a man of action. He had been very upfront about the fact that he was already married. He told her that he was in the process of getting a divorce. The two of them immediately began a relationship that quickly became very intense. It surprised her at first because she had never done anything like that before. It was all very exciting to her and she actually enjoyed the fact that it was devilishly bad.

They met that day at Chez Paris, a pretentious little French restaurant in Vallejo. The restaurant specialized in small portions and large prices but neither Barbara nor Henry cared about the expense because it was all on the house. The Solano Board of Supervisors was considering a measure that would exempt eateries from the County sales tax. The idea was that some of the Supervisors were alarmed at the increase in fast food outlets throughout the County. They made the point that it was somehow contributing to moral decay within the community. People didn't sit down and eat with each other. It was uncivilized. The solution was to exempt restaurants from taxes if the patrons had to sit down indoors in order to dine. At this time very few fast food restaurants had any indoor dining. You either sat outdoors at a picnic table or you ate in your car. The supervisors had the purest of motives. They only wanted to protect the public from itself. It was merely coincidental that 3 of the 9 County supervisors owned their own sit-down restaurants. The owner of Chez Paris was anxious for the measure to be approved and he knew that Henry's support for it could be crucial. The staff at the restaurant fell all over themselves trying to make the couple's visit enjoyable. Barbara was impressed with the power that Henry had over these people and Henry loved to show off for her.

The couple had finished their meal and they were exchanging amorous glances and sexual innuendoes across the table as they sipped cups of coffee. It made Barbara feel like a teenager again to be so openly passionate in a public setting. Then a rather tall man strode into the restaurant and Henry suddenly became distracted.

"I hope you don't mind," Henry started to say to Barbara. In reality he couldn't have cared less whether she minded or not but there were certain pretenses that even *he* had to maintain.

"I hope you don't mind, but I've asked a friend to join us here for a few minutes. It's business and he's only in the area for the day."

"No, of course not," Barbara responded automatically. Then she thought about it and she wondered if that really was such a good idea since both of them were married to other people.

The tall man came up to their table. Henry stood and made the introductions.

"Barbara, this is Jeremy Daniels, he's the Director of Finances for the State Democrat Party. Jeremy this is Barbara Groves, she's a *close* friend."

Barbara could feel her face turn red with embarrassment. She couldn't have felt any-more ashamed if he had simply introduced her as a prostitute. She tried to control herself. She told herself that this was something that she would have to encounter from time to time if the two of them continued their relationship.

Jeremy politely shook her hand and sat down to join them at the table. He didn't seem to be even notice the "close friend" crack that Henry had made.

"Are you a Democrat, Miss Groves?" Jeremy asked with a broad smile on his face.

He called her "Miss" Groves. She appreciated that he was being polite by implying that she might not be married after Henry had practically hung a scarlet letter around her neck.

"I'm not really very interested in politics," she said. Mike had always taken care of political matters for the family.

"Well you should be, it's very important. Henry here could be one of our raising stars." Jeremy continued to smile as he looked over at Henry, then he continued.

"Henry, I only have a few minutes and then I have to get going to a rally over in Fairfield. I'll get right to the point. The Democrat Party in the State of California is about to split from the National Party. LBJ (Lyndon Baines Johnson, President of the United States) has become a pariah. His war in Vietnam has gotten so screwed up that he's going to bring the entire party down with him if we don't drop him like a hot potato. There are a large number of us from around this area that want to take the party in a new direction. The foundation of our platform is going to be to continue the social reforms that LBJ has started but to immediately end the fighting in Vietnam. In order to do that, we're going to need new people to represent the party in the State Legislature and in the Congress. Anyone who has supported LBJ's Vietnam policy is out. We need to start over with people that are not tainted by their support for the war in Vietnam. Do you understand what I'm saying Henry?"

Henry really wasn't sure where Jeremy was going with this but he nodded anyway.

"Yes, I think so," Henry said slowly.

"We need new leaders, Henry," Jeremy continued. "Leaders who can inspire passion and excitement in the voters and frankly," he looked back at Barbara and lowered his voice to just above a whisper. "Frankly, we need people who can make the public forget that it was our party that started this whole mess." He laughed.

Both Barbara and Henry were a bit surprised by his candor.

"Let's see if I understand this," Henry said. "Kennedy started the US involvement in Vietnam and Johnson expanded it. Both of them were Democrats. The Democrats have controlled *both* houses of Congress for the last seven years and they signed off on the

Gulf of Tonkin Resolution that allowed Johnson a free hand in Vietnam but now that it's screwed up they're going to blame it on the Republicans? How is that possible?"

"Simple," Jeremy answered. "If we change course right now to a more radical position of advocating the immediate pull-out from Vietnam regardless of the consequences, the Republicans are sure to oppose us. When they do, it becomes *their* war. The majority of the news media is with us on this. They support the creeping socialism that our party has brought about. The war in Vietnam is an aberration. We want to be the party of social change so we're going to give the war to the Republicans."

Henry leaned back in his chair and thought for several minutes. He struggled to comprehend what he had just heard. The sheer audacity of the concept was incredibly appealing to him.

"It's not really such a complicated process, Henry," Jeremy went on again. "Create a diversion. We're going to propose a more massive redistribution of the wealth in this country. We'll expand Johnson's war on poverty with the notion that we can wipe out poverty simply by giving money to poor people. They will vote for our party regardless of Vietnam if we promise to take care of them. It's an old adage; if you steal money from Peter to pay Paul, you can be assured of getting Paul's vote. Once again, the Republicans will oppose us and when they do, they become the party of the wealthy and we become the party of the average guy. They become the party of war and we become the party of peace."

Henry replied." What makes you think Johnson's war on poverty will be any more successful than his war in Vietnam?"

Jeremy was incredulous, he looked over to Barbara as if to ask her for help and then after a short pause he said, "We don't have to *win* anything." "All we have to do is to show that we have good intentions, that we care."

"What do you want from me?" Henry said finally.

"Leadership, Henry," Jeremy said slowly. "We want dynamic leaders at every level of government to turn the party in a new direction. There's an anti-war protest at the main gate of Travis Air Force Base this afternoon over in Fairfield. Another unit is shipping out to Vietnam through there this afternoon. Have you ever publicly spoken out against the war?"

"No, I never really thought much about it either way."

"Well, start thinking! The party is ready to support you for the State Senate seat from this district if you have what it takes. I want you to say a few words to the group that we're gathering for this rally. I want you to excite the crowd. I want you to inspire them. Can you do it?"

Henry was stunned. "I'm not really sure, I mean… I don't really know too many specific facts about the war."

"This isn't a MENSA convention, Henry. They're a bunch of pot-smoking kids who are afraid of being drafted. I don't want a lecture; I want passion. What do you say?"

Henry was unsure that he was capable of speaking passionately about anything.

"Opportunity is knocking, Henry. Are you going to answer the door?"

Before Henry could answer Jeremy stood and extended his hand toward Barbara.

"It was nice to meet you, Miss Groves. Talk to him, will you? This is important. Henry I'll look for you at the main gate at 3 o'clock. I have to get going and make sure that all of the preparations come together. We're bringing in three bus-loads of kids from Berkley to fill out the crowd of locals." And then he was off.

Henry was quiet for a few moments.

"Barbara, come with me," he said finally. "If you drive I can think about what I want to say."

"I really can't, Henry. Kathy has been alone all day with the other kids already. I have to get home." At fourteen, Kathy was her eldest daughter.

"The kids are fine, why don't you call home and check up on them. Tell them you'll bring them some pizza or something when you come home. This shouldn't last very long. You'll be back before dark."

Against her better judgment, Barbara did as Henry suggested. There was a pay phone in the restaurant and Kathy sounded fine. She enjoyed playing the role of mother to the other two. Barbara assured her that she would be well paid for babysitting the other kids. She promised to be home by dark.

They stopped by Henry's office enroute and he tried to jot down a few ideas on paper. Nothing much really came to mind. Barbara tried to offer him some of her thoughts on the topic but he completely ignored her. It reminded her of the way Mike treated her on important matters. She wondered to herself why she had agreed to go along with him. By the time they finally got to the main gate at Travis, it was nearly 3:45.

"This has to be the most pathetic anti-war rally I've ever seen," Henry said as they approached the gathering.

The road was four lanes wide in each direction at the main entrance to the Air Force Base. The rally had been shoved off to the right shoulder of the road to keep it from blocking any of the traffic that was headed onto the base. There was a long flatbed truck trailer that served as a stage.

A large contingent of police was on hand to insure that the situation remained peaceful. At least two-dozen uniformed Air Force Air Policemen with M-16's stayed back behind the gate. They had been ordered to maintain a low profile as long as the protestors remained off of the Base. A Second Lieutenant was in charge of the detachment of soldiers. The situation warranted an Officer of higher rank but it was a Saturday afternoon and none of the Senior Air Policemen wanted to be bothered. It was generally agreed that the local cops and the State Police would manage the situation. Thirty or forty California Highway Patrolmen and a handful of cops from the City of Fairfield kept watch on the rally outside the gate. To many on-lookers it appeared as if there might be more policemen than protestors. It all seemed much ado about nothing.

As Barbara and Henry stood and watched a thin kid with long hair and thick glasses was at the microphone reading a speech that he had written on a dozen or more pages of notebook paper. He was nervous and read his words with a monotone voice. Henry wasn't even sure *what* the kid was babbling about. He rattled on about the history of the military draft. He mentioned President Diem, the CIA, inequalities and immorality several times but he was about as exciting as a glass of warm milk.

Most of the police were standing well away from the protestors talking among themselves. They appeared to be about as disinterested as everyone else was. There was a camera crew from a local television station there as well. They had their equipment out and were ready for anything but after more than a half an hour of this, they started to take their equipment back into the van that they had come in.

This really was the slow season for protests as well. With only a little more than a week to go before Christmas, most people had other things on their minds. Henry caught sight of Jeremy on the other side of the crowd. Jeremy just shook his head and frowned. Henry thought for a moment and then he strode up to the stage. He climbed up on the trailer and grabbed the microphone away from the kid, as he was in mid-sentence.

"American businessmen are getting rich off of the blood of innocent Asians!" He shouted into the microphone.

People all around began to look up.

"This year another 20,000 Vietnamese civilians were killed to boost the profits of Lockheed and General Motors. The CIA started this war because the Military Industrial Establishment needed to generate sales of their weapons! The people of Vietnam are fighting for their freedom. They're fighting to free themselves from ***American*** oppression. The government of the United States manufactured paranoia about the Soviet Union trying to dominate the world, but the only country that is actually fighting for world domination is the United States."

The TV News crew began to get their equipment out again.

"This fascist government of this country has oppressed and suppressed more people around the world than Adolph Hitler did at the height of Nazi Germany! Look around; they sent their jack-booted thugs here to control what we say and what we do," he gestured towards the policemen that surrounded the assembly.

"Oh crap," one of the highway patrolmen said as he tossed his cup of coffee to the ground. "Here we go."

Henry saw the reaction of the crowd and it inspired him even more. Jeremy was smiling.

"This base is the conduit. The Air Force and its people spread American imperialism around the world like a virus."

The crowd was becoming visibly agitated and the police began to close in around them to contain it. Someone threw an empty bottle at a policeman near the road. Henry was really rolling now ranting about conspiracies, racism and global domination. If someone had written down the text of his remarks it would have been clear that they were simply unrelated generalities but it wasn't the context of this speech that inspired the crowd. It was his emotion.

Jeremy quietly slipped behind the line of policemen that was forming and stayed well clear.

"We have to get this guy off of the stage before we have a full-fledged riot on our hands," A young Highway Patrol Sergeant said to the officers standing next to him. "Come with me!"

Three burly Highway Patrol Officers quickly climbed up on the stage and disconnected the microphone from the amplifier. Then they went over and grabbed Henry by the shoulders and began drag him from the stage.

"They try to intimidate us with their firepower," he shouted. "The fascist regime," Henry continued, "hides behind these gates while they send another 5,000 storm-troopers to rape and kill the people of Vietnam. Well we don't have to accept it. We can fight back!"

Henry was in a frenzy now! He struggled with the officers but it was hopeless because all three of them were much larger than he was.

"Power to the People, Death to the Pigs!" he shouted over and over as they dragged him away.

And that's how it started. The crowd of protestors that just five minutes before had appeared to be on the verge of dozing off to sleep came to life with a surge of violence and outrage. Twenty or more people attacked the policemen that had Henry firmly in their grasp.

"F***ing PIGS, let him go," someone shouted above the others in the melee. The policemen took offense at being called Pigs and they lashed back at the crowd swinging wildly with their batons and nightsticks. Rocks and bottles began to fly from all around almost as if there had been a hidden arsenal of the weapons just waiting for the opportunity to be unleashed.

The policemen fell back and the crowd surged forward toward the gate of the Air Force Base. The Lieutenant in charge of the military policemen at the gate was totally unprepared for the crisis that he faced. He formed his men into line across the wide road that led into the base. They had their M-16's at the ready but the young military policemen were as frightened as their Lieutenant was. They had never trained for anything like this. The Lieutenant radioed for help but the situation was developing far too quickly for anyone to arrive in time to assist.

It was pandemonium in the street now as rioters threw anything they could get their hands on toward the policemen. The first Molotov cocktail (an empty bottle filled with gasoline and a burning rag) landed just short of the Guard Shack in the center of the roadway at the main gate. The next landed dangerously close to the line of Air Force Policemen that were now arrayed in front of the gate. The soldiers looked to their Lieutenant for guidance on how to respond but he was as confused as they were.

The Highway Patrolmen tried desperately to stop the crowd short of the gate but the protestors moved too quickly. The rioters ran toward the Base preceded by a barrage of rocks and bottles.

Several of the Air Force Policemen were hit by debris as they stood in place. The situation was critical now. The Lieutenant had been told that under no circumstances was he to allow any of the protestors to get on the Base.

"FIRE!" someone shouted above the din of the melee and the line of troops erupted with a volley of rifle shots directly into the crowd. The explosion of gunfire caused the entire crowd to fall silent for just a second then there were screams, pleas for help and utter chaos.

Barbara felt uncomfortable about attending the rally at all. She was, after all, still the wife of an Air Force Officer. She thought for a moment that if Mike's superiors ever found out about it, he might be in some trouble. She pondered the matter as they drove to Fairfield. She decided that she liked the idea of making trouble for Mike for a change.

"Besides," she thought, "how will anyone ever know that I've been here?"

Barbara had been surprised when Henry walked away from her without saying a word. She was even more surprised when he got up on the stage and began his tirade. She saw how quickly the mood of the crowd changed and she was frightened by it. She was slowly moving back towards the area where she had parked her car when the policemen wrestled Henry away from the microphone. She was thoroughly confused at that point, not wanting to simply abandon Henry to his fate but hoping to avoid the violence that was sure to occur. In the end, she had no real choice, the crowd quickly turned into a violent mob. Rocks and bottles seemed to be flying everywhere. She tried to get back but a large rock hit her hard just above her right eye. She passed out.

When she awoke again, it was dark and she was in the Emergency Room of the Our Lady of Mercy Hospital in Vacaville, the city just to the east of Fairfield. The hospital in Fairfield had been overwhelmed by the situation and quickly began to farm out less injuries to the surrounding communities. Barbara's wound produced a lot of bleeding just as most head wounds do but it really wasn't as serious as it looked. She had a mild concussion and was disoriented for some time. The Doctor wanted to keep her in the hospital overnight for observation. It was after 9 P.M. when Barbara fully regained her senses and she was frantic. All that she could think about was getting back to her children. Kathy had been alone with the two younger ones all day. As she argued with the attending Physician to be released someone brought up her purse and asked if it belonged to her. Someone near where she was picked up had found it. The purse was dirty and had been torn slightly. All of her money had been removed but mercifully her car keys were still in it.

She asked to use a telephone so that she could call home but the receptionist in the E.R. refused to let her use the phone on her desk. Instead Barbara was directed to use one of the pay phones in the lobby. The lobby was filled to capacity with injured and sick people. There were two pay phones but one of them was broken. An irate patron had pulled the receiver out of the unit. There was a line of five other people waiting to use the phone. She begged them to allow her to make the next call stating that it was an emergency. They all agreed that their calls were emergencies as well and she was directed to the back of the line. She left the E.R. in tears. She didn't know where she was exactly or how she would get back to her car.

That's when the photographer snapped the picture. The photographer was a freelancer that often sold his work to the local newspapers. He had shown up at the hospital in Vacaville purely by mistake. He had been told that some of the shooting victims had been brought there when in fact they were all at the hospital in Fairfield. He stayed around for a few hours hoping to get something worthwhile and was about to leave just as Barbara exited the hospital. Here was an attractive middle-aged woman leaving the hospital, confused, in tears with bandages around here head and her stylish dress torn and soaked with blood. This was the face that the news media wanted to put on the incident. Barbara normally looked as if she could have come right off of the cover of the *Ladies Home Journal*. She was the face of Middle America, such a contrast to the drug-addled, slovenly young people that made up the bulk of the rioters at Travis. Most west coast newspapers had the picture on their Sunday morning front pages. The rest of the nation would have to wait until Monday. Some of them added captions that the police had caused Barbara's injuries others simply inferred it.

Barbara ran through the parking lot of the hospital looking for a ride back to her car. She eventually found a nurse who agreed to take her back to Fairfield. It was after 12:30 A.M. when she finally got home. Her kids were not there.

Kathy Groves had been expecting her mother to come home at any time all day long. She became really nervous when it got dark and Barbara had still not come home. After several more hours the girl was nearly hysterical. The only thing she could think to do was to call her Aunt Rebecca in Baltimore. It was after midnight on the east coast and Rebecca had absolutely no idea what could have happened to her sister. She tried to calm Kathy down but eventually she suggested that Kathy call the local police. It was after 11 when the kids were taken to foster care for the night. By the time Barbara got home, the police told her that her children were being taken care of and that she should wait until the following day.

It had been an incredibly bad day for Barbara but she had all night to reflect on it. She was up all night with her stomach seemingly tied in knots.

It was well after mid-night when Henry Gonzales walked out of the Solano County Jail and got in the car with Jeremy. Jeremy's lawyer had arranged Henry's bail. The two men said nothing initially as Jeremy drove off.

"Well," Henry said finally, "what do you think?"

Jeremy smiled and said, "I think I'm riding with the next State Senator from the 24th district."

"*State* Senator? I'm thinking House of Representatives, Jeremy."

"My, aren't we ambitious all of the sudden?"

Henry smiled.

"You *are* going to have to be careful next time, Henry," Jeremy went on. "General Motors getting rich from the war?"

"It's all I could think of at the moment. I saw somebody's car."

Jeremy snickered at that.

"We'll stay away from General Motors for the time being. The U.A.W. (United Auto Workers) is one of our biggest contributors."

Henry nodded. "What *next* time are you talking about?"

"You're not just a low-level public official anymore; you're a radical anti-war activist. You're famous; or you will be. The D.A will probably charge you with inciting to riot and conspiracy. Don't worry about it though I have a friend at the ACLU that will handle it for us. We'll make a first amendment issue out it. The D.A. will be lucky to get you for disturbing the peace. But, the FBI is going to be watching you from now on."

Henry thought to himself for a moment.

"You know, Jeremy I've done a few things in the past that might be…" Henry struggled for the right word, "in the gray area when it comes to legal use of authority. Is there any way that we could…?"

Jeremy cut him off, "Henry, do you think that I just picked your name out of a hat? We've been watching you. We know what you've been up to. Don't worry about it. Every public official helps himself to a little here and there. It's just the price of…public service."

Henry liked that answer.

Jeremy went on, "that woman that you were having lunch with; is she married?"

"Yes. Is that a problem?"

"It might be."

"Then she's gone," Henry casually waved his hand.

Jeremy grinned, "that's what I was hoping to see; dedication."

"Did anyone get killed at the riot today?" Henry asked.

"No, four people were wounded but all of them should recover. It looks as if the Air Force cops can't shoot any better than the civilian ones."

"Dammit!"

IX: JOLLY ONE-NINE

(14100L, Saturday 16 Dec 1967, Ban Bak, Laos)

HURRY UP AND wait could easily have been the motto of the rescue forces. Jolly 10 and Jolly 19 had launched along with the four Sandys from NKP. Each of the HH-3 helicopters carried a crew of four; pilot, co-pilot, flight engineer and a Para-rescue jumper (PJ). Everyone's adrenaline had been surging right after the take-off and on the way to the target. Then Sandy 7 decided that the area needed to be worked over to silence the guns that were active and for just over a half an hour, emotions were put on hold. The two helicopters took up an orbit about eight to ten miles northwest of the survivor and remained ready to sprint into the area for the rescue as soon as Sandy 7 cleared them.

The rescue men were all veterans; they had done this many times before. They were anxious to get in and get the downed pilot but they trusted Sandy 7. "Iron" Mike Groves (Sandy 7) was an icon in this business. All of them had worked with him and they trusted him without question. They all knew that he would never expose them to any unnecessary danger. So they waited.

Jolly 19 was the low helicopter, meaning they would be the primary pick-up for the mission. Jolly 10 was merely a back up in case something happened to Jolly 19. If everything went as planned Jolly 10 would just orbit at the holding point while Jolly 19 went in for the pick-up. There was no particular significance to the order; it was simply the way that they operated. The duties were shuffled back and forth between the helicopter crews and this was Jolly 19's turn as primary.

Sergeant Dave Kearney was the flight engineer on Jolly 10. 21 years old from Conroe, TX, he was the youngest of the men involved in the operation. Dave was the product of a typical middle-class family. He was instilled with a simple value system that cherished, God, family and country; in that order. His father had served in the Army in World War II and although he had never seen any combat, he had fulfilled his responsibility to his country when he was called.

Dave was typical of so many young men his age. He had above average intelligence but didn't particularly excel at anything academically in High School. He simply couldn't seem to find the motivation. After graduation his parents told him that he had better enroll in college or he would end up being drafted into the Army. He took some classes at a local Junior College but found them to be as boring as High School had been. He dropped classes and drifted from one job to another for the first year unable to find any real direction for his life. Then in June of 1965 his best friend was drafted and Dave knew that he would have to do something. He was unsure of what he wanted to do with his life but he was certain that he didn't want to be in the Army. Four years in the Air Force seemed like a better alternative to two years in the Army so he enlisted. Technically the Air Force and the Navy never had to draft personnel to fill their ranks but realistically, many of the men who enlisted were merely doing so to avoid being drafted into the Army or Marines.

Basic training at Lackland AFB in San Antonio, TX had been relatively easy. While he was there Dave was picked to be part of a test program. Many highly experienced personnel manned the flight engineer program in the Air Force so the career field tended to be top-heavy with very senior NCOs. Someone in personnel thought that perhaps they should try to get some enlisted folks from the lower echelon to fill in the gaps at the low end. Eight airmen were selected right out of basic training to go through the helicopter flight engineer training.

Dave had never even been on a helicopter before much less flown in one. It took a bit of getting used to. The first time Dave got on an HH-3 he was appalled to see that the cabin floor was spotted everywhere by hydraulic fluid that had leaked from the ceiling.

"Is this normal?" Dave had asked his instructor motioning to all of the spilled fluid.

"No. This is one of the good ones. Most of them leak really badly," The Instructor said as he laughed.

The course had been very demanding. Of the eight, Dave and his roommate were the only two who successfully completed it. They succeeded because they worked together and they were both determined not to fail. Dave was sent right to Thailand out of training. He wasn't particularly thrilled with his new job until after his first rescue.

Two months previously his copter had been primary for a rescue of a Navy A-4 pilot from deep inside North Vietnam. The look of gratitude on the pilot's face as Dave hauled him into the copter was worth a month's pay.

The Pilot embraced Dave and said, "I must be queer because I think I love you." They all laughed but there was a sincere sense of overwhelming gratitude. Dave knew that he had found his niche in life. He fought to save lives not to take them. In a war that seemed to make no sense what so ever; *this* made sense. This was combat for the most noble of reasons as far as Dave was concerned. No pilot ever made a disparaging remark about the rescue squadrons. Dave wore his squadron patch with great pride from then on.

Capt. Dan Hudson was the pilot and aircraft commander of Jolly 10 and 1 Lt. Harry Linderman was the co-pilot. Master Sgt Chris Dvorak was their PJ[4]. They all had their own way of dealing with stress in situations such as this. Hudson and Linderman had the habit of discussing the most mundane topics while they waited. They talked about their kids or sports or even the weather. Dave thought that it was strange at first, that they could be facing the fight of their lives at any moment and the two of them would be discussing something as boring as, the best time of year to plant roses in your garden back in the States but he came to realize that this was simply their way of keeping their emotions in check.

Dvorak, the PJ, had the curious ability to fall asleep anywhere at any time but when it was time to go into battle; he was instantly alert and ready for anything.

As the two helicopters loitered waiting for Sandy 7 to bring them into the fight, Jolly 10 stayed above and well behind Jolly 19. The crews of both helicopters were monitoring the situation on the radio. They could hear Nail 28 directing one flight of fighters after another onto suspected gun positions in the valley.

Dvorak was curled up in the aft corner of the cargo compartment, napping next to his gun on the ramp. Dave stood at the opened boarding door looking around at the countryside beneath them as the two pilots discussed their next assignments after they rotated back to the U.S.

"I'm not really sure what I'm going to do, Harry," Dan Hudson said. "If I stay in the Air Force I'm almost certain to come back here for another tour and I don't really want to. My kids barely know who I am now. The last time I was home my wife asked our youngest, "Where's Daddy?" and he went over and pointed to the picture on the television set."

"What makes you so sure you're going to have to come back here? No one has had to do a second tour yet unless they volunteered," Harry said.

"This war isn't going to get over anytime soon and face it, there's really no place else to go in the search and rescue business."

"Well, next year is an election year, maybe LBJ will lose and we'll get someone in who can win this thing."

"I wouldn't count on that. Johnson may be a lousy President but he's a great politician. We're going to be stuck with him for another four years unless something really big happens to change the situation. The average American probably doesn't even realize how badly he's already screwed this war up," Dan said.

"I'm not so sure," Harry replied. "It's still another eleven months till the election and lot can happen between now and then."

"Dave, what do you think? I say LBJ gets re-elected next November, Lt. Linderman isn't so sure. What's your opinion?" Dan asked over the interphone.

---

4 PJ stands for Para-rescue Jumper. These are the Special Forces of the U.S. Air Force. It is the mission of the PJs to go in on the ground if needed to rescue downed aircrew. They receive training in emergency medical care as well as special weapons and tactics. They are required to be "jump-qualified" meaning they have received the same type of training as Army airborne units do. Hence the "Jumper" part of the name.

"Don't ask him," Harry said as he laughed. "He's from Texas. He probably loves LBJ."

Dave had a slight Texas drawl in his voice as he spoke.

"I don't pay too much attention to politics, sir, but I'm not a fan of LBJ either," Dave answered as he moved into the cockpit. "My Daddy went to High School with Coke Stevenson and they were good friends."

"Who in the hell is Coke Stevenson?" Harry asked.

"Coke Stevenson is the man who ran against LBJ in the Democratic Primary for the Senate seat in 1948," Dave explained. "Texas hasn't elected a Republican to the Senate since the reconstruction era so whoever won the nomination on the Democrat side was virtually assured of winning the seat. It was a really close election. I mean ***really*** close! It looked as if Stevenson had won by a handful of votes when Duval County reported that they had 202 last minute votes all but one of which was for Johnson. That gave him nomination from the Democrat Party and he went on to win the Senate seat in the general election. Later on it was discovered that the 202 last minute voters were all Mexicans and they had all voted in alphabetical order. Some of them were dead and many of the others weren't even in the country on Election Day. Stevenson fought it all the way to the Supreme Court but Johnson had one of the Justices in his back pocket and they refused to even hear the case. Years later, on his deathbed, the precinct leader from Duval County admitted that they had rigged the election. Not just the 202 votes, but also thousands more. No one really paid much attention and they sarcastically called him "Landslide Lyndon" from then on. My Daddy says LBJ is the biggest crook that's ever been President!"

"Is that a true story?" Harry asked skeptically.

"Dave shrugged. "I don't know, sir. My Daddy believes it. Heck, he thinks Johnson probably killed JFK."

"Oh, come on now!" Harry was really incredulous.

"Well think about it, sir. As majority whip in the Senate, Johnson was the second-most powerful man in the country in 1960. He would have easily won the nomination if Kennedy hadn't come along but Kennedy *did* come along and took it from him. A lot of people think that Kennedy only offered LBJ the Vice-president slot because he thought he would pass it up. He was being polite. They hated each other. Why would LBJ, a man who, by his own admission, loves power; quit his powerful Senatorial position to be Vice-President, a position with virtually no power? Johnson was a very powerful man in the entire country but he was especially influential in Texas. Kennedy was killed in Texas and then the Dallas Police Department allows the only suspect in the case to be murdered in their own headquarters before he really has a chance to say anything. I don't know but there are a lot of coincidences there. I think Adolph Hitler said something about, the bigger the lie, the easier it is to get away with."

"Do you really think LBJ had a hand in Kennedy's assassination?" Harry asked.

Dave shrugged again. "I don't know, sir. He sure as hell benefited from it."

"Look, " Harry suddenly changed his tone. "He's our commander in chief and we shouldn't be talking about him like this. Hell, he did his time in World War Two didn't he? I think I remember something about him getting some medal for bravery under fire. He knows what we're going through and he's not going to allow us to be pushed around by a ninth-rate power like North Viet Nam!"

"I wouldn't get too excited about Johnson being a war hero if I were you," Dan said, getting back into what had become a two-way conversation. "I know a little something about LBJ's *heroics*. A few years ago I ran into a Lt. Col at a bar who had flown B-26's during the war. He had flown with LBJ on Johnson's one and only combat mission. He told me that after the war started, Lyndon realized that he would have to have some sort of military experience if he wanted to stay in office once it was finally all over. The vast majority of men in Johnson's peer group all served in the war in one capacity or another and they wouldn't look favorably upon anyone who had sat out the war in the safe confines of Washington D.C. So Johnson used his friendship with FDR to get himself commissioned in the Navy as a Lt Commander. FDR then sent Johnson and two other Congressional ***heroes*** to the Pacific on a ***fact-finding*** mission. The whole purpose of the junket was for these politicians to get themselves bloodied up a little bit so they could enhance their political resumes. The Colonel told me that the three of them spent the better part of three weeks in the bar trying to build up their courage. Then finally, they decided that they would go along with the B-26's on a combat mission to observe the enemy first hand. The three politicians each went in a different aircraft. The Colonel that I talked with had the ***pleasure*** of Johnson's company on-board his aircraft. It was supposed to be an easy mission but it became quite desperate as they encountered ferocious ground fire. One of the B-26's was shot down. The Colonel's plane was shot up pretty badly and lost an engine. He had to nurse it nearly 400 miles to get it back to their base. Johnson departed the next day. He went to Mac Arthur's headquarters to ***de-brief*** the General before continuing back to Washington. Mac Arthur, hoping to make some political points for himself, awarded Johnson the Bronze Star for his bravery under fire. No one else on the mission got anything. This Colonel was still really pissed off about it as he told me the story. He said that LBJ told a reporter once that he really didn't deserve the medal, but he had it publicly awarded to himself on three different occasions anyway."

"Are you sure about that?" Harry asked.

"Yeah, I checked it out," Dan said. "It's true."

"It sure fits with what I know about him," Dave added. "It's like my Daddy always told me; once you start to lie it's really hard to stop."

They all were silent for a few long seconds.

"You know, guys," Dan said. "I hate to change the subject but that weather is really building to the west. There's a solid wall of rain now moving this way. If we don't get in there soon, we're not going to get in at all."

They all agreed that Dan was right. The opportunity for a pick-up was rapidly closing. Not thirty seconds later Sandy 7 was on the radio.

"Saddle up, boys. We're going in!"

Jolly 19 turned sharply to the southeast and was quickly surrounded by the four Sandys. Dan kept Jolly 10 back behind the others in the holding area.

"Dave, go back and wake Chris up. I want to be ready in case we're needed," Dan said. Dave hustled to the back of the cabin and seconds later; Chris Dvorak was manning his gun on the tail ramp. Dave was at the sliding door by the hoist and all four of the crewmen on Jolly 10 listened attentively as Jolly 19 and the four Sandys pulled away.

Jolly 19 dropped down to treetop level and accelerated to maximum forward speed. Even at that, the big chopper was still the slowest and most vulnerable aircraft that had flown over the valley all day, including the O-2. The Sandys had to keep their speed up higher than Jolly 19 so that they could maneuver if a threat was encountered. They formed a revolving curtain around the big helicopter taking turns leading and then falling back behind Jolly 19.

A few minutes later Dan Hudson watched the flight as they disappeared over a small ridgeline to the southeast and descended into the river valley.

"Cyclone 32 this is Jolly 19, get your smoke markers out and stand by, we're two minutes out from your position."

Seconds later the radio came alive with calls from all of the five rescuers simultaneously.

"JOLLY Break Left, Break Left, You're taking fire from your right 4 o'clock!"

"Sandy 7, roll out. I'm on your left wing. I'll be guns in five."

"Sandy 9 has a 14 point 5 at my 3 o'clock; I'm in hot on it from the east."

"Oh, F***, we're hit."

...

"Sandy 12, watch out there's more tracers from your right 5...."

"Somebody get that ass****!

"Sandy 12 come hard right. Come hard right, **NOW**!"

"Dammit!"

"Sandy 7 is off high to the southwest. I'll be back in behind you One-five."

"You're in sight 7. I'm going to come off to the left."

"Sandy 15 do you have a shot on the gun at your 11? He's right below you!"

"Negative, Negative."

"OK I'll take him. I'm in hot with guns, Stay clear."

...

"Jolly you're trailing smoke!"

"Jolly 19 is hit. I say again; Jolly 19 is hit we're losing power."

"Sandy 9, Stay with Jolly!"

The radio calls had been coming rapid-fire. The situation sounded chaotic and it was obvious to Dan Hudson and his crew that the rescue operation was in terrible trouble. Dan dropped the collective[5] and Jolly 10 fell toward the trees racing in to join the others.

---

[5] Helicopters have two control columns. A joystick in front of the pilot position works similarly to the joystick on an airplane. A second column on the left side of each pilot position is called the collective. It essentially controls the pitch of the main rotor blades. Pulling up on the collective increases the pitch of the

"We're coming back to the northwest. Jolly one-zero this is one-nine we're hit I think they got our transmission I'm losing power. I'm not sure if I can make it back over the ridgeline to the northwest."

"Roger, 19. Jolly 10 is coming to join up on you."

"Negative, Negative Jolly one-zero," it was the voice of Sandy 7 on the radio. "Jolly one-zero stay west of the ridgeline. The whole valley is alive with fire again."

Dan Hudson thought about disobeying. He desperately wanted to get in and help in case Jolly 19 went down. He continued on toward the ridgeline. Harry Linderman looked over at him but said nothing. A few moments later the issue was decided for him though as Jolly 19 managed to limp back across the ridgeline. Sandy 9 was right with him. Jolly 19 was trailing a thin but definite stream of wispy gray smoke behind them. They barely stayed above the trees.

"Jolly 19, this is 10, I have you in sight. I'll fall in behind you. If you can keep it airborne for a few more minutes there's a large clearing at your 11 o'clock for three miles. I can land right next to you and have your crew on board in thirty seconds."

"Keep it airborne for a few more minutes; easy for you to say!" the voice of Jolly 19 sounded strained. "I'll see what I can do. We're losing power and the pedals are fighting me. I think we might have taken a hit in the tail rotor! Just stick with me if you can."

"I'm on you like glue, pal," Dan calmly replied.

A fixed-wing aircraft is a flying machine. A helicopter is a machine that can fly. An airplane uses the forces of nature; a helicopter overcomes them. The crew of Jolly 19 was quickly learning the difference. The helicopter had ceased to be a valuable obedient tool and had become a 22,000-pound whirling mass of metal pieces. Still, the damaged helicopter was their only hope of a quick escape from danger for the moment. Every second that they stayed airborne took them farther from the valley and closer to salvation. The helicopter was dying but for the time being it was still doing all that it could save them.

"Jolly 19, is everyone OK? Anyone wounded?" Dan radioed.

"Davis got hit but it's not serious."

Technical Sergeant Fred Davis was the PJ on board Jolly 19.

"Did you hear that, Chris?" Dan said over the interphone.

"Yeah. I'll be there with the med kit as soon as we touch down."

"Great! Dave, I want you to get over to them too. See if you can help them get their classified together but don't dawdle. This LZ (landing zone) could be hot! Let's see how quickly we can get airborne again after we touch down."

"Okay, boss," Dave replied into the interphone. "Keep the meter running, we'll be over and back in a flash."

"Take your rifles and be careful. I don't want to have to write any letters to your parents. Either one of you."

The trio of aircraft flew into a wall of rain. It brought visibility down to only a few hundred feet. Sandy 9 couldn't continue to keep sight of the slower helicopters and he pulled off and went back to rejoin the other Sandys. Bits and pieces of Jolly 19's trans-

---

blades and causes the helicopter to climb. Pushing down on the collective decreases the pitch and causes the helicopter to descend.

mission began to fly off behind them but somehow, the wounded helicopter managed to stay airborne.

The pilots of Jolly 19 had been pulling hard on the collective levers hoping to gain some altitude but it had been nearly hopeless. They had managed to climb out of the valley but they had been losing power slowly ever since. The copter was actually beginning to contact the tallest tree branches as it flew to the northwest. Somehow they held the helicopter up long enough to barely clear the tree line on the edge of the clearing that Dan had described. The pilot of Jolly 19 just slightly eased off on the collective just as the tail rotor cleared the trees. The helicopter began to sink rapidly. The pilot came immediately back in with full collective but there was nothing left.

There was time for just one quick radio call, "Jolly One-nine is going down!"

The accident report called it a "controlled impact" but that was being very generous with the word 'controlled'. The big copter slammed down hard onto the ground, blowing two tires and collapsing the right main landing gear. The crew was badly shaken but mostly unhurt. They quickly shut down the motors and applied the brake to the main rotor to halt its rotation. Jolly 10 touched down just twenty yards in front of them seconds later. Dave Kearney and Chris Dvorak raced out the tail ramp of the copter before the wheels touched the ground. The two men hit the ground running and were clamoring into the boarding door of Jolly 19 even before the two pilots were out of their seats.

Chris Dvorak immediately went aft to attend to Fred Davis, the wounded PJ. As Chris approached him he was feverishly working on the .50 cal. gun on the tail ramp with only his left hand. His right hand hung limply at his side. There was blood all over the rear cabin of the helicopter but Fred appeared to be in no immediate distress.

"Fred, where did you get hit?" Chris yelled. He had to shout to be heard above the noise from the rain.

"The bastards got me in the hand," Fred sounded more annoyed than hurt. He stopped working on the gun and held his wounded right hand up for Chris to see. Fred's right hand was badly mangled. It appeared as if a large caliber bullet had gone completely through it, shattering most of the bones in the process. "The wound is not serious," Chris recalled hearing over the radio. "Not serious?" he thought. Fred would be lucky if he would *ever* be able to use his right hand again. The wound must have been incredibly painful and yet Fred showed no sign of being in distress. Chris wondered to himself whether Fred was in shock or just had a great tolerance for pain. He concluded that it didn't matter either way because they had to get back to the other helicopter immediately. He would attend to the wound there. Chris took out a large bandage from his medical kit and hastily wrapped it tightly around Fred's right hand.

"What the hell are you doing?" Chris asked as he motioned towards the gun.

"I'm trying to get the bolt out. I don't want the gooks to get my gun," Fred replied.

"Well, I don't want the gooks to get *us* let's get out of here."

Fred paused for just a moment as he considered their situation and he quickly decided that Chris was right. The two men hustled forward in the cabin of the helicopter.

There weren't many classified documents onboard the Jollys, mostly authenticators and code words that changed daily but they could be very useful to the enemy that was trying to capture the downed pilot. Dave and the other engineer had already secured everything by the time the two PJs came forward toward the opened boarding door. The co-pilot had been injured in the crash landing and Dave helped him out and over to the other helicopter. The rain was coming down in sheets now.

As they approached the tail ramp of Jolly 10 Dave could see Lt. Lindermann standing behind the .50 cal gun scanning the tree line for any enemy soldiers to appear. Dave chuckled to himself. They were good friends and Linderman was a very good pilot, but the Lieutenant looked completely out of place behind the big gun. Dave wondered to himself if Lindermann knew which end the bullets came out of.

It had been just over two minutes from the time that they hit the ground but it seemed like the longest two minutes in the world to Dan Hudson. All he could do was sit and wait.

Dave was the last one back up the tail ramp of Jolly 10. He quickly grabbed a headset and got on the interphone.

"Captain Hudson, everyone is on board. We're secure in back. Get us out of here!"

Seconds later the huge blades of the main rotor bit into the moist air again and the big chopper lifted slowly with its added burden. Dan Hudson pushed the nose slightly down allowing the helicopter to pick up some forward speed before he pulled hard on the collective and climbed away from the clearing.

Captain Dan Hudson hated to admit defeat but everything seemed to be conspiring against them. The weather was moving rapidly toward the valley. The Sandys had expended most of their ordnance and still the valley was not secure. Dan had concern for the wound to Fred Davis' hand and his need for immediate medical attention. He didn't mind risking his own life but now he had to consider the lives of the crew of Jolly 19 as well.

Still, returning to base without the downed pilot would be an admission of defeat and Dan simply could not allow himself to give up. He radioed to Sandy 7 that he was willing to try for a pick-up as soon as he could be cleared in.

Fortunately, Mike Groves (Sandy 7) was the voice of reason. He appreciated Dan's enthusiasm but he told him to return to base. They would have to try again later.

As painful as it was to all of them to leave one of their comrades behind there seemed to be nothing else that they could do. It was a long quiet flight back to NKP.

X: THE RAIN

(1512L, Saturday, 16 Dec 1967, Ban Bak, Laos)

TOM MORGAN (CYCLONE 32) had been hiding at the edge of the clearing for over a half an hour. He was euphoric when he heard Jolly one-nine radio that they were only two minutes away from him. He had his smoke flares out and was ready to pop the tops off as soon as the helicopter got close. He was certain that he could hear the sound of the giant helicopter as it approached. Then he heard the guns begin firing from the ground in the distance. He couldn't be sure how many there were, but he was certain that there were at least two or three. Within seconds the radio came alive again with calls back and forth between the Sandys as they engaged one gun position after another. He prayed that somehow the small rescue force could withstand the firing and make it in to get him. He tried to make a bargain with God. If the rescuers made it to him he would change his life in whatever direction God wanted of him. Then came the came the sickening radio call, the one that he had prayed that he would not hear; Jolly 19 was hit. Tom tried not to despair too quickly but in his mind he knew that the rescue attempt was over at that point. The valley was simply too hot for the rescuers. It seemed that no matter how much they blasted the area, more gun positions just continued to pop up. Now Tom had to consider that he was responsible for the entire crew of a rescue helicopter being shot down as well. His mind simply could not bear the anguish. He sank down to his knees as an overwhelming feeling of hopelessness swept over him.

Tom felt that, if there was a God, he must be a really sadistic creature. Was God toying with him the way a cruel child would torment an insect? Did God create hope within him just so that it could be snatched away again?

"I hope you're enjoying this, God!" he thought to himself as he looked skyward. "I hope you're really having a good time watching me suffer."

Slowly the noise of battle abated and the valley was quiet once again. Nail 28 was on the radio again and he told Tom that the crew of Jolly 19 was safely aboard the other helicopter and they were on their way back to base. At least that had turned out well. Tom didn't have to feel responsible for their deaths too.

Ten to fifteen minutes after the last of the airplanes departed the valley. Tom heard voices and movement all around him again. He assumed that they were taking cover whenever the airplanes were overhead and as soon as it was clear they re-emerged and started looking for him yet again. Soldiers began to appear on the far side of the little clearing where Tom laid. They appeared in groups of two or three and continued to come out until there were thirty or forty of them visible to Tom. His first thought was to run as far and as fast as he could away from them but he managed to control his panic this time.

As he watched a small man spoke to the group. He was obviously in charge. He shouted orders and the others seemed to respond. They split into groups of four or five and the small man pointed to the direction for them to go. At one point the man shouted something and then pointed straight at Tom. Tom's heart felt as if it was in his throat. For an instant he was sure that the man had spotted him. Again, his impulse was to just get up and run for it but he fought it and stayed down on the ground. A group of six men moved away from the others and began walking briskly right toward Tom. The small man continued to shout orders and point in various directions. Tom knew that he hadn't been spotted yet, but he couldn't remain where he was much longer. Staying as low to the ground as he could Tom moved away from the clearing. He tried to move quickly but it was difficult to do as he crawled through the dense jungle. He wondered if they might be attempting to herd him again as they had earlier. Was there another line of troops coming in the opposite direction? He had no way of knowing but he moved as cautiously and quickly as he could, away from the soldiers that he knew of.

He could hear the soldiers behind him now! They were moving much faster than he was. He could hear them slashing through the jungle pushing the dense underbrush aside as they paused from time to time to examine someplace that might be big enough to conceal a man. He kept moving.

Then he could hear their voices. They were talking quietly among themselves. They weren't as loud as the soldiers who had chased him to the river but they made no attempt to conceal themselves either. Tom knew that he could not possibly outrun them. If he could hear them, they must be able to hear him too. There was really no choice. Tom came upon an especially thick clump of brush and dove inside it. He curled himself up into a tight ball and held his gun out toward the soldiers. He debated the wisdom of attempting to fight it out with the soldiers as his heart pounded inside his chest. He thought that he might reasonably be able to shoot one or two of them but the sound of gunfire would attract everyone within a kilometer of him and he knew that there were dozens of enemy soldiers nearby.

The soldiers got closer. Tom could see the silhouette of one of them through the bush. The man was talking softly with someone nearby and casually looking left and right as he walked. He paused and inspected an area just 10 yards from where Tom huddled. Tom had only a few seconds left to make his decision. Should he fight it out with them or simply surrender? If they were North Vietnamese they would probably beat the hell out of him before they sent him back to endure years of prison in Hanoi. If they were Laotian they would kill him on the spot. Tom couldn't tell the difference between the two and neither of the choices was particularly pleasant. The gun in Tom's hand trembled uncontrollably but it remained pointed in the general direction of the soldier's head. A little more pressure on his trigger finger and the man would be dead.

The man looked through a thicket of bushes to his right and carelessly prodded it with the bayonet on his gun. Convinced that it held nothing the soldier moved again toward Tom.

Tom could make out the details of the man's face now. His eyes had no emotion in them as they darted back and forth. The man seemed to be uninterested in his work. The tremendous contrast between the two men's emotional states could not been more distinct. Tom's heart felt as if it was about to explode within his chest and his pursuer appeared to be bored with the entire process.

The soldier walked up to bushes where Tom crouched. If Tom had stretched his arm out he could have touched the man's right foot. There were only seconds left to decide what to do!

Suddenly there was another sound. It started softly but quickly grew to a thundering crescendo. The entire jungle was alive now with a cacophony of noise. It was the wall of rain that had been moving toward the valley and it stuck like a bolt of lightning. This was no light rain. It was a deluge and the sound was thunderous, like being beneath a giant waterfall. Every tree branch, every leaf, seemed to echo with sound as the water washed over them.

The soldier stopped where he was and looked upward. His entire body seemed to sigh as if to say that his task would *really* be unpleasant now.

The rain had unexpectedly presented Tom with another option but he couldn't hesitate. Tom sprang forward as the soldier looked upward. The deafening noise of the rain concealed the sound of his movement. In an instant he was behind the soldier concealed once again by a small clump of bushes. Tom held his breath for a moment and time seemed to stand still as he waited to see if the soldier or one of his comrades had seen him. He closed his eyes tightly and prayed that somehow they had overlooked him.

The soldier shouted something that was barely audible over the din of the rainfall. He shook his head and then angrily used his bayonet to probe the bushes that had concealed Tom just seconds earlier. Convinced that there was nothing there, the soldier moved on, away from Tom shaking his head as he went. Now soaking wet and cold, it was clear that he was not overjoyed with his lot in life at that particular moment.

Tom sat motionless for several minutes. The soldiers were past him now and he could breathe again. He thanked God for sparing him once again. He apologized for the unkind things about the Almighty that had gone through his mind just a few minutes earlier. He stretched out on the ground, allowing the downpour to wash the mud and sweat off of his body. He was wet and shivering with cold but still the water seemed to revitalize him. Tom took a moment to reflect upon his situation. Twice, he had been within a few feet of his pursuers and twice they had failed to find him. He wondered how much longer his luck could hold out. He was struck by how badly he had miscalculated his enemy. There was a feeling on the American side that the North Vietnamese loved the jungle; that they thrived within it. From Tom's limited experience, that didn't seem to be the case. These men appeared to hate it as much as he did.

Frank Robertson (Nail 58) had returned to the area in his O-2. He had raced out from NKP hoping to affect the rescue of his friend Steve Turner (Nail 44) or the other pilot that had been shot down. Enroute he passed Jolly 10 and the four Sandys. They briefed him about what had happened at the river and told him that the weather had gone down. Frank had plenty of fuel left so he continued on to the area and relieved Rick Zeimmer in Nail 28. The weather over the valley was so bad that Frank had to orbit near the Dallas holding point. He tried contacting Cyclone 32 and Nail 44 on the radio. The quick briefing from Nail 28 had left little hope that Steve Turner (Nail 44) was still alive, but Frank had nothing else to do for the moment. The storm was badly interfering with the radio reception so even if they had been alive and trying to contact him it was unlikely that he would have heard either of them. So he orbited safely away from the weather and waited.

Tom quickly realized that he couldn't waste time reveling in his latest evasion of the enemy. He had to move while it was still raining. His only fear was that the noise from the rain would conceal the enemy as well as him. He might just stumble right into a group of them. He tried to move quickly but carefully, constantly watching everywhere around him for any sign of activity. As before, his movement was difficult due to his injuries and the terrain and now he was shivering uncontrollably as well. He was moving west hoping to exit the river valley and be rescued just as the helicopter crew had been. His progress was painfully slow. The rain was so intense that at times it seemed that Tom was swimming as much as crawling along. Everything was slippery and the ground turned into thick muddy ooze.

Tom froze in his tracks as he came to the edge of another small clearing. The tall trees cleared away but there was still a great deal of vegetation close to the ground. This was the reason that the jungle looked so impenetrable from the air. It would be difficult if not impossible to see the height differential from the air.

Tom was sure that he had seen something just ahead of him. He slowly sank to his knees and kept his eyes fixed on the area. He paused for what seemed like an hour but in reality was only about five minutes. It was difficult to see clearly through the intense rain. Just as he was about to continue on his way he saw motion again in the exact same spot. It was a man and he was carrying a heavy box as he walked back toward a thicket of bushes near the center of the clearing. As Tom looked closer he could see what appeared to be a large caliber gun concealed in the vegetation. The man unceremoniously put the box down near the gun and then turned around and retraced his steps. The boxes unmistakably contained ammunition for the gun and the man was stockpiling reserves. Tom studied the scene even more closely. He could make out two gun barrels protruding from the bushes, pointing upward at about a forty-five degree angle. This was definitely an anti-aircraft weapon. As Tom continued to observe the area two more men came out of the same area where the other had disappeared. They were carrying an even larger box between them as if it was a stretcher.

Tom assumed that this was a new gun position and that the men were preparing it for the next round of aircraft that came over the valley. He had to admire their work. The gun was very cleverly concealed. It was difficult to see from the ground just twenty or thirty yards away yet it had a fairly good field of fire overhead through the break in the tree line.

Tom paused to think for a moment. There was a part of him that wanted to take action. He was tired of being chased through the jungle like a frightened rabbit. He wanted to do something to help save himself. This was one of the guns that had tormented him and his fellow pilots. It would surely be a factor if he was anywhere near it when his rescuers returned. He considered for a moment how this scene might play out in a Hollywood movie. The hero would undoubtedly find a way to overpower one of the enemy soldiers; take the man's rifle and use it to shot any of the others in the area. Then, he would use his own smoke flare to destroy the cache of ammunition and the anti-aircraft gun simultaneously. It would have been wonderful Tom thought and the audience in the theater would have loved it. Unfortunately, the reality of the situation was quite different. Tom had no real training in hand to hand combat and with his injuries he would be at a real disadvantage in a fight. He had his pistol but he had never fired a gun at anyone before and with his hand shaking from the cold as it was, hitting a target was by no means a sure thing. He couldn't be sure how close other soldiers were. Certainly the boxes of ammunition were coming from somewhere; was there a truck nearby with a whole platoon of soldiers? Just how explosive is a box of ammunition? They blew up very readily in the action movies but everything blows up in the movies. Would a smoke flare generate enough heat to set off all of the ammunition? He had no way of knowing the answers to any of these questions.

For the time being, Tom was certain only that they didn't know where he was. Discretion certainly seemed to be the better part of valor. John Wayne would have found a way to destroy the gun and safely escape but Tom knew that he wasn't John Wayne. Instead Tom took out his map and tried to estimate his position as best he could. He wasn't really even sure where he was but he took a best guess and noted the position. He would pass the position to one of the FACs when the time came. Slowly and very cautiously, Tom moved away again working his way to around the clearing to the west.

He made slow but steady progress. At one point the terrain began to rise steeply in front of him. Tom could have continued on a more level path by changing direction and moving off to his right or left but he recalled something the instructors in the survival school had told him. If you are faced with a choice between an easy path and a more difficult one, take the more difficult path. The logic was that the path would be just as difficult for your pursuers and they might just get lazy and opt for the easier way. So Tom began to climb. Walking on his injured ankle had been difficult when the terrain was relatively flat. Walking on the sloping terrain was even more painful. The benefit was that the added exertion of climbing helped to warm his body. He was still soaking wet from the rain but he was no longer felt the cold. Up until this point Tom had been walking and crawling and essentially compressing his injured left ankle with every step but as he climbed the ground became soft and mushy. At one point his left foot sank deep into the mud and it formed a huge suction around his boot. Without realizing what had happened Tom took another quick step forward with his left leg. The grip of the mud was tight and the effort abruptly stretched his injured ankle. A searing pain shot through Tom like a bolt of lightning. It took all of his self-control to keep from shouting out with the extreme pain. He instantly felt the blood begin to rush from his head. He knew that he was going to pass out but it happened so quickly that there was nothing he could do to prevent it. Tom collapsed, unconscious, into the mud.

Frank Robertson (Nail 58) was slowly moving his orbit closer to the valley, following behind the storm as it continued its movement on to the east. He called periodically for Cyclone 32 and Nail 44 on the radio but got no response from either. As he flew in circles alone in the O-2, he had time to reflect on his friend, Steve Turner (Nail 44). It was Turner who had checked him out on his first missions over "the trail". Turner was one of the most mature and most cautious pilots in the squadron. He had admonished Robertson and all of his other students to be extremely careful; to stay well-clear of the guns that seemed to pop up everywhere along the trail. He was not the type of pilot who would take unnecessary chances.

Turner had been Frank's flight commander and the two of them had become quite close over the months. Frank felt as if he had come to know Turner's family as well as he knew his own. Now it seemed as if Steve was gone and Frank knew that he would have to write something to Steve's wife and sons even though he had never actually met them. The thought of it made him physically sick.

Robertson was conflicted as he flew in circles. Part of him wanted simply to mourn the passing of his friend; to return to base and to remember the good times over a drink with the rest of the squadron. Still, another part of him refused to believe that Turner was dead. The time seemed to stand still for Frank and the continued silence on the radio only made it worse.

After more than an hour he was very concerned that both pilots might have been lost, but still he kept trying to contact them.

Tom held Nikki close in his arms and kissed her with all of the passion in his soul. He could feel the warm tenderness of her lips against his and he held her even closer. Finally he opened his eyes and took in the soft outline of her face. She looked even more beautiful than he had remembered.

"You broke your watch," she said finally.

It seemed like an unusual thing for her to say at this moment when he was so filled with emotion.

"Yes, I guess I did," he said, sounding a bit confused.

"You left me, Tom. Why did you leave me?" Nikki said sounding more hurt than inquisitive.

Tom's throat instantly had a lump in it that felt like the size of a soft ball. His voice was choked with emotion.

"You know I had no choice. I had my orders before I even met you."

Nikki seemed not to hear anything he said.

"Don't leave me again, Tom. Please don't leave me again."

"I won't. I promise I won't," he managed to reply.

"Come back to me, Tom. Come back to me Cyclone 32"

"Cyclone 32," Tom thought to himself? "Why is she calling me Cyclone 32?"

Then he heard it again but the voice had changed. He opened his eyes and he was lying face down in the mud with his head resting on his left forearm. The rain had stopped but he was still soaking wet. The wristwatch that he wore on his left wrist was just inches away from his eyes. The crystal of the watch was broken. He must have broken it when he fell down.

"Cyclone 32 this is Nail 58. Do you read me, over?"

The voice was in the earpiece from the radio.

Slowly Tom gathered his thoughts. The pain in his ankle was almost unbearable but he knew that he had to get through it.

"Nail 28, this is Cyclone 32 you're weak but readable, go ahead."

"Cyclone 32, Nail 28 is RTB (return to base) this is Nail FIVE-eight."

Tom realized that the FACs must be rotating in and out. This was the third one that he had spoken to.

"Sorry, Nail 58 I have you now, go ahead."

"Cyclone what is your condition?"

"I've hurt my ankle really badly. I'm going to have a hard time moving from my present position. Other than that I'm okay."

"Okay, Cyclone I copy that. Are you safe where you are now?"

"I guess I'm about as safe as I'm going to be anywhere down here."

"Good, just hang in there. We're going to do everything that we can to get you out. Stand-by for just a minute, I need to tell Dragnet that you're still okay. Just sit tight I'll get right back to you."

Tom could see a small ledge off to his left so he dragged himself to it. He could see most of the river valley beneath him from the ledge. He couldn't see anyone but he could hear voices in the distance and the sound of automobile engines. The way the sound echoed through the valley it was difficult to accurately judge the direction but the motor noises seemed to be coming from near the river.

A few minutes later Nail 58 was back on the radio.

"Cyclone, I've got some bad news. It's going to be dark soon and Dragnet doesn't think there's enough time to mount another rescue attempt. I know it's tough, buddy but it looks as if you're going to have to spend the night down there. Are you going to be alright down there for the night?"

Tom was saddened and angry. He suspected that there would not be another rescue attempt until morning but now the realization that he would have to spend an entire night down here was almost more than he could bear. He was angry at how cavalierly the decision seemed to be made for him.

It took several moments for him to compose his thoughts. Once he got beyond his own despair and emotions he knew that the decision was the right one. It would take a major effort to rescue him and he had no right to expect anyone to try again so soon.

"Cyclone, did you copy my last transmission?"

"Yeah Nail, I got it. I understand."

"I'm really sorry. If it helps to have someone to talk to, I'll stay here with you on the radio for as long as I can."

"It helps'" was all that Tom could manage to reply.

At that moment, for some unknown reason, the soldier's creed just popped into Tom's head. He hadn't even heard it since his Junior year in college.

"I am an American fighting man," he thought to himself. "I am a member of a team. I serve the people of the United States of America. I will never accept defeat. I will never quit. I will never leave a fallen comrade. If captured, I will continue to resist." Tom had never committed it to memory. It wasn't the entire text nor was it precisely accurate but it *was* the essence of it.

They were just words in a book when he had read them in the secure comfort of his college classroom. Now they seemed to be much more. All at once he realized that he had been very selfish, thinking only of his own personal welfare and well-being. His fellow pilots had done their best to live up to the creed so far that day. Countless times the fighters had braved the gunfire to save his life. One of them had made the ultimate sacrifice on Tom's behalf. They had already done far more for him than anyone could have expected. Tom felt that if they could live up to the code as bravely as they did, then he could too.

"Nail, there is a lot of enemy activity down here. I can hear trucks down near the river. Is there anyway you can get some air support in here before it gets dark?"

Frank Robertson (Nail 58) was a little surprised by the sudden change in the tone of Cyclone 32's voice but it lifted his spirits too.

"Maybe, let me talk to Dragnet and see if there's anyone around here."

Several minutes later, Nail 58 was back on the radio.

"Cyclone, I have Cutlass 36 coming this way. They're a flight of two Marine A-4's. They should be here in about ten minutes. Can you give me some idea exactly where the trucks are?"

"Yeah Nail, It sounds as if they're moving slowly southbound along the west bank of the river. I'd guess they are about two clicks north of what's left of the bridge right now."

"Roger Cyclone, stand-by for a minute I'm going to come in and try to get a better look."

"Nail, you'd better be careful this valley seems to be filled with guns."

"I copy that, Cyclone. I'll be up at about 5,000 feet that should keep me safe from anything up to a fourteen point five[6]. If anything bigger than that starts to fire at me I'll get out quick."

"Roger that, Nail. I'll try to watch your back for you."

Tom could see the little airplane high above him moving slowly overhead. He watched the valley below him carefully for several long minutes but saw no gunfire toward the plane.

"Cyclone, I can't drop any ordnance down there until I have some idea where *you* are and the bad thing about a radio is that anyone can be listening. If you start telling me where you're located and the Gomers are listening in, they may be able to figure out where you are as well. Let me think about this for a minute."

From the briefing that he had gotten from Rick Ziemmer (Nail 28) he was fairly certain that Tom was on the west side of the river but he wasn't going to take any chances.

"Okay Cyclone, I think I have an idea. Can you visualize a map of the United States in your head?"

"Affirmative," Tom sounded a bit confused.

"Do you know approximately where Kansas City would be on that map?"

Tom knew that Kansas City was fairly close to the geographical center of the U.S. He thought he knew what Nail 58 was up to.

"Yeah, I know where Kansas City is."

"Good. If I was to go from Kansas City to San Francisco would that be the same general direction that you are from the river?"

Tom had to think for just a moment. San Francisco is west of Kansas City and he was west of the river.

"That's affirmative!"

"Okay great. Now we need a reference for distance."

They needed the length of an object that both of them would know without any doubt but it had to be something that the enemy was not readily familiar with. It was Tom who spoke up first.

"Nail, do you know the length of the runway at NKP?"

Tom knew that NKP was home base for the Nail FAC's, so Nail 58 should know the length of the runway without having to think about it. Tom knew it because NKP was their primary divert field and he had been there just the day before when his plane went down.

"Yeah Cyclone, I know the length."

The runway at NKP was 8,000 feet long.

"Alright Nail, do you know the general direction from Kansas City to … Minneapolis?"

Minneapolis is north of Kansas City.

"Yeah Cyclone, go ahead."

---

6 A fourteen point five (14.5mm) is a heavy caliber Soviet machine gun. The maximum effective range was about 3,500 feet.

"Okay Nail, from the big bend in the river go toward Minneapolis one runway length and then toward San Francisco about half a runway length."

"Okay Cyclone, I have that approximate position."

It was 8,000 feet north of the bend in the river and 4,000 feet to the west. Frank scanned the area. As they had been talking Tom had gotten his signal mirror out. The signal mirror is the most primitive signaling device that the aircrews carried but under the proper conditions it could be the most effective. The storm had taken most of the clouds along with it as it moved to the east. The sun was unobstructed now but it was getting low on the western horizon. Tom was on his back trying to maneuver the mirror so that it would reflect on the little O-2 that was almost directly above him.

"Nail, I have my mirror out look for a flash."

Frank strained as he looked down toward the area that Tom had described. Seconds later he saw a brilliant flash of light from the ground. It lasted only a fraction of a second but it was clear to Frank that this was Tom's signal mirror.

"I've got it, Cyclone! I see your position. Great work! Stand by a minute while I plot it"

Tom was overjoyed as well. It made him feel good to know that for the first time that day someone actually knew where he was.

Frank quickly plotted the position on his map and he was a bit dismayed. Tom was just outside of the minimum safe distance for napalm but Frank's experience told him to be especially cautious. This sort of thing could go very wrong very quickly.

"Cyclone, these A-4's are carrying so pretty heavy-duty ordnance. It may get a little hairy down there for you. Are you sure you want to do this?"

There was a slight pause on the radio.

"Yeah Nail. I'm sure."

"Okay buddy we'll try and make it count. Give me a couple of minutes to work my way over to the east side. I'm not quite as fast in my O-2 as you are in your Thud."

"Right at this moment, you're moving a heck of a lot faster than I am, Nail"

Frank Robertson banked his plane steeply to the left and used his binoculars to scan along the west bank of the river. It took a few long moments but then he spotted what he was looking for. A line of at least four trucks was making its way through the vegetation just twenty or thirty feet from the riverbank. They were very well concealed by the jungle.

"I've got 'em, Cyclone. Good call, I don't think I would ever have found them on my own. As soon as the Marines get here we'll put on the greatest fireworks show you've ever seen."

"I can't wait."

Not long after that, Cutlass 36 flight came up on the radio with Nail 58. They were A-4 Skyhawks loaded with two BLU-32 (napalm) canisters and eight Zuni, five inch rockets. Due to the bad weather everywhere they had been airborne for some time already and were anxious to expend their ordnance and get back to base. Frank quickly briefed them on a separate radio frequency for security reasons. Tom couldn't hear any of it. Frank described the situation to them in detail and made certain that they knew where Tom was.

"Cutlass 36, this is *danger close*. I want you to run in from north to south only and I'm not going to clear you until I can see that you're lined up on the target."

"We understand, Nail. Let's get this show on the road."

"Cutlass, stand by for my mark. I'm in high from the south."

Back on Tom's frequency;

"Keep your head down, Cyclone. It's show time!"

Frank rolled in the O-2 from high above the river and fired one smoke rocket at the lead vehicle and then another at the last truck in the line. He pulled back up and watched as the rockets hit the ground. He wasn't trying to hit them he simply wanted to give Cutlass flight a reference on the ground from which to guide them. To his surprise, the two smoke rockets had neatly bracketed to the target. The second rocket nearly hit the last truck in the line. Frank was jubilant.

"Nail 58, I see your smoke."

""My smokes bracket the convoy. Hit My Smoke! Cutlass 36 you're cleared in from the north."

"Cutlass three-six is in from the north."

Cutlass 36 rolled the small Skyhawk jet over onto its side and rapidly descended toward the valley picking up airspeed along the way. At about 500 feet above the ground he shallowed his dive to about ten degrees and raced in toward the target at over 400 knots.

Frank watched carefully to insure that the A-4 was lined up on the target. When he was certain that it was, he radioed again.

"Cutlass three-six your line-up looks good. You're cleared in hot!"

"Three-six is in hot."

The wingman, Cutlass 37 rolled in just thirty seconds after his leader. Frank checked his run-in heading and then cleared him hot as well.

Napalm is delivered from a very shallow high speed dive in order to get maximum dispersion.

Tom had seen the two small jets orbiting high above the valley far off in the distance. He saw the lead jet roll in and dive down toward the ground but he lost sight of it as it disappeared behind some tall trees in the distance. A few seconds later he heard one and then two guns begin to fire from the jungle off to the north. All at once the streaking form of a jet was visible just out along the west bank of the river. The plane couldn't have been more than 200 feet above the ground as it moved quickly toward the convoy of trucks. It was so low that it couldn't possibly miss it's target.

Another gun, this one much closer to Tom, began to fire just as the sound of the speeding jet became audible. Tom watched as two silver canisters dropped from the jet and tumbled toward the ground. As they struck the trees they both erupted into a wall of orange flames and black smoke. There was a "whooshing" sound that was mostly drowned out by the chorus of other noises. The wall of fire quickly rose to over fifty feet in the air. A few seconds later Tom could feel a wave of intense heat wash over him. It was the most awesome display of firepower he had ever witnessed from the ground. Just as the fire began to settle down another jet streaked in from north. Tom had been so overwhelmed by the explosion that he didn't even seen the second jet until it had already released it's payload.

The jungle near the river erupted into flames once again and Tom could hear several secondary explosions from the convoy as the trucks and their cargo caught fire and detonated as well.

The gun that he had passed earlier was only a hundred yards or so away from his position on the ledge and it was hammering away at the two Skyhawks as they rocketed away from the valley.

After a few seconds the firing stopped and Tom could hear faint screams and shouts from the convoy. He actually felt sorry for the men who were anywhere near the conflagration.

"Nail Five-eight, Cyclone three-two, over"

""Go ahead, Cyclone."

"That was some pretty nice shooting. Do they have any ordnance left that can take out a gun sight?"

"That's affirmative, Cyclone. What do you have in mind?"

"There's a twin fourteen point five mount about a hundred yards northeast of my position."

"Yeah Cyclone, I saw it firing but I'm not sure that we can take it out without hitting you."

"I know, Nail, but as it stands right now I can't move and if that gun is still here in the morning it's going to cause havoc for anyone who comes in to get me. If you're up to it, let's take it out now."

"Okay, hold on a minute. We'll see if we can hit it with some twenty mike-mike."

"Okay, Nail."

Frank briefed Cutlass flight again. This time he warned them that the survivor was exceptionally close to the target and that they would have to be especially careful. He suggested that they roll in from the north again and aim short of the target initially and then walk their tracers into the gun position. The leader of Cutlass flight agreed to give it a try as long as the target was clearly marked for them. Frank concurred and told them to stand-by for a mark.

"Get real small for the next few minutes, Cyclone. I'm in for the mark."

The O-2 rolled over and dove from nearly directly overhead the gun site. Frank silently prayed that he could come close to the target without hitting Tom. Initially the gun hadn't fired on the little O-2 but when Frank dove straight at it, it became obvious that he had seen the gun and was targeting it. The guns immediately started firing at Frank's airplane.

"Oh F***," was the only thought that went through Frank's mind as the green-colored tracers started coming his way. They looked like green flaming golf balls to Frank. The nose of the O-2 was pointed nearly straight down and Frank realized that he would be within of the effective range of the guns before he could pull out again, but there really was no choice at this point. He was committed to the attack. It was a terribly unfair mismatch. Frank was shooting only a marking rocket while the gunners on the ground were shooting live ammunition. The tracers whizzed past him just off to his left as he quickly tried to settle his aim on the target. Frank had been hit by ground fire before and he knew the sickening sound that bullets made as they impacted the thin aluminum skin of the O-2. He expected to hear that sound again at any second, but he focused all of his attention on the target. When he was certain of his aim, he pressed the ***pickle*** button and fired a single rocket right back down at the gun site.

With the rocket safely away, Frank pulled back hard on the yoke while simultaneously rolling to the right. It was the most aggressive maneuver that he had ever done in an O-2 and he belatedly wondered if the little plane could withstand it.

The airplane audibly creaked and groaned from the stress but against all odds the O-2 somehow survived the attack and Frank's acrobatics. Frank started breathing normally again.

The gun crew was very experienced and capable but they had never fired at a target as slow as the O-2 before and they ended up giving it far too much lead.

Once the O-2 was climbing back up safely away from the guns Frank looked back to the ground for his smoke rocket. To his astonishment, he saw a plume of white smoke from the rocket rising just about twenty feet north and west of the gun site. He had been remarkably accurate once again with his rocket.

"Cutlass 36, do you see the smoke?"

"I have your smoke, Nail."

"Okay. The target is the gun sight ten meters southeast of my smoke. You're cleared to roll in from the north. Stand-by for clearance to fire."

"Cutlass 36 is in from the north."

Seconds later…

"Nail, I have the target. Am I cleared to fire?"

Frank looked over his alignment again, took a deep breath and prayed.

"Cutlass 36, you're cleared hot with twenty millimeter."

"Cleared hot!"

The gun crew saw the A-4 too late. They were still trying to track Frank's O-2 when they realized that he had already called in the fighters onto their position.

Tom could see the gun barrels quickly depress and slew wildly to the north.

Guns are still the most accurate weapon that the airplane possesses. Using the tracers a pilot can actually see where his bullets are going and make adjustments. The first rounds from Cutlass 36 impacted just north of the target and he quickly corrected. moving them right onto the guns. A deadly rain of cannon shells enveloped the entire gun position.

Tom looked on in awe as a cloud of smoke and dust covered the entire clearing where the gun was positioned. He had fired the gun many times but he had never seen them from the "business end". It was a remarkable sight. Tom's eyes were glued to the gun sight for several long minutes. It seemed to Tom that the lead A-4 had just cleared the target when the wingman opened up on it. Just as before his shots were deadly accurate. There was no response from the gun site.

The two A-4s blasted high and away from the valley as Tom continued to stare at the clearing where the guns were located. To his astonishment, just minutes after the last shots had been fired he saw the gun barrels moving again.

"Nail five-eight, this is Cyclone. That was some pretty good shooting but I can still see movement from the guns. I don't know how they survived that, but I think we need to hit them with something heavier."

"I copy that, Cyclone. You're not making this easy, Pal. Stand-by, one."

A few minutes later Nail was back on the frequency with Tom.

"Cyclone, Cutlass flight is bingo[7] fuel now but they've agreed to one more pass to expend their rockets. It's against my better judgment but if you're willing to take the chance, I'll send them in."

"Do it, Nail"

A minute later Tom watched as the lead A-4 rolled in from high above the valley from the north again. He was diving down at a much steeper angle than he had for the strafing runs. Rockets can be nearly as accurate as guns on a fighter and generally, the steeper the dive angle the more accurate they were.

This time the gun crew was ready. They quickly spotted the A-4 and opened fire. This was a classic shoot-out with the guns firing upward for their lives and the speeding A-4 diving right into them. There was a tremendous "**crack**" as the A-4 salvoed all eight of it's rockets.

Tom's entire world appeared to explode in smoke and flames.

"Cyclone 32, this is Nail 58. Do you read me?"

"Cyclone 32, this is Nail 58. DO YOU READ ME?"

Tom could hear the voice in the distance. It was annoying. His mind was in a fog and all he wanted to do was to just keep his eyes closed and sleep.

"Cyclone 32, this is Nail 58. **Respond**, over!"

The voice was becoming even more insistent. Tom gradually came to his senses. He forced his eyes to open. His head ached and he could feel warm blood running down over his left ear.

"Nail 58, this is Cyclone. I'm okay," he finally managed to say.

"Oh, thank God! I thought we'd killed you."

"Nope, not yet anyway," Tom said hoarsely.

"I'll get back to you in a minute, Cyclone. I have to let Cutlass know that you're alright. They think they might have killed you."

Tom had to struggle to stay awake and alert. He tried to assess his condition. His entire body seemed to ache. He was covered with dirt and debris. He thought about digging himself out and then realized that it might actually help to conceal him as he lay on the ledge. Besides, he was too tired to make the effort anyway. The blood over his ear didn't seem to be too bad so he just lay quietly and turned his attention back to the gun position.

---

[7] Bingo means that a fighter has only enough fuel remaining to get back to base and land.

A fire was still burning there and ammunition was going off sporadically from time to time. He couldn't see the gun barrels any longer. A wave of satisfaction swept over. It wasn't exactly the way John Wayne would have done it, but the end result was that the gun position was destroyed and he was still alive and free; at least for the moment.

The shadows were getting longer in the valley now as the sun set behind the ridgeline to the west of Tom's position. Nail 58 was back on the radio a few minutes later.

"Cyclone, this is Nail. I'm back. Cutlass flight was relived to hear that you are alright. They were really worried about you."

Tom smiled to himself. It was odd how people that he had never met could be so concerned about his welfare.

"Tell them that the Marines are okay in my book. I'm going to erase that stuff I wrote about them on the bathroom wall."

They both laughed at that.

"Cyclone, you were off the air for a good five minutes, maybe ten are you sure you're alright?"

They'd been calling each other by their call signs and it seemed to be getting absurd to Tom. There was a man on the other end of the radio link and Tom suddenly felt that he needed to know who he was.

"My name is Tom," he said.

Frank was surprised by the response. He thought about it for just a second and then concluded that even if they were both captured, they were allowed to give their names to the enemy so he didn't see any harm in it.

"I'm Frank," he said over the radio.

"It's nice to meet you, Frank."

"Thanks," Frank smiled to himself. "It's nice to meet you too."

There was a short pause. Tom noticed that he had a terrible headache in addition to his previous injuries. He was still somewhat dizzy and wanted desperately just to close his eyes and sleep. He forced himself to remain awake and alert.

"Yeah, Frank I guess I must have been hit in the head by something and blacked out for a bit. I seem to be making a habit of that."

"Are you okay, now."

"NO! I need a shower and a stiff drink. Can you get me that?"

Frank realized just how helpless he was to do anything for Tom.

"No, I guess there really isn't much I can do for you," Frank said sounding a bit dejected.

"It's okay, Frank. I can't tell you how much it helps just to hear a friendly voice. Don't worry about me, I'm still good for the time being."

Tom knew that he needed to stop complaining about his own problems.

"You know Frank, you nearly got shot with that last rocket. You need to be more careful if you don't want to end up down here with me."

"Yeah, that was kind of a mistake. I miscalculated my dive angle and rolled in sooner than I should have. I'm going to have to add a few thousand feet to my orbit the next time for the wife and kids!"

Tom got a little choked up again when he thought about his own wife.

The two of them talked back and forth for nearly half an hour. They both were conscious of security concerns, but their exchange was much more personal than it had been up to that point. Frank had been uneasy that Tom would use up all of his radio's battery life. He knew that the radio used four times as much power to transmit as it did to receive. Tom assured him that he had two more batteries.

"Did you know Nail 44, Frank?" Tom asked after some time. "Yeah, I know him really well. He's my flight Commander."

"He saved my life, Frank. They had me. They had me good. There was no way I was going to get away. I called to Nail 44 and told him how desperate my situation was. A few minutes later he came barreling down the river. He was right down on the deck just a few feet above the water when I first saw him." Tom paused for just a moment. It was difficult to relive the incident but he felt as if he needed to tell someone exactly what had happened.

"The gomers were shooting at him from both sides of the river. I don't know how he survived as long as he did. I saw some rounds hitting his plane just as he fired his rockets." Tom paused again, trying to talk through the lump in his throat. "It was re ally spectacular, Frank. There was a group of soldiers just fifty yards or so from me and he just laid into them with a dozen or so rockets. I don't think any of them could have survived that, but then he didn't pull up. He just drove his airplane right into them. I couldn't believe it. There was nothing left, Frank. There was absolutely nothing left."

There were tears streaming down Frank's face as he visualized the scene of his best friends death.

"I don't think that he meant to do that, Frank. I think that they probably shot him, he was incapacitated and he couldn't pull up."

Tom paused for a moment as he waited for a response from Frank.

"Did he have a family, Frank?" Tom asked.

Frank fought his own emotions, trying to sound as close to normal as he could.

"Yeah, he did," was all that he could manage to say.

"I'm really sorry, Frank. If I had known what was going to happen I would have let them get me," Tom said.

Frank could tell from the tone of Tom's voice that he was sincere. He knew that he had to change the tone of their exchange for the good of both of them.

"Look, Tom we can't change what's happened. You're still alive and free. We need to be sure that you stay that way. I know exactly where you are. If you can survive the night there, there's a damned good chance that we can get you out first thing in the morning."

"Yeah, we're going to need some help with the weather, though. It's usually pretty crappy in the mornings around here isn't it?"

"Yes it is," Frank said. "You're going to have to talk to God about that. I'm good, but I'm not *that* good."

"I'll see what I can do."

It was dark when Frank finally decided that he had to return to base and Tom felt as if he was saying good-bye to his closest friend. Frank assured him that he would be back at first light in the morning and then he was gone.

The sound of the O-2 faded off in the distance and the valley was shrouded in utter darkness. The only light was from small fires that continued to burn from the demolished gun site and the convoy near the riverbank.

Once again, Tom felt very much alone.

XI: THE LETTER

(1640L, Saturday 16 Dec 1967, NKP, Thailand)

Mike Groves (Sandy 7) pulled the big Skyraider into it's parking spot and shut off the radial engine. The motor coughed to a stop and the prop slowly wound down and stopped it's rotation. For the first time in hours the big airplane was quiet and still. Mike just sat in the cockpit for a few moments enjoying the silence and reflecting on the mission that he had just completed. It had been a very frustrating afternoon. He was lost in thought for a few minutes.

"What the hell did you do to my airplane, Colonel?" Sgt Carl Peterson asked as he climbed up on the wing and stood next to Groves.

"What are you talking about, Carl?"

"The bottom of the left wing-tip looks like it's made of Swiss cheese."

"Really?"

"Yeah, it's looks as if you took some hits. Was it a rough one today?"

"Just a little," Mike said as he tried to force a smile.

The crew chief helped Mike unstrap and get out of the cockpit.

"Ya know, sir I just finished patching her up from the last time."

"War is hell, Carl."

They both walked over and inspected the damage to the wing.

"Hell, this is nothing, Carl. A little *Bondo* and some paint and she'll be as good as new."

"*Bondo*!? You must think I'm a real shade tree mechanic, sir."

"No I just know that you can work magic when you need to. Can you have her ready for me for the first go of the day tomorrow?"

"The first go of the day! Colonel this isn't just sheet metal damage. I'm going to have to get the fuels guys, flight controls and probably electrical out here to do this for me. The sheet metal guys have had to do so much work on her that they hate me now. Sgt Hall said it would be cheaper just to sell it for scrap and start over."

"You let people talk about your airplane like that?"

"I have to, sir. He's a Master Sergeant, he outranks me."

"Oh!"

"We have a couple of spares, sir. Heck, they all look alike. Why don't you take one of them?"

"Carl, I'm going after NVA regulars. I don't want just any airplane. I want the best airplane on the base."

Carl smiled skeptically. It was a transparent attempt to appeal to his pride.

"I'm going to be up all night with this, sir," said as he shook his head.

"Carl, I'll throw in a case of beer if you guys can have her ready for me first thing in the morning."

Carl was a bit embarrassed that Mike felt as if he needed a special reward simply to do his job.

"That's okay, sir. Save the beer for New Years. I'll go whine to the Chief and we'll have a small army working on her all night if we have to. She'll be ready for you in the morning."

Mike grinned broadly.

"You're a good man, Sgt. Peterson."

"Yeah," Carl smiled slyly. "Did you kick some ass today?"

"No, I think we got *our* asses kicked today, but we're going back tomorrow and I actually feel sorry those poor bastards that we're going after. We're going to kick their butts all the way back to Hanoi."

The Crew Chief looked at the battered airplane with pride.

"She's a tough old bird, Sir. She's mean and ornery and she's not much to look at but she'll bring you home every time."

"Yes, she does," Mike agreed.

"Don't worry, Sir. She'll be ready for you in the morning."

"Thanks, I'll see you in the morning."

Mike made his way back to the squadron building. He wanted to simply jump into the shower and relax for the rest of the evening but it was not to be. The Squadron Commander had been away for a week already for a conference in Da Nang and so Groves, as second in command, was doing both his own job and the Commander's. He really shouldn't have been flying at all. There was a mountain of paperwork that had accumulated that he needed to attend to but flying came first to Mike Groves and paperwork second. He checked in his parachute and life-support gear and then headed to the intel shop for debriefing with the rest of the Sandys from his flight. Twenty minutes later Mike was on his way to his office. Since it was late on a Saturday night the squadron building was dark and mostly deserted.

There was a large open area where the operations desk and it's accompanying schedule board were the heart and soul of the squadron. All of other offices were empty on this day.

Sergeant Greg Rossi, the Squadron clerk, was busy behind the ops desk. Since it was Saturday Rossi was dressed in civilian shorts and a tee shirt instead of his uniform.

"What are you doing here? It's Saturday afternoon, don't you have anything better to do than hang around here?" Groves asked.

"Sir, someone has to keep this place running. You think the Air Force is all about flying and fighting, but it isn't. It's about filling out forms and filing paperwork," Rossi said trying hard to sound serious.

"Actually sir," he continued. "I just came in to pick-up some of the mess that we left behind last night and then I got busy trying to sort through some of the stuff in your *in* box."

"If you think we're going to pay you any overtime for this, Rossi, you're crazy," Groves said as he walked into his office. Actually he was very proud of young Sergeant Rossi.

Rossi had come to the Squadron nearly a year earlier. A nineteen-year-old kid assigned to be the Squadron administration clerk, probably the least-glamorous job in the Air Force. In a unit filled with macho fighter pilots everyone had given him a hard time about being a TW[8]. But Greg took it all in stride, worked hard and made himself virtually indispensable to the unit. He seemed to know everything that was going on in the squadron. Groves and the Squadron Commander had tried to repay him by insuring that Rossi got the assignment of his choice once he left Thailand. Greg had opted to be cross-trained into the radar maintenance career field and he was scheduled to start school at Lowry AFB in Denver, Colorado as soon as he departed NKP.

Groves looked at the stack of paperwork that had accumulated on his desk, shook his head and sighed. It would be a long night, he thought as he sat down. Rossi popped his head into the doorway a few seconds later.

"I took the liberty of signing some of those fitness reports for you, Sir. The Wing admin shop has been all over us because they're so late. I put them on the bottom of the stack if you care to see what you've signed. I thought those Intel folders might be important so put them on top. I told you about them the other day. 15th Air Force wants you to write some comments on them and then send them back. If you just want to scribble some notes onto a piece of paper I'll type it up and get them off of our backs. They've called twice already this week asking for them. Most of the other stuff is just routine but it tends to pile up if you don't stay on top of it."

"Yeah, Yeah, I know all about it." Groves looked tired as he answered. "Why don't you take-off, you shouldn't be wasting your time here on a Saturday night. You don't have that many left here. Hey, just how short are you now?"

"Twenty-five days, not counting today, Colonel. But who's counting?"

"Twenty-five days, huh? What are we supposed to do when you leave?"

"Oh, I'm certain the Air Force will be able to replace me in no time. I'm just a tit-less WAF, sir. You could shake any tree and three more guys just like me would fall out."

"Yeah probably. It'll just be another F***ing New Guy for us to train, though. Hell, it's taken almost a year to train *you*!"

---

[8] In 1967 women were not yet fully integrated into the USAF. All women in the Air Force were known as WAFs (short for Women's Air Force). A TW is a slang term meaning Tit-less WAF. Essentially a man who was doing a woman's job.

"I'm sure you'll manage, sir. Oh, by the way, I stopped at the Post Office and picked up your mail. It's there on your desk too!"

"Yeah. Okay, thanks, Greg. Let me get started and see how much of this crap I can wade through tonight."

Groves quietly worked for the next hour reducing the stack of paper and folders to a more manageable height. He found that he was able to accomplish much more on the weekend since there were fewer distractions.

Finally, he needed to take break for a few minutes. There were two personal letters on his desk. Once he recognized was from his fourteen-year-old daughter, Kathy, he opened it and sat back in his chair to read it.

Dear Dad, Dec 1, 1967

How are you? I have the best news! Jason Calder is this really cute guy in my math class. I think I told you about him in my last letter. Anyway, Jenny McCauley told me that Jason told her, he thought I was nice, so I managed to sit next to him in class. Yesterday, he asked me if I wanted to go to the movies with him and his family next Saturday. Yay!! It's not really a date because his family will be there but it's a start.

Mom keeps saying that I'm too young to start dating but it's only because she wants me to baby-sit for the boys all of the time. She's gone all of the time anymore.

The boys are being jerks, as usual. The other day they were playing football in the house and Mikey stepped on two of my records and broke them. Then Mom got mad at *ME* because I hit him. It just isn't fair. I wish *you* were here.

Mom does nothing but complain anymore about how she hates being here and how happy she would have been if we were living in Washington near Aunt Becky. I really get tired of hearing about it. She sounds like a broken record most of the time.

Oops sorry, Dad. I forgot, it's Saturday. I'm working on the decorations committee for the winter formal and we're having a planning meeting tonight here at our house. I have to get things ready. The dance is probably the biggest one of the year and it's just next week. I'm really hoping that Jason will ask me to go with him and that "Attila the Mum" will let me go.

I really miss you, Dad. I love you and I hope you can come home soon.

Love, Kathy

P.S. I really had a great time in Hawaii. Can we go again? Love you.

Mike sat silent for a few minutes just looking at the letter. His daughter was talking about going on dates! With Boys! When did this happen? It seemed like just yesterday she was running away from the boys at school because she thought they had cooties. Now, all of the sudden, she wants to date them. Mike shook his head slightly in disbelief.

He took out a blank sheet of paper.

Kathy, 16 Dec 67

I just got your letter and it really brightened my day.

It doesn't surprise me that the boys are interested in you. You're a beautiful girl and I'm not just saying that because I'm your Dad. Just take it slowly. Boys that age can be pretty foolish. I know that you think you're pretty mature but you still have a lot of growing up to do. Just be patient. There are plenty of boys who will find you attractive.

Give your Mom a break too. She's had it pretty rough this last year. She was excited about moving to Washington and then I changed everything at the last minute on her. I know that she's mad at me about it and she has every right to be. I want you to understand why I did it. Honestly, there is a part of me that took this job because I saw it as my last opportunity to get to command a squadron. I've never aspired to be Chief of Staff of the Air Force or even to be a General. The only thing that I've ever really wanted from the Air Force was to be the Commander of a flying Squadron. I've stepped on some people's toes in the past and I was hoping that if I did well in this assignment I still might be able to achieve that goal. But in a larger sense; I took this job because it's important work. If I was working at the Pentagon, my job would have been some meaningless effort, shuffling papers. I do important work here.

Just today one of our pilots was shot down and we went in to get him out. The Vietnamese had fortified their position and one of our helicopters got shot up pretty badly. We had to turn back. We'll try it again tomorrow morning and I'd be willing to bet you that we'll get him home safely. Do you see what I mean? It doesn't really pay me anymore and I'm not likely to get promoted but this work actually has some importance to it. I hope that you understand. Maybe someday Mom will too.

Of course, I miss all of you terribly and I wish that I was there with you but we'll get through this. I'm going to retire from the Air Force and take a job that will allow us to live in the Washington D.C. area. I'll be home so much that you'll all get tired of me. You'll wish that I'd leave for a while just to give you a break. I think that will make Mom happy; at least I hope it will.

Good luck at your dance. I hope you have a great time. Wish I could be there to see it. Take pictures.

I love all of you.

Dad

Mike sat quietly looking over the letter before he carefully folded it and placed it in an envelope. He made sure that he addressed it to Kathy. He didn't mind if the rest of the family read it but, it was important for her to get her own mail. It made her feel more grown up. He really needed to write a letter to Barbara but the letter to Kathy had taken so long to write that he felt as if he should get on to something else.

Still, the letter to Kathy had broken Mike's train of thought and he wasn't too anxious to get back to the boring Air Force paperwork.

The other letter was from an old friend, Roy Pearson and it was typed on the Stationary of Garretson Aviation Inc.

Mike, 4 Dec 67

This is just a quick note to confirm our Telecon of 1 Dec. We are looking forward to having you on the Garretson team. Andy "Beaner" Borrega is in charge of our section in Washington DC. You should remember him from Nellis. He's a great guy and you'll be working for him initially. I've talked with him and he's looking forward to working with you again.

I really wish you would reconsider working for me in the flight test group at Edwards. I think you'd be a lot happier flying airplanes than kissing congressmen's behinds but I understand your family situation. Just keep it in mind.

The official offer of employment should come to you from the company within a week or two. Everything is a little slow between the holidays, so be patient. You're in. It's great to have you on the team.

Roy

Just as Mike finished reading the letter, Major Kenny "Buck" Rogers came into the office. Rogers was in charge of the squadron scheduling section.

"Hey Mike, can I interrupt you for a minute? I have the schedule for tomorrow."

"Yeah, Bucky. Come on in let me see what you have."

Groves was happy for the interruption.

"Knudson and Reed are DNIF[9] so I really had to scramble for bodies to fill all of the lines."

"DNIF? What's wrong with them?"

"F***, I don't know! They probably have the clap or something. All I know is that it's getting really hard to do my job when we are so under-manned."

"Yeah, ain't life a bitch?" Groves said as he looked over the schedule.

"You've got me scheduled on an interdiction line?" Groves asked sounding a bit perplexed.

"Yeah, well you flew that SAR mission today, I thought you'd want a change of pace."

"No Buck. Change me with Dickinson on the first line here. We didn't get that kid out today and we're going to have another go at it again tomorrow. I think I got a pretty look at the area and I want another shot at it."

---

9 DNIF an acronym for Duties Not Including Flying. It means that a pilot is sick.

"You're the boss." Rogers couldn't have cared less. He erased Dickinson from the first take-off of the day and penciled in Groves. "Does the rest of it look okay to you," he asked.

Mike quickly scanned the rest of the schedule.

"Yeah, that's fine Buck, thanks."

"Great, I'm out of here! I'll drop a copy of this off at the command post and then I'm going to the club. You coming?"

"No, I'll be over before long. I have a few things to catch up on here first," Mike motioned toward the stack of paperwork.

"Hey Mike," Rogers said as he walked out of the office. "Don't stay too long. That first line has 0500 brief time, I wouldn't want you to violate your crew rest."

They both knew that Mike was already violating his 12-hour crew rest limit.

"Don't worry I'll be right behind you. I'm finishing up now."

Mike looked through the papers on his desk. It was really hard for him to get going again after having taken a break.

A few minutes after Rogers left, Groves heard,

"Squadron Atten-Hut!" someone outside in the lobby area yelled to no one in particular.

It is customary to call the unit to attention whenever an Officer above the rank of Lt. Col. entered the building.

"Great, another interruption," Groves thought to himself as he walked out of his office to see who it was.

Colonel Gary Hartzell was the Commander of the 1st Special Operations Wing of which the 601st Special Operations Squadron was a part.

Groves walked out and casually saluted his superior.

"Colonel, what brings you down here on a Saturday night?" he said.

"I thought I'd find you here, Mike. Do you have a few minutes so we can talk?"

"Sure, come on in," Mike led the way into his office. "Have a seat, sir," Mike motioned toward his chair behind the desk. It was the most comfortable chair in the room. Instead Hartzell sat down in one of the smaller chairs in front of the desk, so Mike took the cue and sat in his own seat behind the desk.

"Mike, what's this all about?" Hartzell asked holding a form up for Groves to see. Groves recognized the form immediately. It was his application to retire from the Air Force.

"Well, sir. I don't mean to sound glib but I think it's fairly self explanatory."

The Colonel looked at him for a long moment before he went on.

"We're in a no-sh** shooting war and Mike Groves wants to be a civilian?" Hartzell sounded incredulous. "I don't buy it, Mike. What is this really about."

"Sir, with all due respect, this isn't a war. It's an abortion! Some politician's idea of a war where you can fight someone without really pissing them off."

All of the frustrations of the day just seemed to quickly come to the surface within Mike.

"We're not allowed to mine their harbors or sink their ships. We get fired at and we practically have to call the White House for permission to shoot back. We've already promised the enemy that we'll never invade their country. This isn't a war. It's Johnson's recipe for defeat."

"Is that what has you upset, Mike? You're angry about the way Washington is running the war? Well, all of us are upset. The Air Force needs you. We need guys like you more than ever *because* we have to fight this thing with one hand tied behind our backs. You can't win by quitting, Mike."

"Sir, sometimes the deck is stacked so heavily against you that you can't win at all, but that's not why I want to retire."

"You want your own squadron don't you Mike?" Hartzell nodded as if he knew a great secret. "I saw that TAC headquarters assignment that came down for you a couple of weeks ago. I think I know what you're getting at. If it will help I'll go camp out on General Jacobs doorstep until he puts you on the Squadron Commander's list. Hell, you deserve it as much as anyone does."

"A year ago; hell, a few months ago, I would have jumped at that offer, sir but not now. I don't mean to sound unappreciative but that's not what this is all about."

"Well, what is it about then, Mike? I've been pretty honest in dealing with you. I think I deserve at least an explanation."

Mike was clearly uncomfortable for a moment or two.

"Colonel, I've spent the last twenty years of my life trying to be the best pilot and the best officer that I could. I always assumed that being a good husband and father was something that came without effort. I never really devoted myself to either of those causes. Now, my kids are growing up and they don't even know me and I don't know them. My marriage is on the rocks. I'm fairly certain that Barbara wants to divorce me. I'm not sure if it's already too late to save it but I think I have to try. I'm forty-four years old and I've managed to screw up nearly every part of my life. I'm through playing soldier. I need to go home."

Hartzell had never really heard Mike talk about his personal life before. He realized now that "Iron Mike" wasn't nearly as devoid of emotions as he would have liked people to believe. He sat quietly for a moment just looking at Mike.

"I'm sorry about your marriage, Mike," Hartzell said eventually. "I didn't know that it was that bad. Hell, you never say anything!"

"It's just the way I am, sir"

"Yeah, I know, "Iron Mike" Groves, nothing ever bothers him," Hartzell added gruffly. "You're sure about this, Mike," he said in a softer tone, as if he was speaking with an old friend.

"Yes Sir."

"Okay then, I'll forward it up the chain."

Hartzell stood up and walked toward the door.

"You know, Mike it takes a special kind of woman to be married to someone in the military; to deal with all of the crap that throw at them."

Mike nodded in agreement but said nothing. It was clear to Hartzell that Mike was back in the "Iron Mike" mode. The brief glimpse into his personal life that Mike had allowed him to see was over. He didn't seem to be open to any marital advice from Hartzell or anyone else.

Still Hartzell felt as if he should at least offer.

"Mike, if there's anything that I can do to help you..."

"I appreciate that, sir. Thank you."

Mike sat quietly for the next several minutes. He looked at the remaining stack of paperwork and decided that he had done enough for one day. He moved the pile off to the corner of the desk and then carefully put the letter to Kathy in the pocket of his flight suit.

Mike had just gotten up to leave when the phone rang. He debated whether or not to answer it. He finally picked it up.

"Six-oh-first SOS, this is Lt Col Groves."

"Colonel, this is Lt Col. Randy Morris, I'm the Commander of the 355th at Udorn. One of my guys got shot down today in Laos and I was hoping to find someone there who could tell me what was going on. I was told that your squadron was involved in the rescue attempt, this afternoon."

"Was the call-sign of your pilot, Cyclone 32?"

"Yes, it was!"

"Well, I can tell you about as much as anyone. I was leading the flight of A-1's that went in to get him."

Mike was tired and he really didn't feel like going through everything again so he related the events of the afternoon to Morris as quickly and completely as he could.

"Okay then," Morris said after quietly listening to the entire story. "What's the plan for tomorrow?"

"The plan is to go in first thing in the morning with everything we have, kick the sh** out of the gooks, and bring your boy home."

"Sounds pretty simple."

"Sometimes it is," Mike said as he smiled to himself.

"We have our first four lines dedicated to this SAR mission. I'll be leading the flight myself. Our call sign will be Fang 11 flight. We're planning on taking off at dawn and hanging on to the tanker until you call us."

"Well, that sounds great, but the Nail FACs are actually running the operation I won't really get involved until the area has been softened up a bit."

"I understand, Colonel. I tried calling over there but no one answered at their squadron. I was a little surprised to find you at work, this time of night."

"Yeah, no rest for the weary, you know. I won't be here much longer either."

"Okay, I won't keep you any longer then. I'm looking forward to seeing you out there. Is there anything else that I can do to help?"

"Well, I don't know how much influence you have but we really aren't getting the job done on these guns with iron bombs. We need CBU. If you have any control over your ordnance loads get them to hang some CBU-26, or better yet CBU-52 on your jets."

"Alright, I'll see what I can do."

Morris hesitated for a moment as if he was struggling with what he was about to say next. Mike was anxious to go.

"By the way, Colonel I don't know if this means anything to you but, our guy that got shot down is a really good kid. He's really young, right out of pilot training with a new wife and I just,…well you know. We'll do anything it takes to get him back."

Mike was tired but he was touched by the sincerity in the man's voice.

"Colonel," Mike began, "I know what you mean, but we'd go through hell and back to save him even if this guy was the biggest prick in the Air Force. That's just what we do."

"I know you would, Colonel. Thanks a lot. I guess we'll see you out there tomorrow. Good-bye."

""Good Bye."

Mike was on his way out of the squadron a few minutes later. He planned to go by the post office and mail the letter to Kathy first and then head over to the "Sandy Box", as the Officer's Club was called. As he walked along in the darkness he saw an O-2 come in and land in the distance. He thought to himself that he was surprised to see the O-2's flying this late. Normally, they didn't fly after dark.

The O-2 was flown by Frank Robertson (Nail 58). He touched down after spending more than eight hours in the air that day. He was tired and hungry and very determined to be the first one out again in the morning.

(1838L Korat RTAB, 16 Dec 1967)

Lt Col Morris began calling 15th Air Force headquarters in Da Nang just after finishing his conversation with Mike Groves. He needed to get the FRAG changed so that his airplanes would be armed with CBU instead of iron bombs as Mike had suggested. He spent nearly an hour getting switched from one person to another and everyone claimed that they could not make the changes that he requested. Finally, he hung up the phone in disgust. He was accustomed to the bureaucratic run-around since he had been in the Air Force for nineteen years but it still frustrated him. He had one last idea. He would find Chief Dugan, the Wing's Chief of Maintenance and see if he knew someone who could help.

He found the Chief at the NCO club nearly twenty minutes later. Chief Dugan was at a smoky table enjoying drinks and a game of Pinochle with three other senior NCOs.

"Chief, can I talk to you for a minute?" Morris had to yell to be heard over the noise in the club

"Sure thing, Sir. What do you need?" Dugan said without getting up.

"Chief, one of our pilots was shot down today."

"Yeah, I know, 745."

"What?" Morris wasn't sure what Dugan had said over the crowd noise.

"Aircraft 60745 was the one that was shot down. You know the pilots, I know the airplanes."

"Oh! Well, he's down on the ground in Laos, running for his life from the Communists. We're going in with the first four lines tomorrow and try to rescue him but the planes are fragged to go with M-117 seven-fifties and I need to change that to CBU's. I've been on the phone for the last hour with 15th Air Force and I can't get it done. Do you have any connections in Da Nang that might be able to help?"

"Is it really that important, Colonel?" Dugan asked.

"Yes, it is," Morris was a bit shocked by the question.

"Okay then, come with me," Dugan said as he stood up slowly.

"I'm going to make a phone call," Dugan yelled to be heard over the crowd. "Go ahead and deal the next hand and Jerry, you make sure they don't look at my cards. I'll be back in a minute."

Morris followed Dugan through the crowd to the lobby of the club. It was quite a bit quieter in there. Dugan went up to the reception desk where a middle-aged Asian woman greeted the guests and checked their membership cards.

"Let me see that phone a minute, Darling," Dugan said casually to the woman.

She handed him the telephone and he quickly dialed a number.

"This is Chief Dugan, Let me speak to Sergeant Foster."

...

"Fred! This is Chief Dugan, how the hell are you?" It was obvious to Morris that Dugan had had more than just a few drinks already.

"Fred, are your guys done loading those first four lines for tomorrows go yet?"

...

"Well, tell them to stop right now. There's been a change to the FRAG."

Morris looked shocked but said nothing

"Yeah, that's right. You need to download the seven-fifties and upload with, CBU-26?..." he looked at Morris for help.

"Fifty-two," Morris whispered.

"CBU-52, Fred. Load six CBU-52 on the centerline MERs and another two on the outboard wing pylons."

Dugan looked at Morris to see if he approved of the change that had been ordered. Morris just grinned and nodded.

"Yeah, I don't know Fred. Some a**hole in Da Nang I guess. They must think we have nothing better to do than change everything around at the last minute. Probably some kind of a f***ing test to se if we can do it. I'll send over a copy of the revised FRAG later."

...

"Yeah, I know, Fred. They change anything else tonight and I'll tell them to shove it up their butts!"

...

"Okay, Fred. You do good work, Sarge. I'll see you later."

Dugan hung up the phone and grinned.

"Is there anything else you needed, Colonel?"

"No," Morris was shocked and at a loss for words. "How are you going to send him a revision to the FRAG?" asked finally.

"Hell, Fred doesn't know how to read a FRAG. We just tell him what needs to be done. He and his guys will be so busy the rest of the night that he'll forget all about the copy that I promised him."

"Okay, but don't those bombs have to be accounted for somehow?"

"Sir, 15th Air Force is so screwed up I don't think they're really sure how many airplanes we have, much less how many bombs that fit on them. We drop bombs everyday, who is to say how many of each type we should have on hand? Maybe someday someone will figure out that we should have more CBU's than we do, but that won't be for at least another six months to a year and you and I will both be back in the States by then."

The Chief grinned happily.

"Go get your boy out of there, Sir. We don't need the gooks to get any more of our guys. Now if there's nothing else I can do for you, I have a game of pinochle to get back to."

"No, that's it," Morris said, still somewhat in awe.

"Colonel, why don't you come in and join us for a drink?"

"Maybe another time, Chief. I have to fly in the morning. Thanks a lot for the help."

"Glad to help, Sir. Good luck tomorrow."

XII: CONSOLATION

(Saturday 16 Dec 1967, 1930L, Westwood, Ca)

NIKKI WAS ALONE in the apartment. Her three roommates had been gone all day. It was out of the ordinary for the three girls simply to take off without saying anything but, it had happened before. It was just as well as far as Nikki was concerned. She was too ashamed to talk to any of them about what had happened the previous night anyway. She had some of her textbooks out on the desk in her room and was trying to do some studying for her finals but it really wasn't going very well. She quietly reflected upon her actions in the previous 36 hours. She tried to think of some way to rationalize what had happened and how the situation might resolve itself. She was not a particularly religious person but failing to come to any happy conclusion for her plight, she prayed for guidance and forgiveness.

She was somewhat annoyed when there was a knock at the door. It was probably one of the boys who lived in the apartment next door to them. They were harmless enough but they were constantly coming over and bothering the girls for one thing or another. Most of the time they just wanted to talk or go somewhere and Nikki wasn't really in the mood for either one of those at the moment.

When she opened the door, she was surprised to see a woman wearing Air Force uniform and an older man in a plain black suit with a clerics collar. Nikki didn't know the Air Force rank insignias but she assumed that the woman was an Officer. The woman was thirty-ish and appeared to be all business. The man was much older; probably sixty-something and he seemed completely out of place with the woman. He looked like a kindly grandfather-type to Nikki.

"I'm Major Sanderson from the Public Relations division at the Los Angeles Air Force Station," the woman began. It was clear from her tone that she liked being in charge. "This is Lt. Col Callen from the Base Chaplains Office." The man smiled and nodded slightly. The Major seemed very cold and business-like. The man was instantly likeable.

"Are you Mrs. Nicole Morgan?" the Major asked.

"Yes," was all that Nikki could manage to say.

"We need to speak with you. May we come in?" the Major went on.

"Yes, of course," Nikki said. She was concerned at first and then she realized that this must be about Tom's incident yesterday. He had said on the phone that the Air Force would probably send someone to tell her about it. Now, here they were, a day late and a dollar short, so to speak; trying to console her about something that she was already well aware of.

"Is this about Tom having to eject yesterday? Nikki thought that it would be best to stop the whole process before they even got a chance to get started.

"Because I already know about it. He called me yesterday and told me everything." Nikki stated.

"He called you *yesterday*?" The Major was incredulous.

"Yes, Tom called me early yesterday morning and told me that his airplane had crashed but that he was alright."

The Major was clearly shocked by Nikki's declaration. She hesitated for a moment as she thought. She looked at the Chaplain and then back to Nikki.

"Ok, well someone has made a mistake then because we were told that this had just happened," The Major was clearly annoyed.

"I don't think so," Nikki continued. "Tom told me that he wouldn't be flying for a few days because he sprained his ankle."

The Major looked over at the Chaplain for help but he just smiled and shrugged.

"Happily, it looks as if we were miss-informed," the Chaplain said as he smiled. "It wouldn't be the first time that the Air Force had made this kind of mistake."

"Well, let me get to the bottom of this," the Major said. "May I use your phone?"

"Go ahead," Nikki waved toward the telephone by the couch.

"Give me a few minutes," the Major said as she sat down and quickly dialed a number on the phone.

Nikki and the Chaplain stood in the middle of the room. It seemed a bit awkward for a moment.

"I'm Nikki, it's nice to meet you, umm,…sir."

"They call me Father Pat." The Chaplain smiled warmly as he extended his hand to her. "You can just call me Pat, if you prefer. I actually am retired from the Air Force and I'm not really much for the protocol."

"Ok, *Father* Pat, then." she said. She was a little uncomfortable with the "*Father*" part but it seemed disrespectful to call someone of his age simply by his first name. "Would you like to sit down?"

"Yes, thank you."

Instead of going to sit in the living room the Chaplain pulled out one of the chairs at the small dining table and sat down. It seemed a bit less formal than sitting in the living room; more relaxed, as if he was an old friend who had just come over to spend a little time with her.

Father Patrick Callen's looks belied the vast experiences that he had accumulated in his sixty-eight years. As a young man he was unsure of exactly what he wanted to do with his life. When the United States joined World War I in 1917, he was eighteen years old. He was caught up in the patriotic fervor that swept the nation. He had a lust for adventure and wanted to be part of the "War to end all wars". He enlisted in the Army just in time to be sent to France to fight the Kaiser during World War I. He had fought in several battles and seen the horror of war first-hand. Pat had been badly wounded at the fighting around St Michel. Many of his closest friends had been killed in horrible ways and Pat had lost all desire to continue living. While he was in a field hospital awaiting evacuation a young Chaplain had inspired him and given him the courage to go on. The experience had changed his life. Pat decided to devote the rest of his life to fighting for God. He continued his education after the war and was ordained in the Catholic Church some six years later. His experience in the military had shaped his life. He was determined to be a military Chaplain like the one who had helped him. He felt as if he owed a debt to the man.

Pat always preferred to be up front with the troops where he felt he was most useful. He served through World War Two, landing in North Africa with an armored unit during Operation Torch. He stayed with an infantry unit as they advanced through Sicily and then on to Utah beach on D-Day with the Rangers. He was in the thick of the fighting in the Ardennes Forest when the Battle of the Bulge erupted. He transferred to the Air Force when it became a separate branch of the military in 1947. He had been on the ground in Korea but he was kept in the rear area due to his age. He was retired from active duty when the war in Vietnam started but he did what he could to help out, volunteering to work with the Chaplains Office in Los Angeles. Being a part of the military had become a part of his life that he couldn't just walk away from.

Throughout his career, Father Pat had comforted hundreds of young men as they took their last breaths and inspired many others with his courage and self-sacrifice. He had repaid the debt that he owed many times over. Despite his vast experience, he remained a quiet and humble man who did what he could to help others.

"Have you been married long?" he asked Nikki.

"No. We just got married in August. Tom had to leave for Thailand two weeks later." Nikki said.

"That must have been very difficult for you."

Nikki thought for a moment contemplating whether or not he was just trying to make conversation. She decided that he seemed very sincere and she was surprised a bit by his compassion.

"Yes...yes it was." Nikki replied. "I barely had time to get accustomed to the idea of being married and he was gone." She was deep in thought for a moment. "I wonder sometimes if we should have waited."

Father Pat smiled gently, "I can't answer that for you. Only you can tell whether or not that is the case. I *can* tell you from my own experiences that your husband probably doesn't regret it. It's a wonderful thing to have a loving wife waiting at home for you. Sometimes it's the *only* thing that makes life worth living." He paused for just a moment to allow her to think about what he had just said. "You *do* love him, don't you?"

"Why yes. Of course!" she answered without any hesitation.

"I think that's probably your answer then. It may be difficult for a time but few things in life that are worthwhile are ever easy. It's only through struggle and hardship that we learn to appreciate the things of real value in life."

Nikki could feel her eyes begin to well up with tears. He really had no idea how badly fouled up her life had become. She was silent for a few moments.

You're attending school here at UCLA?" Father Pat went on. He could see that he had touched on something sensitive and he tried to lighten the conversation.

"Yes, I'm in my senior year, "she quickly replied.

"So you graduate in June then?"

"Yes...well...that's the plan anyway," Nikki said as she recalled the incident in her Philosophy class.

Father Pat could see that he had stumbled onto something else that seemed to be bothering her. He tried to proceed even more carefully. It was like walking through a minefield.

"What do you plan to do after you graduate?" he asked.

"I'd like to teach elementary school. It's something I've always wanted to do."

That seemed to open a more pleasant avenue for their conversation and Father Pat exploited it. He guided Nikki to talk about her aspirations, her family and her hometown; anything to keep the tone of the conversation light. Nikki was a little inhibited at first but Father Pat had a way of convincing people that he genuinely cared about them and their feelings. She felt more relaxed and her spirits brightened somewhat as she continued. She found herself talking on and on without even realizing it.

All the while, Major Sanderson had been busy on the phone. It was already late on a Saturday night on the west coast and it was difficult to find anyone who knew what was really going on. Eventually she was connected to the Air Force's Command Post at the Pentagon in Washington D.C. A Colonel there was able to sort out the details of what had happened and gave her the correct story. She finally hung up the phone nearly twenty-five minutes later. By then, Nikki and Father Pat were both smiling and Nikki had even been laughing a little from time to time as they traded stories.

"Okay, I think I have the straight story," Major Sanderson said as she stood up. She had her note pad in her hand and she had jotted down some of the details that had been given to her. She had worked for years learning to suppress her emotions the way many of her male counterparts did. She was efficient and unemotional as she spoke.

"I don't know about any incident that took place on Friday morning but try to keep in mind that we are thirteen hours behind the time in Thailand. I was assured that your husband took off on Saturday morning on what was a described to me as a *routine* mission over North Vietnam. During the course of the mission his plane was struck by anti-aircraft fire but he safely ejected from it. He was reported to be alive and in good condition on the ground. He is or *was* in radio contact with rescue forces in the area. Apparently, there was an attempt made to rescue him earlier today but it was unsuccessful. I was told that another rescue attempt is planned for early tomorrow morning."

Nikki was overwhelmed. Her mind raced to process everything that she had just heard. She struggled for words.

"Unsuccessful? Why was it unsuccessful?" She finally managed to say.

Major Sanderson shook her head and shrugged. "I don't really know. I've told you everything that I was told."

"Tom wasn't even supposed to be flying!" Nikki's eyes filled with tears again as she looked to Father Pat.

The next few minutes were very difficult as Nikki's mind filled with possible scenarios and all of them were bad. Father Pat held her hand and did what little he could to comfort her. Both he and Sanderson had been through this sort of thing before.

Sanderson eventually went on informing Nikki about certain legal matters that pertained to spouses of personnel who were missing in action. She assured Nikki that the Air Force would keep her informed as the situation developed. It was all part of a script that Major Sanderson had delivered many times. Half an hour later, she finally expressed their regrets and prepared to leave when it seemed to her as if they could no longer accomplish anything of any value.

Sanderson made her way toward the door and Father Pat got up as well. At the door he spoke quietly to Major Sanderson.

"I think I need to stay here a while longer," he said. "You go ahead; I'll find my own way home."

Major Sanderson looked over at Nikki again, made another apology and left. Father Pat returned to the table, sat back down in his chair and looked Nikki straight in the eyes as he held her hands.

"I know that you have a lot on your mind right now but, I think that there is something else going on here that you need to talk about. I'm a really good listener and I'd like to help you if I can."

"No, ...I can't," Nikki struggled to say through her tears.

"You're not Catholic are you?" Father Pat asked.

Nikki simply shook her head.

"Would it help if I got someone of your own faith? We're not like other clergy in the Chaplain corps. We don't try and steal each others customers," he said as he smiled slightly. "Regardless of the differences in our faiths, we all just pitch in and try to help. We have a Rabbi, a couple of Baptist ministers, an Episcopalian, and a Presbyterian in our office here in L.A. I could even get an Islamic cleric if you can give me a little time."

"No, that's not it," Nikki said.

"Since you're not Catholic maybe you don't understand the way this works. Whatever you tell me is kept in the strictest confidence. I'm not allowed to tell anyone else; God forbids it. And I wouldn't want to get the Boss mad at me."

He smiled and paused briefly to measure her reaction.

"I don't think it will do any good to talk about it," Nikki said finally.

"I can't guarantee you that it will help but I'm pretty sure that it won't make it any worse," Father Pat said.

There was no reaction from Nikki.

"I'm sixty-eight years old. There's not much that you could tell me that I haven't heard before."

He smiled gently at her.

"Do you have any coffee?" he asked.

Nikki was a bit surprised by that question.

"Yes, I think we have some instant," she said as she motioned toward the cabinet in the kitchenette.

"Okay, you get some tissues and I'll make both of us a cup of coffee if you don't mind. I think this might turn into a long night."

And so a cup of coffee and a half box of tissues later, Nikki told him everything that had happened in the past day and a half. She told him about her Philosophy professor, the incident in the bar and the revelation from the Doctor. He listened carefully to everything that she said.

"You must think that I'm an awful person," Nikki said finally; her eyes still filled with tears.

"I don't think that at all," he said in all sincerity.

Father Pat got up from the table and walked slowly around the room as he considered what to say next.

"There's a lot going on here," he began again. "Why don't we take these one at a time?"

"First of all your Professor isn't going to throw you out of the class and he isn't going to fail you either. From what you've told me I think that he's a kind of a bully. He uses his position of authority as a forum to promote his political beliefs and to belittle others. If he's in his mid-forties now then he was eligible for the draft during World War Two. It's my guess that he probably had some kind of deferment and didn't serve or was kicked out. Putting down those who *do* serve in the military assuages some of his own feelings of guilt. It's just a guess but I'm probably fairly close to the mark. The man is a coward. What day is your final in that class?"

"Wednesday," Nikki answered.

"You should walk right into class on Wednesday and take that test as if nothing out of the ordinary had happened. You'll do just fine, I'm sure. Men like him back down when they're confronted courageously as you did."

Father Pat put his hand on Nikki's shoulder and spoke softly as he stood over her.

"Now about last night... Everyone has done something in their life that they regret. I wish there was a way that we could simply re-live some of the moments of our lives and take back the terrible mistakes that we had made. Unfortunately, that isn't possible. About the best that any of us can do in that kind of situation is to ask for forgiveness and to resolve never allow such a thing to ever happen again. From what you told me, **you're** not even sure exactly what happened last night. I don't think it was your intention to do anything wrong, was it?"

"No, of course not," Nikki said emphatically.

"Okay then, it's not going to accomplish anything to sit here and beat yourself up over this. For the time being why don't we vow to never allow yourself to get into that kind of situation again and put it behind us at least for the time being? You can deal with this in good time, but for now we have other things to consider. You have a husband who's running around in the jungle half a world away fighting to stay alive and free. Unless I've really missed my guess, **you** are what's keeping him going right now. Nikki, there are some things in life that we have control over and other things that are far beyond our ability to intervene in any way. In those instances, about the only course of action is to pray and hope that God will somehow intercede for us. Not all prayers are answered but they **are** all heard. In my own life I believe two things without question. The first is that God will never ask more of you than you are capable of giving. God knows you even better than you know yourself. Your problems may seem overwhelming right now but you are strong and you *will* persevere. Second, God has a plan for each of us. Sometimes it's very difficult for us to understand the purpose behind the things that happen to us, but that doesn't mean that there isn't one. So often I've been asked; "Why does God hate me?" "Why is he punishing me so?" God doesn't hate you and you aren't being punished. Think of it like tempering steel. Without the tempering process steel would be fragile and brittle. It would break quite easily. But if you heat it almost to the melting point it will be stronger and tougher and last a life-time when it finally cools."

Father Pat paused again.

"God doesn't think you're a terrible person, Nikki. He loves you. The proof is the baby that you're carrying. It's part of you and Tom and it's a most wondrous thing. It will change your life completely. You're going to be a very good mother. I can tell these things. Start being a good mother right now by being strong for Tom. Whatever happens, you'll get through it."

Nikki hugged him and cried on his shoulder for a long while. In the end, she realized that he had been right. It **had** helped to talk about it.

The two of them talked and prayed together all night long. She watched the sunrise the following morning and surprisingly she felt good about the future for the first time in the last two days. Father Pat had worked his own special brand of magic on her. He had convinced her that there was hope that somehow things would work out for the best.

XIII: THE PROPOSITION

(Saturday16 Dec 1967, Ban Bak, Laos, 1920L"

THE GUN EMPLACEMENT had burned for several hours just below Tom's position on the ledge. Tom had seen silhouettes of soldiers moving quietly around the area, recovering the dead gun crew. The fire had finally burned itself out and the area was eerily silent once again. From time to time flames had flared from the convoy near the river. Tom had heard shouts from there too, but now that area had become silent and black as well.

The darkness was absolute now. It seemed to Tom as if the jungle actually absorbed the light. He held his hand just six inches or so in front of his face and he couldn't see it. It made him nervous initially to be blind to everything around him and then he began to feel more relaxed. He reasoned that if he couldn't see the enemy, then they couldn't see him either. Tom actually began to feel somewhat safe for the first time since he had touched the ground earlier that morning. He wrapped the darkness around himself like a warm blanket.

Then, slowly the jungle seemed to come alive. Tom could hear animals moving all around him. He considered what predators there might be in the vegetation around him. He wondered if any of the predators could smell blood the way that sharks do. He had a lot of dried blood on him and on his flight suit. If an animal attacked him he wouldn't be able to run away. He was too badly injured and it was far too dark to see where he was going anyway. His only defense would be the small revolver that he had gripped tightly in his hand for the past several hours. But, if he had to shoot the gun to defend himself, he would reveal his location. His mind raced again, filled with terrible possibilities. Tom teetered on the edge on panic once again. He finally forced himself to control his fears and think of something else. He tried to focus on the things that were going right with his situation.

His radio was his most valuable tool and it was working flawlessly. He had two extra batteries from the survival kit so whatever else happened, he should be able to talk with his rescuers and they had promised to return in the morning. Frank Robertson (Nail 58) knew precisely where he was and he felt somewhat secure in his present location. He had his signal flares and his mirror, a knife and another can of water. He had a survival bar of food but he wasn't particularly hungry.

Physically, he was in pretty bad shape but it could have been much worse. His ankle was the biggest single problem. It didn't ache as much as it had earlier but that was because he hadn't been walking on it for some time now. His head ached terribly but he was alert and able to think clearly. He didn't seem to be bleeding anymore. He was still damp and shivering from the cold and was about as uncomfortable as he had ever been in his life but he was alive and free, at least for the moment. He tried hard to feel some satisfaction with his current plight.

He thought about Nikki. He thought about how great it would feel to hold her in his arms again. He clearly visualized every detail of his reunion with her. He would tell her all about this life-threatening ordeal and it would only be a distant memory. He would be safe and home again.

The noise startled Tom from his daydream. It was the sound of people, two or three, moving nearby through the jungle. Tom could hear them slashing at the brush as they walked. He strained to see something, anything but he couldn't. He couldn't imagine how were they moving through the darkness without any light. He tried hard to gauge their distance from him. He knew they were close but he couldn't be sure just how close they were.

Then, the noises abruptly stopped.

"Come out!" a voice demanded. "We see you. Come out now and you won't be harmed!"

The voice was speaking in perfect English with just a bit of an Asian accent.

Tom was frozen with fear. His heart pounded in his chest and his mind raced. How had they spotted him? This was the best concealment that he had all day and yet they had spotted him.

"Come out, NOW!" the voice demanded again.

Tom was defeated. All of his hard work and all of his suffering had come to nothing. They had found him anyway. He thought about life in a P.O.W. camp. His mind filled with the thoughts of the horrors that lay ahead for him. He thought about Nikki and being separated from her for years, perhaps forever. Fear, defeat and despair overwhelmed his thoughts. He was about throw down his gun and ask them not to shot but something forced him to stay still. Perhaps the fear had paralyzed him. He couldn't even be sure himself, but he lay motionless and deathly still on the ledge. He didn't even dare to breathe.

Then, after what seemed hours, the men moved away.

Tom was totally confused. They must have been simply moving through the jungle and stopping at random, making their verbal threats, hoping to flush him out. It had very nearly worked. His heart began to return to a more normal rhythm and he could breathe again. He wondered to himself just how much more of this he could withstand.

Tom rolled over onto his stomach and looked out over the ledge toward the valley beneath him. He knew that it was there and knew what it should look like but he couldn't see anything but impenetrable darkness. He tried to keep his mind active. Tom reflected on his fall from grace. He had started the day fearing no one, in command of an ultra-modern war machine that carried tons of high explosives, the master of the skies. Now, he was reduced to hiding beneath bushes and trees wielding only this .38 caliber handgun that he didn't dare shoot.

He thought back to the crash for the first time since he had been on the ground. He clearly recalled seeing the bridge as he orbited above it, just beneath the clouds. He remembered watching Clark roll in for his bomb run. He saw Clark's bombs fly just beyond the bridge and detonate in the river just to the south. He vowed to himself not to let that happen with his own bombs. He recalled being fixated on the target. He had seen the guns fire at Clark, he knew where they were but he was determined to ignore them. He vividly remembered rolling in on the target and there it was! His airspeed was only about 300 knots when he rolled in; far below the 400 to 450 knots that he should have had. The dive angle was more shallow than normal because of the cloud deck and it didn't allow his airspeed to build up, as he was accustomed. He was so intent on scoring a hit that he had pressed below the altitude that he should have released at and essentially dropped his bombs at point blank range, making it nearly impossible to miss. In the process he had made one of the most basic mistakes in combat aviation; he got low and slow in an area that was well covered by enemy guns. It was his own mistake that had gotten him shot down.

Tom then began to wonder if perhaps he had bailed out too soon. If he could have stayed with the airplane just a little longer it might have carried him to the relative safety beyond the valley. He recalled feeling the aircraft shudder as the bullets hit it and seeing the engine firelight come on shortly after that. A firelight is bad but the aircraft probably would have stayed together for another few minutes. Then he remembered hearing the voice of Nail 44 on the radio telling him to bail out. It must have appeared to be fairly dire circumstances if the FAC felt compelled to tell him to get out immediately. Tom decided that there was no point considering it any longer. What had happened was in the past. There was nothing that he could do about it now.

After an hour or so, there were noises again of people moving through the darkness beneath him. This time, Tom could see the beams of two small flashlights moving just twenty or thirty yards away. He could hear their voices talking softly. Tom sensed that there was something different about this group from the others. He wasn't sure at first what it was and then it finally occurred to him that this group didn't seem to be searching the way the others had. They weren't looking for him. They seemed to know where they were going. The men stopped on the edge of the clearing where the guns had been. Within a few minutes they had a small fire going. They sat around it and warmed themselves. There is something primeval about a campfire. It had a way of comforting people even in the most desolate of areas. The men appeared to relax and their conversation sounded more carefree. Tom could hear some muffled laughter from time to time from them. There were four of them and they were only about fifty yards or so from Tom. He was about ten feet above them on the ledge so he had a fairly good view of their encampment.

Before long they were cooking something over the fire. It smelled fishy to Tom and not at all appetizing. He watched the men eat their dinner and then relax farther back away from the small fire.

Not long after that, another man joined the group. The four men started to stand as he approached them but the newcomer casually waved his hand and motioned for them to stay down. Tom assumed that this man was an officer of higher rank, perhaps their commander. The man was about average in height, had a very slight build and wore glasses. Tom thought the man looked more like a banker or an accountant than a military leader.

Lam Quang Son had been busy all day despite the fact that his bridge had been blown apart. His men had helped move various anti-aircraft guns into position, carried ammunition, searched for the downed American and helped to clear dead bodies away. Son had rolled up his own sleeves and pitched in right along side the lowliest man in his unit. He hadn't had any real sleep in over two days and he was exhausted.

Son wasn't supposed to fraternize with his subordinates but these four men were the closest things to friends that he had in this isolated jungle. They had all been with his unit from the start. They were loyal and hard working and he had begun to think of them as his extended family.

"Has anyone said what will become of us, Sir?" one of them asked.

Son knew what they were thinking because he had been thinking the same thing. They were supposed to maintain the bridge for as long as it was needed. It was a job that could have gone on for a year or more but now the bridge was gone. There wasn't anything left for them to do here. He had hoped that they might just be ordered to return home to start another engineering assignment, but he knew that it was far more likely that they would simply be folded into an infantry unit and be shipped south for the coming offensive. He didn't want to demoralize the men unnecessarily so he kept that thought to himself.

"No, no one has said anything yet. It will probably be a few days before we hear anything," Son said. "The good news is that they've already sent our Soviet *friend* back to Hanoi."

They all snickered at that and it seemed to lighten the mood around the small fire.

"Maybe they'll send us back for R& R on the beach near Haiphong," another of the men said.

That evoked another round of laughter from everyone.

"I wouldn't break out your bathing suit just yet," Son said as he grinned.

"How has this battle been going here, Sir?" another man asked more seriously. "It seems as if we've been getting bombed all day long."

Son shrugged. "I don't know, I'm just an engineer; not much of a tactician. We shot down two of their airplanes and they've destroyed our bridge, blasted a convoy of trucks and supplies, and killed nearly a hundred of our men. The General seems to be pretty pleased with it all so far."

That didn't sound like a rousing victory to the four men around the campfire but no one said anything.

"Did we capture their pilot?"

"No, as far as I know he's still running around here somewhere."

"The Americans spend all of this effort just to get *one* pilot back," one of the men asked sounding incredulous.

"Apparently," Son nodded.

"Well, if we haven't captured him, then the Americans will be back tomorrow?"

"It would seem so."

The four men just looked at each other and said nothing. There was a terrible sense of foreboding.

"Tell me about your girlfriend again, Gia," Son asked in an obvious attempt to lighten the mood again. "What is her name, Lan?"

"Lam!" Gia corrected him. "And I don't think I'm want to tell these guys anything more about her. I think Duong is writing down notes about her. He's liable to shoot me some night and take her for himself."

They all laughed again.

"What makes you think I'd have to shoot you just to steal your girlfriend?" Duong asked as he laughed. "You're not exactly the most handsome man in the world!"

"Oh, and you are," Gia chided him playfully.

They talked and laughed for quite some time as the fire slowly burned down. After a while another man approached the small gathering. Son had seen him earlier in the day. He was some sort of party official and Son had avoided him. He was too tired for pompous, egotistical party officials this day.

"You are Lam Son?" the man asked as he walked over to Son.

"Yes," Son said as he reluctantly stood and shook the man's hand.

The man was smaller and more bookish looking than even Son was.

"I'm Hoang Du Tuan, I'm the liaison to this province from Hanoi."

Son was immediately skeptical of the man. He was accustomed to party officials who were constantly over-inflating their self-importance.

"What can I do for you, Mr. Hoang?"

"Please call me Tuan," the man sounded friendly enough. "I'd like to speak with you if I could for a moment, ...privately."

Son was a bit put off by the need to speak away from his men.

"Certainly ...gentlemen, if you'll excuse us," Son made a show excluding his men from the conversation but Tuan didn't appear to notice or to care.

The two men walked away from the fire.

"Son, I have a proposition for you that may be beneficial to both of us."

Son was more skeptical then ever, now.

"My father is Hoang Du Lanh. You may have heard of him, he's very big in the Party back home. As you may have guessed, he got me the position here, I didn't really do anything to earn it."

Son was shocked and confused by the man's candor but he said nothing.

"The point is that I feel as if I need to do something important, something out of the ordinary to prove to my father and to myself that I deserve it."

"What did you have in mind?" Son asked. "And what does it have to do with me?"

"I spent a year with the Army just south of Saigon. I saw first-hand a project that the Americans had started that I thought had the possibility of being very effective in uniting the locals to their cause. The American Marines lived with and got to know the villagers. They helped them improve their farms, built roads and schools; actually made life better for the locals. I think the Americans discontinued it because they have no patience. It would take a long time for the effects of such a project to be realized."

"Excuse me, Tuan," Son asked. "I'm really confused. What does any of this have to do with me?"

"My job here is to work with the Laotians. We take supplies, manpower and intelligence information from them, but there is only so much that can be accomplished at the point of a gun." Tuan paused for a moment to let his words sink in. "I'm a visionary, Son. Someday day this war will be over and we will have to live in peace with the Laotians. Wouldn't it be better if we could somehow improve the quality of their lives the way the Americans tried to improve the quality of the lives of those villagers in South Vietnam? Wouldn't it be better if we gave something back to these people for all of the things that we have taken?"

"What did you have in mind?" Son asked. His skepticism was waning.

"The people here are very poor. There is a series of villages on a high plateau about fifty kilometers east of here where the rainfall is very difficult to predict. They have too much rain in the monsoon season and not enough rain in the dry season. I believe providence has sent you to me. I was told that you are something of an expert when it comes water dykes."

"I wouldn't call myself an expert…" Son began, sounding very humble.

Tuan cut him off before he could finish. "This is no time for false modesty. You worked with the government on the paddy dyke system. That makes you an expert around here. It took a lot of persuading, but I have gotten permission from Hanoi to try building a series of water dykes for these people to see if we can help increase the output of their farms. I need you to supervise this project for me. I have gotten the authority to reassign you to this project but I'm not going to force you to do it."

Tuan reached into his pocket, withdrew a sheet of paper and handed it to Son.

"Here is a letter from your commanding General authorizing me to take you on extended duty for two months.

Son looked at the letter. It appeared to be genuine.

"My, you work quickly," Son said as he stared at the letter.

"The tiger cannot simply wait for his food to come to him. He must pounce when the opportunity presents itself."

Son peered up at him from the letter. He wondered if this frail man was comparing himself to a tiger. He quickly let the thought go. He didn't want to antagonize Tuan. He seemed to be sincere if nothing else.

"Two months!" Son protested. "Two months isn't enough time to accomplish much of anything."

"Let me worry about that," Tuan seemed to have anticipated Sons argument. "The hard part was to get you there in the first place.. Keeping you, should be easy. In two months you'll probably be forgotten in the bureaucratic shuffle." Tuan immediately realized that he may have inadvertently insulted Son by implying that he wasn't really very important. He quickly tried to make amends.

"I don't mean to question your importance. I was just saying that the bureaucracy is often slow and inefficient."

Son smiled at him. If Son had been an egotistic political figure, he would have been very offended, but he wasn't.

"I've been contemplating this project for quite a while but I've never had the means with which to accomplish it. Suddenly, providence dropped you right into my lap. Will you do it for me, Son?"

Son was quiet as he considered the proposal. He knew that it sounded far above his level of expertise and by all rights he should simply admit to this man that he was unqualified for the job.

After a few moments, Tuan went on, sounding much more like a close friend than government official. "Son, you have no mission here any longer. They're going to slap a rifle in your hands and send you to the front. You'll probably be dead in two months. I'm sorry for being so blunt but, you're a trained engineer; use that training for something good. *This* is something good!"

Son knew that he was right. He felt totally inept for the job that Tuan had outlined. He would need far more information than Tuan had provided to have any idea about his chances for success but, he would rather take his chances with this man than with a rifle in the war. He looked over at his four men talking quietly around the fire and suddenly he felt the urge to push his luck.

"I can't do this alone," Son began. "I'm going to need some trained personnel to help me."

Tuan was caught a bit off guard. "How many people?"

Son motioned toward the campfire. "Four," he said.

Tuan knew that he was being used but he wasn't particularly angry about it. He looked over at the men around the campfire and thought to himself for a few moments.

"You'll do it if you can take these four men along? Is that the deal?"

"That's the deal."

Tuan was quiet for some time.

"How long would it take you and your men to get your things together?"

"We could be ready within an hour."

"Okay, Give me a list of their names and ranks. I'll need to make a few radio calls but I don't think it will be a problem." Tuan turned away from the fire and spoke in a lower tone to Son.

"The American airplanes are going to be back as soon as the Sun comes up and I don't want to be anywhere near here when that happens. Get your things together quickly. We'll be traveling all night."

Son and Tuan shook hands and Tuan walked off.

Son shook his head in amazement. He wondered to himself just what had happened in the last few minutes. Perhaps the entire course of his life had changed after just a few words. He looked at his men again and considered how they would react to notion of breaking their encampment and traveling all night long. He knew they were tired but this was an opportunity that they could not pass up.

Tom watched the small gathering beneath him in the distance for at least a couple of hours. He was concerned that they would still be there in the morning and interfere with his rescue. Then incredibly after several hours, the men got up, extinguished their campfire and they disappeared into the darkness away from Tom. Tom felt that his luck seemed to be getting better. At least he wouldn't have to contend with these men in the morning. He lay quietly on his stomach and prayed for the Sun to rise quickly.

XIV: ATONEMENT

Sunday 17Dec 1967 (0600L, San Rafael, Ca)

BARBARA GROVES HAD been up all night. Her head still ached terribly from the rock that had hit her at the rally but her greatest concern was for the welfare of her children. She was a loving and caring mother to her children, despite the problems that she and Mike were having.

"Juvenile Hall," the Police Officer at the desk had said. Her children had been taken to Juvenile Hall for the night. Her children were in jail. The Officer had tried to console her by telling her that the county had no other provisions for the short term care of minors. He assured her that they were **not** really in jail. They were in an overnight portion of the facility that was used just for circumstances like this. It didn't really help her to feel any better about the situation.

She looked at the clock again. The Officer had told her that she could pick up her children at eight o'clock. There were still two hours to go. She wondered if her friend, Cindy Blume was awake yet. Cindy lived in the house just two doors down. It was Cindy who had gotten Barbara started in the real estate business and Cindy was the one, more than any other, who had encouraged her to divorce Mike and start out on her own.

Barbara knew that Cindy was an early riser but Barbara wondered if she would be up this early on a Sunday morning. Barbara was desperate for someone to talk to so she decided to take her chances.

The phone was picked up on the first ring.

"**Susan**?!" Cindy practically yelled into the phone.

Barbara was caught completely off-guard by the reply from Cindy.

"No, it's Barbara. Cindy, is something wrong with Susan?"

"She didn't come home again last night, that's all," the volume of Cindy's voice decreased but the anger in it didn't. "I can't wait until that girl turns 18, then I can kick her out on her own. I ought to ship her back to Utah, to her deadbeat father. Let **him** deal with this crap for a change. She's going to turn up pregnant some day, I just know it! What a nice mess that'll be and it will be up to me to fix it!"

Barbara was completely taken aback by Cindy's rant. She thought about Kathy, her own daughter, and hoped that their relationship would never degrade to such a terrible point.

"Cindy it sounds as if I've caught you at a bad time, I'm sorry, but I really need to talk to someone."

"Oh nonsense, Barbara, this goes on all of the time anymore," the anger in Cindy's voice was spent and she seemed to calm down. "What's the matter?"

"I don't really want to go into it over the phone. Could I come over and talk for a few minutes?"

"This place looks like ground zero right now. Why don't I come over there?"

"Okay, but aren't you waiting for a call from Susan?"

"Oh, to hell with her! She uses this place like her private hotel anymore. I don't really care if she calls or not! I ***should*** just lock her out. That will teach her a lesson! I'll be over in a few minutes."

Fifteen minutes later there was a knock on Barbara's front door.

"My God, what happened to you?" Cindy asked when she saw Barbara.

Barbara's head was bandaged and she looked extremely tired and worn out from being up all night.

"Come in and I'll tell you all about it."

Barbara told Cindy everything that had happened to her in the last twenty-four hours. She told her how she had met Henry for lunch and Jeremy Daniels had joined them. She related the gist of the lecture that Jeremy had given to Henry and then went on to describe the events that occurred at the rally. Cindy seemed to be spellbound by the story.

"Wow," was all that Cindy could manage to say once Barbara had finished. "No more dull housewife for you, eh?" Cindy said as she smiled.

"Cindy, you don't seem to understand my problem. I have to go and get my kids at eight o'clock and they're going to ask me where I was yesterday."

"So?"

"**So**! I can't tell them that I was meeting with man, who also happens to be married, and that we went to a riot that he instigated where I was injured."

"Yeah, that could be a problem," Cindy said although she still didn't seem to grasp the gravity of the situation.

"Don't you get it? I'm married to an Air Force Officer and I'm protesting the **war**?! Not to mention fooling around with a married man. I don't think anyone is going to look at that in a very favorable light. They'll think I'm an unfit mother," Barbara said as she burst into tears.

"Okay, slow down just a minute. You don't have to tell them any of this."

"No?"

"No! Just tell them that you were out with clients looking at houses and you got in a car wreck," Cindy said, sounding quite pleased with herself.

"But, what if they ask me *who* I was with, where we were, the details about the accident and why didn't I call?"

"Who has your kids, Sherlock Holmes? It's just some social worker who's probably pissed off about having to work over the week-end anyway. She'll be glad just to get your kids off of her hands. Don't worry about it."

"Are you sure?"

"I'm sure!"

Barbara was waiting in the lobby of Solano County Juvenile Hall at ten minutes to eight. A woman about the same age as Barbara came out to see her about fifteen minutes later.

"Mrs. Groves, I'm Pam Thatcher," the woman seemed friendly enough. Barbara began to think that this might be just as easy as Cindy had said it would be.

"Please call me Barbara."

"It's nice to meet you Barbara. Call me Pam. First of all, your kids are just fine. I looked in on them on my way out here. They're having breakfast now and we'll let them finish before we get them. I have to fill out a report and there will be a hearing in The Family Court later this week. It's all strictly routine. We just want to be sure that your children are being well cared for."

"I understand," Barbara began to get a little more nervous again.

Pam directed Barbara into her office and asked her to have a seat. Pam sat behind the desk and opened up a small brown folder.

"Okay Barbara, this form is just a synopsis of the events that took place this week-end. I have a statement from your children and now I need one from you. The judge will simply review this with you in the court later this week."

Pam looked up at her and waited for a reply. Barbara took a deep breath and began her explanation.

"Okay, my husband, Mike, is a pilot in the Air Force serving in Thailand now." Barbara hoped to score some points by appealing to Pam's patriotism. "He's been gone for seven, no, eight months now. I've gotten started selling real-estate since then to try and make ends meet. My fourteen year-old daughter, Kathy often baby-sits for her two younger brothers if I have to work on a Saturday or Sunday. I was showing a couple from out-of-state around yesterday. I was gone longer than I had anticipated so I called home to tell Kathy that I would be gone a bit longer but I promised to be home before dark. That must have been at about two P.M., two-thirty at the latest. We were traveling to a house out near Lake Berryessa and we had a car accident. I banged my head," Barbara motioned to the bandages on her head. "I was unconscious for awhile. When I came to, my first thoughts were of Kathy and the boys. I tried to call from the hospital but they wouldn't let me use the phone in the emergency room. I tried to get home as quickly as I could but it took quite some time. It was after midnight when I finally got home and by then the police had already taken my kids here."

"That's just terrible. I'm very sorry for you. Were you hurt badly?"

"Oh it looks a lot worse than it is," Barbara said trying to sound brave.

Barbara was very good at judging people. That was one of the reasons that she had done so well selling real estate. She sensed that Pam was skeptical of her story but she quickly convinced herself that she was simply being paranoid.

"What hospital did they take you to?" Pam asked casually as she busily wrote on the form.

"Our Lady of Mercy in Vacaville," Barbara answered quickly, without really thinking about it. She knew immediately that she had made a mistake.

"Really?" Pam seemed surprised. "You had an accident near Lake Berryessa and they took you all the way out to Vacaville?"

"Well, I don't know, I heard them say something about a contract with the ambulance company. I wasn't thinking clearly so I'm not really sure what the explanation was." Barbara was proud of herself for that answer. She had put her foot in her mouth but she thought that she had pulled it out nicely.

Pam returned to writing on the form,

"I'm a little surprised," Pam said without looking up from the form. "You were unconscious and they just released you from the hospital? I would have thought that they would at least want to keep you overnight."

"Well, they did want to keep me but I was so anxious to get home that I refused to stay. I just got up and left."

"I see. And they wouldn't even let you make a phone call?"

Barbara was really beginning to get nervous now.

"Well…The emergency room was very crowded. There had been some kind of riot or something and the place was over-flowing with people."

"Oh yes, an anti-war protest at Travis became violent yesterday and a lot of people were hurt."

"Yes, I think I heard someone say something to me about that."

Pam seemed to be satisfied with that explanation. She continued to write on the form.

Barbara told herself to shut-up. She really hadn't intended to say anything about the protest rally. She wanted to stay as far away from that subject as possible. Barbara now regretted that she hadn't taken the time to fabricate a story. She sat quietly hoping that the interrogation was over.

"How did you get home if your car was wrecked?" Pam asked carelessly as she continued to write.

"What?" Barbara stalled for time as her mind was racing for an answer.

Pam looked up at her.

"How did you get home if your car was wrecked?"

"Oh! We were in my client's car." Barbara felt as if she had hit a home run with that answer.

"Of course," Pam seemed pleased with that response too.

Barbara still felt as if Pam was just toying with her. It was like a fisherman who was just waiting to set the hook.

"Were they hurt as well?"

"Who?"

"Your clients."

"No, I was the only one hurt." Barbara knew that if she said they had been hurt too, the next question would be about the nature and extent of their injuries. She wasn't prepared for that. Barbara thought it best to say that they were not hurt at all. This was like a chess match and Barbara was trying to stay one move ahead of Pam.

"*Dam it*," Barbara thought to herself. She wished she had thought this through earlier.

"Oh, did they stay then, at the hospital to take you home?"

"What? No, they didn't have to go to the hospital because they weren't hurt."

"Well, how did you get home then, without a car?"

"*She's playing with me like a cat toying with a mouse*," Barbara thought.

"A nurse was on her way home and she gave me a ride!"

"That was lucky. She gave you a ride all the way back home from Vacaville?"

"Yes! No! She gave me a ride to my car," Barbara sounded annoyed now.

"Where was your car?" Pam sounded sickeningly sweet.

"Look, am I on trial here? I told you what happened. I was in a car accident. Alright!"

The smile never left Pam's face.

"Have you seen a newspaper this morning, Barbara?"

Barbara was completely stunned by the question. "*What possible difference could it make whether or not I've seen a newspaper*?" she thought.

"No, I haven't," was all that she could manage to say.

Pam appeared to be very self-satisfied as she reached down into her large purse on the floor and pulled out a copy of the morning newspaper.

She laid the paper out to show Barbara the entire front page. The headline read:

Protest at Travis Turns Violent; Shots Fired

Below the headline was the photograph of Barbara as she walked out of the hospital in Vacaville. It took up nearly a quarter of the page. There was absolutely no doubt that it was her. The caption below it read;

Mrs. Barbara Groves, wife of Lt. Col. Michael Groves, USAF, leaves the hospital in Vacaville, Ca. Groves was injured Saturday along with twenty-seven others, some seriously, when military police and State Highway Patrolmen opened fire on a raucous but mostly-peaceful crowd of anti-war demonstrators.

Barbara was speechless. There was a half page article next to the photograph detailing the events at Travis the previous day. Barbara didn't bother to read any of it. The caption said it all.

Where had the photograph come from, she wondered? How did they know who she was? The caption made it sound as if she had been injured by the police when that wasn't the case.

Barbara let the newspaper lay on the desk. It was as if she was afraid to touch it.

"My husband is a Highway Patrolman," Pam said defiantly. "He was at that rally yesterday and both he and I are greatly offended that you and this newspaper would infer that the law enforcement officers were the cause of the problems there yesterday!"

Barbara just sat with her mouth agape.

"There's at least one big difference between the two of us Mrs. Groves; I support *my* husband and what he does to earn a living!"

"But,...I," was all that Barbara could manage to say.

Pam looked back at the form, disgusted. "I don't care about your politics Mrs. Groves. I care about your children! When you come in here and lie to me the way that did, it makes me wonder what else you're lying about. We're going to return your children to you today but you are on notice that we will take them from you if we can prove that you are an unfit mother. I've put in my report that you've deliberately attempted to miss-lead me. It'll be up to the judge to decide how to proceed from here. I'll tell you right now that most judges don't like being lied to!"

Barbara's head was still spinning from the exchange. She thought about apologizing to Pam and trying to make amends by being nice to her. That thought was quickly replaced by thoughts of revenge.

"*Who the hell does this low-level worker drone think she is reading the riot act to me*?" Barbara thought to herself. "*I have friends. I have connections! She'll be lucky if she still has a job when this is all over.*"

Barbara's children were brought in a few minutes later. From the tearful reunion it seemed apparent that the children loved Barbara very much and she, at least, appeared to love them. Pam was unmoved though. She knew that children this age wanted their parents to love them regardless of how badly they were treated.

Barbara spent the rest of the morning with her children. She took them straight home and tried to put the incident behind them. She did everything she could to restore their lives to the normal routine as quickly as possible. Barbara could not stop thinking about it though. She would have to face a judge later this week and he would probably have a lot more questions for her than Pam had. Barbara knew that she hadn't done very well lying to Pam. She was dreading the thought of having to go through it all again with the knowledge that the custody of her children could be at stake.

There was also the memory of the way Pam had set her up. The more Barbara thought about it, the angrier she became. Pam knew very well where Barbara had been yesterday yet she pretended not to. She set a trap and Barbara had walked right into it. Then she sat there and watched as Barbara dug herself deeper and deeper into the hole that she had prepared. Barbara wanted to wipe that smug look of satisfaction right off of Pam's face more than anything else. There was only one way she could think of to do that.

Barbara recalled an incident that Henry Gonzales had told her about a week or two earlier. The County Attorney came to Henry and asked about some corruption charges that had been made against Henry by a third party. Henry got indignant and reminded the Attorney that he worked for the County Supervisors, which essentially made Henry his boss. Henry threatened to start a campaign to have the Attorney fired and the investigation was stopped. The family courts also came under the supervision of the County Attorney. If Henry could coerce the County Attorney to stop a criminal investigation, it should be very simple for him to stop this proceeding about Barbara's children.

Barbara called Henry at about eleven thirty. She thought that he might still be in jail for inciting the riot, but then she realized that if Henry were as powerful and influential as he pretended to be, he would have found a way out by now.

"Yeah?" Henry sounded groggy as if he had just woken up.

"Henry? It's Barbara; you're not in jail apparently."

"No, they didn't have anything on me."

"Are you okay? Those Patrolmen looked as if they were pretty rough with you?"

"Oh, they were nothing. It was kind of fun."

Barbara left the door open for Henry to ask about *her* condition but as usual Henry was concerned only about himself.

"You were just great yesterday. I've never seen a crowd react the way those kids reacted to you." In reality, she had been horrified by the reaction of the crowd, but Barbara knew that she had to pump up Henry's ego a bit if she was going to get him to do something for her.

"Yeah, well..." Henry was trying to sound modest. It was unusual for him.

"Henry, I really need you to do a big favor for me."

"Oh yeah? Well I need something too. I'll pick you up at Bob's at twelve-thirty."

This was their normal rendezvous routine for an afternoon of passion. They went to the Windward Inn, an unpretentious motel just off of Interstate 80 in Vallejo. The owner owed Henry a debt. Cal-trans had decided to make a free-way off-ramp several years earlier. The planned off-ramp would have curved around the back of the Windward Inn and forced drivers to make a u-turn in order to get to the motel. It would have been much easier for drivers to continue on to other motels just down the street. Henry and a couple of the other County Supervisors had been *convinced* to ask for a re-design of the off-ramp that brought traffic right past the motel. In return, Henry was allowed to come and go through the motel with no questions asked. Even though everyone at the motel knew what was going on, it was still a bit unseemly for Henry and Barbara to arrive and depart in separate cars. Even Henry had to draw the line somewhere. So they started meeting in the parking lot of the Bob's Big Boy restaurant that was just two exits east of the Windward Inn. Barbara would leave her car there and they would both go on to the motel in Henry's car. Outwardly they appeared to be just another couple coming and going from the motel. Barbara had found it exciting at first. It was as if they had thought this up from a James Bond movie; switching cars to be sure that they weren't followed.

But Barbara wasn't really in the mood for these antics today. It was the sex-capades with Henry that had gotten her into trouble in the first place.

"Couldn't we just have lunch somewhere, Henry? I'm not really..."

"Look you want me to do something for you but you're not willing to do anything for me. Nothing in this world is free! Now, do you want to meet me at Bob's or not?"

"Okay," Barbara reluctantly agreed.

"Okay, I'll see you in an hour."

Now, she really was a prostitute, but she told herself that this time she was doing it for her kids. She decided that she was willing to do anything to correct this situation. Barbara wondered how she had ever gotten herself into this position but she soon realized that there was no time for that now. She would have to hurry. Barbara quickly arranged for Cindy to watch her children. She fixed herself up as best she could, working around the bandages on her head.

She paused when she was through and looked in the mirror. She saw a tired middle-aged woman who was about to do something that she knew she would regret later. She felt sad more than anything else. She wondered what Mike would say if he could see what had become of the girl that he had married. She quickly pushed that thought from her mind. She decided that Mike was at much fault for this as she was. She grabbed her purse and hurried out the door.

It was two-thirty in the afternoon as Barbara and Henry stumbled over each other getting dressed again in the cramped motel room.

"Now I need a favor from you, Henry," Barbara said coyly, after a while.

"What is it?"

"Remember how you told me that you got the County Attorney to drop those corruption charges against you?"

Henry had to struggle for a moment to remember precisely what he had told her about the matter. The essential elements of the story were correct. The County Attorney *had* approached Henry and asked some questions about allegations of corruption. Henry *had* become irate and threatened to have the attorney fired. But the conclusion was pure fabrication on Henry's part. Instead of dropping the case the Attorney had become more convinced than ever that the charges must be true. He had actually accelerated the investigation and thought that he was only a week or so away from bringing formal charges against Henry.

"Yeah, I remember."

"Well, when I didn't come home last night my daughter called the police."

"What the f*** did she do that for?"

"She was scared. She didn't know what else to do."

"Okay, so what happened?"

"The police came and took them to juvenile hall for the night. I was there at eight o'clock this morning to get them out."

Henry started to laugh uncontrollably and it made Barbara angry.

"Your kids spent the f***ing night in jail. That's hilarious!"

"What's so funny about it?" Barbara asked angrily.

"I start a riot and get four people shot and I was out of jail in no time. Your kids get scared because Mommy's not home and they spend the entire night in the lock-up."

"It's not funny," Barbara yelled at him.

"Maybe it's not to you, but it is to me."

"Henry, stop it. This is serious! They are going to have a hearing later this week to determine if I'm an unfit Mother."

"I've seen you naked, Baby and I will testify that you are *very* fit, if nothing else." He came closer to her and grabbed her around the waist. Barbara slugged him hard twice in the chest.

Henry backed away from her genuinely in some pain. He finally managed to stop laughing.

"Stop it! This isn't a joke!"

"What the hell do you expect me to do about it?" Henry was angry now.

"I want you to call the County Attorney and have this matter dropped."

"Are you out of your mind? I can't do that!"

"You got him to drop the corruption investigation didn't you? This should be a lot easier than that."

"That was different," Henry sounded defensive.

"How is it different?"

"It just is. I can't do it!"

"You can't or you won't. Henry, this is my children that we're talking about," Barbara said as she started to cry.

"I can't! Get your things. We have to go!"

"Why are you being so unreasonable?" Barbara said as she wept.

"I'm being unreasonable? You want me to commit a crime by telling the County Attorney how to do his job and I'm being unreasonable because I won't do it!"

"Yes, you did it to save yourself, now you can do it for me. It's for my kids, Henry!"

"I don't give a dam about your kids!"

Barbara was taken aback. Barbara's children were the most important things in her life. If Henry didn't give a dam about them, then he really didn't give a dam about her either. If he didn't give a dam about her then he was just using her for sex. She felt abused and humiliated. She wondered how she could have been so stupid.

"I'm leaving!" she said.

Henry was actually somewhat relieved. He'd been wondering how he was going to break it off with Barbara and now she had done it for him.

"I'll take you back to your car."

"No. I don't want to be anywhere near you. I'll take a cab."

Barbara gathered her things and started for the door. Henry blocked the way.

"I'll take you back to your car," he said more forcefully.

Barbara felt threatened by him so she decided to agree. It was only a few miles anyway.

She was silent as they got into the car. She refused to even look at Henry. She felt as if she had been terribly used. She was physically sick and terribly ashamed of herself. She sat quietly sobbing and staring out of the window.

Henry was really quite relieved. He was free. This had worked out perfectly. He didn't have a care in the world. He was in a hurry to drop her off though. It made him uncomfortable to be with her in this state of mind.

Luke Williams had been a long-distance trucker for more than fifteen years. He had started this run in Kansas City earlier the previous day. He had pushed all day and through most of the night to make it to California before the close of business on this Sunday afternoon. He had made his first delivery in Vallejo and was anxious to unload the second half of his cargo in San Francisco before they closed at five o'clock. He was tired and in a hurry as he drove north on the four lane road. Interstate 80 was just ahead. A quick left turn onto the freeway and he would be in the city within an hour. The speed limit was 45 mph and Luke was going about 10 mph over that. Just before he got to the freeway a car pulled out in front of him from a motel driveway on the left side of the road. Luke was distracted and very tired. He didn't see the car until it was far too late. He watched his truck collide with the car as if it happened in slow motion. The car was a black luxury sedan. There was an attractive woman with a bandage on her forehead staring blankly out of the passenger's side window. Their eyes met in the last fraction of a second before the impact. He felt so sorry for her.

XV: PRELUDE

Sunday 17 Dec 1967 (0500L NKP Airbase, Thailand)

In the early morning hours a small army of would-be rescuers was rallying to come to Tom's aid. A much larger army had been working all night to prepare the machines that would take them into battle.

Frank Robertson (Nail 58) was the first one to get to his airplane that morning. Technically he shouldn't have been flying at all. The pilots were required to have at least twelve hours of crew rest in between missions. Frank had landed the night before at nearly seven P.M. Normally he wouldn't have been scheduled to fly the first sortie of the day under those circumstances but there had been a mistake in the scheduling section. Frank's second sortie yesterday was unscheduled and never appeared on the Ops board. When the schedulers made the roster for Sunday's flight none of them realized that Frank had flown a second time on Saturday. The first launch of the day was normally Frank's and none of the schedulers saw any reason not to put him in it. Frank should have told them and seen to it that he was rescheduled for a later flight but he wanted to fly this mission.

Frank had stopped by the Officer's Club for a few minutes after he landed last night. The atmosphere was quite somber, as expected. The gathering toasted Steve Turner (Nail 44) several times but for the most part the pilots were quiet and introspective.

Lt Col Garrett, Frank's Squadron Ops Officer, came up and sat next to Frank at the bar after awhile.

"What time did you land tonight, Frank?"

"Oh, I don't know, sir. Not too late."

Frank knew that Garrett must have realized the scheduling mistake.

"Not too late, huh? You know Frank I should take you off of the morning schedule. It's my responsibility and my neck is on the line too if something happens to you."

"I know that, Sir. But you want to get that guy out of there as much as I do and you know that I'm the best man that you have for the job," It was uncharacteristic of Frank to sound so immodest.

"You know I could put someone in your right seat to hold your hand or better yet I could have someone else fly the dam thing and put *you* in the right seat."

"You could, sir. But you won't," Frank said as he downed the last of his drink.

"What makes you so sure?"

"Because you were a smart-ass Captain once yourself and I'll bet you didn't like having a babysitter in your right seat either."

Garrett just looked at him for a minute.

"God dam it, Frank if you go out and bust your ass tomorrow they'll hang *me* from the highest tree they can find."

"I guess I'd better be careful than."

Garrett looked at him as if Frank was his own son.

"Be careful, Frank."

Then Garrett's look switched quickly back to that of the stern supervisor.

"Now get your ass out of here and get some sleep." Then he raised his voice so that everyone in the bar could hear him.

"Okay, all of you assholes who have five o'clock briefs need to get the f**k out of here. Now!"

It was still dark as Frank settled himself into the cockpit of his airplane. He had a large thermos of coffee that he secured for the moment in the right seat of the airplane. He thought about what Garrett had said the night before and concluded that the coffee would be better than any co-pilot.

Frank was anxious to be on his way. A few minutes later the rear engine of the O-2 roared reluctantly to life and Frank taxied out toward the end of the runway. He started the front engine as he taxied.

Farther down the flightline, Sgt Dave Kearney (Flight Engineer, Jolly 10) made his way to his helicopter. He heard the racket as Robertson's O-2 took off but he didn't think anything of it. The O-2's were always the first ones to take off each morning. He had no way of knowing that he would be working with this particular O-2 later in the day.

As Dave approached the helicopter the area around it seemed to be deserted. Dave peered inside the boarding door and saw Ron Fergusson, the crew chief, balled up in the corner behind the cockpit, quietly napping. Dave climbed up into the helicopter as quietly as he possibly could and crept up next to the sleeping crew chief.

"God dam it, Sergeant Fergusson, what the hell are you doing sleeping on the job!" he yelled into Fergusson's ear.

The startled crew chief nearly leapt through the ceiling of the helicopter. Then he saw that it was Dave who was shouting at him.

"You asshole! You nearly gave me a heart attack. I thought it was that jerk, Master Sergeant Young. He's always on my case."

Dave was nearly doubled over in laughter.

"I've never seen you move so fast, Ron," Dave said as he laughed, "and the look on your face was priceless,"

"Yeah, real funny!" Ron said as he yawned. "Payback is a bitch, buddy. Just keep looking behind you."

Dave slowly managed to stop laughing.

"Have a hard night, Ron?"

"Yes. Not that *you* care. You wrote up the fluctuating oil pressure on the number two so I took some extra oil samples and had them analyzed. They found some metal shavings in them. We wound up having to change the whole gearbox assembly on the number two. What a pain in the ass that was. We broke a spline on the way out and it took us nearly all night to get it back together. Hell, we just finished about twenty minutes ago."

"Is it okay now?"

Ron just looked at Dave as if he had asked the dumbest question he had ever heard.

"Have I ever, *not* had this bird ready for you guys?"

"I guess not. Hey don't be sore about the wake-up call. Shift change is in less than an hour and you can go back to the dorm and get some sleep."

"Not for me. Today is my Friday. I'm catching the C-130 to Bangkok at 0900. I'm going to spend the next two days working on the railroad."

"Laying Thai(s)?"

"You got it! Say, you're off tomorrow, why don't you come down there after you land?"

"Thanks but I still haven't fully recovered from the last time we did that."

"Okay, but you know where we'll be."

Dave started to do his walk around inspection and Ron followed after him.

"Hey, I saw that two-balls-nine didn't come back yesterday, what happened?" Ron asked.

The serial number of the helicopter that was Jolly 19 the previous day was 63-2009. Only the last four digits of the number were painted on the noses of the copters and that is how the ground crews referred to each of the helicopters. Two-zero-zero-nine was known as two-balls-nine to everyone.

"They went in to get an F-105 jock that got shot down in Laos. The place turned out to be pretty hot. They think they took some hits in the transmission. The copter lost power and had to make a forced landing on the way back."

"Did anyone get hurt?"

"Yeah, their PJ got his hand screwed up pretty badly. They were all shaken up a bit."

"Yeah, I'll bet. Did they get the -105 guy?"

"No. We're going to try it again today. We're the primary for the pick-up *this* time."

"Wow. You guys better be careful out there," Ron thought that he might be sounding a bit too sentimental so he quickly changed the tone of his voice and went on to explain. "I don't want you to wreck my helicopter."

"We always take the best care of it," Dave said as he smiled.

Still farther down the flightline Mike Groves was sanitizing his flightsuit in the life-support shop. It was a ritual that all of the pilots went through before each flight. They removed all of their unit patches and all of their personnel items, keeping only their military I.D. cards in case they were shot down. Mike stood quietly in front of his locker placing everything neatly on the shelf. As he removed his wedding ring, he paused for a moment to look at it. He thought back to the first time that he had ever seen his wife, Barbara, nearly twenty years earlier. He thought that she was the most beautiful girl he had ever seen. He remembered how the two of them had been inseparable for the first year or so that they were together. He pondered it for a few moments and concluded that it would have been impossible for them to maintain that level of passion. They would have burned out like an over-heated star. He concluded that he still loved her though. It certainly wasn't as intense as it once had been but it was a more sustainable level of passion. He realized that he had taken her for granted and he was determined not to do it anymore. He needed to sit down when he got back from this mission and write her a long letter. He had been working over the precise wording in his mind for the last couple of weeks. It wasn't easy for Mike Groves to admit that he had been wrong, but he resolved to do it.

"Are you coming, Mike?" his wingman asked as he stood by the door to the flightline.

"Yeah, I'm right behind you."

Mike started for the door when the life-support Sergeant yelled to him.

"Hey Colonel, there's a phone call for you. He said he was a General."

"*That's just what I need now*," Mike thought to himself.

He reluctantly walked back and took the phone from the Sergeant.

"Lt. Colonel Groves," he said as he held the phone to his ear.

There was a slight pause on the other end of the line.

"Groves, this is General Allen at 15th Air Force in Saigon. I understand that you're running the SAR mission down at Ban Bak this morning."

""I'm leading the Sandy's, yes sir."

Groves didn't feel as if he should have to explain to a General just how the FAC's would be running the show initially.

"Well, this thing has gotten some high-level attention in Washington. They seem to think this may be part of a much larger campaign to build-up NVA forces in the south."

For once I would agree with them, Sir." Groves knew that he must sound a bit impertinent but he didn't really care anymore. He had already submitted his resignation. What were they going to do; fire him?

"They want me to throw six Arc-light[10] sorties at that little valley. That's enough firepower to blow that place into the next time zone!"

"That's probably a good idea. Just let us get our survivor out of there and you can have at it, Sir."

"Well, that's the rub Colonel. They don't want to wait. They want me to bomb it now."

"You can't do that, Sir. You'd kill our guy too!"

---

[10] Arc-Light was the code-name for B-52 sorties. At this point in the war the B-52's were flying out of U-Tapao RTAB, near Bangkok. A B-52D was capable of dropping 108 500lbs. Mk 82 bombs.

"I know that. That's why I'm calling you. I can stall a bit but I can't stop this. Apparently it's coming straight from the White House. I've managed to convince them that we can't be ready to go until noon-time but I can't put it off any longer than that! In other words Colonel, you either get your boy out of there by noon or you don't get him out at all!"

"Whose side are you on, anyway?"

The General was unaccustomed to being talked to this way by a Lt Colonel but he had heard about Mike's reputation for speaking his mind.

"Look Colonel, I'm sticking my neck way out just to buy you these few hours."

"With all due respect, Sir; *we're* sticking out far more than just our necks. You know that the weather stinks around here this time of year we may not even get a shot at a rescue all day long. Just put this thing on hold until we can get him out."

"I can't do that Colonel. These Arc-Light sorties take a lot of prior coordination. I can't just *put it on hold*. Besides, the Pentagon is breathing down my neck on this!"

"A little too dangerous for you, General? Maybe you should try having your ass shot off everyday like we do and then you can talk to me about danger!"

"Watch it, Colonel. You're crossing the line, here!"

"God dam it, General; if you won't let us win this war at least let us take care of our own people!"

"It's not my call to make!" The General was yelling into the phone. "Now, you have until noon and then the game is over. If you're half as good with your hands as you are with mouth you should be able to fly right in and save this guy. You have your job to do and I have mine. Twelve o'clock, Colonel. That's it! Good-bye!"

The phone clicked loudly as if the General had slammed down the receiver on his end. Mike was angry at first and then, surprisingly, he felt very pleased with himself. It wasn't often that he got to speak that way to a General. He liked this new carefree attitude.

Mike had a broad grin on his face as he walked out to the flightline. The Life-support Sergeant just watched in silent amazement.

At Korat RTAB Lt Col. Morris walked up to his airplane just as the sun was rising. He had to smile to himself as he looked at the canisters of CBU suspended beneath the big Thud. Morris made a note to himself to buy Chief Dugan a drink when he got back later that day. Morris checked the aircraft forms to make sure that the airplane was ready to go; did his walk around inspection of the big jet and then climbed up and strapped himself into the ejection seat.

At precisely 0630 Morris raised his arms above his head so that the crew chief on the ground could see him and smacked his right fist into the palm of his left hand. It was the signal to connect high-pressure air to the engine for start-up. The massive turbine shuddered as the air rotated it for start. Once it was up to speed Morris pushed the throttle up and the engine came to life.

Several minutes later Morris signaled the crew chief to remove the chocks and the big jet slowly lumbered out toward the end of the runway.

As he taxied slowly, the rest of the flight moved into position behind him. They moved in one by one with a precision that the Thunderbirds or the Blue Angels would have envied.

As they approached the end of the runway the jets moved into the bomb arming area for their "last-chance" inspection. The planes pulled up next to each other and Morris could look down the line and see each of the pilots in the other three airplanes. Morris raised his hands above the canopy rail to show to the personnel on the ground that he was not going to activate any switches or controls. The flight controls and actuator doors on the airplane moved quickly and powerfully. If they struck someone on the ground they could easily cause a serious injury or even kill. The team chief of the armoring crew stood where he and the pilot could see each other. He stood with his arms crossed at the wrists. It was the signal for Morris to keep his hands in view and not to touch anything. Once the team chief was satisfied that it was safe, he nodded to his crew and four men quickly ran under the jet and pulled the safety tags from the bomb fuses and the bomb racks. Each of the tags has a long red streamer attached to it with the words "Remove Before Flight" printed on it in large white letters. As they pulled the tags off the armourers accomplished a quick, final check to insure that everything was set properly. There were two crews of armorers and they finished their work on all four airplanes within just a few minutes. Each of the armorers had a handful of the red streamers when they were finished. The team chief and Morris exchanged a quick salute and then Morris looked down the line at his wingmen. He knocked on the right side of his helmet with his right fist and then held up two fingers for the rest of the flight to see. This was the signal for the pilots to change their radios to channel two.

"Fang one-one," Morris broadcast on the tower frequency.

"Two!"

"Three!"

"Four!"

The responses were short and quick.

Morris added power and his jet began moving toward the end of the runway. Each of the other F-105's moved in behind him once again.

"Fang one-one, flight of four Thuds is ready."

"Roger, Fang one-one. Taxi into position and hold"

"Fang One-one is on to hold."

The four jets moved out onto the runway. At the signal from Morris all four canopies began to close in unison. The first three jets lined up across the runway in echelon. Fang one-four lined up farther back between one and two. Morris could easily look back and see two and three; he had to strain to look back far enough to see number four. The four jets sat and waited for clearance to take-off.

"Fang one-one flight, the wind is two-six zero at fives knots you're cleared for take-off on runway two-four," the tower controller radioed.

Morris quickly looked back toward his wingmen and each of them nodded in turn that they were ready to go. Morris cocked his head backwards as far as he could and then brought his chin quickly all the way down to his chest. As he did so, he released his brakes and smoothly pushed the throttle up all the way to the forward stop.

"Fang one-one is rolling on two-four."

The first two jets began to move down the runway as if they were welded together. There were two quick bangs as the afterburners lit and Fang one-one and one-two were on their way. Five seconds later the pilot of Fang one-three made the same exaggerated head nod to his wingman and the two of them moved in unison as they too began their take-off roll. Once airborne each flight lead made a quick upward movement with his head to signal for landing gear retraction.

The second element rejoined quickly with the first and the four Thuds were on their way to rendezvous with the tankers.

Frank Robertson was anxious to get to the target area. He was concerned that Tom may not have made it safely through the night. He had no way of knowing about Tom's status until he got close enough to talk with him on the radio. He pushed the little O-2 to move faster. The weather was about the same as it had been the day before. A solid overcast layer for as far as Frank could see.

Frank checked in with Dragnet just as he always did.

"Dragnet, Dragnet, this is Nail five-eight."

"Nail 58 this is Dragnet, authenticate for me Alpha Seven."

It was a coded response to insure that everyone was who they said they were on the radio. The code sheet was simply a grid with all of the letters across the top and the numbers zero through nine down the side. The pilot merely had to cross reference the letter-number combination and then read off the letter that intersected with both. The letters within the grid changed everyday but the basic method was always the same.

"Dragnet I authenticate Golf."

The controller in Dragnet quickly confirmed that Frank had responded correctly.

"Good Morning, Nail five-eight. Looks as if you could be pretty busy this morning."

"Yeah? Well I might be if this lousy weather would clear up."

Frank was working his way around low clouds, trying to maintain visual contact with the ground out in front of him. It was becoming more and more difficult as he got farther to the east. The cloud layer kept forcing him lower and lower.

"You must have some friends in high places, Nail."

"Why do you say that?"

"I have one flight of Thuds, two flights of Huns[11] and a flight of A-4's that have all been dedicated to you."

"Wow, I'm overwhelmed."

"That's not all. We just got a tanker with a probe and drogue[12] that's been given to us as well so they can hang around and wait for the weather to clear if we need to."

---

[11] The F-100 was known familiarly as "The Hun".

[12] The F-100 and the U.S. Navy airplanes did not use the rigid boom refueling method that is now common to all U.S. Air Force aircraft. Instead, a flexible hose with a basket on the end was attached to the boom. On the KC-135 tanker. the attachment had to be done on the ground before the tanker took off. The rigid

"Okay why don't you go ahead and give me their line-ups."

Frank wrote the line-up for each flight with a grease pencil on the large pane of glass on his left side. This way they were easily accessible and could be quickly erased and replaced with new ones as the situation developed. The line-up consisted of Call-sign, aircraft type, ordnance load, and playtime. Playtime is the amount of time the fighters would have available for the attack, once they left the tankers.

Fang One-one	Monk Four-six	Dodge Six-six	Ferret Two-zero
4 x F-105s	4 x F-100s	4 x F-100s	2x A-4s
8 x CBU-52	2x Mk 84[13]	6 x Mk 82	6 Mk 82
20mm	20mm	20 mm	20 mm
30 mins	20 mins	20 mins	30 mins

Frank was a bit in awe of the firepower that he had at his disposal.

"I got it all Dragnet. Thanks. I'm going to be off frequency for a few minutes. I'm going to call Cyclone and make sure that he's okay."

"Roger that, Nail."

Frank changed frequencies and took a deep breath. He silently prayed for just moment that Tom had made it through the night. He hoped that all of their preparation would pay off.

"Cyclone three-two this is Nail five-eight. Do you read me?"

"Good morning, Nail. This is Cyclone three-two. Frank is that you?" Tom responded.

The response was much quicker than Frank had expected and Tom sounded as if he was in good spirits too. Actually, Tom had been awake all night. Without a watch, he had no idea of what time it was. It seemed to him as if the sun would never rise. He had turned on his radio nearly an hour earlier in anticipation of the call from Nail five-eight.

Tom tried standing on his ankle once during the night but it was too painful for him to try to walk on. He knew that if he took off his boot the pain would ease but his ankle was likely to swell up, possibly large enough that he wouldn't be able to get his boot back on again. He didn't want to risk that so he tolerated the pain instead. The constant sounds of people and animals around him kept him terribly on edge.

"Yeah, it's me Tom. How was your night?"

"I've had better ones."

"I'll bet! Hopefully you'll have a better one tonight. I've got half of the f**king Air Force and part of the Navy standing by to get you out of there, buddy. All we need now is just a little help with the weather. What's it look like on your end."

Tom was over-joyed to know that he had not been forgotten. He was so elated, he could have cried but he managed to control his emotions.

"It looks pretty lousy down here, Nail. I've got a solid low overcast ceiling."

---

boom required more skill and attention from the pilot of the receiver aircraft but the Air Force preferred it because it allowed higher transfer rates for their larger aircraft.

13 Mk 82 is the standard 500lbs iron bomb. Mk 84 is a 1000lbs iron bomb.

"Yeah, it's been like that all the way for me so far but don't despair. The sun is up now and once it gets a chance to warm things up I think we'll get some breaks."

Tom could hear the drone of the O-2 now and he knew that Frank must be nearby even though he couldn't see him.

"Tom what's the enemy situation like down there right now?"

"There was a lot of activity during the night. But it's been really quiet for the last hour or two."

"Are you still in the same place you were when I left last night?"

"Affirmative!"

"Okay, just sit tight and try to stay off of the radio for now. If we get a break in the weather we'll get right in and get you. If you know any weather prayers, this might be good time for them."

"I'll see what I can come up with."

Tom stayed quiet and still. He still felt the constant stress of impending capture and imprisonment but the sound of the O-2 droning in the distance was reassuring.

Jolly one-zero and Jolly two-two had taken off just after sunrise. They re-positioned themselves to the small airfield at An Khe. An Khe was a CIA listening post high atop a mountain in Northern Laos. The mountain was defended by CIA and Laotian mercenaries. From An Khe, CIA and Defense department operatives could monitor most of the radio traffic in North Vietnam. The adjoining airfield was intended for quick escapes in case the defenders at the base of the mountain were ever over run. The rescue helicopters occasionally used it as a forward operating location. From the base at An Khe they were only about a fifteen minute flight from Ban Bak.

The two helicopters landed at An Khe and immediately topped off their fuel tanks. After the initial flurry of activity they just sat and waited for the word to launch from Nail five-eight.

Dave Kearney walked to the back of the helicopter where Chris Dvorak, their PJ, was cleaning the .45 cal. automatic pistol that he carried with him.

"Hey Chris," Dave said casually as he sat down next to Dvorak on the opened tail ramp of the helicopter.

"Dave," Chris looked up momentarily, smiled just a bit and then resumed his work on the gun.

Chris was a bit of an enigma to Dave. He had only been on the crew for about two months now and he was a very quiet person. Most of the time Chris answered questions with only one or two words. He didn't seem to be unfriendly; just quiet. Dave knew that Chris was on his second term of enlistment in the Air Force. He was married and had at least one daughter but that was about all that Dave knew about him.

"Do you think we'll be able to pull this off this morning?" Dave asked.

Chris looked up from his work and scanned the sky for a few seconds.

"I don't know," Chris shrugged. "It sure doesn't look very promising right now."

"I heard on the radio this morning that there was another big anti-war protest somewhere in California the other day. They said a couple of people got shot."

"Yeah, well they can shoot them all as far as I'm concerned. They're just a bunch of dope-smoking cowards anyway," Chris said as he continued to clean his gun.

"Doesn't it bother you though that we're risking our lives over here everyday just doing what our country had asked us to do and Americans back at home are protesting it? Nobody protested like this during World War Two!"

"That was different. The Japanese attacked *us*, and then Hitler declared war on us. Everyone knew that we had to fight them or they would take us over. The North Vietnamese never attacked us. They didn't even have the ability to attack us. We're fighting to stop the communists from dominating the rest of the world. It's a little more difficult concept get your arms around."

Chris seemed to be especially talkative this morning.

"So you're in favor of the war then?"

"No, I'm in favor of *me* going home but that isn't likely as long as this war is going on. If they would just give us the word, we could be in Hanoi in two weeks and there's not a dam thing the North Vietnamese could do to stop us. Then, we could all go home. The worst thing about this war is that there is no way to know if we're winning. During World War Two everyone knew that when we got to Berlin it would be over. There were setbacks along the way but you could see that we were making progress. It was the same thing in the Pacific; once we got to Tokyo the war would be over. When will this war be over? We're not trying to go anywhere. I thought at first that this was some kind of noble venture but after what I've seen, I don't care about the Vietnamese and they don't seem to care about themselves. They have the most to lose and to gain but we seem to be doing most of the fighting."

"True, but didn't we need help from the French to win our independence from England?"

"Help is one thing. This is something else. The French didn't have to come over to us and tell us that we needed to rebel; we started it on our own. The French didn't get involved until much later and even then, we did most of the fighting. The Vietnamese weren't crying out for democracy; we just decided to cram it down their throats for their own good."

"You *do* believe that they will be better off under democracy don't you?"

"Yeah, maybe; but they have to come to that conclusion themselves and until they do we're never going to get anywhere with them. You can't save people who don't want to save themselves."

"If you're so unhappy why did you re-enlist?" Dave asked.

"I got married and we had my daughter, Vicky. She was born with a heart condition and she needed a lot of medical care. I would never have been able to afford it all outside of the military, so here I am."

"I'm sorry, Chris. I didn't know."

"It's okay. She had an operation and she's healthy now. She may need another operation when she gets a little older but the doctors think she's going to be just fine."

"That's good. It's too bad though that you had to stay in the Air Force if you didn't want to."

"I had to work somewhere," Chris' tone seemed to soften. "I guess that this is about as good a place as any. The only thing that really bothers me though is being away from my wife and daughter," Chris looked over at Dave and smiled. "I got a letter from my wife yesterday. Vicki took her first steps last week," Chris said as he grinned. "It kind of broke my heart that I missed it. There was a time when we didn't think that she would live long enough to take those first steps. It makes you realize just how precious life is and every day that I'm over here is another day that I can't spend with them. I guess that's why I'm a little ornery today."

Dave was completed taken by surprise. He had never seen Chris show any kind of sentimentality before.

"Do you have any pictures of them?" Dave asked.

Chris looked at Dave for just a moment trying to assess whether or not Dave really was genuinely interested in his family life. He decided that Dave was.

"Yeah, I know we're not supposed to carry personal items like this into combat, but I never go anywhere without this," Chris said as he reached into the pocket of his flight suit. He pulled out a small plastic photo album. The two of them spent the next several minutes talking quietly back and forth on the tail ramp as Chris proudly showed Dave his two favorite girls.

By 0800 the weather was still too bad to attempt a rescue but Frank Robertson (Nail 58) was using the time to his advantage to plan out the attack. He had watched this area for weeks now and it was finally beginning to pay off. Frank could see the subtle but definite signs of human activity in the area. There was a large clearing on the east side of the river that Frank had named "The Pork Chop" because of it's general shape. As Frank looked at the pork chop this morning he could see that a large number of trees had been cut from the western edge and that a new clump of bushes had appeared near the center of the clearing. Frank was certain that this was a hidden gun position. There were other small changes that Frank had perceived. He was sure that he had spotted at least three new gun positions. He marked the positions on his map. Farther west, closer to the river Frank could see that vehicle traffic had widened one particular gully that he had looked at every day for weeks. It was likely that there were still vehicles nearby.

Frank snickered to himself. The NVA must have thought that they were very clever but they weren't clever enough!

Frank kept a constant watch on the cloud cover above the valley as well as the goings on beneath him. By 0830 he thought he spotted something that he had been hoping for all morning. The clouds were moving from west to east and Frank saw an area beginning to thin out just to the west of the valley. He estimated that it would be clear over the valley within the next twenty to thirty minutes. It wouldn't remain clear for long because the hole in the cloud cover would continue to move but it might just be clear long enough to accomplish their mission. He decided to risk it.

Mike Groves (Sandy 7) was still sitting on the ground at NKP. He had spoken to Frank Robertson (Nail 58) earlier and told him about the 12 o'clock deadline that had been imposed upon them. Nail 58 had called back a bit later to inform them that Tom was still alive and free on the ground but that they would have to wait for the weather to clear before a rescue could be attempted.

Each of the four Sandy pilots had performed a pre-flight inspection of his aircraft and then they stood by waiting for word from Nail 58 to launch. The planes had taxied to the alert pad just off of the approach end of the runway. They could be airborne in minutes and they would rendezvous with the helicopters just north west of Ban Bak. It was turning into a very long morning.

Mike sat on the ground with his back against the left tire of his airplane. Major Greg Forsythe paced slowly back and forth in front of him as the two men talked.

"How old are you, Greg?" Mike asked.

"Thirty-eight."

"You still have a few years then."

"A few years, till what?"

"If you're like me, you'll wake up one morning and realize that you're forty-something and statistically speaking your life is half over; maybe more than half over! You kind of look back on your life and reflect on what you've done and where you've been. Wonder where you might have done things differently," Mike seemed to be a bit distant as he talked.

"Is this what they call a mid-life crisis, Mike? Because I don't think I want one."

"It's not a crisis. It's more of a "how goes it" on your life."

"So what did you come up with?"

"Oh, I don't know," Mike looked off in the distance as he talked. "I was thinking back. Sixteen years ago my brother-in-law was going to open an accounting firm and he offered me half of it if I wanted to buy in. I only had four years in the Air Force at the time so I wasn't really committed to a career yet. I could have borrowed the money if I had wanted to but I decided against it. It turned out to be pretty successful; even better than he thought it would be. He was home every night with his family and he wound up making a lot of money." Mike smiled as he continued, "there's some stress I suppose but your rival accountants aren't trying to *kill* you; at least not in the literal sense."

"And you think you should have gone in with him? An accountant, Mike? You think you should have been an accountant?"

Mike just shrugged.

"Yeah, I can see it now, Mike. Twenty years from now you'll be sitting in your rocking chair on the porch with your grandson on your knee regaling him with the story of how you saved your clients a thousand dollars one day! Wow! That should keep him on the edge of his seat."

"What are you trying to say, Greg?"

"I'm saying that there are two kinds of people in life; participants and spectators. Most people are just spectators. You're a participant! You've done more in your forty-three years than most men do in a lifetime. You *may* never have two cents to your name but the memories that you have are priceless. You grabbed life with both hands and drank it in! Every pilot in the squadron wants to be just like "Iron Mike" Groves."

Mike grinned. "If that's true, than they don't really know very much about me."

"Don't start feeling sorry for yourself, Mike. It doesn't suit you."

"I'm not feeling sorry for myself," Mike assured him.

After a few moments Mike spoke again; "you're quite a philosopher, Greg!"

"Yes, well I like to think of myself as a modern-day renaissance man."

They both smiled at that.

"Colonel Groves!" The Sergeant in the small alert building stood by the door and yelled toward Mike. "Nail five-eight is calling you on the radio."

Groves quickly got to his feet and hurried into the small building.

"Sandy Seven this is Nail five-eight."

The signal was very weak but readable.

"Go ahead, Nail."

"I think that there is a chance that the weather may break temporarily for us in about twenty to thirty minutes. This could be our only chance so I want to hit them with everything we have. I need you to take off and get down here as quickly as you can."

"We're on the way!"

Five minutes later, Mike Groves led the way as the four A-1's were airborne enroute to Ban Bak.

XIV: "FIGHT'S ON"

Sunday 17Dec 1967 (0905L Ban Bak, Laos)

TOM HAD BEEN frustrated all morning. He had made it through the night by telling himself that his rescue would come as soon as the sun came up. Now the sun had been up for several hours and still there was no rescue. Yet, he knew as well as anyone that they were going to need some better weather before they could proceed so he kept quiet and silently prayed for a break in the cloud cover overhead.

Tom had a very uneasy feeling that he couldn't explain right away. It seemed obvious that the enemy troops weren't looking for him as diligently as they had been the previous day. He initially thought that they had assumed that he had moved too far from the valley and they were looking in the wrong place for him. Then he had a more ominous thought. What if they were using him as bait to lure in more airplanes into their trap? The battle had been intense yesterday and the NVA had done quite well against the American warplanes. They had had all night to bring up more guns. It was possible that the entire valley was littered with heavy gun positions now. He tried to push that idea out of his head. There was nothing that he could do about it and he had to try to maintain a positive attitude.

As the morning progressed, Tom's prayers were answered. The overcast above the valley began to clear and Tom could see large patches of blue skies above him. He felt certain that his rescue was at hand.

Frank Robertson (Nail 58) had been busy all morning, spotting potential targets and developing a plan of battle. He spoke with Mike Groves (Sandy 7) on the radio as the four Skyraiders raced toward the valley.

"Sandy 7, this is Nail 58."

"Go ahead, Nail 58."

"I think we can avoid some of the problems that we had yesterday if we overwhelm their defenses. We need to hit them as hard as we can with as much as we can in a very short period of time."

"Okay, what do you have in mind?"

"We'll use the river to avoid conflicting with each other. I'll hit any targets that pop up on the east side of the river and you can have all of the targets on the west side. I'll make sure that my fighters don't go west of the river and you guys don't fly to the east. We'll hit them hard and fast and just race right in and pick up Cyclone before they know what's hit them."

Mike agreed that the plan sounded reasonable. Frank went on to describe a gun position that he had identified on the west side of the river. Frank said that he could mark the target for the Sandys if they could hit it on their first pass over the valley. Mike agreed to make it his first target.

The weather was clearing rapidly now.

Frank then called and brought the fighters down from the tankers. He stacked them in holding patterns directly overhead the valley. He briefed all of them on what he had in mind. It was a bit unorthodox to try to cram so many airplanes into such a small space at the same time so he wanted to insure that everyone was alert and attentive to what was happening.

By nine o'clock everything was ready. They were just waiting to hear from Sandy 7 when he was five minutes out. That would be the signal to start the attack.

Frank called Tom one last time.

"Tom, I'm going to hand you off now to Sandy 7. He'll be up on this frequency in just a couple of minutes. They're going to come in and get you, buddy."

"Thanks, Frank. Whatever happens, you've been great."

"You can tell me all about it at the club tonight."

Jolly 10 and 22 were racing south. In the cabin of Jolly 10 all four crewmen were huddled in and around the cockpit listening carefully to the briefing on the radio and remaining usually quiet themselves. Captain Dan Hudson sat in the right seat, Lt Harry Lindermann was in the left and Dave Kearney and Chris Dvorak stood just in the doorway to the cockpit. They were the low copter today, meaning that they would be the first one in. If everything went well Jolly 22 would just remain behind as a back up the way they had yesterday.

The terrain seemed familiar to all of them since they had been there just the day before. It was Chris Dvorak who broke their silence.

"Hey look up there," he said as he pointed ahead and to the right of the helicopter. "Jolly 19 is still there."

All four of them looked where Chris was pointing. Far off in the distance they could just barely see the helicopter tilting over slightly on its right side in the clearing where they had rescued the crew the day before.

"Okay were getting close," Dan Hudson said. "Let's get to battle stations, guys. Everybody on their toes. It sounds as if we're going straight in for the pick-up."

Dave moved quickly to the boarding door just behind Hudson and checked his M-16 to insure that it was cocked and ready to fire. Chris hustled to the back of the copter, opened the tail ramp and checked over his .50 caliber machine gun one more time. Jolly

10 was ready for action. All four of them were quiet and tense as the big helicopter raced along south toward Ban Bak.

The four A-1 Sandys joined up with the helicopters just a moment or two later. Two of them accelerated quickly out in front of the copters and the other two weaved back and forth staying behind them.

"Jolly one-zero, this is Sandy seven, are you guys all set to go?"

It was reassuring to everyone to hear the calm, authoritative voice of Mike Groves (Sandy 7) on the radio.

"Affirmative," Dan Hudson radioed in reply.

"Okay, Jolly two-two you can take spacing and wait for us here," Sandy 7 was back on the radio again. "Jolly one-zero, follow me."

Jolly 22 wished them good luck and then pulled away above and behind them. Dan pushed up the speed of his helicopter all of the way to the red line as they descended to just twenty or thirty feet above the treetops. He and the crew of Jolly ten watched as the two leading Sandys pulled away and then climbed slightly to clear the ridge line on the west side of the valley.

Frank Robertson soared high over the valley in his little O-2. He was anxious to engage the enemy. He thought about Steve Turner (Nail 44) again briefly and he wondered if somehow it was possible that Steve was watching over him today. He hoped that Steve would have been proud of him. Frank felt confident that his plan was sound but he knew only too well how good plans could quickly go awry once the bullets started flying.

"Sandy 7 is five minutes out!" Mike Groves radioed.

"Roger that, Sandy look for my mark as you come in to the valley," Frank replied.

Frank had been trying to hold himself on a particular spot on the ground. It was similar to playing a game of billiards; he wanted to be able to take the first shot and come out in a good position to take the second one.

"Fight's On, Charlie!" Frank said silently to himself. The little O-2 rolled over on to its right side and dove steeply toward the ground.

"Fang one-one, you're cleared in from the south. The FAC is north and east of the target. Stand-by for my mark!" Frank said over the radio. It was difficult to contain the excitement that he was feeling. Normally he would have waited for the smoke plume of his marking rocket to blossom before clearing in the fighters, but speed was the most essential element of his plan. He wanted the bombs to hit the ground as soon as possible after the smoke rocket hit.

"Roger, Fang one-one is in high from the south with the FAC in sight."

Frank quickly lined up his target in the sight and fired a single rocket toward it. He could watch the rocket as it raced toward the ground, its fiery tail made it easy to follow. Frank was sure that the mark would be close to the target so he pulled up and began to position himself for his second shot.

Seconds later Randy Morris in Fang one-one was on the radio again.

"Fang one-one has the smoke."

Frank rolled quickly back to his left to assess the spot on the ground.

"From the smoke go fifty meters north west. Target is a gun position in the trees. You're cleared in hot with CBU!"

"Fang one-one is in hot!"

Frank quickly rolled the O-2 back to the right and took aim at his target on the west side of the river. He steadied the O-2 on the target and then fired another rocket. He watched this one fly all the way to impact and he was satisfied with the result.

"Sandy seven your target is marked with white smoke. From the smoke look one hundred meters east-southeast. Target is a gun in the trees."

"Roger Nail, I have the smoke."

Tom had been watching everything from the ground. He had heard the constant drone of the O-2 over and around the valley since sunrise. The NVA must have known that Frank was there too but they didn't fire at him; hoping to remain concealed. Just a few minutes ago Tom had heard the sounds of jet aircraft above the valley. He could see them from time to time as they soared high above him moving back and forth between the clouds. They were much too high for the guns to hit so everything on the ground remained quiet. Tom watched Nail 58 roll in for his first mark toward a target on the far side of the river but he couldn't hear any of the exchange between Frank and the fighters because they were on a different radio frequency.

The morning had started out so peacefully and quietly and now all of hell seemed to erupt over the valley. There was a sharp bang that echoed across the river as Frank's smoke rocket hit the ground and exploded. Before the smoke from the first rocket had even begun to blossom Frank fired another rocket much closer to Tom on the west side of the river. There was another loud bang as this second rocket hit. Before there was time to fully process what was happening, an F-105 came screaming in low over the valley from the south. It was moving so fast that it was difficult to see it clearly. Tom could make out enough of the image though to see the two-letter code printed on the tail of the fighter. He knew that the airplane was from his own unit at Korat and his heart leapt for joy at the sight. The big fighter streaked in just above the trees and released a number of silver canisters from beneath it. Then the afterburner of the fighter lit with a loud bang and the airplane raced away climbing steeply to the north. The canisters tumbled to the ground and for a fraction of a second it appeared as if nothing was going to happen. Then all at once there was a tremendous roar as hundreds of tiny bombs detonated one after another. From Tom's position on the ledge, it appeared as if the entire area was blanketed with smoke and dust. Before the dust had a chance to settle another F-105 came screaming in from the north to hit the same target again. The noise level over the valley was deafening now as the guns on the ground came to life.

The gunners on the west side of the river were manning a twenty-three millimeter cannon. It was the largest gun in the entire valley and it required two men to operate it and another four to keep it loaded with ammunition. They had watched the O-2 all morning and they might have had a few good shots at it but they were under orders not to reveal their position until ordered so they had remained quiet. They had been watching the same sights and listening to the same sounds that Tom was. They watched as the O-2 had marked another gun position on the far side of the river. When the second smoke rocket landed just a hundred meters from them, they knew that they had been spotted and an attack would soon be coming their way. They looked frantically all around. They saw the O-2. They saw the first two F-105's and they saw an F-100 diving down at another gun emplacement on the far side of the river. They could see several other jets orbiting above them like vultures from time to time. But they never saw Mike Groves (Sandy 7) coming at them from behind just above the treetops.

Groves (Sandy 7) had to climb just a little in order to see the smoke from Nail 58's rocket. "One hundred meters east southeast," the FAC had said. Groves quickly searched the area. Then he saw it. It was a big gun. The barrel was pointed away from Groves, out over the river, traversing back and forth but it had not opened fire yet. It appeared as if they were still searching for a target.

"Sandy 7 has the target," there was no emotion in his voice as Mike spoke on the radio. It was all strictly business. "This one's mine. Take spacing and cover my six Sandy one-five, I'm in hot with guns."

"Roger."

Groves adjusted his flight path to his left a bit as he lined the big Skyraider up on the target. He could see the gunners clearly now as they searched for a target. They still hadn't seen him yet. Groves saw one of the gunners turn and face him when he was less than a mile away. The man pointed and must have yelled something because the others looked back behind them. Groves was sure that he could see the horror on their faces as they began to slew the big gun around to face him. It was too late!

Groves pulled the trigger in the control stick and the four twenty-millimeter cannons on the Skyraider roared to life. The airplane shuddered from the recoil but it continued to race on toward the gun position. The area around the gun was quickly concealed with dust and debris but Mike knew that at this range the fire from his cannons could not possibly miss. He fired a volley of 2.75" rockets armed with anti-personnel warheads to add to the carnage that he was sure was happening at the gun site. As he raced directly over the target, he released two more five hundred pound bombs with delayed fuses to 'seal the deal'.

"Good hits! Good hits, Sandy 7!" Sandy 15, Mike's wingman, sounded exuberant on the radio.

"Hit 'em again Sandy 15."

"It looks like you destroyed it, Mike."

Mike spoke slowly and distinctly to insure that his wingman knew that this was not a request.

"Hit them again!"

Mike was taking no chances. The 23 mm gum could rip the helicopter to shreds with just one or two hits. He wanted to insure beyond any doubt that the gun was out of operation.

"You're the boss. Sandy 15 is in hot with guns."

Mike circled back around to scan the area for any more threats to their operation and he radioed to Tom as he flew.

"Cyclone three-two, Cyclone three-two this is Sandy seven, how do you read."

Tom had been watching in awe as the battle unfolded around him. Frank Robertson (Nail 58) had already attacked and destroyed one gun emplacement on the far side of the river using F-105's. Then he had marked another and was attacking it with a flight of four F-100's. These Huns were dropping Mk. 84 2000 lbs bombs and the blasts from their explosions were incredible. It seemed to Tom as if a small nuclear weapon had gone off each time one of the bombs exploded. There was even a small mushroom-shaped cloud that accompanied each blast to add to the effect. The sheer volume noise was unbelievably intense.

From where Tom lay it appeared as if Frank was doing a fairly good job of keeping the guns quiet. There were a few shots fired at the airplanes, but for the most part their fire was wild and inaccurate. Tom was so attentive to the sights and sounds around him that he nearly missed the first radio call from Sandy seven. The faint voice in the earphone brought him back to his senses.

"Sandy seven, this is Cyclone three-two. I have you loud and clear, go ahead."

"Roger, Cyclone, the helo is two minutes out, stand by for contact with Jolly one-zero."

Mike made it a point to fly directly overhead Tom's position at just fifty feet above the ground.

Mike couldn't see Tom as he lay in the bushes but he thought he knew where he was. Just as he came over Tom's position, he radioed again.

"Cyclone three-two do you have me in sight."

"Affirmative," Tom was elated. He practically yelled into the radio to be heard over the roar of the A-1's engine. "If you were any closer I could have shaken your hand."

Mike smiled to himself.

"Okay, sit tight. Get your marker flares out and be ready to pop them. It won't be long now."

"Jolly one-zero this is Sandy seven."

"Go ahead seven."

"I've confirmed the survivor's location. It's right where we were briefed. Come in and get this guy."

"I'm pedaling as fast as I can," Dan radioed back.

Jolly ten had to climb slightly to clear the ridgeline and as they did so Dan and Harry got their first look at the river valley. The once-peaceful valley was alive with activity again. On the far side of the river two separate fires were already burning and airplanes were diving down attacking another. There were jets of various types swirling around in the air over the far side of the river; diving, turning, and climbing. It looked like organized chaos to the two helicopter pilots. On the near side of the river there was a large column of smoke rising from the jungle just a mile and a half in front of them. They could see Sandy 7 and Sandy 15 as they fired rockets at something else in the dense jungle beneath them; two or three miles ahead of the racing helicopter. It was like the scene from a movie but it was far more intense than any movie could have imagined. Harry Lindermann just looked over at Dan from the left seat but said nothing.

Dan looked slightly to his right and saw a small ledge on the side of a hill about two miles away. It was just as Nail 58 had described it to them.

"I think that's the spot," Dan said as he pointed toward it.

"Yeah, it could be," Harry agreed. He wasn't really convinced because it all looked the same to him.

Cyclone three-two this is Jolly one zero we're less than two minutes out from your position. Pop your smoke! I say again; POP YOUR SMOKE!"

Tom was overjoyed; he could see the big helicopter as it sped towards him. He put his finger in the pull-tab of the marker flare and prepared to open it. He paused for just a moment. He knew that once he pulled the top off of the flare everyone, friend and foe alike, for miles around would know exactly where he was. He took a deep breath and pulled the tab. Instantly a cloud of orange-colored smoke began to rise out of the small canister. Tom held the canister away from himself and waved it back and forth so that the cloud would grow even larger.

Dan strained hard to see the marker smoke but it was Dave at the boarding door of the copter who saw it first.

"I've got orange smoke on the hillside, one to two o'clock for two and a half miles," Dave announced over the intercom.

Dan had been looking at the wrong hillside. He looked a little more to his right and he saw the orange smoke.

"I've got it," Dan replied and he nudged the helicopter to the right and flew straight for the smoke.

All at once Chris Dvorak was on the intercom from his position on the tail ramp.

"Break left, break left, Captain Hudson, we're taking fire from our five o'clock."

Dan could hear Chris open fire with the fifty cal. on the tail ramp. Without even thinking he pulled the big copter hard to the left and then back slightly to the right in an attempt to fool any gunners that might be trying to track them from the ground. Then Dan just held on to the control stick and prayed that they wouldn't be hit.

As quickly as it started, the firing from the gun on the tail ramp stopped.

"What's going on back there, Chris?" Dan asked on the intercom after a few seconds.

"A group of assholes with AK's just opened up on us. I got a couple of them and the two Sandys back here are kicking the crap out of them now. We're okay."

Dan breathed a sign of relief and turned the helicopter back toward Tom.

Frank Robertson (Nail 58) had been working like a madman bringing the fighters down to attack one target after another. There had been no let up in his attacks and so far it seemed to be working. The fighters had destroyed two known gun locations and two more probable locations. They had encountered only minimal opposition from the ground so far. Frank had been watching carefully but he hadn't seen any anti-aircraft fire going across the river toward the rescue forces.

He took a moment to glance over to the west. He saw a small cloud of orange smoke near Tom's position on the hill and he could see that the helicopter was just about a mile away to the north. Very soon now the helicopter would have to slow down and go into a hover above Tom. Frank knew that this was by far the most critical time for the rescue. As the helicopter hovered stationary above Tom it would be a huge, easy target for anyone with a gun. Tom got on the radio to the fighters again.

"Okay, this is it guys. Two minutes left in the fourth quarter. It's now or never. Fang I need whatever CBU you have left and I need it now! Just saturate the entire area and keep their heads down."

"Roger, Nail we'll come in line abreast from the south and drop everything we have left. Fang flight rejoin on me echelon right. We'll be RTB[14] on the way out."

This was truly unorthodox; a flight of four F-105's coming in to attack simultaneously in formation. Frank shook his head slowly as he pondered the possibly but he decided that the unorthodox had worked well for them so far, so it was worth a shot.

The order to rejoin had caught the other three members of Fang flight by surprise. They were widely split up as they circled the target area but each of them moved quickly back towards their leader as soon as the command was given. It took a fair amount of acrobatics and there was a tense moment or two as Fang one-two and Fang one three came very close to colliding with each other in their haste to rejoin on their leader. But in the end, the four Thuds formed a rough line that covered most of the east bank of the river valley. Once they were lined up, Morris pushed up the speed and dove for the deck. The four Thuds came screaming in from the south along the river. When Fang one-one dropped his remaining two canisters of CBU the rest of the formation dropped all of theirs as well. Fang one-three and one-four still had their full compliment of eight canisters. The result was a curtain of steel pellets from the CBU that covered everything for nearly a full square mile. There was simply no safe place to hide on the east side of the river and there was no more ground fire observed from there for the entire remainder of the day.

Dan Hudson could see Tom laying on the ledge now. Tom had been well concealed but he had come out of hiding once he popped the smoke flare. Dan pulled back smoothly on the stick and began to slow the speeding helicopter down.

"I see him on the ledge, Dave. Do you see him?"

"Yeah, I got him, sir. I'm ready with the hoist."

The helicopter quickly decelerated and slowly came to a stop a hundred feet above Tom' position.

"Stop it there, sir," Dave yelled into the interphone. "We can't get any closer the main rotor is going to hit those trees if you come any more to the right."

"Okay, this will have to do then."

From where the helicopter came to a halt the end of the hoist would touch down about forty or fifty feet from Tom at the base of the hill. They would have preferred to bring it right down on top of him but the rising terrain and tall trees to the west of his location prevented that. This was about the best that they could do.

---

14 RTB means return to base.

Tom saw the helicopter go into a hover and he staggered to his feet. He had a tremendous amount of pain from his ankle but the thought of rescue outweighed the discomfort.

Suddenly Tom heard shots behind him and his left shoulder felt as if a sledgehammer had hit it. He fell forward and rolled onto his back as he hit the ground. Fifteen feet away was a soldier coming towards him with an AK-47 in his hands. The man pulled the trigger of the gun again but it didn't fire. He quickly realized that he must be out of bullets and stopped where he was to pull another magazine from a pouch on his belt. Tom lay on the ground just looking at the man as he tried to quickly reload his weapon. Tom raised his right hand, the hand that had held his small pistol in it for nearly a full day now. The soldier was surprised. He hadn't seen the gun in Tom's hand until now. Tom pointed the gun at the soldier and fired six times right into the bewildered soldier. He would have fired more but the gun only held six rounds. It took all of the effort that Tom could muster to shoot the soldier. He collapsed back onto the ground staring weakly at the helicopter that was just beyond his reach.

"God dam it! Where did he come from?" Dan yelled into the interphone.

"I don't know but it looks as if he brought some friends," Dave said as he leaned out of the doorway with his M-16 in hand. There were three other soldiers working their way through the jungle toward Tom. Dave opened up on them with his M-16. He promptly cut down two of them and the third man quickly turned and ran off into the jungle in the opposite direction. Dave looked down at Tom and he could see that Tom didn't have the strength to make it any closer to the helicopter.

"Chris, I think we're going to need you. He's hurt pretty bad," Dave called over the interphone.

"I'm on it!" Chris responded as he grabbed his medical pack and his M-16. He hustled forward toward the door.

Dan turned toward Harry in the left seat of the cockpit.

"Harry, go back and get on the fifty. Shoot anything that moves!"

Harry nodded and quickly got up from his seat and headed to the gun on the tail ramp. Just yesterday, Dave had wondered if Harry knew which end the bullets came out of. Today, Harry would leave no doubt that he did. He was soon blasting away with the fifty-caliber gun.

Dave stood in the doorway and worked the hoist.

Tom lay on the ground. He felt a terrible despair. The helicopter was so close but he just didn't have the strength to move any closer to it. Then Tom saw something that absolutely amazed him. One of the crewmembers of the helicopter got on the hoist and started to be lowered toward him.

"Is this guy insane?" Tom wondered as he watched the man touch the ground. This is the last place in the world that any American airman would want to be and yet here was this man coming down voluntarily, to this hellhole to save Tom's life. Tom was simply overwhelmed with emotion.

Chris quickly got off of the hoist and ran up the hill to where Tom was laying.

"Are you okay?" Chris asked as he looked at the wound in Tom's shoulder. The AK-47 is a very powerful weapon and Chris felt certain that the bullet had gone all of the way through the shoulder. There as a lot of blood but he could take care of that once they were on-board the helicopter. Chris quickly pulled some cotton wadding from his medical kit and reached under Tom's flight suit to pack it in place around the wound to control the bleeding. Tom was certainly in great pain but, he just winced.

"Yeah, I'm okay," Tom said weakly. "I just don't seem to be able to get to my feet."

"That's what I'm here for. Let me give you a hand," Chris said and he started to help Tom to his feet.

Dave was firing his M-16 out the door of the helicopter again. Chris froze where he was and looked up at the helicopter. In the right seat of the cockpit Chris could see Captain Hudson wildly pointing out in front of the aircraft and then holding up four fingers for Chris to see. Apparently the soldier that had run away earlier had returned with three of his buddies. Chris shook his head in disgust. This was not good.

Chris put Tom gently back on the ground and then reached into the holster on his belt to remove the .45 caliber automatic that he had cleaned so fastidiously just that morning. He cocked the pistol and gave it to Tom.

"Here you go Lieutenant. This one has some bullets in it. Just in case you need it."

Then Chris took his own M-16 that he had slung over his back and turned to face the enemy. Dave had the best vantage point from his perch in the helicopter and he had the four soldiers pinned down with his accurate fire. Chris knew that they couldn't simply hold off the soldiers, they had to take them out quickly. The copter was far too vulnerable in its hover and more enemy soldiers were sure to come at them if they stayed long enough.

It wasn't a question of courage for Chris. It was simple necessity. He got up and charged toward the four soldiers that were now prone on the ground. One of them instinctively got up to challenge Chris, and Dave instantly shot the man where he stood.

The other three were bewildered by the speed and audacity of Chris' attack. Chris shot two of them before they could even react. The third managed to shoot Chris in his left arm. Chris went down hard on the ground, obviously in a great deal of pain. He managed to keep firing at the soldier though who was now hiding behind a large tree. Both Chris and Dave were shooting at the soldier but they couldn't hit him because of the tree that shielded him.

Dan Hudson felt helpless and vulnerable as he held the copter in its hover above the ground.

"God dam it, Dave, shoot that guy," he yelled over the interphone.

"I don't have a shot. That tree is in the way!" Dave replied.

Dan had to think quickly.

"Harry, do you have your safety harness on?" Dan said over the interphone. The safety harness was a tough canvas strap that prevented the crewmen from falling out of the helicopter.

"Yeah, why?"

"Hang on!"

Dan kicked the left rudder pedal hard and swung the tail of the big helicopter around 270 degrees to the left. Dan planned it perfectly moving the copter ahead as it pivoted. When the copter came to a stop again in the air Harry Lindermann was looking straight down at the soldier behind the tree. In an instant, they had neatly out-flanked him. The astonished soldier looked up at the big helicopter and realized that he as staring down the barrel of a fifty caliber machine gun. His rifle was still pointed towards Chris and he quickly moved to take a shot at Harry as he stood on the tail ramp. Harry hesitated for only a moment before he fired the gun and literally blew the soldier to pieces.

"I got him!" Harry sounded elated in the interphone.

"Okay, hold on again. We're coming back."

Dan neatly pivoted the helicopter back to the right and wound up almost exactly where it had been just a few seconds earlier.

Dave watched Chris get up slowly and stagger back to Tom. The two of them tried with all of their strength to help each to stand up-right but they both were too badly hurt. Dave couldn't bear to watch them struggle.

"I'm going down," he said into the interphone. Before Dan had a chance to respond, Dave grabbed onto the metal cable and slid down it to the ground.

Dave quickly moved up the hill to the two struggling men. With Dave's help, the three of them managed to get to their feet and they half walked and half tumbled down the hill where the penetrator was laying on the ground. The penetrator was a three foot cylinder attached to the hoist cable at one end. On the other end were three seats, just metal plates actually, that folded up toward the cylinder. The penetrator wasn't really designed to carry three people at once. It was much too small for that. The three seats were merely intended to make it easier for a survivor to locate and pull down one of them. It could carry two in a pinch if the two riders held on to each other. Dave had never seen three people even attempt to ride the penetrator at the same time before but he was desperate. Dave helped Tom onto one of the seats and then quickly positioned Chris on another. He had the two of them hold on to each other in a bear hug. Dave managed to put both of his feet on the third seat and he stood up, holding on to the cable. He quickly signaled to Dan to raise the raise the hoist. There was a second set of controls for the hoist in the cockpit and Dan moved the control to the up position. Both Dan and Dave knew that they were well beyond the maximum weight limit for the hoist motor but it was a chance that they had to take. The cable slowly retracted toward the door of the helicopter. The ride seemed to take forever but in reality it was only fifteen or twenty seconds.

All he while the four A-1 Sandys had been flying around the stationary helicopter forming a rough circle of swirling warplanes around it. They attacked anything that moved on the ground.

Off to the left of the helicopter a group of soldiers moved into the same clearing that Tom had called the air strike on the previous night. They had a 12.7 mm machine gun that could easily rip through the thin metal skin of the helicopter. Harry had the best chance to spot them but they were too far off to his right. He never saw them. Fortunately, Mike Groves (Sandy 7) saw them. He instantly realized the danger that the gun presented to the helicopter and its crewmen. He was determined not to let that happen. Mike rolled in towards them just as they finished mounting the gun on its tripod. The soldiers were quickly faced with a dilemma. They could easily take out the helicopter with a few well-placed shots but they would almost certainly be shot in the process. The helicopter crewmen were nearly back inside the helicopter and it would soon be on its way out of the valley. If they shot at Sandy seven they would allow the helicopter to escape but they might save themselves. In the end, self-preservation won out and the soldiers swung the big gun around to face Sandy 7 as he raced towards them. Both sides immediately opened fire at each other and both appeared to score hits but it was the powerful Skyraider that won the day. The soldiers were cut down where they stood by the 20 mm cannons from Sandy 7. Just for good measure, Mike released a 500 lbs bomb on them as he roared overhead. The blast destroyed their gun. Mike pulled up at the last possible second to avoid the helicopter as it waited in its hover. He flew over the top of Jolly 10, missing them by only twenty or thirty feet.

In the cockpit of the helicopter, Dan had been watching the three men come up on the hoist on the other side. He didn't see Sandy 7 until the big Skyraider roared overhead missing them by what seemed like just a few feet. Dan instinctively ducked down in his seat, as if that would have done any good.

Dave jumped toward the open doorway of the helicopter as soon as he was close enough. Then he pulled the other two men into the relative safety of the helicopter.

"We're in!" he shouted to Dan.

Dan immediately began moving the big helicopter forward, accelerating as quickly as he could. As soon as he had some forward airspeed he turned the helicopter around in a big left hand turn and headed back away from the river. The copter began to climb rapidly, leaving the small river valley behind it.

"Jolly 10 is egressing to the northwest. We got him!"

XVII: TRIUMPH

Sunday 17 Dec 1967 (0944L Ban Bak, Laos)

Frank Robertson was ecstatic in the cockpit of his O-2 when he heard the radio call from Jolly 10 that they had gotten Tom. He yelled out loud and shook his fist in jubilation. He looked upward towards heaven and said "this one was for you, buddy," as he thought of his friend Steve Turner (Nail 44).

Once Frank had finished his work over the valley, he relayed the news to all of the fighters that had participated in the air battle.

Not surprisingly, Lt Col. Morris in Fang one-one seemed to be especially pleased with the good news. The four Thud pilots had been in their cramped cockpits for hours now but the good news lifted all of their spirits and made it all seem worthwhile.

"You guys were fantastic, Fang," Frank said over the radio. "I think that wall of Thuds coming up the valley really broke their backs."

"You were doing some nice shooting yourself there, Nail," Morris replied. He had been in many battles and he wanted to insure that all of the members of the team were congratulated for a job well-done. "Hey, can you pass on our thanks to Mobil six-six and six-seven. They were the tankers that we worked with this morning. They did a great job. Tell them, if they can get to Korat tonight, the drinks are on me."

"I'll do it," Frank promised. "I have to warn you though. I know some of those guys and they'd probably walk to Korat if the drinks are free."

Morris laughed under the oxygen mask that was strapped tightly against his face. "I hope they do," he said.

Sandy 7 and 15 had raced ahead of Jolly 10 as soon as the helicopter had circled back to the north and began to exit the battle area. They cleared the way for the helicopter while the other two A-1s quickly fell in behind. They maintained a secure ring around the helicopter until it was clear of the valley and well-above the range of any gun in the area.

Jolly 22 joined up with Jolly 10 and the two helicopters sped back to their base at NKP. Once the situation was safe, Sandy 7 and his three wingmen climbed above and behind the two copters and opened up their formation for a more leisurely flight back home. Mike Groves (Sandy 7) had been very quiet on the radio. There had been no statements of congratulations back and forth. This was not unusual for Mike Groves. His flights were always very disciplined and Mike always told his fellow pilots that the mission wasn't over until they were back in the chocks.

About ten minutes out from landing, Mike radioed to his wingman, "Sandy 15, you have the lead on the right."

It was unusual for Mike to ever give up the lead of his flight to anyone. He always wanted to be out in front, leading the way but none of the other three pilots in the flight really thought much about it.

Mike's landing was a little rough. He bounced the big Skyraider a couple of times but, they all had a bad landing now and then and again, no one really thought anything about it.

Normally, the fight would rejoin at the end of the runway and they would all taxi back to the chocks together. This time Mike turned off of the runway earlier then the rest of the flight and taxied quickly back to the chocks by himself. He should have called ground control and asked for clearance to taxi in, but he didn't.

In the control tower, the supervisor was angry as he talked to the Sergeant that was working ground control.

"I thought I told you to hold those A-1s and let this C-130 taxi out ahead of them!"

"I told him to hold his position but he hasn't responded," the bewildered controller said. "He hasn't said anything on the radio."

"Who the hell is that?" the supervisor demanded.

"I think it's Sandy 7," the controller answered.

"Sandy 7? God dammed "Iron Mike" Groves! He must think he's running this airport. Well, he isn't! I'm going to go down and give "Iron Mike" a boot in his ass. See how he likes that!" The supervisor stormed off while the confused controller just watched in silence.

Sergeant Carl Peterson directed Sandy 7 back into it's parking spot. He was amazed as he marshaled the aircraft to see small shards of metal hanging from beneath the wings. The airplane had been badly damaged again. He signaled for Mike to stop the airplane once it was in it's proper place and then signaled to cut the engine off. The big Skyraider fell silent as Carl leaned down under the wings to put the chocks in place around the wheels. Up closer to the damage Carl could see that the airplane had been hit numerous times by small arms fire. Carl could only shake his head in disbelief. The airplane was damaged much more severely than it had been the previous day. He wondered if he would ever get it back into flying condition.

Once the chocks were in place, he walked around the back of the wings and climbed up to the cockpit. Mike was just sitting still inside the airplane as he often did after a particularly tough mission.

"Colonel, I thought you said you were..." Carl stopped in mid-sentence when he came up next to the cockpit. The entire front of Mike Groves flightsuit was covered with blood. There was blood all over the side panels and the floor in the cockpit too.

"Oh my God, Colonel, what happened to you!" Carl finally managed to say. "We've got to get you out of there."

Mike was trying to take off his helmet but it appeared to take more strength than he had available. Carl helped him slowly remove it from his head.

"If you think *I* look bad, you should see the other guy," Mike sounded as he was fighting for his breath, but he still managed a weak smile.

"Colonel, it looks like you've lost a lot of blood. I need to get you out of there." Carl reached in to help Mike unstrap from the airplane but Mike winced in pain as soon as Carl touched the seat belt harness. Carl immediately stopped what he was doing. He wasn't sure what he should do next. He knew that they had to get Mike out of the cockpit, but he was obviously in a great deal of pain and Carl didn't want to make it any worse.

"I'm okay, Carl. I'm just a little tired. That's all," Mike said. He sounded weaker than before.

Carl just stood there for a moment, not really knowing what to do. Finally, he turned and yelled toward the A-1 that was parked next to his. Ssgt. Tony Capece was working underneath it.

"Tony, call an ambulance," he shouted.

Tony walked out from under the airplane looking a little bewildered as he wiped the grease off of his hands. He wasn't really sure what Carl had said.

"What?" Tony yelled back.

"Call a f**king ambulance, Tony. Do it now!"

Tony seemed to understand. He took off running toward the small maintenance building that sat just across the flightline from the parked airplanes.

Carl turned back toward Mike as he sat in the cockpit.

"Dam it Colonel, you never listen to me. I *told* you to be careful," Carl said with tears in his eyes now. It was clear to Carl that Mike was going rapidly down hill.

"You were right, Carl," Mike said. His voice was just above a whisper now.

"Right?" Carl was confused. "Right, about what?"

"She brought me home," Mike said as he patted the side of the airplane. Mike managed to force another smile.

Carl just stood by the side of the cockpit for a moment unsure of what he should do. He recalled when his grandfather had passed away just three years earlier. The older man had an irrational fear of being alone when he died so Carl had simply held his hand as the old man passed away. It seemed to help. So Carl gently took hold of Mike's hand. He knew that it was pointless now to do anything else.

"I'm here with you, sir," was all that Carl could manage to say through the terrible lump in his throat.

"I just need to close my eyes for a minute. That's all. Let me sleep for just a minute and then you can wake me up. I'll be fine."

Mike tilted his head back so that it was resting against the headrest on the seat. Then he closed his eyes for the last time.

XVIII: REDEMPTION

Sunday, 17dec 1967 (Westwood, Ca 1500L)

NIKKI WAS TRYING to study some more for her final exams when her three roommates burst into the small apartment accompanied by a couple of the boys who had been at the bar the other night. Fran, Marcia and Debbie were talking loudly and laughing. It appeared as if they had all had a fairly enjoyable weekend.

Nikki got up from the couch where she had been working and walked over to see what they had been up to. She was still a bit bewildered that they had been gone all weekend.

"Where have you guys been?" she asked.

"We went to Lake Arrowhead," Marcia said as she laughed. "John's parents have a cabin there and we've been skiing all week-end. Fran tried to call you to tell you where we were yesterday morning but you didn't answer the phone."

"Oh."

"Did you have a good week-end, Nikki?" Fran asked.

"It was okay," Nikki said. She certainly didn't want to go into the details in front of everyone.

"I guess you got quite a surprise yesterday morning, huh?" Debbie said slyly and everyone seemed to laugh.

Nikki could feel her face turn beet red as she blushed. She realized that they all seemed to know much more about what had happened than she did. She quickly concluded that Jeff must have told them. She was flustered and couldn't think of anything to say.

"Wait a minute," Fran said. She could see that the comment had embarrassed and upset Nikki. "How much do you remember from the other night?"

They all stopped and listened for Nikki's response, which embarrassed her even more.

"I don't think I want to talk about it right now," Nikki said as she turned and started toward her bedroom.

Fran quickly caught up with her and grabbed her gently by the shoulders. Fran was by far Nikki's best friend of her three roommates.

"Wait a minute, Nikki," she said. "I was afraid of this! This is why I hate practical jokes. I told you guys not to do it," Fran said as she looked back angrily at the others. "Nikki, how much do you remember from the other night?"

Nikki had tears in her eyes as she turned back to look at Fran.

"I remember getting up to leave the bar, and then I don't remember anything else until I woke up yesterday morning."

Fran seemed to have quickly analyzed the situation and she knew instinctively what must have been going on in Nikki's mind.

"Oh my God," Fran said and she hugged Nikki. "Nothing happened. Do you hear me? You didn't do anything wrong!"

"What?" Nikki was totally confused now.

"Come here and sit down. I'll tell you what happened."

Fran gently pulled Nikki over to the table and sat her down. Everyone except for Fran seemed to have a sly smile on their face as if they knew something that Nikki didn't.

"You got up from the table to leave and you immediately passed out," Fran said.

"Nikki, you really should have something to eat before start drinking next time," Marcia interjected as she smiled.

Nikki just looked at Marcia and said nothing. She didn't intend to do any more drinking for a while, or ever!

"Anyway, you passed out right in front of one of the waitresses and she spilled half a pitcher of beer on you."

Nikki was even more embarrassed than before. The others could see that she was upset but they couldn't help but laugh little as they remembered the incident.

"So we all decided that we should leave and bring you home at that point. When we got you home we were going just to put you to bed in your clothes but you smelled like a brewery so we decided to try to take your dress off and to clean you up a bit first. The boys wanted to help but we made sure that they stayed out here." Fran looked sternly at the two boys that were still in the apartment kitchen with them. "It took quite an effort to undress you and clean you off. You were flopping around like a rag-doll and remember, we had been drinking too! I looked around for your pajamas but I couldn't find any so eventually we just decided to put you to bed as you were..." Fran smiled a little. "Au natural. Then we came out here for a while and talked and drank for a bit longer. John said that his parents had a cabin up at Lake Arrowhead that we could use and we decided to go there for the weekend. As we were getting ready to leave, I guess Jeff had been drinking a bit heavier than the rest of us. Anyway, he walked right into the bathroom door and knocked himself out."

"He was out cold, Nikki. You should have seen it," Debbie said.

"So at that point, someone," Fran looked at one of the boys and frowned. "Someone got the brilliant idea that it would be really funny if they put Jeff in bed with you."

Nikki was stunned.

"How could you possibly think that was funny?" Nikki said as she looked at the others around the table.

"Oh come on," Debbie said. "Look at the absurdity of it. You, sleeping with some guy that you met in a bar? It would be like," Debbie had to pause for a moment to think of just the right analogy. "It would be like Mary Poppins having a one night stand."

Nikki was still too shocked for words. She wasn't sure if she should be angry that they had played such a cruel joke on her or to be happy that she hadn't really done anything to be ashamed of other than drinking a bit to excess.

"It seems a lot funnier after you've had a few drinks," Marcia offered. "We didn't mean to upset you."

"I told them not to do it," Fran said. "But, I was out-voted. Jeff wasn't under the blanket with you, Nikki. I made sure of that. He was so drunk that he couldn't have done anything to you even if he had wanted to."

"Jeff showed up at Arrowhead yesterday," Marcia said. "He didn't seem to know anything about what had happened. He said that he woke up yesterday morning and you were gone. He had no idea that you had ever been there."

Fran looked at Nikki with all of the sincerity that she that she could manage.

"You didn't do anything that you need to be ashamed of, Nikki. Nothing bad happened."

XIX: HOMECOMING

Sunday, 24 Dec 1967 (Victorville, Ca 1400L)

FINALS WERE OVER and school was out. Nikki was living back at home for the Christmas break.

The Air Force had been quick to tell her that Tom had been shot down but then they refused to tell her anything more. The White House had become involved after that phone call to the Pentagon on Saturday night and everything concerning the operation was immediately classified. The President was alarmed that it had taken such a large operation to rescue Tom. He was afraid that the news media would find out about the secret war in Laos. So he just restricted any information about what had happened including the news that Tom had been rescued.

True to his word, Father Pat did what he could to keep Nikki informed about the situation, but even he couldn't find anything out. It was very frustrating and troubling to Nikki. She became more distraught with each day that passed without any news.

She had taken her philosophy final just as Father Pat had told her. The professor seemed to be a bit sheepish when she came into the classroom. He avoided making any eye contact with Nikki and simply grunted a little as she handed in her finished test. She wouldn't know the results for another week or two, but she felt as if she had done reasonably well. At least well enough to pass the class.

She was working this afternoon at the restaurant in Victorville, and business had been unusually brisk. There was the normal church crowd that seemed to show up every Sunday and then there was also the last minute shopping crowd who had waited until Christmas Eve to finish their gift shopping. Most of the customers were families. The kids tore up the restaurant leaving piles of debris in their wake and the parents were demanding and really didn't tip all that well. It was turning into a very long day for Nikki but the hectic pace forced her to think of something other than Tom and his well-being.

She had just picked up a particularly large order for a family of eight when she noticed Linda, one of the other waitresses just standing very still, looking toward the door of the restaurant with her mouth agape as if she had just seen a ghost. Nikki glanced back over her shoulder and saw Tom standing in the doorway.

"Oh my God," was all that she could manage to say. She literally dropped the plates that she was carrying onto the table and ran toward the door with tears streaming down her face.

Tom was in his uniform. His left shoulder was heavily bandaged and he was using a pair of crutches. Nikki ignored all of that, she ran up to him and hugged him as tightly as she could. They held each other for a long while and neither one wanted to let go of the other. It wasn't long before most of the women in the restaurant were crying tears of joy for both of them.

Nikki and Tom would remember it as the one year that each of them got the gift that they had prayed for.

XX: REFLECTION

Saturday, 17 May 1989 (Dak Thuo Province, Laos 1010L)

LAM QUANG SON stood quietly on the small hill overlooking the river. He was admiring the wooden bridge that spanned the river. It was only a bit over 70 meters in length but the bridge had had a profound impact on the two communities on either side of the small river. In the past, the two small villages had been virtually cut off from each other during the rainy season when the river was swollen with water. Now, both villages had access to each other all year long.

Son had always dreamed of building bridges and while this wooden structure wasn't exactly what he had envisioned, he was pleased with it nonetheless. There wasn't a single nail or screw in the entire structure and yet it was strong and durable.

As he looked at the bridge he recalled that evening conversation and a most unlikely turn of events that had brought him to this country twenty years earlier. He thought back to the pontoon bridge and the mistake by the Soviet man that had led to its prompt destruction. He wondered how much differently his life would have turned out had the pontoon bridge not been destroyed that day. He concluded it was pointless to wonder. There were too many variables to solve the problem. He remembered the constant air strikes by the Americans and their tremendous zeal to get their comrade safely back. That had always struck him. How bad could the any people be who were so willing to sacrifice themselves for their brothers, he wondered?

His wife came up behind him, as he was deep in thought.

"I think you love that bridge more than you love me," she said as she slipped her arms around his waist.

"Not more," Son said as he turned to hug her in return, "just in a different way."

Just as predicted, his government some twenty years earlier soon forgot Son. The local Laotians greatly appreciated him though. He engineered a simple system of dykes that had greatly helped the local farmers. Son became one of the leaders of this small community. He managed to bring his wife and three daughters to live with him not long after he arrived. They had adapted quickly to the simple life style in Laos and were one of the most well-known and well-liked families in the region. Five years ago Son had started planning for the bridge to span the Xianphong River. The structure had been completed just six months ago.

"If you stand here any longer you'll be late for your daughter's wedding," his wife said.

"I know, I know. It just gives me a great deal of satisfaction every time that I look at it," Son said.

"Your daughters give you great deal of joy too. I know that. Now, let's get going."

The two of them turned away from the river and walked arm in arm toward the village.

XXI: PRODIGY

Saturday, July 25 1999 (Norton AFB, Ca 1530L)

It was the change of command ceremony for the 63rd Aeromedical Evacuation Squadron. It is traditional for the out-going Squadron Commander to say a few words of thanks and then the in-coming Commander makes a short speech. The out-going Commander Colonel George Montoya, was just concluding his remarks.

"...and so when General Jameson asked me who I would pick as my replacement as Squadron Commander, there was really only one name that came to mind, Kathy Iverson. No one has worked harder, no one has done more for the Squadron and no one is more qualified for the job. Apparently the General agreed with me. So while I have some regrets about leaving this Squadron, I'm certain that I'm leaving it in very capable hands."

There was a brief ceremony as Colonel Montoya turned over the Squadron colors to Colonel Iverson. At the conclusion of that, Colonel Kathy Iverson stepped up to podium to make a short speech.

"I would like to thank all of you for attending today. I am greatly honored to be your new Squadron Commander. We have some special guests in the front row here that I wanted to share this day with. They are the most important people in my life. Of course, my husband, Phillip Iverson. He has always been there for me whenever I needed a friend for the last sixteen years and I'm certain that I wouldn't be standing here today had it not been for his continued support and reassurance. The next two very special people here are Nikki and Tom Morgan. I love both of them as much as I love my husband. Those of you that know me know that I don't talk very often about my personal life. I've been told that it's a trait that I inherited from my father. But, I would like to take this one opportunity though, to share some of my family history with you. Both of my parents died when I was just a teenager. Ironically, they both died on the same day at opposite ends of the world. My younger brothers and I went initially to live with our Aunt in Baltimore. But she was divorced with two children of her own and so it was very difficult for her. Then Nikki and Tom came into our lives. Tom had been a pilot during the Vietnam War and my father was killed on a mission trying to rescue him. Nikki and Tom eventually adopted us and raised me, my two brothers and three of their own children. They gave all of us their unwavering love, support and guidance. I'm not sure how I would have survived that most difficult period of my life without them. Nikki has always been as much of a best friend to me as a mother. She has always maintained that things happen for a reason. I like to think that my father saved Tom's life so that he and Nikki would become part of my life. In his last letter to me my father wrote that it was his one desire to command a squadron in the Air Force. He never got that opportunity, so I'll pick up where he left off. I hope that somehow he can see us here today. It is *my* greatest desire that he would be as proud of me as I am of him."

Kathy somehow managed to avoid breaking into tears as she delivered that very emotional part of her speech. She regained her composure and went on to thank Colonel Montoya for his confidence in her. She told the members of the Squadron that she was anxious to work with them in her new role as Commander. She concluded by describing how honored she was and she vowed to do her best to be worthy of it.

There was a small party afterwards. In the corner of the room, one of the young Captains in the Squadron was talking to a very attractive and seemingly unattached young lady.

"Oh no. I'm not in the military," the lady explained. "I'm just a school teacher…like my mother."

"Who's your mother?" the Captain asked.

"She is," the lady pointed across the room to where Tom, Nikki and Kathy were talking with a group of people.

"They're your parents?" the Captain seemed a bit confused.

The lady nodded and smiled, sweetly.

"Then I guess you're Colonel Iverson's…?"

"Sister," The lady finished the sentence for him. "Yes, I am."

The Captain appeared to be intrigued by that.

"Well, hi." he said. "I'm Matt Trapaga."

"I'm Sandra but everyone calls me, Sandy."

AUTHORS NOTE

All of the characters in this story are fictional. All of the major events are true. They all occurred, they just didn't all occur at the same time as they do in the story. The aerial sequences have been cobbled together from many different actual sorties in an attempt to give the reader a feel for what it was like to fly and fight in the Vietnam War.

In January of 1968 the Army of North Vietnam launched a devastating attack that became known as the Tet Offensive. Two main axis of attack came through the Ban Bak region of Laos and were directed toward the city of Hue and toward the U.S. outposts at Lang Vei and Khe Sanh. Lang Vei was, in fact overrun by a Communist force led by PT-76 tanks. There were many more strikes elsewhere throughout the entire country of South Vietnam. The scope of the attacks was shocking to the U.S. military and to the American public but most of them were quickly contained. The U.S. Embassy in Saigon was attacked but the Viet Cong attackers never got inside the embassy building. By every standard, the Tet Offensive was an overwhelming defeat for the North Vietnamese Communists yet it actually turned the tide in their favor. It was a tactical defeat but a strategic victory. How could this have happened? It happened because the Johnson Administration had been lying to the American public about the progress of the war in Vietnam for years. They assured the public that the Communists were on their last legs; that victory was close at hand. This huge offensive proved that these claims were untrue, yet ironically, after the Tet Offensive, it probably was true but the American public refused to buy it. As he watched the fighting to retake the city of Hue, America's most respected journalist, Walter Cronkite, told the American public in his evening news broadcast, that the war in Vietnam could not be won. Americans trusted him and from that time on there was never any hope of defeating the Communists, America simply wanted to find some way to extract themselves with some measure of their pride still intact. Republican, Richard Nixon was elected President in 1968, promising peace with honor and in January of 1973, he delivered on that promise. He "***Vietnamized***" the war; giving the Army of South Vietnam the equipment and training that they needed to defend themselves and pulling U.S. ground troops out of Vietnam. The Communists launched a second major offensive in early 1972 and the South Vietnamese

Army nearly crumbled, but with massive firepower supplied by U.S. air power and the backing of a few key American ground units, the offensive was halted. In October of 1972 the North Vietnamese were ready to end the fighting. They agreed to the Paris Peace accords and the war should have ended there. But the South Vietnamese balked at the terms of the treaty and it wasn't until after the federal elections of 1972 that Nixon convinced them to agree. Nixon was reelected by a landslide over Democrat, George Mc Govern but the elections put an even more liberal and more-extreme group of anti-war Democrats in control of Congress. They were stating publicly that they intended to terminate all funding for the war when Congress re-convened in January. In essence, they were going to pull the rug out from under Nixon. There was no need to negotiate a settlement to the war because the Democrats were going to surrender. When Nixon returned to the peace table in December of 1972, the Communists refused to sign anything or to even talk anymore. Nixon had to work fast and just before Christmas of 1972 he untied the hands of the U.S. military and allowed them to bomb any target in North Vietnam that they wanted to.

The first B-52s showed up overhead the City of Hanoi on the evening of 18 Dec 1972. There were hundreds of U.S. prisoners of war who were being held in and around the city; some of them had been prisoners for years. They all had the same thought as saw the huge bombers overhead and heard the battle erupt around them; "***Pack your bags, we're going home!***"

The B-52's came back for ten more nights. By the end of the eleventh night there were no more targets in North Viet Nam for them to bomb. Suddenly, the Communists wanted to negotiate again. They signed the treaty and returned our P.O.W.s. Nixon held the Russians and the Communist Chinese at bay and accomplished in a week and a half what Johnson had failed to do in five years.

America's direct involvement in the war ended in 1972. The Communists broke the treaty and launched a third offensive in 1975. This time Uncle Sam wasn't there to back up the Army of South Vietnam and they folded like a house of cards. They couldn't drop their weapons fast enough and run away. The Communists had won the victory that they had pursued for so long. The blood-bath that many had predicted **did** occur and the worker's paradise that they created is still one of the poorest countries on the face of the earth.

The liberal news media loves to say that U.S. military was defeated in Vietnam yet the U.S. military wasn't even there when the Communists won their eventual victory. For those of us that served in the Viet Nam war it has been a terribly unfair and bitter insult to brand us as the only generation of American servicemen ever to have lost a war.

Surprisingly, the military that the United States committed to fight in Viet Nam was probably the best that this country had ever fielded at the beginning of any war. There was a strong cadre of battle-experienced Officers and NCO's. The average education level of the enlisted ranks was the highest it has ever been. The U.S. Military was tough and confident when Johnson took the position of Commander in Chief. Five years later it's confidence was badly shaken and morale was at an all-time low. Many American people openly displayed their anger and outrage towards those who served in the military. In the leftist view of the cold war, the United States was an aggressive imperialist nation and the military was it's enforcement arm. In their view, the U.S. Military was not really any different than hired thugs who relished any opportunity to bully the down-trodden people of the world.

Still, contrary to most Hollywood movies, most Viet Nam veterans did not return from the war as drug-crazed serial killers. In fact statistics prove that Viet Nam era veterans have a lower rate of criminal behavior and felony convictions than their peers who did not serve in the military. Most, simply did their jobs in the military as best they could and then returned to civilian life.

Atrocities are committed in every war and Viet Nam was no exception but considering the duration of the war and the number of people involved, there were fewer atrocities committed in Viet Nam than in most other wars. One positive outcome of the war was the out-pouring of love and gratitude that occurred years later when this country fought another war in the Middle East. The Viet Nam vets made sure that their sons and daughters who fought in the Gulf Wars would not be treated as shabbily as they had been.

In a survey taken in 2002, 63% of college students in the U.S., who actually professed to know anything about the U.S. involvement in Vietnam, blamed Nixon for the debacle that occurred there. It is so ironic that it's laughable. Only by analyzing and understanding our mistakes can we keep from repeating them.

Democrats controlled both houses of Congress during the entire Vietnam War and they controlled the executive branch until January of 1969 yet, in the minds of Americans, they are absolved of any blame for the disaster that occurred there. It is a real tragedy that most young Americans are blissfully unaware of the truth that the debacle in Viet Nam was caused by Lyndon Baines Johnson, a liberal Democrat from the State of Texas.

Johnson was easily the worst American President of the twentieth century. His absurd theories of military strategy and his outrageous lies cost the lives of over 58,000 Americans for absolutely no reason at all. The blame for the American failure in Viet Nam rests squarely on his shoulders. It must be added that the senior members of the military stood silently by as Johnson mis-used and abused the U.S. military in Viet Nam. Their silence was interpreted by the majority of the American public as agreement with Johnson's inane policies and so they must bear a measure of responsibility for the failure as well. If one or two of our "***brave***" Generals or Admirals had had the courage to "fall on their swords" they might have been able to force Johnson to change his ways.

The vast majority of Viet Nam vets served their country with honor. Many performed heroically and with great valor. All of them wanted to believe that they were fighting for a righteous and just cause. In the end the cause was not worthy of them or of their sacrifice. They were no better and certainly no worse than the men and women who have rallied to the flag of the United States whenever they were called throughout our history.

As the hopelessness and absurdity of the war became apparent to them, they fought more for each other than for *the cause*. In the air battle, this translated into some of the most daring and desperate rescues ever attempted in any war. It is my sincere hope that this story will help the next generation of Americans to understand and appreciate their great courage and devotion to duty.

J.C.

ABOUT THE AUTHOR

JAMES CASEY SERVED in the Air Force during the Viet Nam War, loading bombs on B-52s. He was awarded an ROTC Scholarship and graduated from Loyola Marymount University in 1978. Commissioned in the Air Force he flew the F-15. He currently works as a 777 Captain for a major airline.

ABOUT THE AUTHOR

[illegible]